D0057519

EBERRON

JAMES WYATT

DRAGON FORGE

DRACONIC PROPHECIES

BOOK TWO

DRAGON FORGE

The Draconic Prophecies· Book 2
©2009 Wizards of the Coast LLC

Cover art by Raymond Swanland
Map by Robert Lazzaretti
Original Hardcover Edition First Printing: June 2008
First Paperback Printing: April 2009

9 8 7 6 5 4 3 2 1

ISBN: 978-0-7869-5105-5
620-23970740-001-EN

U.S., CANADA,
ASIA, PACIFIC, & LATIN AMERICA
Wizards of the Coast LLC
P.O. Box 707
Renton, WA 98057-0707
+1-800-324-6496

EUROPEAN HEADQUARTERS
Hasbro UK Ltd
Caswell Way
Newport, Gwent NP9 0YH
GREAT BRITAIN
Save this address for your records.

Visit our web site at www.wizards.com

For Amy

PART

I

Three drops of blood mark the passing of the Time Between.
The three dragons are joined together in the blood,
and the blood contains the power of creation.
One drop is shed where the Dragon Above
pierces the Dragon Below,
the Eye stabs at the Heart.

Blood joins them, and so begins the Time Between.
One drop unites Eberron with the Dragon Below.
Blood is drawn from a serpent binding the spawn of Khyber
and the fiend that is bound.

Bound they remain, but their power flows forth in the blood.
One drop unites Eberron with the Dragon Above.
The touch of Siberys's hand passes from flesh to stone,
held within the drop of Eberron's blood.

The Time Between begins with blood and ends in blood.
Blood is its harbinger, and blood flows in its passing.

CHAPTER
1

General Jad Yeven strode into Kelas's study and stood at attention, waiting for his superior's acknowledgment. His eyes scanned the familiar room—the large oak desk with its sheaves of parchment, the bare plaster wall behind. Nothing was out of place.

"Take off that face," Kelas snapped. "I hate talking to dead people."

Yeven's face changed—its distinctive nose smaller and hair growing out of the general's severe military cut. The changeling stood a little less erect.

"What face would you prefer?" he asked.

"Haunderk."

The changeling sighed. He preferred changing in front of a mirror, especially for Haunderk. He wanted every freckle in place, the eyes just the right shade of amber. Those details could come later, though—as far as Kelas cared, the tousled sandy hair, pasty white skin, and light brownish eyes were enough. The general's bulky muscles melted into a wiry frame, and he compounded his slouch by losing a handbreadth of height. Haunderk took shape, and he found himself wrapped in the comfort of a familiar body and personality. The general's austere military uniform began to chafe.

"That's better," Kelas said, smiling. "There's the spy I trained."

Forcing his face into a smile was far easier than changing his entire appearance.

Kelas stretched, resting his feet on his desk and his hands behind his head. "Have a seat, Haunderk."

Haunderk sat straight in the wooden chair across the desk

from Kelas. The desk was almost bare—dark, polished wood, with only a single sheaf of papers off to one side. What had Kelas been doing when he entered?

"I have learned nothing of Gaven's whereabouts," Kelas said. "You don't have any news?"

"Nothing. The last time I saw him, I expected him to either die or become a god." Detachment, he reminded himself—Haunderk's face made it easier. Emotion would cause trouble. Suffering. Report the facts.

Kelas scoffed. "And he lacked the sense to do either."

Haunderk couldn't decide whether he agreed or not, so he said nothing.

"What about the woman?"

"Rienne."

"Yes. She didn't say anything about plans, goals? Dreams?"

Haunderk cast his memory back over the time he'd spent with Rienne, from Stormhome to the battlefield at Starcrag Plain. What stood out in his memory was not anything she'd said, but her kindness to him, her acceptance—even once she knew he was a changeling. He realized that he didn't want Kelas to find her, then chastised himself for letting his emotions interfere with his work.

He decided on a straightforward, honest answer. "At the time, they were both very focused on immediate concerns."

"If I had any idea of the extent of Gaven's understanding of the Prophecy, I would have given you different orders."

"No," Haunderk said. "It was important to bring the general to you at the moment of his defeat. If he'd had time to repair his ego, he would never have cooperated with you."

A question tugged at the corner of his mind. Would he have been able to betray Gaven if Kelas had ordered it?

He stifled the question. He was a professional. He would do what he was ordered.

"And how is General ir'Brassek now?"

"Haldren is firmly in our camp. He's still driven by ambition, but he knows the best way to achieve what he desires is to work with us." Detachment, again.

"Good. The queen still wants his head—and Yeven's, for that matter."

"She needs someone to hang, to appease the Thranes," Haunderk said.

"And to show that she's still in control. If the other nations see Aundair's army acting without her command, it will seem as though we have already seized control."

"That army took heavy losses at Starcrag Plain."

Kelas nodded. "The Thranes did as well, or they might already have retaliated."

"I wonder what makes Aurala angrier—the army acting without her command, or its failure."

"It's not a bad situation for her. The renegade generals let her deny any responsibility for what happened. If they'd succeeded, she could have claimed credit. With their failure, she doesn't have to take the blame. Although she'd be happier if she could bring the generals forward and punish them publicly."

"Too bad I didn't bring Yeven in alive. And we still need Haldren's help." Haunderk was cold-hearted, efficient.

Kelas ran his fingers through his short black hair. "I think it's time for General Yeven to meet another untimely end," he said.

Easy enough for a man already dead. Just a question of how to do it. "A trial and execution? Or an arrest gone awry?" No regret.

"We don't need to stage it. I'll report that our agents located him, he put up a fight, and we were forced to kill him. We've kept his body preserved, so we'll wheel that out and the queen will have a renegade general."

"And the illusion of control." It was a good plan, but for some reason it made Haunderk sad. "It's done, then, unless there's anything else the general needs to do before his demise."

Kelas put his feet back on the floor and leaned forward on his desk.

"No, he has served his purpose."

Haunderk felt his pulse start to quicken, and he took a slow breath to calm it. Keeping his voice steady, he said, "You have another mission for me?"

"It's time to put the next stage in motion."

Haunderk's hands went cold. "Striking west. You've found a pretext?"

"That's your mission. I received a report this morning that something is brewing in the Demon Wastes. One of the chieftains of the Carrion Tribes is emerging as a sort of warlord. He's conquering nearby tribes and uniting them under his banner."

"Uniting them? The Carrion Tribes?" Haunderk found that hard to believe. The tribes were constantly warring with each other. Many of the tribes' leaders had the blood of demons running through their veins, and the tribes lived by violence—mindless slaughter, more to the point.

"Apparently so. Clearly, this is an exceptional chieftain. We don't know much about him, or what he hopes to accomplish. Most likely, he's just looking for status and power in the Wastes. He might think to strike against the orcs of the Labyrinth."

The orcs were the only common enemy the Carrion Tribes shared. Haunderk saw where Kelas was heading. "But if we can make him strike farther east . . ."

"If he attacks the Eldeen Reaches, we'll have the pretext we need. An attack on the Reaches is a threat to Aundair's western border. Queen Aurala will be justified in sending troops into the Reaches to ensure the safety of our borders."

"And my mission?"

"Go to the Demon Wastes. Find this warlord. Help him see beyond the Labyrinth. Goad him into attacking the Reaches."

Haunderk sat back in his chair, drawing another slow breath. The success of this mission was crucial to Kelas's plans. But Haunderk's survival was by no means a prerequisite for success. All his work required was that he let this warlord learn he was a spy from the Eldeen Reaches. And the most likely way for him to obtain an audience with the warlord was to be captured—and recite his lines under torture.

Then die.

He kept his face impassive. "Is there anything else?"

Kelas smiled. It was a smile that had won over many enemies, softened much hostility. Haunderk felt nauseated.

"No, that's all," Kelas said. "What will you need for the journey?"

Haunderk looked up at the ceiling, trying to focus on the task at hand. The eastern part of the Eldeen Reaches was much like Aundair, heavily agricultural. The west was largely wilderness, tended by druids and rangers. Haldren's aborted attempt to restart the Last War, launching an invasion of Thrane to the east, had caused a diplomatic furor that still raged. That meant the borders were closed.

"Crossing the Wynarn is going to be tricky," he said.

"Fly to Wyr. I'll have someone south of the city to ferry you across the river."

Haunderk closed his eyes, visualizing a map of the Reaches. "Then down to . . . there's a village not far south of Wyr, on the Eldeen side."

"Riverweep. I'll get you papers to ride an Orien coach from there to Varna and on to Greenheart."

Haunderk nodded. House Orien operated the lightning rail, but the lines of conductor stones that made that magical conveyance possible did not extend past the Aundairian border into the wilds of the Eldeen Reaches. Roads did, though, and the Oriens also carried passengers on more mundane carts and wagons. Magebred draft horses could pull an Orien coach from Riverweep to Varna in about three days, with overnight stops in villages along the way. A far cry from the five hours it would have taken on the lightning rail, but fast enough for this purpose.

"What name do you want on the papers?" Kelas asked.

What name? He'd need a new one. He didn't want any of the others to die.

"I'll let you know."

"Very well. From Greenheart you'll be on foot all the way into the Demon Wastes. You should find some help to make sure you stay alive until you get there."

Until I get there, Haunderk thought. Then it doesn't matter any more. "I think that's all I need, then."

Kelas put his hands on his desk, looking down at the smooth

wood. Then he stood and smiled again. Haunderk jumped to his feet.

"I don't think I've told you how much I appreciate your work all these years," Kelas said. "You've been an enormous help."

"Service to the Royal Eyes is my life," Haunderk said. "It's all I've ever known."

Kelas's smile faltered, and Haunderk could see the effort it took to force it back onto his face.

"Very good. Farewell, Haunderk."

Haunderk turned and left the room, putting General Yeven's face back on as he left. Might as well wear the face of a dead man.

* * * * *

General Jad Yeven stood before a mirror in his apartments, stripped to his plain breeches. Tall, soldier-straight, with a sculpted face—the face of a leader. Strong, well-defined muscles covered his chest.

"Who are you?" he said. "Jad Yeven, you're dead."

He let the general melt away. Fine blond hair grew out from the general's severe cut, and he let a day's growth of beard follow. Tanned, weathered, and handsome. Still strong, though not as muscular as Yeven.

"Darraun Mennar. You're dead, too." He had found a body on the battlefield that bore a passing resemblance to Darraun, and tinkered with it to cement the resemblance. Had Rienne found the body?

Darraun melted away. Hair darkened to a tawny brown, and spilled down a slender back. Round and soft—the face, breasts, and hips. Not too shapely—the body of a soldier.

"Caura Fannam." She stared for a long moment at her face in the mirror. "You weren't around long enough to die," she said. "You were very kind."

Her eyes burned as Caura melted away.

"Too kind. You cared too much. Nothing is permanent, and no one lives forever. Remember that, or you will suffer."

Short—as short as possible, but broad, strong. A dwarf, male again, with brown skin and black hair. Muscles like polished marble.

"Auftane Khunnam, damn you. You started all this. All those months you spent with Janik and Mathas and Dania—" His voice broke at the sound of her name. A paladin of the Silver Flame, Dania had sacrificed herself to destroy a rakshasa, a demon that had possessed Janik's wife—the wife of the man she loved. A year later, thinking of it made a knot in his chest, a feeling he couldn't quite understand. Such a sacrifice made no sense.

"And you repaid their kindness by stealing the torc from her lifeless throat and disappearing," he whispered, leaning close to the mirror.

"I did my job," he retorted, stepping back. "I didn't let emotion get in my way."

He snorted, and Auftane melted away.

"Haunderk Lannath." Taller again, sandy hair, white skin. He put every freckle in place and found the perfect shade of amber for his eyes.

"You were born for this, trained your whole life to be a spy. You belong to the Royal Eyes. Do your damned job."

Haunderk's face dissolved.

"Who are you?" The voice came from a face that was between faces, as pale as Haunderk's but longer and thinner.

"Aunn. My name is Aunn." With some effort, he shaped his face until it had no shape. Colorless eyes stared out from a blank field of gray skin. White hair fell in tangles over smooth shoulders.

"This is my face." He stared long and hard at the unfamiliar visage, so blank, as if it were waiting for features to be impressed upon it. Waiting for an identity. "Who are you?" he whispered.

He straightened and began to change. "You're a spy, damn it—an elite agent of Aundair's Royal Eyes. You have a job to do. Ugly work," he said, "so you need an ugly face."

Tall and strong. Weathered skin, tan and hard. Dark hair covering a muscular chest. A thick neck, then up to the face. A nose crooked nose from being broken in many brawls. A wide mouth, then a thick beard that went too far up the cheeks. A shaggy mane of dark hair. Then the eyes—the eyes always needed the most attention.

"Pitiless eyes," he said. Pools of liquid metal formed in his blank white eyes, dark and hard as steel. "No fear, no mercy."

For just an instant as he looked in the mirror, he saw the Traveler—the divine changeling, the great trickster. She wore the face of a half-elf with short red hair, bathed in silver light, and her mouth was bent in a half-smile.

"Who are you?" He didn't know if the voice was his or the god's.

"Kauth Dannar," his ugly face answered. "A mercenary during the war, now a drifter, a thug, and an adventurer. Get out of my way."

He struck the mirror with the back of his fist, sending it crashing to the floor. It exploded in shards of glass, and Kauth Dannar strode out of the room.

CHAPTER
2

Gaven lay in a swinging bunk below the decks of the *Sea Tiger,* one arm behind his head, the other wrapped around Rienne. Her head rested on his shoulder, her black hair spilling over his arm and off the edge of the bunk. He savored the quiet—the soft creak of the ropes moving with the galleon and the splashing of the hull cutting the water. Moonlight gleamed on Rienne's dark skin.

"Jordhan says we'll be in the Dragonreach soon," Rienne said. "Then on to Argonnessen."

"Here's what I don't understand. All the ten seas connect to each other, right? So how do you know when you leave one and enter another? What's the difference between the Lhazaar Sea and the Dragonreach? Or if we kept sailing around Khorvaire, how would we know when we left the Dragonreach and entered the Thunder Sea?"

"It's not much different than traveling on land," Gaven said. "How can you tell when you leave Aundair and enter Thrane?"

"Soldiers come and demand your papers?" Rienne lifted her head and smiled at him, shifting to prop herself up on one arm. The movement sent the bunk into gentle swinging.

"You know what I mean. There's no difference in the land. Sometimes you cross a river, sometimes you go through a mountain pass. But many times the lines are totally arbitrary—the border is set where each nation's control ended at the close of the Last War."

"I understand that. But there aren't any nations in the seas to fight over borders."

"True, thank the Sovereigns. In that case, it's more a matter of how sailors define them. The Lhazaar Sea is full of whales, and that's how the Lhazaars make their living. They don't go whaling in the Dragonreach, though, because they'd find their harpoons stuck into a dragon turtle. Or bouncing off its shell, more likely."

"Is that what it is? Different creatures in different seas? So we'll know we're in the Dragonreach when we spot our first dragon turtle?"

"Not just that. If you sail east from Lhazaar, you eventually get into the Sea of Rage, and pretty soon you realize you've gone too far when you sail into a freak storm or a giant waterspout. The seas are different. They behave differently. Almost like people."

"Some are more tempestuous than others," Rienne said. She started tracing a finger along the winding lines of the dragonmark on his chest.

Gaven closed his eyes and enjoyed the touch of her fingers on his skin. In his mind, he could see the movements of her fingers, and the patterns of his dragonmark took shape.

The words of creation. He had been seeing them etched into the land and sea ever since he walked the twisting Sky Caves of Thieren Kor—every part of the world spoke to him of its past and what it might yet become. The Prophecy of the dragons was written upon the world itself. But he had never realized before that it was written on him.

He saw it now, in the fine lines that weaved across his skin, from just under his chin and down his neck to cover his chest and the upper part of his arm. He saw in those lines all that he had been and was becoming—his past and his potential, his beginning and what might well be his end. He saw the thread of Rienne's fate bound up in his own. A chill shot up his spine, and he shuddered.

"Sorry," Rienne said. "Did that tickle?"

He looked up at her smile, and those lines of his dragonmark that spoke of her stood out clear and strong in his mind. He reached up and wove his fingers into her hair, then pulled her down to kiss him.

* * * * *

"You're awfully quiet," Rienne said, stroking Gaven's cheek with the back of her hand. They stood at the prow of the *Sea Tiger*, watching a pod of dolphins riding the bow wave.

"Thinking," he said.

"Mm. Why not let me in on those thoughts?"

Gaven sighed, then smiled at her. "I'm sorry. I spent so much time alone in Dreadhold that I'm still getting used to having someone to talk to."

"I understand. But I'm pretty tangled up in your plans right now—I hope you can share them with me."

"Of course, love." Gaven kissed her forehead, then turned to look out over the open sea. The last of the Lhazaar islands had already vanished behind them into the haze of the horizon. Somewhere ahead of them in the apparently boundless sea lay the land of dragons. "I'm just trying to figure out what all this means."

"All this what?"

"The Prophecy and my place in it. Your place in it. What's happening to the world."

"That's why we're going to Argonnessen, right?"

Gaven nodded. "I feel as though the world is coming to a crucial moment, a . . ." He looked up at the ring of elemental water that churned in a circle around the *Sea Tiger*'s aftcabin, helping to propel the ship across the sea. "It's like the moment when you turn an hourglass over and the sand starts running the other way. I don't know if I can explain it any better than that. The Time of the Dragon Above has ended, the Storm Dragon made his appearance in history. And the Time of the Dragon Below is coming, with the rise of the Blasphemer. That means this is the Time Between."

Rienne's brow crinkled and she looked away. "And what happens in the Time Between?"

"That's the thing," Gaven said, leaning against the bulwark. "I know some words of the Prophecy, a hint of their layers of meaning. But I don't really know what they mean as a whole. When I was in Dreadhold, I dreamed all the time about the Storm Dragon and the Soul Reaver and the events of the Time of the Dragon Above. And I've had a few visions about the Blasphemer—terrible visions. The Time Between is a mystery to me."

"What do you know of the Prophecy about the Time Between?" Rienne asked. Gaven could hear the trepidation in her voice.

"A great deal of blood," he said. He closed his eyes, remembering the twisting tunnels of the Sky Caves of Thieren Kor. He could almost feel the stone beneath his fingertips. " 'Three drops of blood mark the passing of the Time Between.' Three events involving bloodshed of some kind. 'Ten eyes gaze brightly upon the City of the Damned,' whatever that means. But I don't know what it's all about. I don't know what I'm supposed to do any more."

"So we're going to Argonnessen to learn what the dragons say about the Time Between."

"Right." He looked back down at the water. The dolphins had abandoned their play, and there was only open ocean as far as he could see. "It's strange," he said. "For the better part of thirty years I was haunted by dreams—by nightmares about the fulfillment of the Prophecy. I lived the death of the Soul Reaver countless times, felt the monster's tentacles clawing at my face and wriggling into my mouth—" He shuddered.

Rienne put a gentle hand on his back.

"Now the dreams are gone," he said, "and some part of me misses them."

"Because you were so used to them?"

"Not just that. It also gave me a much better sense of what I was doing—it gave me a purpose, a goal, even something like a plan, though I often felt—"

"Like you were writing the script as you went along?"

"Exactly. But at least I had an idea of where the play was heading. Now I don't even have that."

"So that's what you're hoping to find in Argonnessen?"

"I suppose it is." He turned and smiled at her. "But this time without the nightmares."

Even as the words left his mouth, he remembered a dream that had haunted his sleep on the lightning rail. A blasted canyon, a wound torn into the earth. Dragonfire fueling a great furnace. A blast of fire jetting up to engulf him.

"What is it?" Rienne asked.

"Just a headache," he said, forcing the smile back on his face. "Too much glare off the water. Let's go below."

* * * * *

"Land ho!"

In the aft cabin, Gaven looked up from the charts spread out before him and smiled at Jordhan.

"Well done," he said. "Your prediction was dead on."

Jordhan walked to the hatch and peered out at the sailors on deck. "I told you, I know the sea," he said, "and after all these years I hope I know how to read a chart."

"As far as they go," Rienne said, still frowning at the charts. They traced the outline of a large island and two smaller ones to its north, then a longer coast that Jordhan said was the mainland.

"We're lucky to have these. House Lyrandar has done some trading with the people of the Seren Islands here. If anyone else has, I don't know about it."

"People?" Rienne asked. "Elves from Argonnessen? Or Lhazaarite colonists?"

"Neither," Jordhan said with a frown. "They're human, but they don't look like Lhazaarites. Well, they act like Lhazaarites—they're pirates and raiders."

"Sounds like we should avoid the islands," Gaven said. He leaned over the table for a closer look at the charts.

"Yes, I'd much rather head directly into the land of dragons than face pirates and raiders." Sarcasm dripped from Rienne's voice.

Gaven looked up at her. "Why invite more trouble than we're already bringing on ourselves? Besides, if we head straight for the mainland, we don't put Jordhan and his ship in as much danger."

"Just yourselves," Jordhan muttered. He had insisted on bringing them to Argonnessen, pointing out that only a Lyrandar galleon could make the journey—and no other Lyrandar would give aid to Gaven. Even so, he wasn't happy carrying them on what he believed to be a suicidal journey.

Gaven clapped his old friend on the shoulder. "You've carried us into danger many times, and we've always emerged alive."

"Yes, and in all that time, how many dragons have you faced?"

"Two."

Jordhan's eyes widened in amazement. "Two?"

"There was a young red that attacked our airship as we neared the Starcrag Plain. It wouldn't have been too much trouble if it hadn't thrown Rienne overboard. Before that, I fought Vaskar in the Sky Caves of Thieren Kor."

"But you didn't kill him," Rienne pointed out.

"I drove him off. If he hadn't fled, I would have killed him."

Jordhan gave a low whistle. "Two dragons is more than most people can claim."

"But we're about to journey into the dragons' homeland," Rienne said.

"As I said before, no dragon will find me an easy meal."

Jordhan forced a laugh. "Perhaps some will relish the challenge."

Gaven had enough of Jordhan's dire predictions, and he turned back to the charts. "The coast here is marked as Totem Beach. Do you know what that means?"

"They say that great stone statues are arrayed along the beach—enormous dragon heads looking out over the sea. The Serens come to the beach to worship the dragons."

"Another place to avoid," Rienne said. "Perhaps we should just avoid the whole continent. What happens if we just keep sailing south?"

"No idea," Jordhan said. "Probably we freeze to death."

"Will you two stop it?" Gaven snapped. "I wouldn't lead either of you into the jaws of the Keeper. It looks like Totem Beach is the only place we can safely make land. I'm not going to ask you to sail beyond what's on this chart in hopes of finding a safer harbor. Totem Beach is our destination."

"Any particular location strike your fancy?" Jordhan asked.

"The closest." Gaven pointed at a spot on the charts. "Here."

Jordhan nodded and gathered up the charts. "I'll show the helmsman." He pushed his way out the hatch.

"I'm sorry, Gaven," Rienne said, running a hand down his

arm. "I got caught up in Jordhan's gloom, I suppose."

He circled her in his arms and held her to him. "Do you trust me, Ree?"

"Of course I do," she murmured, returning his embrace.

"And you understand why I'm doing this?"

"I think so." She paused. "Actually, I'm not sure I do. I know what you want to accomplish. But I don't understand why." She pulled free of his grip and turned away. "Why should the Time Between have anything to do with you?"

Gaven scowled. "True. The Storm Dragon might not have any part to play in the Time Between."

"The Storm Dragon." She turned back to look into his eyes. "Is that how you think of yourself now? You filled that role in the Prophecy, but has it consumed who you are?"

Gaven pulled a chair away from the table and sat down, staring blankly at the charts.

Rienne moved behind him and ran her fingers through his hair. "Sometimes I look into your eyes or lie in your arms and we're young again—it's almost as though none of this had ever happened. I feel you right there with me, and I see all the things I love about you." She kissed the top of his head. "Other times, though, I don't know who you are. You're off in the world of the Prophecy and destiny, the schemes of dragons—a world I don't understand. You look at me and I'm not sure you even see me."

"For twenty-six years—"

"I know, love. All the years you were in Dreadhold, the Prophecy consumed you. You dreamed about it at night and pondered it during the day. But you're free now. You have to free your mind as well."

Gaven turned to face her and shook his head. "You don't understand."

"No, I don't. I wasn't there. I haven't endured what you have. But look." She slid her sword from its sheath and ran a finger along the edge. "We balance on the razor edge between past and future, but that edge is what matters. Where is your blade in this instant, and where is your enemy's blade? You can't spend your life worrying about the mistakes of the past and the mysteries of the future."

"I have to think of the future." He stood up and turned to face her. "I know the Prophecy better than any person alive—probably better than most dragons. I have the power of the Storm Dragon at my command. If the world is careening toward disaster, I have a responsibility to try to stop it. No one else can."

Rienne's gaze dropped from his eyes to his neck, to the top of his dragonmark emerging from his shirt. Gaven saw a weary sadness settle onto her face, and his heart ached.

"Perhaps I'm fated to be the supportive wife after all, trailing behind you and helping in any way I can."

Gaven cradled her cheek in his hand. "No, Ree."

"It's what I'm born to, really. An heir of the Alastra family, which has always served the Lyrandars and always will. I followed you through all those adventures into Khyber. And when you were gone I did my family duty."

Gaven dropped his hand to the hilt of her sword, but she grabbed his wrist.

"What are you doing?" she demanded.

"Let me see your sword."

"See it or hold it?"

"Just see it."

Rienne released her grip on his wrist, took a step back, and lifted Maelstrom for Gaven to see. She held it delicately with both hands, almost reverently. It was an exquisite blade, the finest example of an art that had long been forgotten. Intricate patterns wove across the flat of the short blade, complementing the faint blue damask of the steel. Both sides carried razor-sharp edges, and it tapered gracefully to a deadly point. The guard was carved in the stylized form of a dragon's head, as though the blade emerged from its mouth. A pair of wings arced down around the blade. The hilt was wound with smooth leather, and the pommel resembled the dragon's tail, curled around an enormous blue-white pearl.

"It's a beautiful weapon," Gaven said.

"Yes. What about it?"

"Is this the weapon of a supportive wife?"

Scowling, Rienne swung the blade around—dangerously close to Gaven's face—and slid it into its sheath in one smooth motion. "It's my sword, so perhaps it is. What's so damned important about Maelstrom? You said something about it before."

"The day you first touched that sword, you set a course for a much greater destiny. It's a sword of legend, Ree. Great things have been done with it, and more greatness will yet be accomplished. Can't you feel that?"

Rienne slid the sword, still in its sheath, out of the silk sash wrapped around her waist. She ran a hand lovingly along the leather scabbard and its gold tooling. "Of course I can. But the greatness of my sword says nothing about me. If I fall in battle tomorrow, some other hand will wield this sword—perhaps the greatness will be theirs."

Gaven shook his head. "It's the sword of a champion. No lesser hand could wield it. You won't even let me touch it."

She clutched the scabbard to her chest and looked down at the floor.

"You and Maelstrom are linked in destiny," Gaven said, "as surely as you and I are."

"There's comfort in that, anyway." She looked up and met his eyes, and a smile spread across her face.

Just as Gaven bent to kiss her, Jordhan appeared in the hatch.

"Are you two still in here?" the captain said. "We're starting to circle the Seren Islands—you should come see. There are precious few who have ever laid eyes on these shores."

CHAPTER
3

Kauth stared out the window as the coach approached Varna. The Wynarn rushed past in the opposite direction, gray with the grime and muck of the city, carrying it north to Eldeen Bay. Across the river was Aundair, the stretch of woodland that stood on the banks of Lake Galifar. He found himself wondering if he would ever lay eyes on Aundairian soil again. Then he shook his head to dispel that thought and looked around the carriage again.

His travel so far had gone exactly according to plan. He rode an airship from Fairhaven, Aundair's capital, to the last town on Aundair's side of the river, Wyr. Under cover of darkness, he walked a few miles upriver and found another agent—he didn't know the woman's name—who rowed him across on a small raft. The rather sudden appearance of heavy clouds to blot out the moons made him suspect his accomplice had ties to House Lyrandar.

He had made camp on the Eldeen side of the river and walked into Riverweep with the farmers bringing their goods to market. By luncheon, he had secured a seat on a coach bound for Varna. A wagon the size of a small house pulled by a team of magebred draft horses. And the next morning, as the coach pulled out of whatever farming village it had stopped in for the night, he had spotted the shifter.

The descendants of werewolves and other lycanthropes, shifters looked like hirsute, somewhat savage humans—most of the time. In the heat of battle, they showed their heritage. Some grew sharp claws, and the jaws of others grew into muzzles full of deadly teeth. They were more common in the Eldeen Reaches than anywhere else in Khorvaire. There, they lived in bands, almost packs, in the wilder lands, coming into more settled areas to trade furs and meat for grains and cheeses. A shifter traveling alone, though, was exactly the kind of person Kauth was looking for—a man with no ties, with plenty of experience surviving in the wild, and tough enough to survive the journey into the Demon Wastes.

So he kept an eye on the shifter for the rest of the journey. The man was tall and strongly built, and armored in a shirt of gleaming silver chainmail made from light, flexible mithral. Two long-bladed knives hung at his belt, and he carried a quiver of red-feathered arrows on his back. A long bow, unstrung, leaned against the window beside him. His mane of brown hair was streaked with blond and woven into two thin braids that hung in front of his slightly pointed ears. He had amber eyes that never seemed to lift their gaze above the floor. Whenever Kauth tried to catch his eye, the shifter simply ignored him.

He hadn't moved since Kauth had last studied him. He sat across the aisle running down the center of the coach, as alone on a bench as Kauth was. Leaning forward, the shifter rested his head on the seat in front of him, staring down at the floor, his hands clenched as if in prayer.

Kauth felt the coach slow, and he looked back out the window just in time to see the river and the forest beyond it disappear as they passed through the walls of Varna into the city. The quiet fields and ranches gave way to the noisy bustle of city life—people on the move, buying, selling, and crafting.

He suddenly felt very tired, and he leaned his head against the glass. Here was a city full of life and energy, people going about their lives trying their hardest to find fulfillment and happiness in the circumstances they were given. And if his mission succeeded, the city would soon be a ruin—either besieged by Aundairian forces or razed by the hordes of the Carrion Tribes.

Nothing is permanent, he reminded himself. Change is part of the cycles of time. Creation, destruction—one flows into the other and neither is cause for joy or grief. Detachment is the key to peace and understanding.

He glanced back to the shifter's seat. It was empty. He leaped to his feet and scanned the coach, but the shifter had vanished. He threw himself into the shifter's vacated seat, heedless of the stares he drew, and peered out the window. A quick glimpse confirmed his fear. The shifter had leaped off the moving coach and was doing his best to lose himself in the crowd.

Kauth cursed under his breath and ran to the front of the coach. The busy street passed by more quickly than he liked. Shifters had a natural agility that would have made the jump relatively easy for his quarry, but it made him nervous. For a moment he questioned whether this particular shifter was worth the risk of a broken bone.

I'll get a lot more than a broken bone if I try the Demon Wastes alone, he told himself.

Drawing a deep breath, he jumped. He landed hard but kept his feet. Scanning the street, he spotted the area where he'd seen the shifter, and wove his way back through the traffic.

He was glad he'd chosen a tall body for this persona—it gave him a slightly better view over the crowd. And he was looking for another tall man, so he focused on other heads that jutted up from the masses. A mane of brown hair streaked with blond caught his eye, and he altered his course to intercept the shifter at a side street.

He lost sight of his quarry on the way, but kept on course until he reached the other street. He stopped at the corner and scanned all around, to no avail.

"Damn," he muttered.

A hand gripped his shoulder and a voice growled in his ear. "Why are you following me?"

Kauth spun around and found himself face to face with the shifter. The man's amber eyes bored into his, and his teeth were bared in a very animalistic display of aggression.

"I need your help," Kauth said, spreading his hands, palms out.

People aren't so different from animals, he thought. Displays of aggression and peace, rituals of dominance and submission. Do animals manipulate each other, though? Do they pretend to be submissive to lull the dominant ones into a false sense of control?

The shifter's eyebrows rose. "My help? What in the ten seas do you need me for?"

You're so accustomed to being useless, Kauth thought. You'll do whatever I ask you to.

"I need strong allies for dangerous work," he said. "You struck me as a man who could handle the work."

"I assume you're not talking about menial labor." The shifter's hand rested on the hilt of a long knife at his belt.

"Can we talk somewhere more private?"

The shifter looked him up and down. His eyes lingered for a moment on the flanged mace at Kauth's belt and the crossbow slung over his shoulder, then he gave a slight nod.

"I'm Sevren Thorn," he said, extending a hand.

Kauth clasped it and smiled.

Who are you? he thought.

"Kauth Dannar."

* * * * *

Sevren Thorn was a desperate man, quickly won over. Kauth said he was a scout for the Wardens of the Wood, the druidic sect that maintained order throughout the Reaches. Rumors of war were building, not just in the east near Aundair, but also on the Reaches' western border. He had been charged with infiltrating the Demon Wastes to determine the truth of these rumors.

Sevren drained his third pint of the dark, bitter ale common in the Reaches as Kauth sipped his first with distaste. "So is it just the two of us?" the shifter asked. "Or are you looking for more strong allies?"

How many people am I willing to lead to their deaths? Kauth thought.

"More would improve our chances," he said. "But too many will draw attention. Do you know anyone who might be interested?"

"I have a couple of ideas. People I've worked with before. People who have some trouble fitting in to city life, like me."

"Can you contact them?"

"It might take some work, but I'm sure I can track them down. That's what I'm good at."

"I'd be glad to meet them," Kauth said.

* * * * *

The next evening, he draped himself in a heavy cloak and altered his face and form as much as he could while wearing Kauth's metal-studded leather armor, and then he made his way to the same tavern. From outside, the tavern's location offered a splendid view of Lake Galifar and the light of the Ring of Siberys gleaming on its waters. Inside, though, the few small windows in the fieldstone walls were paned with smoke-blackened glass. One roaring fire threw its flickering light over the crowded room, casting large and looming shadows.

He spotted Sevren Thorn and his two companions as soon as he entered, but he didn't look directly at them. He sat at the bar and ordered a pint of the vile ale before turning to survey the room. The shifter was at ease with these friends, laughing loudly at some joke, his head thrown back. The changeling smiled despite himself—he had quickly come to like the shifter, whose ready laugh was one of his most endearing traits.

His companions looked like very much the same kind of man, perfect for this mission. One stood out immediately from the crowd. First because he evidently thought drinking was a serious, even dangerous business. He wore heavy armor, well-crafted plate with one pronounced shoulder plate. Second, he was an orc, gray-skinned, hideous, and huge. He didn't even smile at whatever had made Sevren laugh so loudly.

The other man was human, but he stood out from the crowd no less than his companions. He wore a flamboyant emerald green shirt beneath a black vest embroidered in gold. His head was bald except for an arc of black hair sprinkled with gray running around the back, baring an elaborate black tattoo of angular patterns that covered his scalp. Kauth recognized the tattoo as an arcane symbol, suggesting the man had some kind of magical ability. Thick eyebrows rose from the bridge of his nose to a high point before bending back down at the ends. His mouth was twisted in a sardonic grin—some barb of his had doubtless spurred Sevren's laughter.

Satisfied, the changeling slipped out of the bar, leaving his ale on the counter. He stood in the shadows outside and slid into Kauth's familiar form, then stuffed the cloak into his pack. Running a hand over his face to make sure he hadn't missed any details, he walked back in the door as though he had just arrived, pretending to scan the room until he spotted Sevren.

He walked to their table. "I'm Kauth Dennar," he said.

Sevren stood with a smile and clasped Kauth's hand in greeting. "This is Vor Helden," he said, indicating the orc.

Kauth nodded at the orc, puzzling over the odd name. It didn't seem Orc.

"And this is Zandar Thuul." Sevren clapped the other man on the shoulder. "Have a seat."

Kauth settled into the empty chair across from the shifter and smiled at the other men. "Sevren told you about the job?"

"He did," the orc, Vor, answered. "And I'll be blunt. You need me. You'll never get through the Labyrinth without me."

Kauth's eyebrows raised, and he noticed Zandar's mouth quirking into the same grin. "You're a Ghaash'kala?" Kauth asked. The Ghaash'kala tribes patrolled the broken land between the Demon Wastes and the Eldeen Reaches. Zealous believers in an obscure religion, the Ghaash'kala orcs tried to ensure that no evil escaped from the Wastes—and that no one entered that land of corruption. They would be the first casualties of Kauth's mission, if he succeeded.

"He was," Zandar said.

Vor glared at the human before turning back to Kauth. "I was born among them, and I know the Labyrinth well. I no longer carry the privilege of calling myself a Ghaash'kala, or of using my full name."

Kauth nodded, deciding not to press him further. That explained the simple name, anyway. "I'll be glad for your help," he said. He looked at Zandar. "How about you?"

"What about me? You want me to tell you all the reasons you should bring me along? I'll keep you alive—that's all."

"And how will you do that?"

"If anything tries to kill you, I'll kill it first."

"Quite a boast from a man who doesn't carry a weapon," Kauth observed.

In answer, Zandar pointed his finger at the half-drained mug of ale in front of Vor. A stream of shadow shot from his hand and shattered the mug. Shards of pottery flew everywhere, and ale sprayed all over the orc. Vor jumped to his feet, reached across the table, and hauled Zandar up by his collar.

"I've had enough from you, warlock," the orc snarled. "I'll be damned before I take another journey with you."

Zandar didn't seem the least bit intimidated. "Aren't you damned already?" He sneered. "Hasn't the Silver Flame abandoned you?"

Vor threw him back into his chair. "Kalok Shash is testing me," he said, but the fire was gone from his eyes. He settled back into his chair, his plate armor clanking.

Interesting, Kauth thought. An exiled Ghaash'kala warrior, sworn to protect the world from evil, and a warlock, a pracitioner of an arcane tradition said to come from fiendish pacts. Certainly both men would be useful—as long as they didn't kill each other.

"Don't mind them," Sevren said, smiling at Kauth. "They do this all the time. It's like they're married."

Vor glared at him, but Zandar leaned toward Kauth. "It's just so much fun to see him riled up. I've never seen a paladin with such a temper."

"A paladin?" Kauth arched an eyebrow at Vor.

Vor glared at Zandar. "I was," he said.

CHAPTER
4

"Totem Beach," Jordhan announced, his voice hushed with awe.

Gaven could only stare. An uneven row of monolithic dragon heads towered over the sandy beach. Their necks rose up from the sand and the sea, and their heads glared down at the approaching ship. The *Sea Tiger* was miles from shore, but the gray stone dragons still seemed impossibly large. Gaven couldn't imagine how human hands could have shaped such immense figures, and he had never thought of dragons as sculptors. But there they were—standing watch over the beach to accept the sacrifices of the Serens, or to warn away intruders. Or both.

It was awe-inspiring—and completely unfamiliar. Gaven had hoped that laying eyes on Argonnessen would trigger some memory of the land. He had harbored the memories of a dragon for all those years in Dreadhold, but now that those memories were gone, he couldn't remember anything of Argonnessen. He couldn't even remember whether the dragon in his mind had ever been there. Totem Beach did nothing to jar his memory, and he grew increasingly convinced that the dragon had spent its whole life in Khorvaire. Mostly, as far as he could recall, in the lightless depths of Khyber.

"We might have trouble," Rienne said, pointing off to port.

Gaven squinted against the morning sun and saw the object of her concern—a three-masted longship sailing toward them. "The Serens?"

Jordhan shielded his eyes with his hand and followed Rienne's finger. "Yes, that's one of theirs. You can tell by the long prow and the distinctive shape of the sails. They—"

Gaven cut him off. "Will they attack us?" The Seren ship was smaller than the *Sea Tiger*, but that long prow was built for ramming, and with enough speed she could tear a hole in the galleon's hull.

"Only if they can catch us," Jordhan said with a grin. He spread his arms to indicate the grandeur of his ship—her three masts and the elemental ring of water surrounding her. He had every reason to be proud of her.

"We can outrun them to the coast easily enough," Rienne said, "but then what? When we disembark, we'll be on the beach and you'll be at anchor, and we'll both be easier targets."

"I could sink them," Gaven said. The idea was distasteful, but if it meant that Jordhan and his crew were not at risk, he'd do it.

"Don't be so sure," Jordhan said. "Their ships are built to weather storms. I've never heard of the Dragonreach lying as still as it has these past few weeks."

Rienne put a hand on Gaven's shoulder. "You can thank the Storm Dragon for that."

Gaven leaned on the bulwark and surveyed the coast. Beyond the sandy beach, a cloud of mist hung over what looked like thick jungle, obscuring the horizon.

"I wish I had a better sense of the land."

"You're looking at as much as the charts show," Jordhan said. "The beach with its watchers, then a strip of forest. That mist might be a permanent feature."

"That's one thing about the weather," Gaven said with a grin. "It always changes."

He closed his eyes and felt the air around him, the wind blowing toward the coast. He spread his arms and drew a long breath, then let it out slowly.

I am the storm, he thought. I am the wind.

The skin of his arms tingled, and his dragonmark grew warm. For a moment he held a swirling ball of air in his outstretched arms. With a sharp breath, it gusted out before him. He took a step back against the force of it, then planted himself more firmly on the deck. He felt Rienne's hand on his back, lending him her strength.

The wind grew into a gale blowing out from the *Sea Tiger*'s prow. He opened his eyes and watched it churn the sea into foaming waves, then kick up blasts of sand on the beach. Branches thrashed wildly, and the mist roiled before dissipating completely in the face of the mighty wind.

Beyond the forest, the land rose up in a wall of forbidding mountains, high enough that their peaks were cloaked in snow. Gaven staggered back another step, as though the mountains pushed back against his blast of wind.

"Ten seas," Jordhan breathed. "How are you going to get across those?"

Gaven ignored him, keeping his mind focused on the wind. The mist draping the forest blew off in wild streams away from the central point directly ahead of the ship's prow. The mountains indeed formed a wall following the line of the coast, rising higher toward the east. As he watched, dark shapes took to the air, spreading wide wings to ride the wind rising off the mountains. Dragons.

"There, to the east," Rienne breathed in his ear.

Gaven focused more of his attention to the east. The Seren longship's sails flapped fiercely, and the wind turned her broadside to the *Sea Tiger* as the Seren crew fought to furl the sails and bring their oars to bear. Gaven kept his eyes on the horizon and saw what Rienne had seen. After reaching their highest point, the mountains dropped abruptly on either side toward the sea.

"Good eye, Rienne," Jordhan said. "There's an inlet or bay there, and I'd wager it cuts through the mountains."

Gaven slumped against Rienne, and the wind died as suddenly as it had begun.

"Get us there," he said, panting for breath.

"I'll do my best," the captain answered.

"You'd better get your charts," Rienne said. "You're going to be adding to them."

"Let's hope they find their way back to Khorvaire."

* * * * *

Despite their taste of Gaven's power, the Serens shadowed the *Sea Tiger* along the coast, trying to keep between her and the beach. The Serens knew the waters better than Jordhan's charts could show him, and the captain's caution kept the galleon from outdistancing the Seren longship.

"If we hit a rock or even a sandbar out here, we might as well have sailed into the jaws of the Keeper," he said. "No one will come to rescue us, and we'll find no harbor to repair the hull."

"We're no better off if the Serens ram us," Gaven pointed out.

"I'm fairly certain you can prevent that."

"Probably. But they have oars as well as sails, and I'm not going to underestimate their determination to drive us away."

Jordhan sighed. "We're going as fast as I dare. They haven't caught us yet."

As fast as Jordhan dared proved to be fast enough. The captain dropped anchor at night, refusing to sail the unfamiliar waters in the dark. Gaven stayed on deck through the night, tracking the shadow of the Seren ship by the light of the Ring of Siberys, but they came only a little closer, keeping a safe distance from the *Sea Tiger* while still guarding the beach. By the middle of the next day, the inlet was in clear view—wide and calm, flanked by jutting pillars of natural stone like twin sentinels guarding the entrance to Argonnessen's inner reaches.

As they approached the inlet, the Serens fell farther behind, until the longship was nothing more than a dark speck amid the sea spray on the horizon.

"I think they've turned back," Rienne said.

Jordhan nodded. "It wouldn't surprise me. They're superstitious about this land. As far as I know, Totem Beach is as far as they go inland."

"With those mountains as barrier, I can hardly blame them," Gaven said.

"Perhaps that's all there is to it. But I suspect they wouldn't enter this inlet—they wouldn't dare trespass on the dragons' land."

"What remarkable discretion," Rienne said.

Gaven scowled at her, but she smiled and put a hand on his arm.

"You know I'm joking," she said. "We're in this together."

He put an arm around her shoulder and gazed ahead at the sentinel pillars. On the western side of the inlet, the stone was clearly part of the mountain range that shadowed Totem Beach. At that point, the sea pressed in close to the mountains, squeezing out the beach almost completely. The mountains, for their part, grew shorter as if giving way to the sea's advance into the inlet, but offered one last proclamation of their strength with this outcropping. On the eastern side, though, the stone towered over a surrounding blanket of forest. The mountain chain continued on the other side of the inlet, but much farther inland.

As they sailed closer to the pillars, the land beyond took shape. The inlet proved to be a wide channel cut deep into the mainland. On either side, the mountains sloped up to form a daunting barrier, but ahead the land rose more gently—Gaven was confident that they had found a way in to the land of dragons.

With the inlet beckoning, Gaven found it hard to stand still. He paced the deck through the afternoon, his eyes fixed on the gap in the mountains. It was a threshold few had ever crossed before him, an entrance into an almost unknown land. Even more, he felt something beyond the inlet calling to him, enticing him with a deeper understanding of the Prophecy. He kept the sails full of wind, but the *Sea Tiger* couldn't sail fast enough to satisfy him. He tried to persuade Jordhan to keep sailing through the night—the entrance was so close!—but the captain refused. He spent another restless night sleeping in fits, then getting up to pace the deck some more.

Late the next morning, the pillars rose up on either side of the *Sea Tiger*. They were miles apart, but they still seemed threatening as they loomed above the ship. Gaven watched them drift slowly past—then started in amazement.

The stone of the pillars was striated in varying shades of gray, brown, and red. The sides facing the inlet had strangely smooth walls—but they were carved with the enormous faces of dragons. They were clustered near the tops of the pillars, far above the reach of any human hands. Dozens of them, and no two the same. Long horns and short ones curled and coiled, or jutted straight back or to the sides. Scaly ridges jutted at every angle from cheeks, jaws, chins, and ears. Each one had its own attitude, its own personality. Gaven pointed them out to Jordhan and Rienne.

"Just like the ones on the beach," Jordhan said.

Rienne shook her head. "But these aren't totems for the Serens."

"It makes me think," Gaven said. "Perhaps these and the ones on the beach were made for the same purpose."

"To warn intruders away," Rienne said.

"Exactly. They say quite clearly that this land belongs to the dragons."

As if in response to Gaven's words, a dark shape rose up from the top of the eastern pillar. It was long and serpentine, and its wings were like fans extending along its sides, tapering down to the end of its tail. It snaked through the sky high above them, weaving great circles in the air.

Gaven clenched the bulwark. "It's just taking our measure."

"I hope you're right," Jordhan muttered.

"I hope I'm wrong. I'm here to learn from the dragons. I'd rather talk to one now, or fight it if I have to, than fight three dragons later when they decide to attack us."

Jordhan shrugged. "All I know is I'd rather live a little longer, even if it's only a few hours. I mean to squeeze every last drop out of life before I'm dragon food."

"No one on this ship will be dragon food," Gaven said, louder than he meant to. "Just keep sailing, Jordhan."

The captain's face darkened, and he stalked back to the helm without another word.

"Damn," Gaven muttered. "I didn't mean to—"

"It's been a long journey, Gaven," Rienne said. "We're all getting a little testy."

"At this rate, we'll kill each other before the dragons have a chance."

CHAPTER
5

Kauth stared out the window of another Orien coach as it rolled past an apparently endless series of trees. This time, though, Vor sat stiffly beside him, and Sevren and Zandar joked in the seat behind. Perhaps a dozen other passengers half-filled the enormous coach, watching the countryside drift slowly by or talking quietly with each other. Even a team of magebred horses pulled the coach at what felt to Kauth like a snail's pace. The first five days outside of Varna, the view had been monotonous—farm after farm on the starboard side, and the broad expanse of Lake Galifar to port. The other side of the lake was too far away to see, except for the peaks of the Blackcaps jutting up in the middle. Leaving the unremarkable village of Niern that morning, though, the coach had finally turned away from the coast toward Greenheart, and fields soon gave way to the dense forest that made up the heart of the Eldeen Reaches.

The trees crowded close in to the road, as if they resented the civilizing influence that had cleared away their brothers and sisters. Their leaves blocked the sun, shrouding the forest in a perpetual twilight. At times, branches scraped against the roof of the coach or broke against its sides. Wild animals watched the coach without fear—at one point, passengers on the port side had screamed in terror as an enormous Eldeen bear shambled up beside the coach, staring at them eye to eye. Other, stranger things flitted through the forest at a safer distance, some wearing more or less humanoid shapes, others more like beasts. Sometimes the trees themselves walked, shadowing the coach on its course.

Around midday, the coach lurched to a stop. A nervous hum of whispered conversation rose immediately in the coach, and Kauth shot a glance at Vor. The orc looked at him, nodded, and heaved himself to his feet—plate armor and all. He strode to the front of the coach, and Kauth grabbed his crossbow as he got up to follow.

"Wait." Zandar grabbed his arm.

"There might be trouble," Kauth said, whirling to face the warlock. "I'm not going to let Vor face it alone."

"Neither are we," Sevren said. He bent his bow and looped the string around the free end. "But Vor prefers to face trouble head-on."

"While we sneak around behind," Zandar said, jerking his head toward the back of the coach. "This way."

Sevren followed, and Kauth trailed behind to the door at the back of the coach and out into the shadow-cloaked woods. The air was warm and heavy, quiet with the expectation of a summer thunderstorm. Vor's voice, coming from in front of the coach, was muffled but clear.

"This coach is under my protection," he called out. "You will face me before you harm a single person aboard."

The only sound Kauth could hear in response was a harsh hiss that pulsed with anger.

"It's the Children of Winter," Sevren whispered, and Zandar nodded.

"What does that mean?" Kauth asked. The name sounded familiar to him—he thought perhaps it referred to one of the druidic sects of the Eldeen Reaches.

"It means bugs," Zandar said with a grin. "Lots of big bugs."

"Let's move," Sevren said.

He and Zandar moved to opposite sides of the coach and skulked into the shadows of the trees. Kauth decided to stick with Sevren, trailing several yards behind. The shifter held an arrow nocked in his bow, and made only the slightest rustle as he moved. Kauth felt clumsy by comparison.

Another rattling hiss made him start, then Sevren cried out. An arrow flew wild, and something yanked the shifter off his feet and into the air. The forest blocked Kauth's view, so he broke into a run.

He cleared an ancient oak and stopped short. An enormous

green mantis, taller than an ogre, held Sevren in two scythelike claws. Four other legs held the insect's slender body off the ground, and its long abdomen jutted out and up behind it. Sevren had managed to pull out two long knives, but it was all he could do to keep the mandibles at the bottom of the creature's triangular head from tearing open his belly.

Kauth lifted his crossbow to his eye and sighted along the shaft of the quarrel, aiming for one of the insect's enormous eyes. Just as he tightened his grip to loose the bolt, a centipede the size of his finger dropped onto his hand from a branch above. He jerked, and his quarrel soared over the mantis's head.

"Bugs, indeed," he muttered, shaking his hand to throw the centipede off. In the same moment, something landed on the back of his neck and bit, sending a jolt of pain down his spine.

Swatting at whatever had landed on him, he stumbled away from the oak where he'd stopped. Glancing back at it, he realized that the tree was alive with centipedes, writhing and crawling over every inch of bark. He shuddered, brushing at his arms and chest, then he remembered Sevren.

Just as he turned, Sevren fell from the mantis's claws, the creature's head falling with him. The creature jerked spasmodically, lashing out with its claws as it staggered forward. One claw raked across the shifter's chest, but Sevren lashed out with a knife and cut it cleanly off. With a final shudder, the mantis fell to the ground, its legs twitching in the air.

Kauth ran to the shifter. "Let me look at you," he said. "How bad are your wounds?"

"Don't worry about me!" Sevren snarled. "We need to get to Vor!" He sheathed his knives, retrieved his bow from where it had fallen, and set off, nocking another arrow as he ran.

The shifter leaped over ferns and roots without breaking stride, and Kauth found himself lagging again. When he lost sight of Sevren, he felt the forest close in around him. Everywhere his eyes fell, he saw some kind of crawling thing—spiders the size of his fist skittering along branches, thick millipedes snaking amid the fallen leaves, beetles whirring their wings in the air, a scorpion the size of a dog creeping slowly alongside his path.

He felt them all watching him—thousands of eyes following his every movement, sizing up their prey. His skin crawled, and every few steps he swatted at some real or imagined vermin pricking his exposed skin.

He broke, panting, out of the forest and onto the road in front of the Orien coach. Vor stood directly in front of the coach, the ground around him littered with the shattered carapaces of enormous spiders and insects of every description—as well as one crumpled gray-cloaked human form. Two more of the hooded figures dodged the sweeping strikes of his greataxe, trying to slash through his armor with their curved blades. A wasp the size of a horse darted around him, lunging at him and then flying back out of his axe's reach, the droning of its wings drowning out the sounds of the battle.

Two men and a woman, all wearing the unicorn symbol of House Orien on their shoulders, stood behind Vor with light-weight blades in their hands. They jabbed at the hooded Children of Winter and the pack of scorpions and spiders at their feet, but it was clear that if the defense of the coach had rested in the hands of these warriors alone, it would already be overrun. The horror-struck faces of the other passengers peered out the windows at chittering swarms and gigantic vermin crawling over the carriage's sides and windows.

Sevren and Zandar ranged back and forth at the edge of the forest to line up clear shots against the Children of Winter and their many-legged minions. Sevren kept his bow in his left hand, but he alternated between pulling it back to loose an arrow and yanking out his knife to cut down a foe that came too close. His arrows feathered several corpses littered over the road, and a few more lay along his path at the side of the road.

Zandar held no weapon, but he fired blasts of shadow from his hands, like the one he'd used to shatter Vor's mug back in Varna. When an enemy got too close, he lashed out with a hand curled into a claw, drawing streaks of shadow and blood across the chest or face of his foe. He had evidently reached the scene before Sevren—without the distraction of the giant mantis, it was easy to imagine how—and his body count was higher.

A clump of four gray-robed women kept their distance from the melee, standing back to back in the midst of a swarm of red-hued wasps that buzzed constantly around them but evidently caused them no discomfort. They had thrown back their hoods to reveal long, wild hair. Two were withered crones, but one looked more like a plump baker or farmer than a sinister priestess, and the fourth was no more than twenty. The women chanted a constant stream of ritual prayers, pointing here and there around the field of battle. Wherever one pointed, vines and roots sprang out of the forest to grab at one of Kauth's allies, a blast of wind made someone stagger backward, or another giant vermin skittered out of the forest. Kauth had found his place in the battle. Dropping his crossbow and sliding his mace out of its loop at his belt, he ran at the knot of women.

As soon as he reached them, he wished he hadn't. The swarm of wasps descended on him, stinging every bit of skin they could find. Their stings burned like fire, and they buzzed in his ears, crawled to his eyes and mouth, and began working their way under his armor. He managed a swing of his mace at one of the crones, knocking her back against her comrades, then he staggered out of the swirling, droning cloud.

The crone he had hit spoke a word, and a ball of flame appeared in her outstretched palm. Snarling at Kauth, she hurled the fire at him. He sprang out of its path, but another dancing flame appeared in the druid's hand.

"Sea of Fire," Kauth muttered. "That's not a bad idea."

He backed away, stopping short at a chittering sound behind him. He swung his mace as he turned and was rewarded by a crunching sound of chitin and the squelch of a spider's soft body beneath. Jumping across the wolf-sized spider's corpse, he ran another ten yards or so, fumbling around in the quiver at his belt to find the right wand.

He drew out a slender length of cherry wood topped with a fire opal, turning it over in his hands to feel the magic inside it. A weaving pattern of fiery lines took shape in his mind. Pointing the red gemstone at the cluster of druids and their living shield, he loosed the knot of magic in the wand, letting the fire burst forth.

It shot like a glowing ember toward the druids, then blossomed into an enormous sphere of roaring flame. The women shrieked in pain as the fire seared their flesh. The magical flames dissolved into the air, leaving the druids scorched but standing—but the swarming cloud of wasps was gone. The cinders of a hundred thousand tiny wasp bodies littered the ground.

"Well done!" Zandar called to him, loosing a blast of shadow at the nearest druid. She fell on the ground and lay still. Kauth jammed the wand back into his pouch, shifted his mace back into his right hand, and charged at the remaining three.

Just as he reached them, an arrow thudded into the one on his left, then two more in rapid succession, and she followed her sister to the ground. He shot a glance at Sevren and realized that the battle was winding down. No more vermin harried the shifter or Zandar, and Vor was charging at the remaining women from the opposite side. Kauth sighed his relief, and at that moment a blast of lightning shot out of the sky, knocking him off his feet.

"Gaven?" he murmured, then the world went black.

CHAPTER
6

During the Last War, while he served in Aundair's army, Cart had often marveled at the muscles of the human face. So many small bits of flesh moved the skin, the eyebrows, and the eyes—all combining to form such a bewildering variety of expressions. Humans and the other races like them wore their emotions on their faces, though the dwarves were better at steeling their faces than the others. But to him it was as though they spoke a foreign language he understood imperfectly. When they died, their faces all seemed to freeze in a mask of their horror. Sometimes they looked down at the wound where his axe had slashed them open. Other times they looked at his face.

A mask—that was his face. A smooth plate of metal, incapable of any expression except opening and closing his mouth. A single rune on his forehead marked the place of his forging and an identifying number. His face was quite effective at striking fear into an enemy's heart. It also made it surprisingly easy for him pass lies as truth. But at times, Cart wished for the simplicity of a scowl or a frown to express his displeasure.

Haldren was trying to explain Kelas's plans, the complex machinations the spy had set in motion. Kelas's goal was the same as Haldren's had been, when he first escaped from Dreadhold: seizing the throne of Aundair. But Haldren had relied solely on military power to achieve what he wanted, making no more than a half-hearted attempt to secure allies beyond his contacts in the army. Kelas, on the other hand, not only relied on Haldren's military contacts—those that had survived the last ill-fated excursion, anyway—but also spent most of his effort negotiating, wheedling, manipulating the wizards of Arcanix, the artificers of House

Cannith, and his own allies and underlings among the Royal Eyes of Aundair. It was a world of diplomacy and compromise that was completely alien to Cart's way of thinking.

"Try to understand it as a military campaign," Haldren tried to explain. "Each of these potential allies is like a key strategic objective. Kelas marshals his forces to take each one, mindful of how he distributes them, sometimes giving way at one battlefield in order to win another."

Cart shrugged—one means he did have to express emotion, and one that he found effective. "That's your expertise, Lord General, not mine. I'm a soldier, not a general, not a diplomat. And not an assassin."

Haldren threw up his hands. "Forget it, then. I'll work with Kelas. You just do what you're told."

"I always do," Cart said. It was true—he was made to follow orders, and he took that duty seriously. "You are my commanding officer. But I am your staff—your entire staff—and I cannot advise you in matters I do not understand."

"Clearly, in this realm I do not need your advice."

"Clearly." Cart's jaw tightened. A human like Haldren would not detect the flex of fibers at the joint.

"Dismissed." Haldren spat. He turned his attention to the papers on his desk.

Cart had to give credit where it was due. Haldren had learned to rein in his temper. Of course, that meant he was little more than Kelas's lackey. He did not like to see the Lord General so beaten. Though he had to admit that his confidence in Haldren's judgment had diminished since the debacle at the Starcrag Plain.

He put his hands on Haldren's desk and rose slowly to his feet. Haldren did not glance up. A quick salute, then Cart turned crisply and strode out of the room. He turned just as decisively to the left and made it down past four other doors before he realized he'd gone the wrong way. He stopped abruptly, then pivoted where he stood and walked back the way he'd come. He fought the impulse to slam a fist into Haldren's door as he walked past it.

The halls and offices beneath the abandoned cathedral of the Silver Flame formed a labyrinth appropriate to their new use as

Kelas's base of operations. Cart found himself just as lost among the vaulted passages as he was in the political scheming, and just as frustrated.

He rounded a corner and something slammed into his chest. Not something, he realized—someone. His arms folded reflexively around her as she yelped in surprise, then he gently took hold of her shoulders and steadied her on her feet. Only then did he recognize her as Ashara d'Cannith, Kelas's liaison to the northern branch of House Cannith.

"I'm sorry—" she began.

Cart cut her off as he fell to one knee. "Lady Cannith, the fault is mine."

House Cannith had built him and given him life. Their creation forges had birthed his race. Any dragonmarked heir of the House was his rightful master. The question had never come up, but if he were forced to choose between obeying the Lord General and obeying the most insignificant heir of the House, it would be a difficult decision.

"No, no," she protested. She reached down to his elbow and gently guided him to his feet. "I wasn't watching where I was going. You're Cart, aren't you? Haldren's . . ."

"His advisor, yes." He wondered what she was going to say. Slave? Part of him suspected that, despite the emancipation of the warforged with the Treaty of Thronehold, House Cannith still thought of them more as property than as people.

"I don't know if you remember me, but I was at Bluevine with you and Haldren. I'm Ashara." She held out her hand to him, as naturally as if she were meeting a new friend in a tavern.

"Lady, I—"

"Just Ashara." She smiled, and Cart found himself warming to her.

She was a small woman—her head had collided with his chest, her shoulder hitting the bottom of his chest plate. The lyrelike shape of the Mark of Making swooped across her upper arm. Her brown hair was cut short, and her eyes were the same color, warm and bright in the pale magical light of the everburning torches that lit the halls. Her smile—once again, Cart marveled at the intricacy of the muscles. Her smile reached all the way to the corners of her eyes.

He clasped her outstretched hand. "I'm glad to meet you, Ashara," he said.

"Likewise, Cart." Still clasping his hand, she asked, "Were you on your way somewhere?"

"Out of here, that's all."

"Oh, good. Perhaps you could help me find the exit?"

"I'll try," Cart said. "I confess I often get lost under here. But I think it's this way." He pointed the direction he'd been walking, and they started walking side by side along the hall.

"I feel lost in this whole affair," Ashara said.

Cart turned his head to look at her. She did not seem to be joking, which made her confession surprising both for its content and in the simple fact that she made it to him.

"But you're essential to the whole operation," he said.

"My House is essential. I am not. And this is the first time I've been in this position—negotiating for the House, mediating between Kelas and Baron Jorlanna. I wish they'd just talk to each other and leave me out of this."

"I feel much the same way."

"What's your role in all this?"

"I'm not certain. I work for Haldren, and he keeps asking me for advice in matters I just don't understand. Including," he added, "how to get Baron Jorlanna committed to Kelas's plans. What is it that Kelas wants from House Cannith?"

"Armaments, for one thing. But primarily, just the assurance of Jorlanna's support in the . . . transfer of power."

"And what's he offering in return?"

"In the short term, a new facility. He says he has plans for a new kind of forge, one that will triple the House's production capabilities and enable the creation of entirely new kinds of weapons."

"The Dragon Forge," Cart said.

"So you know about it." Ashara seemed surprised. Tiny muscles lifted her eyebrows higher on her forehead and widened her eyes.

"Only the name. Haldren is accustomed to telling me only

what I need to know." Cart shrugged. "And underestimating what I need to know."

"Sounds familiar. Except that Kelas tells me only what he wants the Baron to know. And Baron Jorlanna tells me what she wants him to know. Precious little passing in either direction. I have to guess the rest."

"What do you know about the Dragon Forge? And what have you guessed?"

"Well, not much more than what I said—higher production, new armaments." She frowned. "The work of artificers and mage-wrights depends largely on the ability to manipulate the magic that's locked inside everything. We sometimes describe it as finding a knot, a tangle of energy in the heart of something and loosing it so the magic can flow properly. What Kelas promises amounts to an enormous knot and the means to open it."

"Why is it called the Dragon Forge? Where do the dragons come in?" Cart asked.

"I'm not certain."

"I would have thought we were done with dragons after the Starcrag Plain." The memory of that defeat still stung. The bronze dragon, Vaskar, had led Haldren into it, lying to him all along. He'd promised Haldren a flight of dragons to guarantee victory, even as he was marshaling a flight of dragons to fight on the Thrane side of the battle as well. All to orchestrate the fulfillment of the Prophecy—a foretold "clash of dragons."

"This world will never be done with dragons, I'm afraid."

"They've been here since the beginning, I suppose they'll be here until the end. But why do we have to deal with them at all?"

"It takes power to seize power. And the dragons have power to spare."

They finally emerged from the old cathedral into a secluded alleyway. Ashara turned her face to the sun and basked in it.

"I hate it down there," she said. "I should have been a Lyrandar, not a Cannith. I'd much rather spend my days on the deck of an airship than down in some forge."

The mention of House Lyrandar made Cart think of Gaven, and he fell silent. At the end of the battle at Starcrag Plain, Cart had left Haldren's side to fight with Gaven, helping him carve a path through the hordes of the Soul Reaver. Down in the Soul Reaver's haunts, he had briefly toyed with the idea of becoming a god himself, imagining what it would be like to be god of the warforged.

From the threshold of immortality to the cellars of the abandoned cathedral. How he had fallen.

"Where are you going now?" Ashara asked.

"A fine question," Cart muttered. There seemed nowhere to go but farther down.

"Would you care to accompany me to our enclave? You could meet the Baron."

Cart had heard Haldren speak of disgust rising in his gut, or the taste of it in his mouth, and indeed he made the same face when he felt disgust at some person or idea that he made when he tasted something he didn't like. Lacking a digestive system or any sense of taste, Cart had never understood the physical sensation of it, but disgust assailed his mind like a wave of unease radiating back from his face.

"No," he said. He had no taste for the scheming, the maneuvering. And he had a sudden sense that even kind, pleasant Ashara was using him, trying to bring him into a position that would bring her advantage. "I enjoyed our talk, Lady," he said, honestly. "I hope to see you again soon. But I must go."

He put his back to the cathedral and the Cannith district and walked away.

He was a good twenty paces away when he heard Ashara's quiet voice. "Good-bye, Cart."

CHAPTER
7

K auth's first conscious awareness was of motion—back and forth, bouncing up and down. Slowly the sensation resolved into the gentle lurch of the Orien coach, continuing along the rough road to Greenheart. The light began to register in his vision, and he opened his eyes. Zandar crouched over him, wearing his habitual sardonic smile.

"He lives!" the warlock proclaimed.

Full awareness of where he was rushed into his mind, accompanied by a surge of panic. He put a hand to his face to check—yes, he was still Kauth. He tried to roll himself sideways and nearly fell off the bench he was lying on. With some effort, he managed to prop himself up on one elbow. His body still screamed with pain, and he grimaced at Zandar.

"You have my thanks, Zandar," he said. "But you're about the last person I'd think to call a healer." He fumbled at his quiver, reaching for one of the wands he used most often, one that held healing magic. It wasn't there.

"Looking for these?" Zandar said, holding three wands out to Kauth. "You can thank them, not me."

Kauth snatched them away. He didn't like the idea of anyone rummaging through his pouches—especially the warlock, he realized. Even if Zandar had just saved his life, he wasn't quite ready to trust the man. Choosing one of the wands, he extended his mind to touch the weave of magic it held, and felt a fresh wave of healing magic wash over his body like cool water against fevered skin. He took a deep breath and sat up.

A murmur of approval arose in the seats around him—evidently several of the nearby passengers had been watching with interest. Sevren and Vor stood in the seat behind him, and even the orc was smiling. Zandar moved from his crouch and sat on the bench next to Kauth.

Zandar leaned close and murmured in his ear. "I'm afraid we've become celebrities on the coach," he said. "Too much attention, if you ask me."

"What happened?" Kauth asked, shaking his head. "It's all a blur."

"The Children of Winter attacked the coach, of course. And we killed them. That makes us heroes." Zandar grinned again. "I've always wondered what that would feel like."

"Who are the Children of Winter, and why did they attack us?"

"Sevren, you want to answer that?"

The shifter leaned over the bench. "They're one of the—" He stopped suddenly, and Kauth turned to look at him. Sevren's amber eyes were narrowed as he looked down at him.

"What's wrong?" Kauth asked.

"What kind of agent of the Wardens doesn't know who the Children of Winter are? Khyber's blood, what Reacher doesn't know them by reputation at least? Who are you really?"

Kauth glanced at Zandar, who sat between him and the aisle. The warlock scowled, and Kauth could almost see his eldritch power boiling in his eyes, churning shadow eager to burst forth and wreak destruction.

Damn Kelas, he thought, and damn the Royal Eyes of Aundair. They should have given me more information.

But they want me dead, he reminded himself.

"All right," he said, looking back at Sevren. "I wasn't completely honest with you back in Varna. I'm not a Reacher. I was born in Stormreach, and I've only been in Khorvaire for a few weeks. I came here looking for work—the kind of work that my experience in Xen'drik might help with. The Wardens hired me for this mission, so I'm a sword for hire, not one of their regular scouts or agents."

"Much like us," Vor observed.

"How much are they paying you?" Zandar asked.

Kauth did some quick math in his head. He had offered them payment of a thousand gold galifars each. It would be reasonable for him to keep two parts for himself. "Five thousand."

Zandar looked to Sevren, and Kauth met the shifter's gaze. Sevren stared at him for a long time. Finally he said, "That's a pretty good story. It'll do for now. Zandar, Vor, you agree?"

The others nodded. Zandar's smile returned to his face. Kauth wasn't sure what to make of that.

"So here's what we're going to do. We'll take that five thousand and divide it in four parts instead of five. We're all equal partners in this mission now. Twelve fifty each."

Just the right amount of hesitation, Kauth reminded himself. "Done."

Sevren extended a hand over the back of the bench, and Kauth clasped it. "Equal partners," the shifter said. "That means I give the orders now."

Zandar laughed, and Kauth just shrugged. "Seems to me you'll do a good job keeping us alive," he said. "I have no problem with that."

"Good. That's settled. Now, back to your question, ignorant Stormreacher."

Kauth laughed. The people of the Eldeen Reaches were used to scorn coming from the self-styled sophisticates of the Five Nations. They all looked down together on the provincials of Stormreach, situated at the tip of the mysterious southern continent of Xen'drik.

Sevren shared the laugh. "The Children of Winter are one of the crazier sects running around the Reaches," he said. "Their leaders are druids, so they have sort of a respect for nature. But they tend to focus on a part of nature's cycle that other sects prefer not to dwell on."

"The dying part," Kauth guessed.

"Exactly. They work with spiders, scorpions, wasps, and centipedes—that sort of thing. That seems to be a matter of personal preference rather than a part of their philosophy, but it certainly helps them terrify the peasants, which seems to be part of their goals."

"So why did they attack the coach?"

Sevren shrugged. "That's what they do. They believe that nature is going to cleanse the land, and they see themselves as agents of that cleansing."

"Hastening the cycle of nature," Zandar observed.

"Something like that."

"I hope they were prepared to meet the end of their life cycles," the warlock said.

Kauth laughed—it was easy to make himself laugh. But as he laughed, he wondered whether his companions were prepared for their own deaths.

Nothing is permanent, he reminded himself.

His next thought disturbed him: Perhaps I should join the Children of Winter.

* * * * *

Greenheart was a stark contrast to Varna and, indeed, to every capital city of Khorvaire. It would be a stretch to call it a city at all. At a guess, Kauth figured that fifty Greenhearts would fit inside Fairhaven's walls, but he thought he might be guessing too low. There were precious few actual buildings—little more than stone huts that looked as though they'd been lifted out of the earth to serve as shelter. Other residents lived on strange platforms in the trees that seemed to be extended from the branches themselves. Nowhere in the town was the work of carpenters or masons readily apparent.

The Orien coach dropped them near the center of town, took on a few new passengers, and started quickly back the way it had come, along the only road into or out of the capital of the Eldeen Reaches. The town center itself was not a marketplace or business district, but a lush green grove ringed with ancient pines. Hard-looking warriors stood guard among the pines—humans and shifters armed with bows and knives, much like Sevren Thorn. Kauth shot a glance at Sevren. Had he once stood as a guardian of Greenheart's sacred grove?

There could be no doubt that this grove was sacred to the Reachers. Even with his limited knowledge of the Eldeen Reaches and their druids, Kauth knew that Greenheart was a center of religion, not politics. The druids of Greenheart supervised the activities of the Wardens of the Wood throughout the Reaches, and that supervision extended to matters of governance as well as spirituality, but this was no many-tiered, rigid hierarchy like Thrane's. The Wardens served as spiritual advisors to their communities and arbitrators of disputes, and the druids of Greenheart offered them support and advice more than supervision or discipline.

"Ah, Greenheart," Zandar sighed. "The only capital city of Khorvaire without a tavern."

"The druids will give us shelter," Sevren said. His voice was hushed, almost reverent, heightening Kauth's suspicion that the shifter had some connection to the guardians of the grove.

"What about the Great Crag?" Vor said. "Is there a tavern in the court of the three sisters?"

The capital of Droaam, a nation of monsters just to the south of the Eldeen Reaches, was little more than a collection of goblin camps and gnoll barracks. Harpies nested in the cliffs of the city, and three hags—the three sisters—governed the fractious nation from a court built among the ruins of the ancient hobgoblin empire of Dhakaan.

"Have you ever seen an ogre drink?" Zandar said. "There must be taverns there to feed those appetites."

"House Tharashk has an outpost there," Kauth added. "I'm sure they maintain something like civilized facilities." House Tharashk, made up of orcs and half-orcs as well as humans, had made enormous profits during the Last War by recruiting mercenaries from among the monsters of Droaam.

"What about Ashtakala?" Zandar said, grinning wolfishly at Vor.

"The city of demons is not the capital of the Demon Wastes," the orc growled.

"Isn't it a legend?" Sevren said. "I've never heard of anyone who's actually been there."

"It's real," Vor said.

Zandar smirked. "Or as real as a million-year-old city populated with masters of illusion can be." He was clearly trying to nettle Vor, and it was working. "Maybe we'll find it on our expedition."

Vor stepped close to the warlock and stooped to look straight in his face. "You had better pray to whatever creatures you serve that we do not," he said. "Or we'll all be damned."

Zandar backed down after that, and Sevren led them to a druid he said would help them stock up for their journey. But Kauth couldn't get Vor's words out of his mind.

* * * * *

Sevren proved to have useful contacts in Greenheart, and soon their packs were loaded with everything they would need for their journey—food, tents, rope, even extra clothes and weapons. Considering that none of the town's buildings were crafted unless by druidic magic, the town was well supplied with the gear used by rangers and druids in the wild.

That evening, they set up their new tents near the edge of town, where the trees started coming closer together and the stone huts farther apart. They had agreed on two tents, each one large enough to hold two of them. Zandar and Sevren shared one, which left Kauth and Vor in the other. Kauth was relieved to see that Vor removed his plate armor to sleep—he had visions of the orc's large shoulderplate jabbing into him as he tried to sleep. Even so, the tent was going to be crowded with the two larger members of the group together.

Kauth stayed awake outside the tent when the others retired for the night. For a while he sat and listened to the sounds of the forest—the chirping of frogs and crickets, the hoots of owls, and the soft, mournful songs of parents lulling their children to sleep. He could grow to like Greenheart, he decided—it had a peace and harmony about it that was sorely lacking in the other parts of his many lives.

With that thought, he began preparing his mind for the night ahead. He would be in close quarters with Vor, and he could not allow his identity to slip as it had on the airship with Gaven and Rienne. He began by reviewing the shape and features of his body, from his unruly hair and steel eyes down to his thick, crooked toes with their ugly nails. Cementing every detail in his mind as he had learned so many years ago.

She was jolted out of sleep by Kelas's voice: "Who are you?"

She sat bolt upright and shouted her answer: "I am Faura Arann."

"Stand for inspection."

Kelas examined every detail of her face and body, measured the length of her hair, checked that her mole had not drifted while she slept. He stood behind her and weighed her breasts with his hands.

"Excellent. Go back to sleep."

Kelas never paid enough attention to the eyes, she thought. It's the eyes that will give you away.

Kauth shook the unwelcome memory from his mind, scowling at himself. He ran a hand over his face to make sure he hadn't slipped.

"Focus," he told himself. He repeated the exercise, from the top of his head to the leathery soles of his feet. Fixed each detail in his memory.

Who are you? he asked himself.

Kauth Dennar, he answered. A mercenary during the war, now a drifter, a thug, an adventurer. Born and raised in Stormreach. I'm working for the Wardens of the Wood.

And leading my friends to their deaths.

"Listen well," Kelas said, leaning over him. "You have no friends. You love nothing, care about nothing. Nothing is permanent— everything changes, everyone will die. If you love, if you care about anything, you will suffer. You will fail!" He punctuated his last words by striking Haunderk's face with the back of his hand.

And what about hate, Kelas? Haunderk thought. Isn't hate a form of caring? You can't hate someone who's irrelevant to you.

"Focus," he whispered through clenched teeth. Once more, from the top of his head to the soles of his feet. And again, reining in his wandering mind.

Nothing is permanent. Everyone will die. I will not fail.

CHAPTER
8

Gaven's assessment of the dragon seemed correct. It circled above them—"like a vulture," Jordhan observed—until they had cleared the sentinel pillars, then flew inland until they lost sight of it. Gaven cursed, but the crew was breathing easier.

Better to deal with the dragons when I'm risking only my own life, Gaven realized. And Rienne's.

The wide channel's waters were still and clear. Coral reefs teemed with life far below the surface, brightly colored fish darting in and out of their aquatic castles. They spotted some larger creatures as dark shadows in the distance—an enormous eel the size of the *Sea Tiger,* and what might have been a dragon turtle that dwarfed her—but those monsters kept clear of the ship.

Jordhan hugged the western edge of the channel as close as he dared, keeping an eye on the coral so it didn't tear a hole in the hull. He stopped the ship when the daylight became too weak for him to see into the depths, but no one aboard slept except in fits, jerking awake at every strange sound or surge of the waves.

At daybreak, Gaven looked around and saw a crew on the brink of mutiny. Lack of sleep and abject terror had begun to overcome even this crew's fierce loyalty to Jordhan. They wanted to sail back to familiar waters—it was written plainly on their haggard faces. He pulled Jordhan into the captain's quarters.

"We have to find a place to disembark as soon as possible," he said as the hatch closed behind him.

"What's the matter?" Jordhan asked.

"Your crew. I don't think you can rely on them much longer."

"You finally noticed? You think I don't know my crew?"

Gaven grimaced. He hadn't intended to start another quarrel with the captain. "What are we going to do about it?"

"They're my crew, aren't they?" Jordhan seemed determined to fight.

Gaven looked more closely at his old friend, and suddenly noticed what he had managed to ignore for so long—the same haggard expression, sunken eyes and hollow cheeks, he'd seen on the *Sea Tiger*'s crew.

Thunder and lightning, he thought. What have I done?

"They are your crew, and this is your ship. I'm sorry I put you through this."

Jordhan's shoulders slumped. "I insisted. You're my friend."

"That means the world to me." He clapped Jordhan on the shoulder. "We'll get through this."

Jordhan straightened, managed a weak smile, and followed Gaven back onto the deck.

That afternoon, one of the sailors charged with watching for dangers to the hull spotted the wreck of another ship, encrusted with barnacles and coral. Her mast rose dangerously close to the surface, so Jordhan steered clear. But as they sailed past, a number of sailors clumped at the bulwark, watching the wreck as they passed, muttering darkly to each other.

Gaven shook his head. He couldn't blame them for their mood. It had been a long journey, they had already spotted one dragon as well as other dangers lurking in the water, and the ship-wreck seemed like a premonition of their own future. Standing beside Rienne, he stared blankly at the wall of mountains rising up to starboard, wondering whether he had made a terrible mistake in bringing them into this danger.

After a moment, his eyes took in the landscape before him. His mind seemed to shift into a different way of thinking and per ceiving, and the mountains were no longer just mountains.

"What is it, love?" Rienne was looking up at him, concern etched on her brow.

"Eternity," he whispered.

She tried to follow his gaze, searching the mountains to see whatever it was that he saw.

"The words of creation, Ree. They're written on the land here—the Prophecy is inscribed in the shape of the mountains and the path of the coast." Before the battle at Starcrag Plain, the rolling hills and fields of Aundair had spoken to him of their past and future, of centuries of turmoil and bloodshed. This land was different, powerfully different.

"Tell me what you see."

"Eternity," he repeated. "The land of the dragons has been since the beginning, and it will be at the end of the world. Change is alien to this land. The Prophecy unfolds around it, not within it."

It was not quite unchanging, he realized. But the pace of its history was slower than in Khorvaire. The echoes of incredibly ancient events still resounded dimly within the mountains. He saw a trace of the battle that had wrecked the ship, a fleeting blur of movement where the destiny and activity of Khorvaire intruded upon the stately majesty of eternal Argonnessen.

"What about us?" Rienne asked. "Surely our arrival here speaks of change, however small."

"A tiny quaver in the voice of the Prophecy. We will leave no lasting mark on this land."

"Which is greater? To leave a great mark on the volatile history of Khorvaire, or to add your voice to the symphony of eternity?"

Gaven furrowed his brow and looked down at Rienne. She tore her eyes from the horizon and met his gaze. He took in her whole face, ran his fingers through her hair. He had always had a vague sense that her destiny was significant, momentous, but it had never been clear to him—or to her. He saw her, for a moment, as a part of this land. She had mastered the discipline of focusing her soul's energy, uniting thought with action. There was a stillness even in her movement, a purity of intention. A thread of eternity woven into her mortality.

"I don't know," he admitted at last.

* * * * *

Early the next morning, Jordhan called Gaven and Rienne to the poop deck and pointed to the coast ahead of the *Sea Tiger*. Gaven scanned the coast, but he found that his eyes were still on the Prophecy, and he had a hard time discerning what Jordhan was pointing at.

"The cove?" Rienne asked.

"I think we've found our harbor," Jordhan answered.

Finally Gaven saw the cove cut into the coast ahead of them. The mountains rose up on the near side of the cove, but on the far side, a beach sloped gently up to level ground.

"The gates to Argonnessen stand open," he said.

The words stirred something in his memory—the gates of Khyber? The Soul Reaver's gates? That portal had figured prominently in the Prophecy surrounding the battle at Starcrag Plain and his fight against the Soul Reaver. But he felt there was something else. . . .

He smiled at himself. A few months ago, the Prophecy had been so vivid in his mind that it leaped to mind unbidden, overwhelming him with visions and dire warnings. Now he searched his memory and caught only the hem of a fleeting thought—the gates to the land of dragons . . . or something like that. He didn't miss the nightmares, the visions that seized him even when he was awake, the constant sense that he remembered events an instant before they occurred. But as he had said to Rienne, he did miss the sense of purpose.

"The gates to Argonnessen," Rienne echoed.

While Gaven was lost in thought, Jordhan returned to the helm to steer the *Sea Tiger* into the cove. Rienne leaned over the bulwark, staring at the distant beach.

She glanced over her shoulder at him with a grin. "You have a way of making everything sound so momentous."

"Don't you think it is? How many people have even seen this land, let alone walked into its heart?"

"Perhaps I've grown jaded. You and I spent years venturing into caverns far below the earth where no one had ventured before. Somehow that never seemed so . . . weighty."

"It turned out to be, though, didn't it? That's where I found that nightshard, the Heart of Khyber."

Rienne's face clouded. That single moment had set world-shaking events in motion—from speeding along the schism of

House Thuranni, to Gaven's sentence in Dreadhold, and ultimately his confrontation with the Soul Reaver. It had caused them both a great deal of pain.

"We were so young," Gaven added. "Too young to appreciate the significance of what we were doing."

"Or perhaps now we're inclined to exaggerate the importance of our tiny quavers in the voice of the Prophecy."

A surge of anger rose in his chest. "You think I'm being arrogant? Is that what you think this is about?"

Rienne turned and leaned back against the bulwark. Gaven expected her face to mirror his own anger. Instead he saw sadness. "I still don't know what this is about," she said.

Her calm demeanor did nothing to soothe his anger. "How many times do I have to explain it to you?"

"Just until you find an explanation that makes sense."

"Saving the world doesn't make sense to you?"

"Saving the world, Gaven? Listen to yourself."

Gaven was completely dumbfounded. "You think that's pride."

"I think the world doesn't need saving. You said it earlier—this place is eternal, and the world with it. Nations and empires will come and go, we mortals will live our lives struggling like mad to leave any kind of lasting mark on it, but the voice of the Prophecy continues. Like the drums and the drone, unchanging beneath the melody."

"Eternity doesn't make that struggle less important. Maybe this isn't about saving the world. But it might very well be about saving everything we know as the world—all of Khorvaire, for example. I think that's important enough."

"And you think you can do that."

"I think I have to."

Rienne turned back and looked out over the glassy water. "I'm sorry, Gaven. It seems my heart's just not in this yet. I don't know what I'm doing here, what my part in all this is."

He put a hand on her back. "I'm glad you're with me, anyway."

She gave a slow nod. Then something caught her eye, and she pointed. "What's that?"

Gaven's gaze followed her pointing finger off to port and upward. Two dark shapes wheeled in the air—dragons. There could be no doubt.

"The dragons are back," Rienne breathed. "Sovereigns help us."

"We'd better tell Jor—"

The voice of the lookout cut him off. "Dragons!"

"Do you have a plan?" Rienne asked.

In answer, Gaven stretched out his fingers, feeling the wind that drove their ship toward the cove. His dragonmark itched again, and the wind gusted briefly, then grew steadily. He felt the wind move through him, felt the storm gathering in his mind. The brilliant blue drained out of the sky, and a veil of gray draped the sun.

"What are you doing?" Rienne said. "They'll think we're attacking!"

Dark clouds gathered above them, responding to the surge of anger he felt. "I'm trying," he said, "to get the ship into the cove." Speaking was difficult. Every word sparked a gust of wind.

Rienne looked toward the cove, then back at the panicked crew. "I'll get the crew below."

The dragons were coming in fast, adjusting their course to account for the *Sea Tiger*'s burst of speed. They would be upon her before she reached the cove. Gaven couldn't read their intent—they might have been coming to parley, or purely out of curiosity. But the sunken ship they'd passed in the channel suggested otherwise. Gaven growled in frustration, and thunder rumbled in the clouds overhead. The winds grew stronger, and the clouds roiled in a great maelstrom.

They were close enough to identify now. One was the same dragon that he'd seen before, at the sentinel pillars. Its wings didn't so much flap as undulate along the length of its serpentine body, and it managed to ride the wind better than the other. Sunlight shone gold on its scales. The new dragon was a bit smaller, but its white body was thicker. It flapped its wings furiously in the wind.

They weren't too large, by dragon standards—both were smaller than Vaskar had been, but Gaven would barely reach the shoulder of either one. The gold dragon had two sharp horns sweeping back from its brow, and a number of small tendrils extending like a beard from its cheeks and chin. A thin crest started just behind its horns and ran the length of its neck, matching the twin membranes of its fanlike wings. Where the gold gave an air of wisdom and subtlety, the white dragon was all predatory hunger. A short, thick crest topped its wolflike head, and thick plating started at its neck and its heavy tail.

The gold circled above the ship, and a moment later the white landed heavily on the deck, right in front of Gaven. The deck creaked as the galleon keeled forward, and Gaven stumbled backward to avoid sliding right into the dragon's claws. The dragon growled deep in its throat, and it took a moment for Gaven to realize that it was forming words in Draconic.

"You should not be here, meat," the dragon said, prowling a few steps closer to Gaven. It ran a blue-white tongue over the teeth on one side of its mouth.

Meat—dragons sometimes used the same word for humanoids as they did for food. A vivid memory sprang to Gaven's mind: Vaskar's bronze-scaled mouth closing around the neck of a wyvern. He shook the memory from his head. He would not be meat, and neither would any other person on the *Sea Tiger*.

"I've come to learn the wisdom of the dragons," Gaven said in Draconic.

The dragon pulled its head back, evidently surprised to be answered in its own language. Then it snarled and snaked forward again. "Then you've made a fatal mistake, meat." It bared its daggerlike teeth and started padding toward Gaven.

"You're the one who has erred," Gaven said.

Thunder rumbled overhead as if to underscore his words, and Gaven thrust his arms forward. A ball of lightning formed around him then hurtled at the dragon as a mighty bolt and a resounding clap of thunder. The force of it knocked the dragon back and over the bulwark. It thrashed about for a moment before catching air under its wings again.

Gaven watched as the dragon flapped up and away from the ship, clearly both hurt and daunted by the blast of thunder and lightning.

"Gaven!" Rienne's voice behind him jolted him around just as a great gout of flame washed over the deck.

The gold dragon flew above the highest mast, blowing a stream of fire from its mouth to cover the whole deck with a blanket of fire. To his surprise, Gaven didn't see any of the crew—just Rienne, standing near the main hatch, surrounded by leaping flames. She cried out.

Drawing a quick, deep breath of the searing hot air, Gaven thrust his arms out to the front and back, and a great blast of wind swept the fire from the deck. Rienne fell to her knees.

Gaven cursed, and lightning flared in the clouds. A flashing bolt speared through the gold dragon, knocking it into the water with a great splash. He ran to Rienne and bent to help her stand.

"Never mind me," she gasped. She pointed weakly behind him.

Gaven spun around just in time to catch the full brunt of a blast of frozen air streaming from the white dragon's mouth. Frost crusted on his eyes and mouth, ice formed in his hair, and a layer of rime coated the deck. He staggered backward a few steps and slipped, landing hard on his back.

"First you dare trespass in our land." The dragon landed on the deck again and prowled toward Gaven. Its voice was a low growl. "Then you have the audacity to *hurt* me. Now I plan to eat you alive."

Gaven struggled to get his feet under him again, but the deck was too slippery.

"Is this dragon *talking* to you, Gaven?" Rienne stepped over him and took up a stance between him and the dragon. She didn't speak or understand Draconic, and Gaven wasn't sure whether the dragon understood Common. But it didn't matter. "What a waste of time," Rienne said, and she and Maelstrom began their deadly dance.

Gaven spoke a quick spell to sheath his body in a shield of flickering violet flames that warmed his body and turned the frost beneath him to water, and then to steam. He sprang to his feet, sliding his greatsword from the sheath on his back. Another arcane word made crackling lightning spring to life along the blade, sparks flying off into the air. He edged forward to stand beside Rienne.

The dragon reared up, batting at Maelstrom with its front claws but unable to stop its incessant whirling. Rienne had already scored its hide with several long gashes, and fear was in its eyes. It spread its wings and flapped them hard.

"Where do you think you're going?" Gaven said in Draconic. He sprang forward and slashed the muscle where the dragon's wing connected to its body, and that wing crumpled at the dragon's side. The dragon roared its pain and fury, then brought its front claws down hard on Gaven.

The sword clattered from his hand as he fell to the deck. The dragon's weight on his chest knocked the wind out of him, but then the beast roared again and drew back, seared by the flames around Gaven's body. Gaven swung his arms and brought his hands together in front of him, and a boom like thunder knocked the dragon backward.

This is harder than it should be, Gaven thought. Have I led these people to their deaths?

The ship rolled beneath him, and Gaven found himself sliding toward the gold dragon on the tilted deck. His sword slipped just out of his reach.

Gaven got to his feet once more. "I'm finished lying on my back now," he growled in Draconic. "Get ready to see what the Storm Dragon can do."

The gold dragon recoiled at that, and the white was still reeling from the blast of thunder and Rienne's unrelenting assault.

"That's right," Gaven growled. "I am the Storm Dragon."

Wind swept around the ship and gathered quickly into a whirlwind that pinned the gold dragon in place, tearing at its wings and snatching the breath from its snout. Lightning flashed within the walls of howling air, searing the dragon's scales. The wyrm opened its mouth, but it had no breath to roar.

With only a glance in its direction, Gaven thrust a hand toward the white dragon and pierced its body with another blast of lightning. It crashed to the deck, and a final slice from Maelstrom made sure it didn't move again.

The gold dragon beat its wings furiously against the whirlwind. Gaven snarled, and a thunderous crash exploded inside the swirling air. The dragon's wings crumpled, and another crack of thunder crushed it. With a wave of his hand, Gaven sent its body hurtling off the deck and into the water.

CHAPTER
9

Past Greenheart, the trees that gave the Towering Wood its name grew taller and broader—older, Kauth realized. An ogre couldn't circle one of their massive trunks with its arms, and one of the giants of Xen'drik couldn't reach their lowest branches. Their broad leaves were larger than a soldier's shield, and their gray-blue bark could have served as armor. At times he felt as though he walked through a grand cathedral, the trees supporting a soaring roof, a place of sacred beauty. In other places, where the trunks grew closer together, it felt more like a labyrinth, when the farthest he could see in any direction was straight up. There the beauty became something awesome and terrible, daunting him with the sheer age of the forest and its trees. It seemed unearthly—strangely enough, considering that it must have been the place in Khorvaire where the world was most like it had been before goblins and humans built their cities and empires.

Sevren led their party along a course as straight as the forest allowed. No paths wound among the trees, excepting places here and there where deer or other animals had trampled the soil and dead leaves down into something like a trail. Still, Sevren's sense of direction seemed unerring—whenever Kauth was able to determine the direction they traveled, they were still heading northwest, the shortest way through the forest to the Shadowcrags and the Demon Wastes beyond.

The woods teemed with life, but the animals kept a safe distance from Kauth and his party. Squirrels scampered up trees at their approach, rabbits broke cover and hopped away, birds fluttered up out of reach. Larger animals stalked just at the edge of their vision, appearing only in glimpses between distant trees.

Kauth found himself most aware, though, of the favored creatures of the Children of Winter—the spiders and scorpions crawling at their feet, hunting their own tiny prey among the detritus of the forest. A centipede the size of a viper writhed its way alongside Kauth's path for a few unnerving moments, and he shuddered at the memory of their confrontation with the druids on the road.

At night they pitched their tents wherever they could find space. Kauth repeated his nightly ritual beside the embers of their small fires, cementing his identity in his mind to make sure he didn't slip out of it while he slept beside Vor in their little tent. His focus grew stronger each night, the unwelcome memories of Kelas and his early training intruding less often into his thoughts. Each night he hardened his heart to the impending death of his comrades, only to find himself warming to them again as they walked through the days.

On the fourth day of their journey, as he laughed at Zandar's latest quip, he wondered how and when he had become so weak.

* * * * *

Six days outside of Greenheart, the trees thinned, and ferns and shrubs crowded into the patches of sunlight in the spaces between. Sevren pointed out scattered blocks of stone—the crumbled ruin of an ancient wall—mostly covered with lichen and creeping vines.

"That explains the thinning trees," the shifter said. "There's probably a paved area not far ahead. The trees will grow through it eventually, but it takes time."

"We should skirt the ruin," Kauth said.

"Are you serious?" Zandar said. "This is our specialty."

Sevren nodded. "We can afford a brief diversion from our journey. Vor?"

"This is how we make our living," the orc said. "If there's nothing of value in the ruins, it won't take long for us to determine that, and we won't have delayed our journey. If there are treasures to be found, it's worth a small delay."

Zandar clapped Kauth on the shoulder. "I'm afraid you're outvoted, friend."

Kauth thought briefly of pulling rank, asserting his role as leader of the expedition. Then he remembered that the others had stripped him of that authority back on the caravan, after they caught him in his lies. He shrugged in resignation, and Sevren altered their course slightly to take them into the heart of the ruins.

Twenty paces past the ruined wall, shattered cobblestones paved the forest floor. Plants sprouted up between the ancient stones, and a few trees—smaller than elsewhere in the forest—pushed the stones apart and buckled them with their spreading roots. Sevren slowed his pace, stooping every few paces to examine a fern or vine. Each time he bent down, his face showed more concern.

Soon the shifter stopped entirely, kneeling on the cobblestones and examining the underside of a pale, almost white fern.

"What is it?" Kauth asked.

Sevren yanked the fern from the ground and stood up. He held the plant out to Kauth, pointing at the leaves. Strange nodules covered them, purplish white and pulsing faintly with life that struck him as distinctly not plantlike.

"We call it the Depravation," the shifter said. "It's the influence of the Realm of Madness. There's probably a portal somewhere in the ruins. Maybe still sealed—or mostly sealed. Possibly broken."

"You think there's a daelkyr here?" Kauth carefully kept the alarm from his voice, though it was written plain on the others' faces. Thousands of years ago, the alien world of Xoriat, called the Realm of Madness, had come close to the natural world—close in some abstract, metaphysical sense that, fundamentally, meant it was easier to cross from one world to the other. What had crossed from Xoriat into the world had given the Realm of Madness its name: tentacled horrors and deformed monstrosities much like the beings that had spilled out of the Soul Reaver's domain in the Starcrag Plain. But the rulers and makers of these monstrous aberrations were the daelkyr, deceptively humanlike beings of incredible power whose greatest skill lay in warping flesh according to their insane designs. With their gibbering hordes, they had devastated the goblin empire of Dhakaan before the druids known as the Gatekeepers had pushed Xoriat away from the world and sealed the portals the daelkyr had used. Even so, their influence still lingered, particularly in the western parts of Khorvaire.

"I suppose there could be, but I don't think it's likely. The Depravation would be stronger, more noticeable."

"What, then?" Zandar asked. He maintained his cocky smile, but Kauth could see the effort it required.

"Some weaker spawn of the daelkyr, I expect," Sevren said.

Kauth pointed at the fern. "So what are those nodules?"

"Eggs." Sevren used the sharp nail of one finger to pry one of the objects loose from the leaf. Tiny tendrils trailed behind it, sliding out of the fern. They seemed to writhe in the air before curling up close to the body of the egg.

Holding the tiny object gingerly between two fingernails, Sevren stooped to pick up a small piece of cobblestone. He laid the egg on the flat stone and pressed his nail into it. There was a barely audible squelch and a violet fluid oozed out. He picked at the shell, revealing a tiny maggot-thing, the same pale purple as the nodule. It was about as large as the husk that held it, suggesting that it had been almost ready to hatch. Indeed, it pulsed with life and began to writhe as soon as the air touched its slimy skin, lifting one end toward Sevren's finger. With a snarl of revulsion, the shifter cut the larva in two. The halves continued squirming for a moment before falling still. Sevren stooped again and used the stone to grind the maggot against another cobblestone.

"What will those grow into?" Zandar asked.

"No idea. Probably some warped form of fly or beetle. A blood drinker or flesh eater."

"So are we continuing into the ruins?" Kauth asked. "Or circling around?" He glanced at his three companions.

Zandar's revulsion was clear on his face—ironic, Kauth thought, considering the dark and twisted forces the warlock dealt with in practicing his magic. Vor's face was impassive, while Sevren looked grim.

The shifter set his jaw and spoke through clenched teeth. "Continuing."

Vor nodded, and Zandar looked off in the direction they had been walking.

"Until discretion trumps greed, we forge ahead," Zandar said. "I'm not letting flesh-eating flies dissuade me. At least, not before they've hatched."

Kauth smiled. These were, indeed, the kind of men he'd been looking for—rootless, experienced, and tough. Expendable, he reminded himself—but not until they reached the Demon Wastes.

"Let me see your weapons," Kauth said.

"What?" Vor asked. "Why?"

"If we're going to fight the spawn of the daelkyr, I want us to be ready. I'll enchant your weapons to strike truer and harder against them."

"I can't argue with that," Sevren said, sliding his knives from their sheaths and handing them to Kauth. Vor followed his example.

Zandar shrugged and gestured toward the dagger at his belt. "If I end up drawing this thing in battle, we've already lost," he said.

* * * * *

As they pressed farther toward the heart of the ruins, scattered heaps of crumbling stone marked the locations of ancient buildings. The vines that covered them were acid green or lurid yellow, studded with spiny thorns, and they bore sharp-edged leaves. Clouds of flies swarmed around the party, tormenting them with painful bites, some even drawing blood.

Sevren held a hand up, bringing them to a stop. Kauth saw what had caught his attention—the foliage was tramped down ahead of them, woody stems snapped and leaves ground into the fractured cobblestones. The shifter dropped to one knee beside the most obvious marks, then followed them a short way to the right. He stood and rejoined them, his brow furrowed.

"It's big," he said. "Walks on two feet, but dragging its arms as it goes. Except where it picks up a chunk of rubble and tosses it aside. A gray render, if I'm not mistaken."

"You can tell it's gray from its tracks?" Zandar asked with a sardonic smile.

"I don't know that for sure, but I've never seen a gray render that wasn't gray."

"How many have you seen?" Kauth asked.

"Just one."

"So what can we expect," the warlock said, "based on your extensive past experience?"

Sevren shot him a glare. "They're big, and strong as a giant. Their name comes from their color, obviously, and from the way they grab and tear. Stay out of its claws."

"The voice of experience?"

"Yes. The other thing is, they have a strange habit of taking up with other creatures, assuming a role like a bodyguard."

"Like a loyal dog," Kauth said.

"Exactly. And about as smart. So it's probably attached itself to whatever spawn of the daelkyr—"

Sevren's hands shot to his ears and his mouth opened wide in a voiceless scream. Vor stepped to his side as Kauth looked around for the source of the attack. The first thing he saw could only have been the gray render Sevren had described—a hulking brute with a hairless gray body, long arms, and short legs. Kauth's head reached about to its gaping mouth, but the thing's sloping forehead and hunched shoulders rose several feet above him. Six small eyes in two columns rose up above the razor-toothed jaws.

Kauth's mace was in his hands before he saw the render's companion—an enormous emerald-scaled serpent almost as large as the gray-skinned brute. It slithered along the ground, holding its head high. A cobralike cowl spread out behind its head, which bore a twisted mockery of a human face, snarling in rage.

Vor stepped forward to meet the onrushing gray render. It thrust its misshapen head forward and tore the orc's flesh with its black teeth, catching Vor off guard—his axe was ready to block a claw swinging in from the side, not the bite coming down from above. Only after the bite connected did the thing bring its claws to bear. Kauth's gut clenched in fear—not for his own safety, but for the fallen paladin's. He cursed his weakness even as he sprang forward to distract the creature before it could tear Vor apart.

His mace's flanges tore into the render's upper arm, and the monster's head turned to him. Vor wrested himself out of the render's grasp and struck a powerful blow with his greataxe, drawing its attention back to him.

Kauth nodded. Back and forth, back and forth, he thought. Keep it constantly distracted so it can't land a solid blow.

He edged around the beast so it was directly between him and Vor, meaning it had to turn farther each time it shifted its attention. He scored a telling blow on the render's back, just behind its arm, and it roared in pain as it wheeled back to face him. He concentrated on defending himself until Vor struck it again.

Back and forth, he thought, and it'll be dead in no time.

Then the pain hit him, in the form of an arcane word that coursed through his body and set his nerves on fire. There was no part of him that wasn't in agony, and he doubled over, clutching at his ears as Sevren had done. Even the gray render's tearing bite didn't increase the pain. He started falling backward from the force of the render's blow, but its claws caught him before he hit the ground. Just as the torturous word faded from his ears and its wracking agony with it, the render's claws tore at him and sent a jolt of a different kind of pain through his chest. At last, the render tossed him aside, turning back to face Vor, and he fell to the ground in a heap.

Kauth just wanted to lie there—it hurt to move even the slightest bit. It was humiliation, though, that made him reach for one of the wands at his belt and send its healing magic into his body. He didn't want to be the one who got knocked out of the fight again, as he had when they fought the Children of Winter. He didn't want to lose the respect of his companions.

The wand's magic coursed through him, knitting his flesh and easing the ache that still throbbed in his skull. He took a deep breath as it flowed like cool water through his veins, bracing and refreshing, then got to his feet.

He heard Vor shout in pain, caught in the gray render's grip again. Shifting his hold on his mace, Kauth swung it as hard as he could into the beast's shoulder. The spikes dug deep, and the club's impact made the render stagger forward. Vor stumbled backward out of its grasp, and then it fell on him. The orc managed to shift its weight to one side and send it crashing to the ground without being crushed beneath it.

Kauth drew a wand again and started toward the orc, but Vor waved him away, pointing weakly at the others. Kauth spun around—focusing on the gray render and the combat rhythm he had found with Vor, he had all but forgotten their two companions and the serpent creature.

Trying to assess the situation was like watching a complex dance. Sevren preferred to dart in, cut with his knives, and dart back out of reach, and Zandar liked blasting the serpent from a safe distance. The serpent wove between them, repeating its word over and over, rendering one man or the other helpless for a few moments at a time. Without Vor at the forefront, none of the battle's participants wanted to stand still next to the others.

The serpent showed the marks of both Sevren's knives and Zandar's blasts, but it was still going strong. Kauth glanced back at Vor. The orc was stooped over, his hands on his knees, catching his breath and readying himself to fight again. He jerked his head back toward the others, so Kauth turned around again and charged the serpent.

Sevren saw Kauth's approach and timed his next lunge so they hit the serpent at the same time. In that instant, the terror of the battle slipped away. Kauth felt like part of a larger creature, each part functioning with perfect coordination. He and Sevren were two claws of the same beast, an irresistible assault. He rode a surge of joy forward.

Then the serpent spoke another arcane word, and it resounded in the air like a clap of thunder. Kauth stopped dead before he could complete the swing of his mace. The thunder echoed through his mind for an instant, driving away any other thought.

In that instant, the serpent drew its head back and spit a gout of black liquid that sprayed over him and Sevren. His skin burned, and he felt fire wash through the veins the healing magic had cooled.

Poison, he thought. I have a wand for that, too—somewhere.

It was a wand he didn't keep ready at his belt, and his mind was still reeling from the serpent's thundering word of power. He fumbled at a buckle that normally required only a simple flick of the fingers to open, even as he saw Sevren double over in pain. The venom made Kauth's stomach churn, but at last he found the wand he needed. Just as he drew it out, though, the coiled serpent's tail lashed out and slammed into his gut, sending him sprawling.

He looked up at the serpent, expecting to see a fanged mouth closing in for the kill. But a veil of darkness covered its eyes, and it flailed about. The tail whipped around wildly, hitting Sevren next, but the serpent moved away from them, trying to protect itself until the darkness cleared from its eyes.

That gave Kauth the time to yank the wand from his pouch and stop the poison, cooling his blood once more. He stepped to Sevren and touched him with the topaz tip of the wand as well. The shifter nodded his gratitude then leaped at the serpent again, slashing furiously with his knives.

Kauth was pleased to see that the enchantment he'd placed on Sevren's weapons made a difference—each blow from his blades brought spurts of blood and hissing cries of pain. He hefted his mace and circled to flank the serpent with Sevren, hoping to find the same kind of rhythm he and Vor had found. He bashed at its coiled body and readied himself for its attack, but it proved more intelligent than the gray render—it kept its attention focused on Sevren, clearly a more significant threat.

Then Vor charged back into the melee. He swung his axe in a weaving loop, back and forth, biting deep into scales and flesh and bone each time. Kauth felt like cheering as the serpent gave a final, gasping hiss and slumped to the ground. Its body flopped around for a moment, uncoiling to show its monstrous length, and it died staring blankly at the sky.

Vor put his hands on his knees again, breathing heavily. His armor was splashed with blood, and Kauth could see several tears in the metal where the render's claws had torn through and cut into him. Kauth produced one of the wands he kept close at hand and set to work on Vor's wounds, knitting flesh back together. The wounds were deep and must have been painful, but Vor never flinched. He accepted Kauth's ministrations with a gracious smile.

Kauth tried, but he couldn't quell his admiration for the former paladin. He wondered what had happened to cause Vor to lose that exalted status. Vor seemed to him like a perfect exemplar of the paladin ideal—dauntless almost to the point of foolhardiness, but staunch enough to keep his ground against overwhelming odds. He seemed completely selfless and devoted to his friends, however much he and Zandar traded jibes.

Vor seemed, in other words, to be exactly his opposite. At the thought, Kauth's stomach churned and he tasted bile. His work on Vor's wounds complete, he turned away from the orc, unable to look at him—a perfect mirror reflecting his own imperfection.

CHAPTER
10

After Kauth had seen to Sevren's broken ribs, the shifter led them to a crumbling structure at the heart of the ruins. It was larger than the outbuildings they'd seen before, and in better condition. A colonnade had once surrounded the building, though many of the columns had fallen into rubble and the roof they once supported was long gone. Some pillars still stood, and the carvings they bore had not completely eroded away. An assemblage of plants and animals—bears figured prominently, along with elks and panthers—ringed the columns, along with abstract symbols Kauth couldn't make sense of, weaving lines forming circular patterns. The face of the building bore similar imagery, with fewer natural elements and more of the abstract designs.

"A Gatekeeper shrine," Sevren said, giving only a cursory glance to the pillars as he led the others to the entrance. "Probably built above a daelkyr portal they sealed."

"And now the seal is leaking," Zandar said.

"Hence the Depravation."

"Can we seal it again?" Vor asked.

Sevren scowled. "I doubt it."

The shrine's entrance was an open archway. Kauth eyed the stones of the arch warily, not certain that the worn keystone was quite serving its purpose any longer. Vor stepped in front of Sevren and entered first, ducking his head to clear the arch. It didn't collapse on him, and Sevren followed, lighting a sunrod to illuminate the darkness inside. Zandar went next.

A smoothly coordinated team, Kauth thought. No discussion— they have a standard procedure and they follow it without question. I'm extraneous.

The thought made him tired—tired of a life he'd spent in the same position. Worming his way into others' confidence. Following other groups without ever being a part of one. Traveling with friends who were not his friends, watching their friendships from the outside.

So this is what lonely is, he thought as he ducked his head and followed Zandar into the shrine.

* * * * *

The ground floor of the shrine was unexceptional. According to Sevren, there was no trace of any creature other than the serpent, no indication that any other living creature had traveled the halls in centuries. The gray render would barely have fit through the arch, of course, but Sevren suggested that the serpent had probably enforced the boundary of its lair.

At the heart of the building, the hallway widened into a stairway descending into darkness. Two large alcoves flanked the top of the stairs. The one on the left had collapsed, and rubble covered anything of interest that might have been there. To the right, though, the stone was intact, and a long, curved sword hung on two chains from the ceiling. Sevren and Vor set about examining the blade, which showed no signs of age, but Kauth's attention was captured by the writing that covered the walls of the alcove.

Coiling, twisting characters of the Draconic language were engraved in the stone, grouped into lines and couplets and verses, spelling out the words of the Prophecy. The writing covered three tall, narrow walls, outlining the destiny of the world.

Tangled up, Kauth thought. I can't seem to escape the Prophecy. If only Gaven were here.

He could read Draconic, but it took some effort, first to decipher the script and then to read the meaning. His eyes swept over the writing, looking for familiar words. *Dragons . . . death . . . confront* or *oppose* or *face*—he hated Draconic verbs. Unwilling to just come out and state their meaning, they shifted and hid behind multiple layers.

Much like me, he thought.

One word recurred with some frequency, but it wasn't a familiar one. He sounded it out carefully. *Hadrash.* Based on a verb, but the *ha-* prefix made it a noun, someone who *drash*es. *Drash*—it seemed related to the word for speaking.

Speak evil? he thought.

Then it struck him. The Blasphemer. Gaven had mentioned a verse of the Prophecy about the Blasphemer. What had he said?

It was the verse Vaskar had used to bring dragons to fight for Haldren's army. A verse whose time had not yet come, Gaven had said.

Kauth scanned for a place where "dragon" and "Blasphemer" appeared in proximity, and found one almost immediately. He put his fingers at the beginning of that line and started sounding it out. "Dragons fly . . ." he whispered.

"What are you doing?"

Sevren's voice shattered Kauth's concentration. He had forgotten the others, who were all watching him now, a range of expressions on their faces. Zandar wore his habitual grin, Vor was impassive, and Sevren looked perplexed.

"You can read that?" the shifter asked.

"It takes some work, but yes."

"You're smarter than you look. What does it say?"

Kauth felt a pressure behind his eyes. He wanted to read, and was irritated at the distraction. "I was just starting to figure that out."

"Does it say anything about the sword?" Vor asked.

"If you shut up and let me read, I'll tell you!"

Vor simply arched an eyebrow at him, and he immediately regretted snapping at the orc. He turned back to the writing, but his concentration was shattered.

He drew a deep breath and turned back to the others. "Could you give me some space, please?" He made an effort to keep his voice calm and quiet. "I'm finding it difficult to concentrate."

"As you wish," Sevren said. He pointed back down the hall, the way they'd come, and they cleared away.

With another steadying breath, Kauth turned back to the verse he had just started reading.

Dragons fly before the Blasphemer's legions,
scouring the earth of his righteous foes.
Carnage rises in the wake of his passing,
purging all life from those who oppose him.
Vultures wheel where dragons flew,
picking the bones of the numberless dead.

It was the verse Gaven had recited. A chill ran down Kauth's spine. Gaven had said its time had not yet come, but how could he know that? Vaskar had persuaded the dragons that it had. It seemed to Kauth that there must at least be a possibility that it could be fulfilled—or that someone could try, as Vaskar had tried to make himself the Storm Dragon.

He glanced back down the hall and saw the others watching him intently. Vor wanted to know if the Prophecy mentioned the curved sword in the alcove, so he scanned the text for that word, *barak*.

He found plenty of swords—*the swords of the legions hew their foes* here, and there, *the swords of his foes shatter beneath their feet.* But he didn't see the singular form anywhere.

He felt more than saw that his companions' restless pacing brought them closer and closer to him, and the pressure behind his eyes grew into a dull ache. He shook his head and turned to face the others.

"I can't find anything about the sword," he said. "I'm sorry."

Sevren closed the gap between them. "What did you find?"

"They're verses of the draconic Prophecy," he said. He started to say more, but bit it back. There was no need to tell them any more.

"What about?" Sevren was relentless, staring intently at Kauth's face.

Kauth turned back to the writing, pointing at the common words he recognized. "Death, battles, swords," he said. "Dragons and war."

Vor grunted. "Typical," he said.

"What do you mean?" Sevren asked.

"From what I've heard, most of the Prophecy is like that. If you predict war, it's hard to go wrong. The best prophecies are easy to fulfill."

Zandar laughed. "Well spoken, Vor. You're starting to sound like me."

The orc glared at Zandar, but Kauth saw a smile tugging at the corner of his mouth. Vor shouldered past Sevren and stood in front of the alcove. "If no one has any objection, then, I'll claim the sword." He reached out his hand, poised to seize the weapon, waiting for his companions' answer.

Kauth and Zandar shrugged. "It's yours," Sevren said.

Vor grabbed the sword and pulled it free of the chains suspending it. He examined the blade, testing the edge and tracing the grain of the steel.

To Kauth's eyes, the sword was far more than well-hammered steel. Magic flowed freely through the blade, and it seemed to come alive in Vor's hands. "A fine weapon," he said. "It should serve you well."

"We've lingered here long enough," Sevren announced. "Down the stairs."

* * * * *

A large chamber at the bottom of the stairs had evidently been the serpent's nest. A pile of rubble in the center of the room had several gaps large enough for the snake to enter, so it could rest safe from intruders. Crumbling tunnels stretched off to either side, but Sevren shook his head.

"Those ceilings aren't safe," he said.

Kauth barely heard him. His attention was drawn to a circular pattern in the wall opposite the stairs. It was no more than a faint tracing in the stone, but Kauth could sense the magic in it even from across the room.

"I think I found the source of the Depravation," he said.

Sevren followed his gaze and spotted the circle in the wall. He spoke, but Kauth couldn't process the shifter's words. Strange whispers hissed in his mind, a babbling ululation in some not-language, incomprehensible and distracting to the point of madness.

Sevren kept speaking, but he wasn't looking at the seal or

at Kauth anymore—he seemed to be muttering to himself. Vor leaned against the wall and clutched his head in his hands. Only Zandar seemed unaffected by the waves washing out from the portal. Grinning mischievously, he strode to the portal and ran a finger along the edge.

Kauth fought to keep his wits. Something was wrong— Zandar's smile was too manic, his eyes unfocused. He staggered forward, but Zandar wheeled around to face him. The warlock spoke words that Kauth couldn't distinguish from the ceaseless babble in his mind, then Zandar's hand burst into flame. Still grinning, Zandar pointed a burning finger, and the fire hurtled at Kauth.

Kauth twisted his body out of its path, but his feet couldn't compensate for the sudden movement and he crashed to the ground. Zandar cackled.

Kauth felt as though he were surfacing from the depths of an ocean of madness, the clear air of reason washing over his mind. The warlock had seemed immune to the befuddling effects of the babble, but it had warped his mind most of all. Indeed, Zandar had turned back to the portal and clawed at the edge of the seal as if to pry it free.

"Zandar, no!"

Kauth scrambled to his feet and lunged at the warlock. His shoulder connected just under Zandar's ribs, and the warlock collapsed around him. They tumbled to the floor together. Zandar curled up around his stomach, trying to draw breath. Perhaps the blow would clear the warlock's head, just as Zandar's attack had helped Kauth shake off the madness.

"Sorry," Kauth murmured as he stood and turned to examine the portal and its seal.

As soon as he touched the seal, an image of its magic flashed into his mind—a tight mesh of magic strands, glowing blue, holding back what lay beyond. Except that the mesh was frayed along one edge.

Sevren was wrong, he thought. I *can* fix this.

He glanced at the place where Zandar had fallen, but the warlock wasn't there. Kauth swore under his breath and wheeled around, the portal at his back, expecting another blast of fire any second.

Instead, he saw Zandar back at the bottom of the stairs, trying to rouse Sevren from his stupor. Vor nodded at Kauth—everything was under control.

The orc's eyes widened. In the same instant, Kauth felt something coil around his neck—something both slimy and sharp. He half-turned and saw a slender tentacle emerging around the seal. The stone disk holding the seal's magic had shrunk, creating a gap the tentacle-thing emerged from. He grabbed it in his left hand and fumbled at his mace with his right.

The pain was excruciating as the tentacle bit into the skin of his neck and constricted his windpipe. Pulling at the tentacle only made the pain worse, and he worried that bashing it with his weapon would have the same effect. Lights swirled across his vision as darkness crept into the edges.

The pressure stopped abruptly, though the pain remained. Kauth looked up and saw Vor standing beside him, the sword he'd found upstairs clutched in both hands. Vor had severed the tentacle, but the end still bit into Kauth's skin and the stump thrashed wildly.

Kauth yanked a wand from his pouch and touched it to his neck as he pulled the end of the tentacle free. Tiny barbs lined the grasping edge of the slimy tendril, and they were quite effective— streams of blood had traced paths down his chest. The magic of the wand refreshed him, and he turned back to the portal, confident that Vor could handle the remains of the tentacle or anything else that might emerge while he worked.

He eyed the portal carefully before touching it again. Had his touch weakened the portal, allowing the tentacle to reach through? Or had the thing beyond somehow sensed his presence and wormed its way through by brute strength or force of will?

It didn't matter, he decided. He couldn't repair the portal without touching it, and if he succeeded, there would be no more gap though which creatures could emerge. He laid both his palms flat against the portal and lost himself in its tightly woven patterns.

"What are you doing?" Vor yelled.

Kauth opened his eyes without moving his hands, and saw that the gap had widened still farther. Three more tentacles flailed around him and Vor, and something with several gnashing mouths and bulging eyes was just visible beyond the seal.

"Hold them back!" he gasped. "I'll seal it."

He closed his eyes again. Pain seared through him as two more tentacles coiled around his neck and one arm, but he didn't stop his work. Vor cut them off again and the pain subsided.

He traced his fingers along the lines of woven magic that formed the seal. It was not unlike spinning wool into yarn, drawing frayed threads out, strengthening them, and knitting them together again. It was slow work, though, coaxing the threads out of their tangles, and the madness that still washed out from beyond battered at the edges of his concentration. Pressure built behind his eyes and flowered into splitting pain, and tentacles kept raking across his skin.

Then it was done. Vor gave a triumphant shout and the babble fell quiet. The magic of the seal pulsed with renewed strength. Kauth turned and leaned his back against it, feeling its power like warm coals behind him. Vor clapped him on the shoulder. Even Zandar smiled with genuine pleasure. Sevren blinked and looked around, trying to make sense of what had happened.

Pride welled up in Kauth's heart. He had proved his worth, after too many battles that left him unconscious or feeling ineffectual. Without him, his companions would be dead or lost to madness. He slid down to the floor, exhausted but satisfied.

I saved them, he thought.

CHAPTER
11

The death of the two dragons heartened the *Sea Tiger*'s crew enormously. Jordhan clapped Gaven on the shoulder and hugged Rienne, all their past arguments apparently forgotten. The sailors spoke excitedly about the gates of Argonnessen, congratulating themselves on being the first natives of Khorvaire to pass through them alive. Gaven was caught up in the revel, singing old shanties with them, joining in the invention of new verses celebrating their victory, and drinking plenty of their liquor as they leaned over the bulwark and watched the cove slowly grow closer.

Long after the ship had dropped anchor for the night, Jordhan broke up the party and sent the sailors to their bunks. Only when he stumbled back to his own quarters did Gaven realize that Rienne had not joined in the celebration—had not, in fact, appeared on the deck all evening. He found her asleep in their bunk, facing the wall. The sight of her brought a surge of anger to his chest.

"Damn it, Rienne," he said. "Why can't you celebrate what we've done? Why can't you believe this can turn out for the good?"

She didn't answer, and later she didn't move when he climbed into their bunk and draped his arm around her. He fell asleep like that, and when he woke up his arms were empty.

* * * * *

Rienne avoided him the next morning. Gaven threw himself into the work of sailing alongside Jordhan's crew, who welcomed his great strength on the ropes, fueled by the anger simmering in his chest. He called the wind to fill the sails, and though lightning flashed in the sky, the ship was never in danger as it flew across the water to the cove.

The crew cheered when he scaled the mainmast to retrieve a rope that had flown wild, and he cast a triumphant glance around the deck, looking for Rienne. She was nowhere in sight, but Jordhan stood at the foot of the mast, his arms crossed. He shimmied down the mast and alighted beside the captain.

"Gaven, go below," Jordhan ordered. His face was the stern mask of the captain, not his customary smile.

Gaven had a sudden urge to strike his old friend, to send him sprawling onto his ship's perfectly clean deck. He was sick of them both, Jordhan and Rienne, with their predictions of doom and murmurs of eternity. He glared at the captain, fists clenched at his side, barely containing his wrath.

"What?" he said, and thunder rolled in the sky.

"You heard me. Go below."

A step brought Gaven closer, towering over Jordhan. "Why?" he asked.

Jordhan didn't bend. "You're putting my ship and my crew in danger," Jordhan declared. "And you're acting like a child. I'll join you in my quarters in a moment."

Acting like a child? The only thing holding Gaven back now was the onlooking crew. In the privacy of the captain's quarters, Jordhan would pay for that remark.

Gaven put every spark of anger he could muster into his glare, then turned and stalked to the hatch. Behind him, he heard Jordhan ordering his crew to furl some sails, to slow the *Sea Tiger*'s headlong rush to the cove.

He threw open the hatch. Rienne leaned back against the table that held what scant charts they had.

"What is this?" he said. "Is Jordhan trying to force us to talk to each other again?"

"I don't care if you speak or not, but Jordhan and I both have some things to say to you." Her face was hard, but her voice was quiet, not confrontational.

"Why don't you start, then, while we're waiting for the captain to finish hobbling his ship and join us?"

"Hobbling his ship? What is wrong with you?"

"Don't ask me questions if you're not interested in the answers.

What do you have to say to me?" He was trying to provoke her, prodding her to display any of the fury he felt.

Her calm didn't waver. "Very well," she said. "I want you to understand what I am seeing and feeling. If you choose not to explain yourself, that's your prerogative. But it only clarifies my most troubling perception: we are no longer partners."

She paused then, waiting for some response. He didn't move, though something joined the storm of anger in his heart—a cold wind akin to dread.

"Back . . . before," she began. Her gaze left his face and fell to the floor.

Before you betrayed me and left me to rot in Dreadhold? he thought. *Before I went mad?*

"When we delved into Khyber together, when we sailed with Jordhan, when we worked for your House together, we were partners. Equals. We fought as a team. You covered my back, and I covered yours. Often literally—we'd stand back to back and face off against a ring of monsters or bandits. We don't fight like that any more. You lose yourself in the wind and lightning and leave me to fend for myself."

Gaven couldn't contain the storm of anger any longer. "You're more than capable—"

She cut him off. "I know I am, or I wouldn't be alive. That's not the point. The issue here is that you used to give a damn about me—you used to love me, and I don't think you do anymore."

"Don't be absurd. Of course I do." He walked past her to the portholes aft and stared out at the sea and storm behind them.

He felt her gentle hand on his back, a touch that had so often steadied him in difficult times. "Are you sure?" she asked softly.

Gaven heard the hatch slam open and Jordhan stomp in. Rienne's hand left his back and he felt suddenly, painfully alone.

"We're risking our lives for you," the captain barked, "but that doesn't mean they're yours to toy with."

The gray water churned in the *Sea Tiger*'s wake, but the storm clouds were fading into the horizon. A weight settled into Gaven's chest, stifling the anger, numbing him to the chill of dread. His shoulders slumped and he leaned his forehead against the wall.

Jordhan continued, a little less forcefully. "We're in uncharted waters. We've seen wrecks in the water, warning us of rocks and coral and posing a new danger of their own. Charging ahead full sail is reckless and stupid, and it puts all of us in serious jeopardy."

"When the dragons attacked," Rienne added, "you didn't give a thought to the safety of the crew. Remember what you said? 'No one on this ship will be dragon food?' You promised more concern for them than that."

Gaven didn't lift his head. "Nobody was dragon food," he said.

"Because I led them below," Rienne said.

He turned. "We fight as a team, as you said. You led them below, while I held off the dragons."

"I was thinking like a team. You were not. I covered your back, and you ignored the rest of us."

"That's not true! I came to help you when you fell in the gold dragon's fire."

"You did spare me a passing thought, I grant you that."

Jordhan looked bewildered, turning his head back and forth to follow their argument. Realizing that he had nothing more to contribute, he pointed at Gaven. "I've got a ship to sail. You two sort this out. And Gaven, you're like a brother to me, but the safety of my crew is my first priority. Don't endanger them again." He spun and pushed through the hatch.

When Gaven turned back to Rienne, her shoulders slumped. "I don't know why I'm arguing with you," she said. "The point was for me to tell you how I perceive the situation. You can't argue me out of my perception, and I shouldn't presume to know what's happening in your head. You tell me you still love me. Fine. That's how you understand it. But it's clear to me that word means something different to you than it does to me."

"Rienne—"

"And I need more than whatever you think you're giving me. I do love you, Gaven, and I'm committed to following you into Argonnessen. I'll cover your back. I hope you can spare a thought to cover mine."

The look on her face as she turned to leave drove a spear into Gaven's chest. For the first time, he saw the weight of the past twenty-six years on her face—small wrinkles at her brow and the corners of her eyes, the marks that grief and worry had etched into her face. Then she was gone, and Gaven was alone.

* * * * *

Back in his quarters, Gaven noticed that Rienne's gear was packed and waiting at the door, ready for their journey. He gathered his belongings, carefully rolling his clothes and packing them tightly into his pack with room to spare. He placed the journey-bread they'd brought from Aundair gently on top and fastened the buckles, tied a bedroll to the top of the pack, and checked the coil of rope and the magic waterskin strapped to the bottom. He was ready.

He considered telling Rienne to stay behind and making the journey alone. He'd survive, he was sure. If she felt no obligation to protect the world from the catastrophe he felt sure was imminent, she could stay on the ship and enjoy her distant view of eternity.

The problem is, he thought, I still love her. I think I do—or why would I feel this way?

A weight greater than his pack had settled into his chest, no longer piercing but just heavy. Walking felt like an effort, and when he sat on his bunk he wanted to lie down and not get up again. I'll have to show her, he thought, prove it to her.

Those were his thoughts when he felt the anchor chain rumble against the hull, heard the splash as it hit the water. He grabbed his pack and Rienne's and ran to the deck.

They had arrived. The *Sea Tiger* was tucked into the cove. Mountains rose up on the starboard side, but a sandy beach sloped up to port, turning at the tide line into an emerald plain. A lush forest hugged the feet of the mountains, alive with birds—or were they dragonets?—hopping and fluttering in the branches at the edge of the plain. The crew, still alive with the energy of the morning, was already lowering a launch into the crystal blue water.

Gaven made his way through the crew to the bulwark and found himself face to face with Rienne. She gave him a weak smile.

"Here we are," she said. "Ready to begin another adventure?"

He returned her smile. "Thank you," he mouthed—his voice failed him. How could he have thought of leaving her behind?

She took her pack from his hand. Two men waited in the launch for them, holding a rope for them to climb down. Rienne swung herself over the bulwark and slid easily down the rope, settling gently into the little boat.

Gaven was about to follow, but Jordhan's hand on his shoulder stopped him. He turned to face the captain, but Jordhan's stern captain face was gone.

"I meant what I said earlier," Jordhan said. "You are like a brother to me. So come back from this trip. I don't want to be the one who ferried you to your death."

"I'll see you again, this side of the Land of the Dead." Gaven extended a hand, and Jordhan clasped it.

"Sovereigns keep you," Jordhan said, "Storm Dragon."

Gaven clapped his friend on the shoulder and climbed down the rope. The launch rocked fiercely when he alighted, and Rienne bubbled with laughter. He took his seat more carefully, and the sailors rowed toward the shore.

Jordhan's last words echoed in Gaven's mind as he watched the beach slide closer.

* * * * *

Gaven and Rienne stood at the tide line, watching the launch crawl back to the *Sea Tiger*. Its departure felt final, like a mausoleum door grinding shut. Jordhan had secured them a return fare, as he called it—two fine silver chains that, when broken, would magically transport them back to Stormhome. Even so, Gaven would have preferred the promise of a ship beneath his feet.

Only when the launch had returned to the shelter of the *Sea Tiger*'s embrace and Jordhan's ship had pointed her prow back toward the open sea did Gaven turn to face the strange land before them. Even the sand at their feet seemed odd, alien—grains of a bluish stone mingled with the more familiar tan and gray to give the beach an azure glow that intensified the blue of the crystal clear water. The coarse grass that fought for a hold in the sand gave way, just ahead, to a lush plain rooted in firmer soil. Tall grass danced in the wind blowing off the water, spotted here and there with the sapphire, topaz, and amethyst shades of wildflowers. The plain hugged the edge of the bay as it continued winding around to their left, cutting deeper into the land—deeper than Gaven had been willing to lead Jordhan and his crew.

To their right, the plain thickened into ferns and shrubs lining the edge of the forest. The trees beyond stood smooth and straight or twisted wildly as if reaching for every scrap of available sunlight, some lithe and some solid, with smooth skin of silvery white or jagged brown bark. From Gaven and Rienne's closer vantage, the flutters in the trees resolved into dragonets, not birds—snaky but elegant creatures with delicate wings and scales of every color flashing in the sunlight. The mountains loomed up behind the forest in a pale blue shadow, draped in the clouds that grayed the sky.

Beneath the rolling plain and verdant forest, the land whispered to Gaven of numberless centuries, millennia in which no native of Khorvaire had set foot on this land. It was not utterly without history, though—there were battles in the memory of Argonnessen, from territorial squabbles between ancient dragons to . . . yes, the clash of armies. This land had its peoples, then, native children who gathered in tribes or kingdoms.

"Lead the way, Storm Dragon," Rienne said.

Gaven gave Rienne a sharp glance, but her face was free of bitterness or sarcasm. Her eyes were wide as she surveyed the forest, and a faint smile turned the corners of her mouth. What does she see? he wondered.

"Your sword is Maelstrom," he said, "but you're an untroubled sea."

"No, love. I'm the still point at the heart of the whirlpool."

"The calm at the center of the storm."

Her eyes met his, then she started walking.

"You said I was leading," he said to her back. With a few quick steps he caught up, and they walked side by side into the land of dragons.

CHAPTER
12

The cathedral in Fairhaven had once been the largest church of the Silver Flame outside of Thrane. Hundreds of Aundairians flocked to its grand dome for worship, and dozens of priests left its chambers and ventured westward to spread the faith. But that was before the Church of the Silver Flame became too closely associated with the government of Thrane. When King Thalin of Thrane died and Aundair's eastern neighbor fell under the rule of the church, Aundair's King Wrogar closed the cathedral and its clerics scattered.

For eighty-five years the cathedral lay vacant, the object of superstitious fear though it was haunted only by criminals and fugitives. Kelas had taken over the labyrinthine corridors below the building, and at least one significant criminal organization claimed some of the upper halls, but the sanctuary with its shattered stained glass and tattered tapestries stood empty.

But it was in that once-sacred space that Kelas assembled all the key players in his unfolding drama. The faded grandeur of the cathedral hall lent an impressive aura to the proceedings, suggesting a royal audience chamber. Clearly it made Kelas feel more important, and it cowed his guests into an almost reverent calm.

Cart stood three paces behind Haldren's chair at the round table Kelas had brought into the sanctuary. Kelas had chosen a round table to give the impression that those seated at the table were all equal, but Haldren had started fuming as soon as he realized that he wouldn't be seated at Kelas's right hand. That position of honor, as Haldren saw it, went to Baron Jorlanna d'Cannith, and Haldren sat next to her.

That meant Ashara d'Cannith stood beside Cart, close enough to whisper up to him, naming the other figures at the table. Cart stood stiffly, uneasy with her presence. He had not seen Ashara in the weeks since they had met in the halls, and he still felt that she had been hoping to manipulate him in this morass of politics. But she seemed to be pretending that had never happened, treating him like a friend. Her proximity only increased his feeling of being adrift in all the plots and schemes of the conspirators around the table.

Cart recognized Arcanist Wheldren, seated at Kelas's left, and Janna Tolden, who had been General Jad Yeven's second-in-command at the battle of Starcrag Plain. Tolden, sitting at Haldren's right, didn't wear a military uniform or any insignia of rank. Ashara mentioned that Tolden had been stripped of her position after that debacle. Certainly better than the fate of General Yeven—the Royal Eyes had hunted him down and killed him, ostensibly because he resisted arrest. Haldren had told Cart that Queen Aurala needed a martyr to blame Starcrag Plain on, and "better him than me." Still, Cart wondered what part Kelas had played in Yeven's death.

To Wheldren's left were the financiers of Kelas's operations. First was a portly man Ashara named as Bromas ir'Lain, head of the small Aundairian branch of the ir'Lains who held so much power in the city of Sharn in Breland. Bromas was a petty noble with little power but a great deal of money, who would easily be motivated to trade some of his vast fortune for a position of power in a new Aundairian regime. Beside him was a gaunt, aging dwarf called Kharos Olan, a powerful merchant who controlled much of the legal trade in Fairhaven and beyond. Olan had both money and power, Ashara explained, but he had lived in the Eldeen Reaches before it seceded from Aundair, and he wanted to see the Reaches returned to Aundairian rule.

Closing the circle was a half-orc clad in furs and steel, with bones knotted into his beard and his unruly mane of hair. His gray skin was stretched over enormous muscles, and the table shook when he slapped it to emphasize a point or communicate his impatience. Kharos Olan and Janna Tolden sat as far from him as possible at the table, suggesting to Cart that he either frightened them or offended them with his odor. Ashara didn't know the half-orc's name, but she explained that he was an exile from the Shadow Marches working in Droaam. He had promised Kelas that he could lead a force of monstrous mercenaries north from Droaam into the Eldeen Reaches in support of Aundair's invasion. He was by far the most unsavory character at the table—an outcast and mercenary lord at a gathering of nobles, merchants, military officers, and a dragonmarked heir. His voice was harsh and his words blunt, but Cart liked him almost immediately. The others treated him with barely concealed scorn, except for Kelas.

Kelas was by no means the orator that Haldren was, but his soft-spoken and friendly manner had clearly won over his audience long before this meeting. He looked around the table and met the eyes of each person, smiling warmly—and then he made a second pass around, acknowledging the aides and advisors who formed a larger ring around the table. That was part of Kelas's power, his ability to connect with the great and small alike.

"Friends," he began, when everyone was seated and settled, "this is a gathering that will be remembered in the annals of history." A murmur of approval rose around the table. "This is the moment when all our plans begin to boil into action."

Kelas stood and extended one arm to indicate the Cannith Baron at his right. "Baron Jorlanna d'Cannith has agreed this day to give the full support of her House to our cause. When our work is accomplished, House Cannith will cease to exist in Aundair. In its place will be a Ministry of Artifice, a prominent branch of the royal government dedicated to advancing the work her House has performed in the past."

The dwarf, Olan, started a round of polite applause. "Merchants like Olan have much to gain," Ashara whispered to Cart, "if House Cannith stops operating like a dragonmarked House. House Orien won't carry Cannith goods any longer, so other merchants will get those contracts. Very lucrative contracts."

When our work is accomplished, Cart thought. Meaning when we've deposed Queen Aurala and ended a thousand years of Wynarn rule over Aundair. Historic work indeed.

"Baron d'Cannith now has an announcement to make," Kelas continued, taking his seat again.

Jorlanna rose. "In partnership with Arcanist Wheldren and the resources of his esteemed organization, we are pleased to announce that the construction of the Dragon Forge is ready to begin." More applause greeted her words, louder this time. "We have all pinned high hopes on the construction of this device. The Arcanist and I have personally reviewed the plans, and we feel confident in assuring you all that those hopes will not be disappointed." She returned to her seat.

"I have asked Lord General Haldren ir'Brassek to secure the construction site," Kelas said. Cart saw Haldren's shoulders tense. "He will lead a party including representatives of both House Cannith and Arcanix, along with sufficient force to take and hold the site in preparation for the construction work."

Cart was baffled. Haldren had not mentioned this to him. Was this a surprise to Haldren? He couldn't judge the Lord General's reaction, especially without being able to see his face. But Haldren didn't start or turn to look at Kelas as he spoke, so Cart figured he probably knew this was coming.

So had Haldren simply been too busy to mention it to Cart, assuming that his advisor would agree to the plan? That was certainly possible. Since their argument a few weeks ago, Haldren had been even less open with his plans. Or did Haldren perhaps not plan to bring him along? No, that was unthinkable.

Cart realized he didn't know where the Dragon Forge would be built. He had assumed it would be in Fairhaven or nearby, but thinking about it, that didn't make sense if dragons were involved. Kelas spoke of securing the site, so it must be a dangerous locale.

Good, Cart thought. An opportunity for action. I've had enough of diplomacy.

* * * * *

Cart's concerns about Haldren leaving him behind proved to be unfounded. Haldren took Cart back to his office beneath the cathedral and informed him of their destination: a sun-blasted canyon at the edge of the Blackcap Mountains, near the Brelish border. The canyon, he explained, was the location of an imprisoned fiend-lord who would provide the knot of magic Ashara had mentioned. According to the scouts Kelas had sent, the presence of the fiend at the site had corrupted the plants and animals that lived nearby—particularly the animals. The reports described wolves that were warped and twisted into demonic forms.

"Our task," Haldren said, "is to exterminate the wolves."

At that, Cart understood why Haldren had not mentioned this task to him before. The bitterness in Haldren's voice said everything he needed to know. The Lord General felt that his skills and abilities were wasted in this mission, which he viewed as a hunting party rather than a military exercise. In Haldren's view, his fall from glory, which had begun at the Starcrag Plain, was complete. He had avoided telling Cart about it out of sheer embarrassment.

Cart could see his point of view easily enough, but he didn't share his commander's bitterness. Any action, even a hunting party, was preferable to the way he'd spent his last few months, sitting around Fairhaven waiting for Kelas and Haldren to finalize their plans and solidify their alliances. He was ready to draw his axe in battle again, to hew through flesh and bone. He was made for battle.

The plan was simple enough. They would assemble their party in Fairhaven. Haldren had already begun choosing soldiers, and Kelas would work with Jorlanna and Wheldren to select representatives from their organizations. Then Arcanist Wheldren would transport their party to Arcanix, using the same magical transportation he himself used in his ventures to Fairhaven. From Arcanix, it was a short march south across dry plains and a few scattered farms. The representative of Arcanix would lead them to the correct location, and they would secure the area. Put in those terms, rather than Haldren's, it was a straightforward military operation. Except that the enemy forces were made up of demonic wolves rather than soldiers of a national army.

Cart couldn't shake the feeling, though, that this plan—like all the plans he was involved in—would turn out to be far more complicated than it seemed.

CHAPTER
13

Rienne suggested that following the forest edge would make it easy to retrace their course if they needed to, and though Gaven couldn't imagine a reason they'd need to, he agreed. The land seemed to welcome them, offering an easy path through tall grass that seemed free of brambles and burrs. Far off to their left, the coast of the bay paralleled their course.

The forest at their right was unlike any other Gaven had seen, shrouded in shadow but alive with color, hung with moss, and steeped in the silence of ages. A hush lingered in the trees, muting the sound of the grass rustling with their footsteps, brooding like a physical presence constantly at their side. Here and there a dragonet perched on a branch at the forest's edge and watched them pass, slowly fanning its wings as its tiny black eyes followed their movement. As colorful as any bird in the jungles of Q'barra or Aerenal, the dragonets seemed like something between a squirrel and a monkey—small foreclaws gripping branches or some morsel of food, needle-toothed mouths preening their scales, the serpentine undulation of their bodies as they scurried and glided among the leaves.

As Gaven and Rienne walked, they sometimes played the games that had occupied them on many treks in the past, jousting with words or exchanging riddles—but they knew each other's riddles, and Gaven was prone to slip into brooding over some riddle of the Prophecy. They walked often in silence, hushed by the stillness of the forest, absorbed in the strange landscape, stumbling occasionally over a tangle in the grass or a root striking past the forest border to invade the plain.

When they made camp under the eaves of the forest, Rienne sang, and the silence fell away.

Clinging to his scraps of sanity in Dreadhold's mighty walls, Gaven had often tried to remember the sound of her voice, but it had eluded him. Her voice was like the perfect steel of her sword, clear and sharp and resonant like ringing crystal, and it cut to his heart. Her tunes were at once peaceful and deeply melancholic, making his chest ache with their beauty. Sometimes she sang old epics or hymns or laments, but often her songs had no words.

When he closed his eyes, he could see the shape of the melodies, tracing bold arcs or curling on themselves. They reminded him of the words of the Prophecy traced on the walls of the Sky Caves of Thieren Kor, the words of creation hidden in the earth itself, but these were characters he couldn't read, secrets of the universe he couldn't decipher. They hinted at the eternity beyond the tumult of history and Prophecy, in much the same way that the anthems and marches of Khorvaire's nations and armies shouted their fleeting, furious existence in the thick of that storm.

Rienne walked and laughed and sang with him like an old friend, but when the embers of their fire died down and they spread their bedrolls on the ground, she did not lie in his arms. So he lay watching the stars and listening to her breathe as she drifted into sleep, and grief weighed on him until he thought he would drown in it.

A few days in, the forest bent their course back toward the beach, and the bay reached for the trees, cutting another cove into the line of the shore. The sound of the tide as Gaven drew nearer to the water put him on edge—the urgency of the waves made his trek without a destination feel like a waste of precious time. For the better part of a day they wore at his mind until he was nearly ready to abandon his quest and teleport back to Khorvaire where he felt he could at least *do* something—he didn't know what, but any activity had to be better than what might turn out to be a walk through an unchanging eternity.

Then they rounded the last hand of the forest, grasping at the beach, and the landscape of Argonnessen came to an abrupt end. The forest fell back from the intrusion of a vast blanket of cultivated fields. Dragon heads carved from great boulders formed a rough ring around the fields as far as their eyes could see, tiny compared with the monuments of Totem Beach but similar in style—except that these all depicted what might have been the same creature, with the pronounced crest of a silver-scaled dragon. Far in the distance, beyond the fields, the bright afternoon light shone along the southern horizon in the shimmering line of a river, and lit the western walls of a city.

Rienne sank to her knees in her amazement. "The Serens?" she said.

"Jordhan seemed to think that they see Argonnessen as sacred ground and won't venture inland any farther than Totem Beach."

"Jordhan could be wrong," Rienne said.

"Besides, the Serens are barbarians. They're sea raiders. Their settlements on the islands are scattered villages, nothing like a walled city."

"Maybe the Serens and these people are two branches of the same family. Maybe one branch settled inland, developed agriculture, and built cities, while the other settled the islands and kept to their raiding. Like the Lhazaar Principalities compared to the Five Nations."

The mention of the Lhazaar islands sent a shudder down Gaven's spine—the prison-fortress of Dreadhold towered over one of those islands. Many nights he had lain in his cot, straining to hear the faint whisper of the waves crashing against the rocks far below his tower cell, struggling to stay awake.

"But even the Lhazaarites have Regalport, Port Verge, and Tantamar," Rienne continued, oblivious to his discomfort. "They're not much, but they're more than the Serens seem to have."

Battles raged in the memory of the land, the clash of armies, the blood of soldiers soaking into the soil. The earth had whispered to Gaven of Argonnessen's native people, and proof of them was spread before his eyes. His earlier shudder lingered in his spine as a chill tingle—an excitement and wonder and dread he couldn't quite pin down.

"The only way to figure out who lives there," he said, "is to go there."

* * * * *

Hugging the edge of the forest, Gaven and Rienne made their way around the fields. Most of the crops growing there were familiar—wheat and barley, grapes and olives. Whoever lived in this city, Gaven surmised, baked bread and drank beer and wine. A few plants he couldn't identify. Moving farther along, they came upon fields of livestock—hulking beasts the size of cattle, but definitely not cattle. Their horns were curved and sharp, their hides covered with brown-black scales, and their shoulders were ringed with a frill of spines. Still farther, they found some fields that were freshly plowed. And there they saw a long line of people stretched across the far side of one field, stooping or crawling along the ground, planting.

It struck Gaven as absurd, somehow, the mundaneness of it. They were in a distant continent, one that no other native of Khorvaire had ever seen, as far as he knew, and his first sight of the people of this land was a row of farm laborers, planting the next season's crops. All their talk of Prophecy and eternity, of exploring new lands and walking into unknown danger, and then they stumbled upon a farm. He laughed.

"What are they?" Rienne breathed. The absurdity had escaped her, clearly—she was intent on the distant figures, shielding her eyes from the setting sun.

"What are they?" Gaven echoed. "They're farmers, laborers. Where's the mystery in that?"

"No, I mean what *race* are they? They're not human."

The smile dropped from Gaven's face, and he squinted at the laborers he'd dismissed. Rienne was right—at first they looked human, tall and as broad as you'd expect from people who made their living by heavy labor. They were too far away to make out more detail than that. The discrepancy was in their heads, when from time to time he'd see them in profile. Rather than the gentle contours of a human face, they had long, rounded snouts.

"Gnolls?" he said. Those barbarians, plentiful in the monster nation of Droaam, had heads resembling dogs or hyenas.

"I don't think so. I've never heard of a gnoll city before."

"They could be slaves of whoever built the city."

"It's not the right shape."

Rienne was right. Gnolls had flat, sloping foreheads, a sharp brow ridge, and a pointed muzzle. These had a single curve from crown to snout, unbroken by a brow. With the addition of a horned frill, they would look just like Vaskar.

"Lizardfolk?" Rienne wondered. Reptilian races were fairly common in the jungles of Q'barra, south of the Lhazaar islands on Khorvaire's east coast.

"No. They look like dragons."

Rienne blinked. "I don't know why I'm so surprised. We just discovered a city in Argonnessen, why shouldn't it be inhabited by walking dragons?"

Gaven was certain now that he harbored no long-lost memories of Argonnessen in the depths of his mind. If he had ever known that Argonnessen was inhabited by dragon-people, he was certain he would remember it now. He watched one of the creatures stand from its labor, stretch long, strong arms, and then freeze. It lowered its arms slowly.

"They've seen us," Gaven said.

"I wonder if we're as strange to them as they are to us."

The one that had seen them was rousing the others, and the dragon-people sprang into action. One took off at a run in the direction of the city, and the rest hustled to a corner of the field.

"I'm not sure I want to find out," Gaven said. "Let's get some cover."

Rienne led the way into the shelter of the forest. Only when the last trace of sunlight was draped in the shadow of the canopy and the stillness of the ancient trees had closed around them did she pause. Gaven turned then and peered back through the brush. The laborers were spreading across the field again, but in a line parallel to the forest edge. They carried spears and halberds with huge, jagged blades.

"They're prepared for intruders," Rienne said. "They think we're scouts from their enemies, perhaps."

"What will they do when they see we're not?"

"I doubt we'll be any less threatening to them."

"Let's get out of here." Gaven strode into the shadows of the trees.

"What?" Rienne said, hurrying after him. "Don't you want to learn more about these people?"

"Not if that means witnessing their combat techniques, or learning how they treat prisoners of war. Hurry!" Gaven cast one last look over his shoulder to make sure the well-armed farmers had not caught up to them. Still a few steps behind him, Rienne glided across the forest floor, her eyes darting to catch every movement in the forest around them. Satisfied that they had a significant lead on their pursuers—if indeed the dragon-headed people were still pursuing them—he charged onward.

"Gaven."

Rienne's voice had the quiet urgency she reserved for truly dire circumstances, and Gaven halted his headlong rush, scanning the trees. He heard the quiet song of Maelstrom sliding from its scabbard, so he pulled the greatsword from his back, though he still couldn't see what had alarmed Rienne.

The first things he saw emerging from the undergrowth and around the thick trunks of trees were arrowheads—obsidian, he guessed, rough-hewn but viciously sharp. Then strong hands clutching the horn handles of curved bows drawn back. Then the dragon-folk stepped into view.

I'd be dead where I stand, Gaven thought, if Rienne hadn't seen them. She is watching my back.

"Easy, Gaven," Rienne said, and Maelstrom slid into its sheath again with a whisper. "If they'd wanted to, they would have loosed their arrows already. See if they speak Draconic."

Gaven dropped his greatsword to the ground and spread his empty arms wide, palms out. "We mean no harm," he said in Draconic.

He saw their eyes widen, and he was suddenly struck by how human they seemed. Their faces were wide, and accentuated by small frills extending back from their mouths. Despite his earlier impression, they did have distinct brows—ridges of scales arching up from their snouts over their eyes and meeting those cheek frills. Behind their brows, they had crests resembling thick, ropy hair, formed of horn or scales. Some of them also had protruding scales that extended down from their chins, and Gaven realized suddenly that those were the males—the bodies of the men and the women were quite different in familiar and quite un-reptilian ways. There could be no question about it in Gaven's mind. The strange creatures that surrounded him in this alien forest were people.

People he shared a common language with.

"What kind of creature are you?" one of the women said in Draconic. Her voice was low but melodious. She wore metal armor, unlike most of the others whose garb was stitched of scaly hide. She held no bow, but carried a shield in her right hand and an axe in the other. Armor, shield, and weapon shared a similar style unlike anything he'd ever seen—graceful curves meeting in points, suggesting tongues of flame. Like the breath of a red or gold dragon.

Gaven opened his mouth to explain what he and Rienne were but found himself at a loss for words. The first word that came to his mind to describe them was "meat"—not how he wanted to identify himself to these people. He turned to Rienne.

"What are we?" he asked. "How do I explain Khoravar to these people?"

"The dragons of Argonnessen certainly know of the elves of Aerenal," Rienne said. "Try it."

"We are travelers-on-the-sea," Gaven said in Draconic. "We have journeyed a great distance to arrive at this land. Some of our ancestors were Aereni." He paused to judge their reaction to this news.

Their wide mouths curved in unmistakable smiles. At the tips of their snouts, the scales formed a beaklike protrusion, but leathery skin behind it parted to reveal knife-blade teeth. Some of them laughed out loud, deep and throaty. Gaven cast his mind back over what he'd said—had he made some gaffe of manners or grammar?

"You talk like a dragon," the armored woman said through her smile.

"Or a character in a bad romance," another one added, letting his bow straighten slightly as he laughed.

Gaven was relieved but confused. He did speak like a dragon—probably because he learned to speak Draconic by holding the memories of an ancient dragon in his mind for twenty-seven years.

He didn't know any other way to speak Draconic, though he had already puzzled out some idioms and colloquialisms he'd never heard before. "Bad romance" was his best guess, and he could only assume that the dragon-man had meant a play or a work of fiction.

He decided to take advantage of the moment of levity. "And you?" he asked the woman, indicating the whole group of dragon-people. "What manner of creature are you?"

"We are *drakatha*, of course," the woman answered. A compound construction—dragon-bred? he wondered. Dragon-spawn? Dragonborn, he decided.

"We know the Aereni from our histories," the woman continued, her face serious again, her fist tight around the haft of her axe. She stepped closer to Gaven. "They are the ancient enemies of the *drakamakki*. Are you their spies?"

Drakamakki. Dragon-kings? Did dragons rule over these people like kings?

"Spies? No," Gaven said. "Our ancestors were Aereni, we are not. We are simply travelers."

"Travelers have an origin and a destination. You have given us neither." Her tone was threatening, and the smiles had vanished from the faces of her entire party. Bowstrings were taut again.

What am I saying wrong? Gaven thought, cursing himself. "We come from beyond the land of the Aereni, far to the northwest." Gaven wished Draconic had a better name for Khorvaire—as far as the dragons were concerned, "beyond Aerenal" was the best description of the location and significance of Gaven's home continent.

"And where are you bound?" The woman stood close now, stooping so her eyes gazed directly into his.

Rienne's touch on his shoulder calmed him in the face of the belligerent dragonborn, but then it tightened in warning. He glanced back at her, just in time to see their original pursuers erupt from the forest and stop in bewilderment.

Shouts rose up from both groups of dragonborn, and a dozen arrows that had been pointing at Gaven and Rienne flew at the newcomers.

CHAPTER
14

The ground rose slowly toward the mountains as Kauth and his allies hurried to put miles between them and the serpent's lair. At first they slogged up long hills that weren't too steep, then circled the edges of dells or made their way down into shallow valleys. After a few days they climbed paths that wound back and forth up hills too steep to take directly. One morning their path led them along the edge of a sheer cliff, still rising, and when they cleared the tops of the trees below them the whole forest was spread out before them.

Kauth paused to lean against a tree whose roots emerged from the cliff into empty air before winding their way back down to fertile soil. He fought to catch his breath, pretending that he was simply taking in the view. That was the problem with taking a form like Kauth's—he looked both stronger and hardier than he actually was. Most of the time it wasn't an issue, but days of hard climbing were taking their toll on his endurance. And Sovereigns prevent some tavern thug from challenging him to a contest of strength!

On the other hand, as Sevren had observed, he was smarter than he looked, which almost made up for his physical shortcomings.

The others stood beside him to admire the view. Zandar was visibly winded—that was acceptable, though, since he was slighter than the others. Vor and Sevren seemed unaffected by the exertion of their climb. And the view was impressive. An emerald mantle covered the hills below them and the gentler land beyond, as far as Kauth could see. The summer sky was a perfect blue, unbroken by clouds, and Kauth realized how accustomed he'd grown to overcast skies while he traveled with Gaven. The man carried the threat of storms with him like a weapon at his belt.

Sevren startled him by leaping up the trunk of another tree and climbing the branches as if they were a ladder until they grew too thin to support his weight. He leaned over the edge of the cliff and looked up.

Zandar called up to the shifter. "What are you doing?"

"Trying to get a sense of the land ahead—or above. We're nearly at the tree line."

"Can you see the pass?" asked Vor.

"Do you think I've led you astray?" Sevren pointed to his right. "It's a little to the north, but I think our course will rake us right to the gates of the mountain."

"Then down into the Labyrinth," Vor muttered.

Sevren scampered down the tree even more easily than he'd climbed it. "Come," he said, and he continued up the path.

Kauth pushed himself to keep up with Vor, just a few paces behind the shifter, while Zandar trailed behind. "And you're leading us through the Labyrinth?" he asked the orc.

"I told you I would."

"Yes, you did. And I'm grateful."

Vor grunted his acknowledgment.

"If we encounter the Ghaash'kala . . ." Kauth wasn't sure how to ask what he wanted to ask.

"We will," Vor said. "They are vigilant, and no one enters the Labyrinth without their knowledge."

"Are you . . . welcome among your former people?"

"No one who seeks to cross the Labyrinth is welcome among the Ghaash'kala."

"Ah." So Vor would be no help in that regard. He had hoped the orc would be able to negotiate their passage in more than just a geographical sense.

Finally, the question he'd been burning to ask the orc since they first met in Varna spilled from his mouth. "Why did you leave?"

Vor looked at him, his face a mask of righteous indignation. Then his shoulders slumped, and he looked away, down at the ground. "It's only right that you should know," he said. "My life is in your hands no less than it is in Zandar's and Sevren's, so you should know what you're holding."

Kauth suddenly wished he hadn't asked. He didn't want to hold the noble orc's life in his hands, didn't want to know anything about the life he was willing to sacrifice for his own purposes. For Kelas's purposes.

If Vor noticed his sudden discomfort, the orc gave no sign of it. "You know about the Ghaash'kala. They come from the same stock as the orcs of the Shadow Marches to the south, and once probably followed the same druidic traditions. Some wanderlust or calling led them to the Labyrinth. One legend claims that they were an army pushing back an invasion of the Carrion Tribes, so zealous in their cause that they chased their quarry back through the Labyrinth to the threshold of the Wastes. The more pious among them claim that the leaders were following the call of Kalok Shash, the Binding Flame, which drew them to the Labyrinth to continue the sacred work of warriors long since vanished from the land."

"The Binding Flame," Kauth said flatly.

"I know what you're going to say—it sounds just like the Silver Flame. Everyone who's not a Thrane or a Ghaash'kala says it. And maybe they're right, for all I know. Certainly since I left the Labyrinth I've come to understand the Silver Flame better."

Kauth could understand the confusion. Two religious traditions known for producing paladins, both of which revered an impersonal force identified as a flame. It was an image with strong religious resonance, he reasoned—fire could represent fervor and devotion, crusading zeal, a purifying furnace, or a punishing force of destruction. Paladins might cling to any of those images, or all of them. Even Dol Arrah, the one god of the Sovereign Host most identified with the virtues of the paladin, was also a sun god, depicted as a knight shining with brilliant light—or as a red dragon, mouth aflame.

Vor was beginning to stray from the original question, and Kauth thought perhaps he could divert the conversation entirely. "What does the Binding Flame bind?" he asked.

"It binds the souls of noble warriors together, the living and the dead, and thus holds back the darkness. In the most literal sense, it binds the evils of the Demon Wastes within its bounds, preventing them from spilling out across Khorvaire. And that is why I am no longer privileged to call myself Ghaash'kala."

Kauth blinked. Had he missed the connection?

"I failed in the most basic commandment of Kalok Shash," Vor continued. "I willingly and knowingly allowed a demon to escape the Wastes. For that crime, I was exiled from my people. I would have been hunted and killed in the Labyrinth, but my knowledge of its ways exceeded that of most of my—most of the Ghaash'kala. I escaped, and now I keep the company of the likes of Zandar Thuul, friend of darkness."

Kauth glanced over his shoulder and was surprised to see the warlock close behind, clearly listening to the orc's words. Zandar grinned, as though he'd just been waiting for a chance to interject another barb at Vor's expense.

"Think of me as a shade protecting the world from the blinding radiance of your soul," the warlock said.

"The world doesn't need protection from me," Vor snapped, "but from the likes of you."

"That's ridiculous. I'm not as bad as the fiends in the Wastes."

"A lesser evil, certainly. But still evil."

"I'm not evil," Zandar protested. "Just . . . practical."

Vor snorted and cast a sidelong glance at Kauth.

Kauth remembered Sevren's comment back in Varna about his two companions: "It's like they're married." Indeed, he thought. Their lives are in each other's hands, and in Sevren's. And in mine.

I'm not evil, he told himself. Like Zandar said—just practical.

* * * * *

As Sevren had promised, he soon led them out from under the shelter of the Towering Wood, high on the slopes of the Shadow-crags. The sky still clung to the blue promise of summer, but the air held the chill of the snow-covered peaks. The trees gave way to fields of purple heather and hardy gray-green grass, littered with bare, dry stones left behind in the summer's thaw.

They had emerged from the forest at the mouth of a gentle valley that beckoned them farther up the mountains. Sevren said that they were approaching one of the few easy passes through the Shadowcrags—easy in terms of the climb, at least.

"It's an easy way into the mountains," the shifter explained, "so it's also an easy way for things that live in the mountains to make their way out. In winter, especially, predators from the heights spill down into this valley and out into the forest in search of prey. In summer, they have plenty of food—mountain goats, elk, and hares. But that doesn't mean they won't take the opportunity to vary their diet. Keep alert."

"What sorts of predators are we watching for?" Kauth asked, careful to keep the trepidation he felt from his voice.

"The hungry kind," Zandar said with a grim laugh.

Sevren ignored the warlock, as usual. "I haven't seen any sign of Depravation, so I don't expect to see anything really strange. Bears, panthers, maybe girallons."

Kauth had heard of girallons—carnivorous, four-armed apes—but never seen one, and he had to admit to some curiosity.

"Be especially on your guard for flying hunters," Sevren added, pointing at Zandar to make sure the warlock was listening. "Griffons, wyverns. Sovereigns protect us if a dragon has made its home in the pass. Ready?"

"Ready," Vor said, and Zandar nodded.

"Ready," Kauth echoed, though he didn't feel it. The mention of dragons and wyverns made him think of Haldren, which reminded him of Kelas and the whole damned mission he was on. He trailed behind Vor as they walked up the valley toward the pass.

They passed through the valley with its wildflowers and herd of elk in a pleasant haze and camped for the night on a level patch of ground beside a bluff that made keeping watch easy. Twice during his time on guard, Kauth thought he saw eyes glowing pale green in the moonlight, but both times whatever creature was watching them kept a safe distance and then withdrew.

By the time they neared the valley's head, snow dusted the slopes just above them. Kauth could see his breath steaming in the cold, and the thin air made his lungs ache. He tried, subtly, to make his chest larger, to expand his lungs and help himself breathe, but his control over his internal organs was imprecise at best. The fact that Sevren and Vor still showed no sign of exertion embarrassed him. Zandar, at least, was gasping more than he was.

They kept climbing until the snow was underfoot, and onward until they slogged through drifts as high as their knees. The sides of the valley grew steeper and closer around them, looming over them, sometimes even leaning together, almost touching above their heads. Bitter winds howled between the canyon walls, freezing Kauth's breath to his face and driving snow into his eyes. Only then, when it was far too late to turn back, did Sevren tell them what the pass was called. Frostburn Cut.

Figures moved in the blinding snow, Kauth was certain of it. A snow leopard perched on an overhang and watched them walk below it, as though hoping one of them would stray from the others and make itself easy prey. Dark and distant wings circled above them, shadows in the snow-filled sky—perhaps the griffons or wyverns Sevren had mentioned. But more unsettling were the figures that were not there. Kauth kept thinking he saw places where the snow did not blow, where it eddied around a form with no shape or substance. No attack materialized out of these strange emptinesses, and Sevren paid him no heed when he mentioned it. So he continued on, casting wary glances around as the day wore on.

When the sun reached the horizon, it flared for a moment beneath the solid cover of slate-gray clouds, a flash of crimson light staining the snow around them like blood. In that instant, a shadow fell across the ground, a shadow cast by emptiness. Kauth had a fleeting vision of a face within that emptiness, a face that gave form to his most primal fears. A great horned bear, snarling in bestial fury, its mouth foaming with blood, and tongues of fire in its eyes—its gaze was fixed on Kauth, he felt it burning into him. Terror seized him like the icy cold.

By the time his cry of alarm had leaped from his throat, the vision was gone. The pall of night draped over them as the red sun vanished, and the form in the snow was gone, not just invisible to his sight, but no longer present even as an absence amid the snow. Sevren's knives were in his hands, but Vor did not seem surprised at all.

The orc lumbered over to where Kauth stood, searching the darkening snow for any sign of the creature that had inspired such fear, and put an arm around his shoulders to steady him.

"We are in the Demon Wastes now," Vor said gravely. "Do not trust your senses."

"Then what under the twelve moons can I trust?" Kauth said, knowing full well the answer.

"Nothing at all, my friend."

Kauth saw something pass across Zandar's face, something not too different from his customary smirk. It reminded him unpleasantly of the warlock's behavior in the Eldeen ruins, when he had so calmly tried to kill his companions. Did Zandar suspect Kauth's secret? His true nature, or the real purpose of their journey?

No, Kauth realized, the warlock's eyes were not on him, but on Vor.

* * * * *

They made camp only when it was too dark to see their way through the pass, and none of them slept except to doze briefly, sitting up, huddling near the fire to ward off the cold. For all their vigilance, no danger materialized in the night, and by morning the snow had slowed and the wind calmed. Their path led them slowly downward, and soon a bare valley, as free of snow as it was desolate of vegetation, came into view.

"Bid farewell to Frostburn Cut," Sevren announced.

"And abandon all hope for your body or your soul," Vor added, "for we stand in the Demon Wastes."

"How charming," Zandar said. "Is that a proverb of your people? I rather like the sound of it."

Vor snarled at the warlock, and Kauth laughed. Zandar had not spoken while they traversed the pass—either because of the thin air and driving snow or because something else weighed on his mind—and Kauth felt relieved to see him back to his normal, sardonic self.

The valley was a fitting introduction to the Demon Wastes. The sky churned with storm clouds, but an angry glow like magma suffused the clouds as though they might rain down fire instead of water. Boulders that might have been the remnants of some incredibly ancient watchtower littered its slopes, and shadows seemed to flit among them in the strange light of the ruddy sky. Not only trees but grass and even lichen had long since abandoned the dusty soil. The air grew warmer with every step they took away from the freezing peaks of the Shadowcrags and toward the wasteland below.

The valley channeled them quickly down the mountainside before spitting them out on a low bluff overlooking a wide, open plain. It was a commanding vantage point, and Kauth was reminded of the view they had enjoyed from the Eldeen side of the mountains, looking out over the vast expanse of the Towering Wood. He could not imagine a starker contrast to that placid scene than the vista spread before him.

If the corruption, the distilled acidic evil of the Demon Wastes, had corroded the earth, burning away what it touched and leaving a blackened, twisting residue, that residue might have resembled the Labyrinth. Mile upon mile of winding canyons, scorched plateaus, and jagged outcroppings stretched from the feet of the Shadowcrags as far as Kauth could see. On the horizon, only tall fires licking at the blood red sky marked the land beyond the Labyrinth.

Abandon all hope for your body or your soul, Kauth thought. *I have consigned us all to damnation.*

PART
II

In the Time Between,
ten eyes gaze brightly upon the City of the Damned,
watching as the pilgrim arrives.

The pilgrim comes to the damned dragon's home,
his dreams full of fire and blood.

The touch of Siberys's hand is upon him,
the storm is in the blood of the Storm Dragon.

CHAPTER
15

The first alteration of the plan was the result of a simple oversight. Arcanist Wheldren was called away to the royal court before Haldren's entire team could be assembled, and the less experienced wizard of Arcanix who was appointed as his proxy couldn't transport the assembled party with a single ritual.

Haldren had assembled his troops in the sanctuary of the cathedral. Cart looked them over and was pleased to see that none of them showed signs of impatience. Disciplined troops would accept a delay, and this mission called for disciplined troops. Ashara smiled at him as his gaze fell on her face. Still uneasy with her presence, Cart had asked Haldren not to include her. But Baron Jorlanna had appointed her, and Haldren couldn't gainsay the Baron. Four squads of veteran soldiers, hardly the best Aundair had to offer but the best Kelas could muster, stood at attention, their eyes fixed on some point at the back of the cathedral. Those four squads were the problem.

With a few hundred extra gold galifars, two arcanists could transport the entire group. With the budget they'd been allotted, they could transport two squads. Haldren quickly decided to teleport the two squads and send the other two by foot. Ten soldiers could hunt wolves as well as twenty, he argued, even if it took them a little longer. The other squads would arrive in time to hold the canyon against any new or renewed threat.

The chain of command, though, required that Haldren wait for Kelas's approval before acting on this change of plans. Haldren's blood boiled while he waited for the runner to return. As a general in the Last War, he gave orders and they were obeyed, and he let the royal treasurers figure out the consequences. This was just one more example of Haldren's total subordination to Kelas. The Lord General believed Kelas delayed his response intentionally, to remind Haldren of his proper place.

Finally Kelas's approval came. Haldren put the more competent of the two sergeants in charge of the overland expedition and sent them out. Then the Arcanix wizard performed his ritual, opening a glowing portal in the air. Beyond it, Cart saw another great hall, richly furnished and inscribed with arcane sigils. Haldren strode through the portal first, leaving Cart in command. That part, at least, went according to plan. Cart was the last one through, and it felt no different than walking across a threshold— a single step that carried him across five hundred miles.

The round chamber on the other side was as large as the ruined cathedral. It filled one floor of one of Arcanix's magically floating towers, with windows on every side looking out over the Aundairian plain, the Blackcrags to the southwest, and the rich blue expanse of Lake Galifar to the west and north. Great columns formed an inner ring, each one carved with a human or near-human figure gazing toward the chamber's center. Gleaming silver traced weaving patterns along the wall, and other metals outlined smaller circles spaced around the rest of the hall. Haldren circled the chamber with a mix of impatience and rapture—he evidently felt or saw something in this arcane paradise that completely escaped Cart.

Another thing that escaped Cart was any means of egress from the chamber. Though there was certainly more to this tower, no stairway led up or down. The windows on every side proved that there were no rooms or stairs beyond the walls of the great hall. They were trapped—the whole party was at the mercy of the wizards of Arcanix, who could seal them in this room forever if they desired.

Fortunately, the wizards evidently had no such desire. The arcanist who had opened the portal from Fairhaven led Haldren to an inlaid copper circle and, with a simple word and gesture, set the ring glowing with a rich green light. Haldren barked the orders this time, sending one squad into the circle first, where they vanished. Haldren and Ashara followed, leaving Cart to order the last squad through and bring up the rear, alongside the young wizard.

Cart had spent so much time in the maze below Fairhaven's cathedral that it seemed he had forgotten what open air and sunshine felt like. Even when he left the dark passages, he hadn't been out of Fairhaven in months, and as green and warm as the city's streets were, they couldn't compare to the feeling of sheer possibility he felt standing once more on a wide plain. Lake Galifar stretched out behind him, so wide that its far shore—its Eldeen shore—was lost in the haze of the horizon.

Eager to start the mission, the quicker to get it over with, Haldren pointed to the south and ordered the soldiers to march. Falling back on habit, Cart marched alongside them—eyes forward, attention only on the cadence of the march. Ashara, though, apparently thought of their journey as a pleasant stroll across the countryside, and walked beside him, chatting as though she were on a casual stroll on any sunny summer day.

"What do you make of these reports of demonic wolves?" she asked.

Cart shrugged. Left, left, left.

"I wonder if there's some wizard behind that," Ashara continued. "They say there's a mad wizard in Droaam who was exiled from the Twelve because of his work in modifying living flesh. This could be the same sort of thing, don't you think?"

"Could be." Left right left.

"On the other hand, maybe we should take the reports at face value. The Dragon Forge is supposed to draw on the power of an imprisoned fiend—why couldn't some taint of its presence affect the creatures around it?"

"That's what Haldren thinks." Left, left.

"He's probably right, then."

Ashara fell silent, a blessed respite from her incessant chatter. Cart let the cadence fill him, move him along in the march, carry him along the road. The greatest joy in the soldier's life, he had often thought, came from working with a single will, perfectly coordinated, with his fellow soldiers. The march was the simplest example, the first step on the way toward a total union of disparate minds and bodies. The squad, the company, the regiment that could march together would someday learn to fight together.

"Why don't you like me, Cart?" Ashara shattered the silence and disrupted his rhythm.

He stopped beside her and gestured for the soldiers to continue. "Lady Can—"

"Call me Ashara, please."

"Lady Cannith," Cart repeated firmly, "we are on a military expedition, not a stroll through a vineyard. Whether I like you or not is irrelevant to our mission."

"It's relevant to me."

For a moment, looking at her so-human face with its contracting muscles and damp eyes, Cart almost believed her. Then, disgusted, he followed the marching soldiers, eager to rejoin their cadence. He didn't notice what Ashara did after that.

* * * * *

The sun blazed overhead when they drew near the canyon four days later, and Cart could see that the heat was wearing on the soldiers. Sweat rolled down their faces, and their discipline was crumbling—several of them stopped to remove their helmets and shake the sweat from their hair. He didn't reprimand them. He knew from experience that if they didn't have a chance to catch their breath while marching, they'd try to do it while fighting. And then they'd die.

The first sign of the wolves came as they were pitching camp that evening. A howl rose from the foothills ahead—an unearthly sound, rumbling with thunder even as it soared to eerie heights of pitch. The soldiers looked up from their work, fear in their eyes. Another howl, and this one was joined by several more, a demonic chorus. The upper notes of their calls clashed in agonizing dissonance even as the lower rumbles flowed together in a rolling boom like an earthquake. An uneasy feeling settled into Cart's chest at that, and a few soldiers looked on the brink of headlong flight.

Haldren kept his head and barked orders. Two rings of sentries would patrol the edge of the camp, in constant motion to ensure alertness, rotating in short shifts through the night. At the merest hint of wolves, the sentries should wake the camp—better to warn of an attack and be wrong than to keep silence and have soldiers die in their sleep. Cart nodded his approval. The Lord General might have found this assignment disappointing, but he took it seriously once it began.

Needing no sleep, Cart patrolled on every shift. Twice, sentries on the opposite side of the camp from him sounded alarms, but either their eyes had been tricking them or the wolves retreated when the soldiers sprang into motion. The sentries described enormous shapes looming out of the darkness, as tall as a man at their shoulders. Cart suspected them of exaggeration born of fear, but he said nothing.

When he saw a wolf himself, he was glad he had not accused the other soldiers of exaggerating. He shouted the alarm as he sprang toward the creature, swinging his axe with all the strength he could muster. Its eyes were level with his own, not so much reflecting moonlight as glowing with their own inner green fire. Its muzzle was scarred with what looked like intentional designs or even infernal runes. Its foreparts were as much bear as wolf, shaggy and strong, ending in enormous paws. As his axe struck its shoulder and knocked it a step sideways, Cart could see that its hindquarters had no fur, but were armored with obsidian scales.

He wondered if the scouts who called these monsters "demonic wolves" had actually seen them or had just fled in terror from their unearthly howls.

In response to Cart's attack, the demon-wolf howled, and it was quickly joined by four or five other voices, surrounding the camp. At such close quarters, Cart could feel the low rumble vibrating in the ground beneath his feet and shaking his resolve. Then, as though it sensed his fear, the creature bared a thicket of pointed teeth and twisted its lips in a fiendish mockery of a smile.

Cart's axe lashed out again, impelled by his revulsion and terror, and bit deep into the wolf's shoulder, spraying a gout of green-brown blood. It staggered back, then pounced at him and knocked him to the ground. As it stood over him, its teeth clattered against his plated body, seeking softer parts beneath.

He had been vaguely aware of other soldiers moving around the camp, and other wolves tearing them down. But face to snarling face with one of the monsters, he drowned in its burning green eyes, terror numbing his senses and rooting him to the ground. He had managed to wedge his shield between himself and the pouncing wolf, but the creature's weight pinned the shield and his left arm tightly against his body. He still had a grip on his axe, but he couldn't bring the blade to bear with any strength.

Instead, he drove the bladed pommel of his axe into one of the wolf's green eyes. It recoiled, and Cart found his feet, glancing around to get the feel of the battle. Once again, the overall plan for their mission would need alteration. Many soldiers were on the ground, and in some cases wolves still stood over them, ripping at their flesh to feed, heedless of live soldiers who jabbed their spears at the monsters.

"Aundair!" Cart shouted, hoping to rally the soldiers' courage, and he charged the wolf he'd wounded. A few weak cries of "Aundair!" answered him, but another chorus of demonic howls drowned them out. The wolf reared up on its hind legs to meet Cart's charge and batted his axe out of the way before clamping its jaws on his shoulder.

Fury began to supplant Cart's fear. Another military debacle under Haldren's command was more than he could bear. He jabbed the pointed tip of his axe into the wolf's belly, pulled it back as the wolf released its grip on him, and brought it around for one final blow with the blade, cutting through the wolf's neck.

Cart spun around to see where he was most needed, and a blast of fire flared in his eyes. When the fire died down, he saw the blackened corpse of another wolf at his feet, and Haldren glaring at him from a few yards away. Just as Cart nodded his thanks, Haldren looked away and loosed a blast of fire to engulf still another of the demon-wolves.

At that, the remaining wolves turned tail and disappeared into the night, leaving a scene of carnage at the camp. Ashara moved slowly among the fallen with a pair of wands in her hands, tending to the wounded and dying. Of the ten soldiers marching with them, two were dead and four were seriously injured. Haldren,

Ashara, and the wizard from Arcanix—whose name Cart could never remember—were unhurt, but Cart and the other four soldiers bore minor wounds testifying to their part in the struggle.

Haldren fumed. "Two squads of soldiers torn to shreds by one wolf sortie." He spat. "And you call yourselves soldiers of Aundair."

The soldiers hung their heads, but Cart could see resentment, rather than shame, on some of their faces.

"Worgs," came a voice.

"What?" Haldren wheeled on the wizard.

He was as young as any soldier Cart had ever seen, a downy moustache clinging to his upper lip. He wore a coat of brilliant red—hardly practical in these surroundings—over clothes too elegant for hard travel. He quailed in the face of Haldren's fury but repeated what he'd said. "Not wolves, worgs."

"Are you questioning my choice of words, soldier?"

This seemed to steel the young man. "I'm not a soldier under your command, General. I represent the Arcane Congress on this mission, and I assert my right to share the knowledge of the Congress when the situation warrants it."

Fire crackled in Haldren's hand and for a moment Cart thought he would actually hurl it at the wizard, but his better judgment prevailed.

"Fine," Haldren said, rage strangling his voice. "Why don't you tell us about these worgs?"

"The scouts who described them as demon-wolves were not far from the truth. They're like wolves with the hearts of fiends, filled with malice and insatiable hunger." The opportunity to discourse on a subject he knew something about evidently strengthened the wizard's nerve—his voice was louder, and his body more animated as he spoke. "Most importantly, they're intelligent. Not geniuses, by any means, but not dumb wolves. They attacked with a plan, and they fled with a plan. We have not defeated them."

"That fact had not escaped my notice," Haldren said, "nor does your learning, while fascinating, illuminate how one attack from these worgs could leave two veteran soldiers dead."

To Cart, this was at last the Lord General's familiar face, at home on the field of battle, harsh in discipline, firm in commands, and tactically brilliant. The worgs' attack had opened Haldren's mind to what Cart had realized in Fairhaven: this was a military operation, not a hunting party. And from what the wizard had said, the worgs were very much like enemy soldiers.

CHAPTER
16

Kauth's initial impression of the Labyrinth did not change when Vor led them down the bluff and into its jagged, twisting passages. There was a wrongness to the place that reminded him of the Depravation around the serpents' lair, but compounded by a sense of brooding evil shrouding the land like a fog. The thick air burned in his nostrils, hot and acidic.

"I will lead you through the passages of the Labyrinth," Vor said, stopping at the entrance he had chosen. They stood at the top of a steep slope that cut down into the earth, closed in by blackened walls. "I know its passages as well as I know my name."

"What is your name, again?" Zandar said.

Vor's growl had always impressed Kauth. It was a sound no human could make, as richly textured as a lion's roar. He resolved to practice the sound in an orcish guise, if he ever had the chance.

"But I remind you," the orc continued, "that I can't predict the movements of the Ghaash'kala. They are likely to find us."

"What will they do?" Sevren asked.

"It depends on which clan finds us. The Khuruk clan will attack without bothering to challenge us or question us. The Darvuks will pause long enough to tell us why we have to die, and they'll try to pepper us with arrows without ever standing in honorable combat. The Maruks will talk first, offering a choice: Commit your lives to the service of Kalok Shash and the holy calling of the Ghaash'kala, or die where you stand."

"I take it you were a Maruk," Zandar observed.

To Kauth's surprise, Vor didn't growl or even snarl at the warlock. "I once had that honor," the orc muttered. His shame was plain on his face, and Kauth felt a pang of sympathy he couldn't quash.

"All right, Vor," Sevren said. "You lead us through the maze, and I'll steer us away from recent tracks and try to keep us out of a Khuruk ambush."

"One other thing," Vor said. "The Labyrinth is treacherous, and it changes often. I know the passages, but I don't know the location of every chasm plunging into Khyber, every river of lava, every gout of flame that might spew up from this accursed land. We need to watch for rockfalls, and if there's any sign of rain, for flash floods. The ground might open beneath our feet."

"Is there anything else?" Zandar said.

Vor's gaze was hard as steel. "And there are fiends in here that will as soon feast on your soul as devour your flesh."

"They'll find my soul scrawny and full of gristle," the warlock said with a grin.

"That won't matter."

* * * * *

For all Vor's dire warnings, he led them safely through the final hours of the day. Kauth quickly lost any sense of direction, and he was certain he couldn't retrace his path. There was only one moment of abject terror, when the left side of the canyon crumbled away beneath his feet. Sevren scrambled to catch him before he slid down the rubble into a black chasm, and pulled him up to solid ground.

"Be more careful," Sevren said, still clasping Kauth's hand.

"You were supposed to warn me."

"Then I'll be more careful for you."

Night fell quickly in the narrow gorge. Sevren and Vor searched for a safe place for their tents, and finally settled on a place where the canyon widened slightly. By pitching their tents in the middle, they figured, they could avoid the risk of rockfalls in the night, and they'd have some warning if anything came up the canyon in either direction or crept down the sides to attack them.

Sevren took the first watch, longer than his fair share. The night was nearly half gone when he woke Kauth.

"See anything?" Kauth asked. He pretended to rub his eyes while checking his face to make sure nothing had changed in his fitful sleep.

"Nothing," the shifter said. "Somehow that only makes me more nervous."

"I know what you mean." The quiet of the night felt like the calm before a storm. "Sleep well."

"Not likely." Sevren crawled into his tent and Kauth was alone.

A field of stars and two moons shone in a sliver of sky framed by the darkness of the canyon walls. The silence was oppressive—except for Zandar's quiet snoring, nothing made a sound. No animals scurried over the canyon walls, no owls called to each other, no frogs or crickets chirped into the darkness. He saw no bats flitting across the stars. The land could not have been more different than the teeming forests of the Eldeen Reaches.

He had to pace to keep himself awake, listening to the soft crunch of gravelly soil beneath his feet. When he heard a quiet tumble of rocks, he first looked down, thinking he'd opened another crack in the earth. Then he realized the sound had come from above him, to his right.

Looking up, he saw a shadow just disappearing behind the lip of the cliff. It looked like a head, probably belonging to a person rather than a predator, which might have pounced rather than taking cover. He scurried to the flap of his tent and whispered Vor's name.

The orc sat up, his new sword already in his hand. "What is it?" he asked, clambering out of the tent.

Kauth pointed to the place where he'd seen the shadow, where a trickle of pebbles still tumbled down the canyon wall. "Somebody's up there," he said.

"Wake the others." Vor strode to the base of the cliff and looked up. While Kauth rattled the peak of the other tent, the orc growled in his native tongue. "Ghazak kurdun!" The phrase defied translation, but it could be a greeting or a challenge.

The rustle of Zandar crawling out of the tent was the only answer. Sevren emerged in silence.

Weapons in hand, they waited, trying not to move or even breathe too loudly. Kauth strained his ears for any sound, any hint of an ambush. Nothing.

Vor was the first to lower his sword, shaking his head. Kauth relaxed, and Zandar let out a long breath.

"What was that all about?" the warlock asked.

"I'm sorry," Kauth said. "False alarm."

"No, it wasn't." Vor was still looking up the canyon wall. "Someone was up there."

"Someone?" Zandar said. "Or something?"

"Ghaash'kala. I'd bet my life. Probably a scout. Probably Maruk."

Zandar looked puzzled. "Maruk? How do you know?"

"They haven't attacked yet."

"Yet," Kauth said. "When, then? Will they wait until morning?"

"Probably not." Vor hefted his breastplate from its resting place in front of his tent and slid it over his head. "Best to get ready," he said, working on the buckles. Kauth and Sevren moved to get the heavier pieces of their armor they removed for sleeping.

Zandar smirked. "I'm ready. What's taking you so long?"

Vor threw a heavy gauntlet at the warlock.

* * * * *

Once they were ready for battle, Sevren decided they might as well pack up the tents and be ready for travel as well. Kauth was tying the last strap around his bedroll when the challenge came.

"Travelers in the Labyrinth!" a low voice resounded in the canyon.

Three shadows loomed in the night ahead of them, tall and broad like Vor. Starlight gleamed on chain links and polished blades, but their faces were in darkness. Feet crunched on the gravel behind them, and Kauth glanced over his shoulder to see two more dark shapes blocking the way back. Four orcs total, he figured, and one human, probably a convert from the Carrion Tribes.

"You stand on cursed ground." The speaker was one of the orc trio, standing a little in front of the others. His voice carried a thick accent, but his Common was impeccable, like a well-rehearsed ritual. "You may proceed no farther into this place of evil, and you may not leave to spread its taint. I offer you a choice: Commit your lives to the service of Kalok Shash and the holy calling of the Ghaash'kala, or die where you stand."

Right to the word, Kauth thought—Vor knew the speech. Did he once lead a band like this one? Was the orc who stood before them now a paladin?

Vor stepped forward. "Durrnak," he said.

The orc leader's face clouded, and he answered in the orc tongue. "Voraash? You dare return? And now you lead outsiders to damnation—you compound your sin. You escaped punishment once, Voraash. You will not escape again."

"You were a friend to me once."

"May Kalok Shash forgive me."

"Durrnak—"

"Silence!" The orc leader's voice was harsh with anger. "You let a demon escape the Labyrinth into the world beyond! There is nothing to discuss."

"A pregnant woman, Durrnak!"

"Carrying the taint in her womb! In her blood! You knew our holy command, and you spurned it. Your sentence is passed, Voraash. You will die here today."

So that's it, Kauth thought—a pregnant woman. He broke the laws of his people, was stripped of his family name and his paladin's honor and sentenced to death in the Labyrinth, because he spared the life of a woman and her unborn child.

Vor's sword—the sword they'd found in the serpent's lair, enshrined among the words of the Prophecy—sang as he slid it from its sheath.

The other orc turned away from him to address the others in his accented Common. "Voraash is doomed," he said, "but your choice remains. You can join us, or you can die here."

"You won't kill Vor while we live," Sevren said.

"Then you will die with him. I am sorry. Kalok Shash grant you a swift death."

What a strange prayer for victory, Kauth thought.

Durrnak hefted his shield, raised his sword, and charged. With a chorus of roars, the others joined the charge, closing in from both sides.

"I think this means the talking's over," Zandar said. A blast of black fire erupted from his hand and engulfed the orc leader, searing his flesh. "And now the party starts."

Durrnak howled in rage but didn't slow his charge. He caught Vor's swing on his shield and drove his own sword at Vor's shoulder, but a quick dodge sent the sword's point sliding off a shoulder plate.

"So this is the company you keep in your exile," Durrnak snarled at Vor, jerking his head in Zandar's direction. Motes of fire still danced across his face and armor. "To what fiend has he sworn his pact?"

Kauth couldn't hear Vor's response, if he gave one. One of the other orcs came barreling into him, swinging his axe with clumsy ferocity. Kauth stumbled back before the sheer force of the charge, then found his feet and stepped to the side, wheeling his mace around to smash the orc's shoulder. They both tottered, off-balance, for a moment in a strange sort of dance, then the orc crashed to the ground. Kauth stepped forward, lifting his weapon, but hesitated too long—the orc rolled away and scrambled to his feet.

"Kauth!" Sevren called. "This isn't a tournament!"

Kill him, Kauth told himself. What's wrong with you?

"Kill him!" Kelas yelled. "Cut his ugly throat."

Haunderk gripped the too-large sword in a shaking hand. He knew the forms, he'd knocked Ledon's sword away and beaten him to the ground. But he'd never dealt a final blow, never killed before.

"What's wrong with you?" Kelas's big hand curled around his, strengthened his grip on the hilt, and drove the blade down. Haunderk watched in terrified fascination as the point dimpled the skin, as blood welled up and the man's eyes widened. He felt the blade pause at the cartilage in the throat, then pierce that too and press on to the bone.

I am Kauth Dennar, he reminded himself. An ugly man made for ugly work. No fear, no mercy.

He remembered the care he'd put into his eyes—hard as steel, pitiless eyes. He hadn't seen a mirror, but he had a feeling those eyes had changed.

The orc circled him warily, then lunged in again and landed a solid blow on Kauth's shoulder. Reflexively, Kauth brought his weapon up to smash the orc's face and hurl him back.

Pitiless eyes.

The orc faced the final blow without any sign of fear, and Kauth delivered it swiftly. Then a flash of light drew his eye to Durrnak, who was still locked in battle with Vor. The orc leader's sword glowed with silver-white fire, and it flared to brilliance as it struck another blow on Vor's upper arm. Vor staggered backward.

Sevren and Zandar were locked in their own battles, Zandar forced to fight with a strange crystal dagger that gleamed purple in the darkness. Kauth drew a steadying breath and circled around Durrnak. Before the orc leader was aware of his presence, Kauth's mace crashed into his skull.

Durrnak fell to his knees. He shook his head then looked up at Vor.

"I gave my life to Kalok Shash and the Ghaash'kala," Durrnak said. "You rob them, not me."

Vor stepped closer. "Forgive me, old friend."

"No."

With a mighty swing of Vor's sword, Durrnak's head rolled from his shoulders.

What happened to Dania?" Auftane asked. He could see her, a crumpled heap on the floor.

Janik walked to her body and fell on his knees beside her. He rolled her onto her back. The front of her armor was covered with drying blood. Janik lifted the helmet from her head and smoothed her red hair back from her face.

In a daze, Auftane shuffled to stand behind Janik, blinking his burning eyes. His gaze fell on Dania's sword, and he bent to lift it from the ground. He saw the magic in it, but what he felt was something entirely different—holy power pulsing through it. He handed it to Janik.

Janik was explaining Dania's sacrifice, how she had taken the evil that possessed Maija into herself, imprisoned it with the magic of the silver torc she wore, then implored Janik to kill her and so destroy the possessing spirit. Auftane couldn't wrench his eyes from the torc. It filled him with loathing.

Vor was staring at him, looking puzzled. Kauth remembered his eyes, pitiless eyes, and shot Vor a cruel grin. As if killing Durrnak were a victory.

Damn fool martyrs, he tried to tell himself. They deserve what they get.

CHAPTER
17

N"o point in trying to sleep any longer," Sevren said. "Kauth, can you go on? You didn't get much sleep."

"I'm ready if you are."

"I'm fine. I thought you looked a little drowsy while we were fighting those orcs."

Those orcs, Kauth thought. As easy as saying "those bugs" or "that gray render." As though they were just monsters or vermin.

"I said I'm ready," Kauth snapped.

Kauth is growing soft, he thought. I need a new face.

Vor led them on as the sky slowly brightened to its unearthly red, and farther on as it grew dark again. The going was hard. The ground in places was littered with rubble they had to scramble over, and in other places it broken by crevices—small ones that would swallow a foot and break an ankle, and large ones that forced them to climb up and around on the canyon walls.

Kauth was glad for the hard terrain. It meant that there was no chance for idle conversation. And it let him try to convince himself that he too was hard—hard as the canyon walls.

But even the canyon walls weren't indestructible—something had cut through the earth to carve the canyon walls. Kauth had first thought of it as concentrated evil corroding the ground like acid, but for just a moment he imagined the holiness of Kalok Shash burning through the corrupted earth like a purifying fire, forming this barrier between the evil of the Demon Wastes and the rest of Khorvaire.

When they made camp that night, Sevren and Zandar laughed and joked. Their victory against that small party of Ghaash'kala had bolstered their confidence, and their healthy fear of the Demon Wastes had evaporated. Vor sat in silence. That was not too far off from his usual behavior, but Kauth suspected that his final exchange with Durrnak—which the others had not heard—was weighing on his mind.

Kauth lay back on the hard ground beside Vor, trying to lose himself in the churning clouds that still glowed dimly red. The gravel dug into his back—such a strange feeling, heightening his awareness of the body that was not his own. He focused on that feeling, mentally tracing the shape of his body and the lines of his face. Trying to keep his mind from replaying their battle against the Ghaash'kala.

Sevren and Zandar were celebrating, but to Kauth the battle had been a disaster. His hesitation to kill the first orc—which Sevren kindly attributed to drowsiness—galled him. It was one thing to grow attached to his traveling companions and to regret the mission that forced him to lead them into certain death. That was bad enough. But hesitating in battle against an enemy . . . It went against a lifetime of training and, worse, could well end up as a fatal mistake.

And then Durrnak's death. Kauth hadn't hesitated in striking Durrnak to protect Vor, but still it troubled his conscience.

Conscience? he wondered. When did I develop one of those?

Auftane gazed at the silver torc, the shape of a serpent coiled around Dania's neck. It was the reason he was there, the purpose of his mission. He had lied his way into Janik's confidence, sailed to Xen'drik and trekked into its depths, fought monsters and demons, and somehow grown to care about his companions—all so he could stand over Dania's lifeless body, trying to figure out how to remove that torc.

Maija stirred, Janik rushed to her side, and Auftane found his chance. He yanked the torc from Dania's neck and broke the thin crystal rod that would teleport him back to Fairhaven.

Sitting up, he reached into the pocket of his coat and pulled out a shard of masonry. It had caught his eye when he stood in the ruin of Gaven's cell in Dreadhold—a piece of Gaven's wall, where he had written all his ravings about the Prophecy and his dreams. He rubbed his thumb over its rough surface and turned it over in his hand, not quite prepared to look at it.

Instead, he turned his head to look at Vor. The orc was lost in his own reverie, his eyes fixed on the ground.

"Why did you let her go, Vor?" he asked. "The pregnant woman?"

Vor didn't move or speak.

"Vor?"

"I heard you." He didn't turn his head. "I didn't know you understood the language of the Ghaash'kala."

Kauth felt his cheeks flush. He had overheard a conversation meant to be private—Vor revealing his deepest and most painful secrets.

"I'm sorry," he said, "perhaps I should—"

Vor cut him off. "Never mind. It's not an easy question to answer."

"I'm just trying to understand . . ." Understand what? What it meant to have principles?

"She begged me," Vor said.

"She begged you? That's it?"

"I offered her the choice, the same one Durrnak offered us today. If she had stayed with us, we might have been able to deal with her child when it came, either purify it or destroy it before it grew too powerful. But she refused. She said that she had friends who could exorcise the evil from the child before it was born and let her give birth to a normal child free of evil's taint."

"And you believed her."

Vor hesitated, tracing some pattern in the gravel. "I'm not sure I did, actually. But I wanted to."

"You wanted to?"

"You don't understand what it's like to live here, Kauth. Wandering the Labyrinth you can go days without seeing another living thing. Anything you do see you usually have to kill. It's a war of relentless extermination. To believe that she could bear a normal, healthy child—it was like believing that something could grow and flower in the Demon Wastes." Vor slowly shook his head. "A damn fool dream."

"As though life could somehow grow out of death," Kauth said. He looked down at last at the masonry in his hand.

. . . recapitulates the serpents' sacrifice, binding the servant anew so the master shall not break free.

The first time he'd seen it, it had made him think of Dania, made him wonder if Gaven had dreamed of her one tortured night in Dreadhold. Had Gaven seen Dania exorcise the spirit from Maija's body, trapping it in her own? She had bound the servant, the lesser evil, before it could carry out its plan to free its master, a still greater evil bound in the depths of the earth.

Could Dania's death have fulfilled some part of the Prophecy? Did it have some greater purpose, something that would give meaning to her sacrifice?

Could life grow from her death?

* * * * *

The night passed without another attack, and by dawn's light Vor announced that they should clear the Labyrinth by the end of the day. That lifted Sevren and Zandar's spirits even higher, but Kauth could think only of the far greater danger that lay on the other side.

Sunlight barely penetrated the clouds that day, and they walked in a strange twilight world of dim red light and greenish shadows. When the day had worn on to what Kauth guessed was its middle, the earth suddenly erupted a few yards ahead of them, cutting off Zandar's laughter. Kauth thought at first that a flow of mud had burbled up from the depths, accompanied by a sound that was not so much liquid as metallic, almost like coins in a pile shifting around each other. The oozing stuff began to pile on itself in a mound, then a slender pillar, and he realized that the flow was composed of brownish black beetles, each one about the size of a gold galifar, massing together into a figure the size of a human.

When only a few beetles still skittered over the ground, the sound grew to a shrill droning as all the ones in the pile lifted their wing casings, becoming a shimmering blur of color. Then silence, and what stood before them was no longer a swarm of insects, but a beautiful woman with the slender grace and elegance of a fey queen or a noble elf of Aerenal. Her eyes were pearly orbs of silver staring wide, her hair was a wild tangle, and she wore a crooked smile that reminded Kauth of Zandar's. The long hem of her tattered velvet gown dissolved into beetles as it swept the ground. She spread her arms wide as though beckoning Vor into her embrace.

"You," the orc murmured.

Sevren threw a sharp glance at Vor. "What's going on?" he said.

A blast of Zandar's dark fire shot over Kauth's shoulder, between Sevren and Vor, and splashed against the smiling woman. Kauth saw beetles fall from her gown and lie still on the ground, but the woman's smile didn't falter.

"It's charmed him," Zandar said. "Take it down."

"You didn't escape," Vor said, his voice choked with grief. He dropped his sword on the ground, pulled himself free as Sevren tried to grab at him, and stumbled toward the beetle-woman.

Zandar blasted her again, and Kauth felt in his pouch for the cherry wand, the one tipped with a fire opal. He drew it out and pointed it at a spot a few yards past where the woman stood. When he loosed the knot of magic in the wand, fire blossomed out from his target point and swallowed the strange figure. More beetles dropped off her and, for an instant, her fair face vanished and she was just a column of beetles again. Then the beetles shimmered and droned, and her lovely face returned. Her smile was gone, but she didn't take her gaze from Vor.

"Your child," the orc murmured. "What happened to your child?" He was just a few steps from her now, and she stepped forward to meet him, to take him in her arms.

Sevren sprang forward to intercept her, slashing his knives through her belly. A few beetles fell from her body, this time with a splash of green-black blood and an angry chittering sound, and she turned her eyes on him with fury. She swung her arm in what would have been a backhanded slap—unhindered by another slash from Sevren's knife, which seemed to pass right through her arm—but her hand dissolved into crawling vermin as it connected with his face. Sevren cried out in pain and shock and he clawed at his face.

Kauth's stomach turned as he saw the beetles burrowing into the skin of the shifter's face and neck. At the same moment,

Zandar shouted and Kauth wheeled to see the warlock stumbling away from a new threat—a towering hulk of a monster, clutching a curved sword in both hands. But for its purple skin, it might have been an ogre or a degenerate giant, something twisted by the evil of the Demon Wastes. A pair of gleaming white horns emerged above its hideous face, which was twisted in a mocking grin as it advanced upon Zandar.

Indecision paralyzed Kauth. The battle seemed to be playing out beyond the grasp of his understanding, and it overwhelmed him as he glanced between the giant demon on one hand and the beetle-woman on the other. Shaking himself, he returned the wand to his pouch, drew out his mace, and ran to help Zandar, entrusting Vor to Sevren's able care.

The giant's smile broadened as Kauth approached. It stepped to one side, putting Zandar between itself and Kauth's approach, then pointed a claw-tipped finger at them. Lightning sprang from its hand and flew in a mighty bolt through the warlock's body and just past Kauth. Zandar dropped to the ground, stirring a grumbling laugh from the giant. Kauth continued his headlong charge, but just as he reached the spot where Zandar lay, his foe vanished.

Cursing, Kauth drew up short and closed his eyes, straining to hear the monster's footfalls. Zandar scrambled to his feet beside him, crunching the gravelly earth but holding in his breath. A few yards away, Sevren was growling his pain, and Kauth could hear the whistle of his blades slicing the air, and the quiet chittering of the beetles. But no sound from the demon-thing.

"Eleni, what happened to the child?" Vor's voice was pleading, pained. "Where is my child?"

Kauth's eyes shot open and he whirled around to look at the orc. The child had been his—he let the woman go because she bore his child! And now he thought this apparition of beetles was her, and he walked willingly into her embrace.

"No!" Sevren and Kauth screamed together. Sevren, closer to Vor, sprang at the orc and knocked him to the ground. Too late—beetles swarmed to cover them both, wriggling between the plates of Vor's armor and beneath Sevren's chain mail shirt, burrowing into the flesh of both men.

Kauth fumbled in his pouch for a wand that would help, unsure how to attack a foe that was burrowing inside his friends. Zandar ran past him and started blasting the ground with black fire, incinerating the beetles that still crawled free. Kauth shuffled forward, painfully aware of the beetles all too near his feet but deciding that the best way he could combat this creature was to make sure Sevren and Vor stayed alive.

At that moment, the demon-giant's sword appeared out of empty air and slammed into his stomach. His armor, reinforced with magic, deflected the edge of the blade, but the force of the blow alone was enough to send him stumbling backward, fighting to breathe. The giant stood before him, visible once again, peering at the blade of its sword as if unsure how it had failed to kill him.

The creature's brow furrowed, and it dropped the sword on the ground. Spreading its fingers wide before it, it blasted a wave of freezing air, engulfing Kauth and his three companions. First pain, then a deadly numbness washed over Kauth. He drew a shuddering breath, and the frigid air seared his lungs. He fell to his knees, clutching at his chest and teetering at the edge of despair. The giant grinned, stooped to retrieve its sword, and lifted the blade over its head for a killing blow.

Kauth could do nothing as the blade descended—the cold had stiffened his limbs, and darkness was trying to claim his vision. He had failed. They would never get through the Labyrinth, never goad the warlord into attacking eastward. On the other hand, he had succeeded in getting himself killed, which was certainly part of Kelas's plan.

Then a flare of silver light drove away the darkness, and he saw Vor standing over him, sparks flying from his sword as the giant's blade scraped along it. Vor moved like a whirlwind of fire, cutting at his monstrous foe with every step, deflecting every blow. Kauth thought he glowed with silver light, much as Durrnak's blade had burned with holy flame.

With numb fingers, Kauth fumbled for the wand that had fallen from his hand, then loosed its healing magic to flow through him. Warmth spread over him and through him, soothing away the cold and the pain. Confident that Vor had the giant's full attention for the moment, he turned to check on Sevren.

To his relief, he saw the shifter getting shakily to his feet. Lifeless beetles, dusted with frost from the giant's wintry blast, littered the ground.

That must explain Vor's recovery, he thought. And Sevren—

Sevren had not recovered. Kauth could see beetles still lodged beneath the skin of the shifter's face and hands, and he moved with what seemed to be enormous effort. He slowly bent to retrieve one of his knives, and just as slowly straightened.

"Sevren?" Kauth said. "Do you need help?" Something was terribly wrong with the shifter, as though the beetles under his skin, rather than his own mind, were in control of his body.

Sevren shuffled forward until he was next to Kauth, then suddenly slashed at him with the knife. Fortunately, whatever was slowing the shifter's feet interfered with his attack, and Kauth dodged it easily.

"What in the—" Kauth said, but another swing cut him off. "Sevren!"

"Heal him!" Zandar shouted from somewhere behind him. "Your wand!"

Kauth glanced down at the wand in his hand. "I have to touch him first," he muttered. Trying to imagine it as a dagger, he dodged another swipe of Sevren's knife and lunged, trying to time the wand's discharge for the instant it touched the shifter.

But it didn't touch the shifter. Sevren jerked to the side just in time, then plunged his knife into Kauth's stomach. The taste of blood filled his mouth, complementing the bitter taste of defeat.

CHAPTER
18

"W hich side are we on?" Rienne asked, turning to look at the dragonborn crashing through the forest toward them.

"Neither," Gaven said. "Let's get out of here." He retrieved his sword from the ground and started in the direction they had been running, but the dragonborn woman moved to block his path.

The initial volley of arrows had little effect—the dragonborn had attacked in haste, surprised by the sudden appearance of one group of enemies while they were in the midst of interrogating another. Most of the woodland dragonborn, as Gaven imagined them, had dropped their bows and drawn huge-bladed swords, charging their new enemies, the farmers. A few hung back and loosed well-aimed arrows into the fray. But the leader's attention hadn't shifted away from Gaven.

"You still haven't told me where you're going," she said, "though you seem in a great hurry to get there."

"I do not"—Gaven suddenly grasped how to form a contraction in their language—"I don't know our destination. We came to learn more about the Prophecy, about the Time Between, but I don't know anything about this land or your people. We are not so much travelers as explorers."

The dragonborn seemed to consider this carefully, while letting her eyes rove across their faces, clothing, and weapons. She seemed oblivious to the battle raging around her.

"We will call you pilgrims, then, and place you under the protection of the city of Rav Magar. But if you accept our protection, you must fight in our defense."

That struck Gaven as odd, but he was willing to accept it. He turned to Rienne.

"She says she'll accept us as pilgrims and protect us, but we need to help them fight these other ones."

"I suppose that answers my original question."

"Right. At least these ones were willing to talk to us." He looked back at the dragonborn, who had listened intently to their conversation but showed no sign that she understood. "We accept your protection and offer our swords to your defense," he said, aware that he'd lapsed back into more formal dragon-speech.

"The left flank could use our aid," the dragonborn leader said. Gripping her axe and shield more tightly, she strode to where one of her soldiers was struggling to beat back the long hafts and biting blades of two of the farmers. The leader opened her mouth and released a blast of lightning that shot through the two enemies, leaving them scorched and dazed but still standing.

So the resemblance to dragons is more than superficial, Gaven thought.

Gaven spoke a spell to shield himself in cold fire and charged after the dragonborn leader, charging the nearest dragonborn farmer. He knocked his foe's halberd aside with a swing of his sword, then brought his blade back around in a deadly cut. Rienne whirled into motion beside him, Maelstrom dancing easily between the farmers' long polearms.

The skirmish was over quickly, before Gaven reached his stride. The woodland dragonborn outnumbered their opponents and seemed to outmatch them in skill as well—not surprising, Gaven supposed, considering that the farmers were laborers who left their fields to pursue Gaven and Rienne through the woods. A few of the farmers ran off into the woods, but fleet-footed woodland dragonborn pursued them.

"Thank you for your help," the dragonborn leader said. She pressed her fists together in front of her chest and bowed slightly to Gaven and Rienne.

Gaven returned the bow. "Thank you for not turning your wrath on us."

"I'm Lissann Orak," she said, "first captain of the Magar scouts. Or Lissa."

"I am Gaven. My companion"—he tripped over that word, unsure of which nuance of meaning to put on that word, finally deciding on the most neutral—"is Rienne ir'Alastra." Hearing her name in the midst of Gaven's Draconic babble, Rienne gave a small bow.

"As pilgrims you are under the protection of Rav Magar, and we are obligated to see you safely there. But we must go a little farther before we can return to our city. Will you accept a delay in our escort?"

"You're asking us? Your people must hold pilgrims in high regard." Gaven wasn't positive he had grasped the right meaning of the word, *hathandra*. "Those who travel" was the simplest translation, but the word carried a definite connotation of a sacred purpose, of being on pilgrimage.

"Our cities are constantly at war, but pilgrims must travel safely," Lissa said.

"So your city is at war with the one back there on the river?"

Lissa nodded. "Rav Dolorr. We've fought them for generations."

Gaven wondered how long a generation was for these draconic people—were they as long-lived as dragons? "How far away is Rav Magar?"

"Twelve days' march."

"Twelve days!"

"For a marching army, yes. Eight for us, if you can keep up with us."

"So that explains why farm laborers had weapons close at hand, so ready to give chase," Gaven said.

"Ah. They were chasing you."

"They saw us at the edge of the forest. They must have assumed we were scouts from your city."

"That is unfortunate," Lissa said. "That means Rav Dolorr is already alerted."

"Yes. When they spotted us, one ran into the city while the rest pursued us."

"That's important news. I have to consult with my *takarra*."

Consult her wings? Gaven wondered. Then he saw Lissa call two other dragonborn to stand beside her—one on either side—and speak with them. Her "wings," then, were something like lieutenants or advisors. The ones who keep her aloft, he thought.

Gaven looked around. He'd been so intent on the conversation with Lissa that he'd all but forgotten about the other dragonborn, who were tending to their wounded and the scout who had fallen. And about Rienne, standing still but expectant beside him. She arched an eyebrow at him.

"They're scouts from another city," he explained, "at war with the one we saw first. We might have ruined their mission when those farmers spotted us."

"What's the destination of our pilgrimage?" Rienne asked.

"I don't know. Didn't think to ask. I know they're planning to escort us back to their city, Rav Magar. I have no idea what there is to see there."

"What did you tell them of our purpose?"

"I don't know," he said, annoyed. "I kept us alive, didn't I?"

"So far. I hope we're as lucky in a city full of these people."

* * * * *

Lissa and her *takarra* decided to head back to Rav Magar, their mission a failure. Drawing near to Rav Dolorr would invite disaster—the city was alerted, and the first group of dragonborn to chase the intruders wouldn't return. Before long, the forest would be crawling with soldiers from Dolorr, better armed, better trained, and in greater numbers than the laborers they'd defeated so easily.

They sped through the forest for the rest of the afternoon, across ground that rose steadily toward the feet of the mountains. Traveling with the dragonborn confirmed the impression Gaven had gleaned from the fields they'd passed—these people ate bread and drank wine, as well as dried meats Gaven couldn't identify and exotic fruits they gathered as they walked. They shared their food with Gaven and Rienne, a welcome respite from their diet of dry journeybread. They stopped traveling when the sky fell dark, set up camp and told stories around their fire, then slept until dawn. Camping under the trees and relieved of the responsibility for keeping watch, Gaven fell quickly into the deepest sleep he'd had since their arrival in Argonnessen.

As much as their eating and sleeping habits seemed familiar, the way the dragonborn interacted with each other was totally foreign to Gaven. It was Rienne, despite her ignorance of Draconic, who observed that their behaviors seemed to be based on relative social status. Lissa was the dominant member of the band, clearly, and each other member made varying gestures Rienne interpreted as marks of submission each time they approached her. There was a clear second tier, the ones Lissa had identified as her *takarra*, who made submissive gestures to Lissa but received them from the others. Once Rienne pointed these out, he could make sense of what were essentially military ranks. She seemed to perceive nuances even in the lower ranks that were beyond him, though. Rienne surmised that they were related more to family status than individual status—and, of course, being a member of Aundair's nobility, she would be sensitive to that sort of thing. Gaven never had any patience for it.

The next day, they emerged from the forest to the bank of a wide, slow river, the opposite bank barely within bowshot, Gaven guessed, and Lissa confirmed, that the river flowed past Rav Dolorr and emptied into the bay. For seven more days they traveled upriver, scrambling up past its rapids and cataracts. Before long they were walking in a narrow gorge that cut through the mountains. Then, at the end of the eighth day, the gorge opened into a wide valley cradling a large, still lake—the source of the river.

Fields spread along the nearer sides of the lake, and herds scrambled over the valley's steep sides—probably goats or sheep, but just shadows on the darkening hillside. The city of Rav Magar grew around the far end of the lake and up the back of the valley. A high wall surrounded the city, spiked with jagged blades reminiscent of the dragonborn's weapons—they might even have been halberds and glaives propped against a battlement. Torchlight flickered through arrow slits cut through the wall, and great watchfires blazed in towers spread along the wall. Similar towers flanked the head of the river where Lissa's band emerged from the gorge.

Gaven glanced up at the sky as they approached the gates between the towers, then stopped, staring. A row of bright disks shone like a strand of pearls stretched across the Ring of Siberys—ten moons all rising full on the same night. *Ten eyes gaze brightly upon the City of the Damned, watching as the pilgrim arrives.* He was the pilgrim, he was sure of it—it was just the echo of a memory, but the verse that had sprung to his mind went on to speak of the Storm Dragon.

Rienne and Lissa stopped together to look back at him, and Gaven hurried to catch up.

Guards challenged them at the gates, but let them pass as soon as they recognized Lissa. They gawked at Gaven and Rienne as they followed Lissa through, and two of them speculated aloud about what they could be, apparently not considering the possibility that Gaven could understand their words.

"They wear clothes like people," one said.

The other snorted. "But they have fur like—" What was that word? *Meat-animals.* Livestock.

"Not much meat on them."

The second guard gasped and pointed at Gaven. "His skin, look!"

His dragonmark. Gaven hadn't thought about how the dragonborn would respond to the mark of the Prophecy on his skin, but Lissa hadn't seemed to give it any notice. He was curious to hear what the guards would say about it, but they just gaped and pointed, and then he was past the guardpost and walking a rutted dirt road along the lake shore.

Lissa noticed the attention his dragonmark drew, and took off her cloak when they were out of sight of the guardpost.

"Better put this on," she said, "and cover it up." She gestured at his neck and arm, apparently at a loss for words to describe "it."

"Why?" Gaven asked. "My mark didn't seem to disturb you or your scouts."

"Disturb is perhaps not the right word. Interest would be better. And it did interest me."

Gaven gathered the dragonborn's cloak—made of linen, apparently woven from flax just like in Khorvaire—around his neck. He let its folds drape over his left arm, where the dragonmark extended down past the half-sleeve of his chainmail coat. For good measure, he pulled the hood over his head, hoping it might reduce the number of casual observers who stopped in their tracks to gawk at the unfamiliar creature. Rienne had the same idea. She had unwrapped the long silk cloth she wore around her waist and was carefully draping it over her head and around her shoulders.

As they drew closer to the city, they fell in among a steady stream of people—dragonborns, entirely—making their way both in and out of the city at the end of the day. There were farmsteads dotting the sides of the valley, hearthfires springing to life inside them as the sun went down, and some merchants and farmers were leaving the city walls to join their families at home in those dwellings. Laborers and travelers were shuffling in, returning from their work as farm hands, masons, or carpenters to their homes safe inside the walls. Like Lissa's band, every one of the dragonborn made or received some gesture of submission while passing another. Gaven tried in vain to make sense of it, then finally resolved to ask Rienne about it later.

The variety among the dragonborn struck him for the first time. Their coloration ranged from Lissa's bronze-gold to dark shades of red, covering a spectrum of golds, browns, and rust along the way. They were generally large and strongly built, but they showed as much variation in height as humans did, even if the shortest of them was as tall as Gaven. Most of them had leathery hide covered with very fine scales, with larger scales on a few areas of their arms and legs. A few had large scales over their whole bodies, like soldiers in heavy armor. The more of them he saw, the more he recognized differences in facial features—the spacing and shape of the eyes, the structure of the frills, width of the head and mouth, and the height of the brow and the length of the snout.

The city itself might have been full of farm hands, merchants, and blacksmiths, but it seemed no less alien to Gaven than the bodies and customs of its dragonborn inhabitants. The city grew like a mountain against the back of the valley, filling the valley floor and then narrowing as it climbed higher to a single palace silhouetted against the sunset at the lip of the valley. Gaven imagined that the structure of the city mirrored the social structure of its people, with the ruler in his palace at the peak, then progressively larger neighborhoods of decreasing status. He wondered if the ruler were a *drakamakk,* a dragon-king—and if a *drakamakk* was actually a dragon, or just an exalted dragonborn with a lofty title?

Whoever sat in the palace, dragons were everywhere in the architecture of the city. Dragon heads jutted out from lintels, dragon claws held signs lettered in Draconic, and dragon mouths belched smoke from chimneys. Dragons dominated pediments on the front of larger buildings, and elegant dragons coiled around the pillars that supported them. They snaked along stairways and over archways, and dragon statuettes crouched outside doorways.

All of the buildings aspired to a monumental style—especially the larger stone buildings with their columns and pediments, but even smaller homes were fronted with fieldstone and boasted pillars and sometimes friezes above the doorways. Yawning archways unblocked by doors seemed to welcome guests to every home.

And among all these strange buildings and carved dragons, the dragon-headed people walked the streets, filtered into taverns, closed shops and retreated to their hearthfires. Gaven felt overwhelmed, and suddenly very vulnerable.

As soon as they were inside the city, Lissa dismissed her *takarra,* who took their scouts off in loose formations toward the heights of the city. When they were gone, she turned to Gaven.

"You are pilgrims, so you will visit and stay at the shrine," she said. "I will lead you there, and then I will have to leave you for now."

"What's at the shrine?"

"You told me you were interested in the Prophecy."

Gaven couldn't believe it. "The shrine is dedicated to the Prophecy?" Was it possible that he could find what he sought in a single place, and so soon?

"Of course," Lissa said, in a tone that suggested she couldn't imagine any other possibility.

"Then we'll be happy to visit it. And stay there."

CHAPTER
19

Kalok Shash!" Vor's roar resounded in the canyon, and it seemed to Kauth that the earth beneath him shook with it. Clutching his belly as he fell to the ground, Kauth turned to look at the orc.

The giant's sword was buried in the orc's shoulder, and Vor was drenched in blood. His left arm hung lifeless at his side, but the sword in his right hand was in the midst of a mighty swing aimed at the stooping giant's neck. Silver light traced the arc of the blade, and it flared into a brilliant explosion as it struck true. The giant toppled, but Vor followed it down to the ground.

"No no no," Kauth groaned. He tried to crawl to Vor, but his arms wouldn't support his weight.

Sevren's foot slammed into his ribs, knocking him over onto his back. The shifter held his knife poised for a killing blow, but his face showed signs of his internal struggle. He was trying to resist whatever compulsion held him in its grip—but he couldn't.

Just as the knife began its downward plunge, Zandar leaped over Kauth and into Sevren, knocking him down. Kauth loosed the wand's healing magic into his body, stopping the blood flowing from his gut, at any rate, though it still left him feeling weak from the blood he'd already lost.

Sevren had the upper hand in grappling the warlock. Though his knife had fallen away somewhere, his claws tore at Zandar. Worse, beetles now swarmed over Zandar as well, burrowing beneath his skin. On the other hand, Zandar completely occupied the shifter's attention, leaving his back open to Kauth's wand.

Kauth struggled to his feet and bent over the shifter. As the wand's magic coursed into Sevren's body, beetles erupted through his skin and fell dead to the ground, leaving bloody ulcers behind. Sevren stopped struggling against Zandar, and the warlock pushed him off. Kauth bent over Zandar next.

"I'm fine," the warlock said, pushing him away. "Check on Vor!"

A surge of grief clenched in Kauth's chest and pressed at his eyes. "It's too late for Vor," he said.

"It can't be! Go heal him!" Zandar's face was twisted in pain that reflected Kauth's own and magnified it.

The beetles that still crawled over the earth came together and started building their slender pillar again. Kauth pulled out the fiery wand again, but Zandar snatched it from his hand.

"I'll kill it," Zandar said. "See to Vor!"

Kauth couldn't argue. Dreading what he would see, he picked his way among the swarming beetles to the fallen orc's side. Fire burst behind him, and he heard the drone of the beetles.

He'd been right—there was no pulse of life in Vor's neck, no breath in his mouth. His eyes stared blankly at the sky. But in this one place, the sky did not seem so dark. Kauth felt a sudden surge of hope—hope, perhaps, for Vor above all. At the last, he had struck the giant with the power of Kalok Shash. The Binding Flame had not abandoned him.

Another burst of fire made Kauth's shadow fall across Vor's face. Then silence. He heard quiet footfalls approach, then Zandar fell to his knees at Kauth's side. Sevren stood behind them. There was nothing to do but mourn.

* * * * *

Vor's lifeless eyes stared at the burning sky. Kauth followed them up as if there were something to see, and lost himself in the churning of the clouds, the strange red light, and in memories of Vor.

Zandar was weeping unabashedly beside him, displaying far more affection for the dead orc than he ever had while Vor was alive. The sounds of his cries seemed a fitting background to Kauth's thoughts.

Vor had died for him. The giant-demon would have killed him

if Vor had not charged in when he did. Kauth had put his own life in danger to reclose the Gatekeeper seal in the serpent's lair and saved his companions, but Vor had been the one standing beside him, hacking off the alien tentacles that wrapped around his neck while he worked.

Why should Vor's death bother me? Kauth thought. I brought him here to die. The whole plan rests on him dying, along with the others. Along with me. Their lives are playing pieces in a much larger game.

He shook his head, still staring up at the clouds.

"Do it now!" Kelas stood behind her, yelling in her ear. "No one lives forever."

Laurann stared into her friend's eyes. She had trained with Kyra for a month. They had been girls together, laughing and laughing over the most foolish things. She had told Kyra things she had never told anyone. Now Kelas was making her kill her friend.

Kyra set her mouth in a thin line, but her eyes betrayed her. The eyes always do.

"You have no friends," Kelas said. "If you cannot kill her, I will make her kill you before I kill her myself. Kill or be killed. If you love you will fail!"

"I'm sorry," Laurann whispered. She drove the knife into Kyra's heart as fast and hard as she could, hoping her friend would die quickly.

Kelas spun her around and punched her face. "You are not sorry!" he yelled. She fell to the floor and Kelas kicked her in the gut. She curled around the blow, gasping for breath, and he kicked her again. "You do not care for this girl! She failed, so she died!"

He kicked her once more, and Laurann rolled over into the spreading pool of Kyra's blood.

How many people had he killed at Kelas's command? He couldn't begin to count. It started when he was barely old enough to wrap his hand around the hilt of a sword. How many times had Kelas beat him for displaying a shred of hesitation or compassion, for caring a whit about anyone? Kelas had worked hard to ensure that Kauth—that *Aunn* in all his faces hated him. Hated him and obeyed him without question.

Always the message was the same: Aundair was everything and the lives of individuals meant nothing. A Royal Eye was willing to sacrifice anything and anyone for the good of the nation, even himself. The needs of the nation and its hundreds of thousands far outweighed the life of any one person.

I don't believe it anymore, he realized. He looked down from the sky to Vor's corpse on the ground, to Zandar weeping over his friend. This, he thought, is what life is about.

I won't do it. For the first time in my life, I'm going to fail. And Kelas can burn in the Lake of Fire for all I care.

He unslung his pack from his shoulders, opened the front pouch, and drew out an ivory cylinder. He unscrewed the lid and shook out a roll of papers, then began to shuffle through them, looking for the one he needed.

"What are you doing?" Sevren asked. The shifter had been standing silently behind him, mourning in his own quiet way.

"I'm going to bring him back."

Zandar looked up at that. His face was a mask of anguish, streaked with tears. His violent display of emotion no longer seemed out of place to Kauth. It was right and good that he should care so much about his friend.

"You can do that?" the warlock asked. The note of hope in his voice convinced Kauth that he had made the right decision.

"I can damn well try." He'd carried the scroll with him for years, hoping he would never have to use it, and never quite sure that it would work if he did. He found the right one, withdrew it from the sheaf, and returned the others to their case.

"How can I help?" Zandar asked.

"Pray for me."

* * * * *

Kauth let his eyes roam over the scroll, blocking out the rest of the world from his mind. A devotee of the war god, Dol Dorn, had scribed it, ornamenting it with images of weapons and marching armies. The priest had probably intended it to be used in the event of a great general's death on the field of battle. Presumably whoever carried it into battle had died before the general in question.

Kauth had purchased it some years ago with money he'd secreted away without Kelas's knowledge.

Kauth had heard other changelings in the Royal Eyes speak of the Traveler over the course of his training, always out of earshot of Kelas and other handlers. The ever-changing trickster of the gods, the Traveler did not answer prayers or accept sacrifice—the Traveler smiled on the self-reliant. The Traveler's ten thousand names were said to hide the secrets of the universe for those who could puzzle them out. The idea of those ten thousand names had always captured Kauth's imagination, and he figured that the best way to glean their secrets was to adopt ten thousand names himself. In thirty years, he had yet to take on a hundred names, and he felt more than nine thousand names distant from the mysteries of the universe.

He wasn't sure whether the Traveler had really appeared to him in a dream. He had been inclined to dismiss that apparition as the product of a fever. But her persistent question—he had always thought of the Traveler as her, though others described him as male in sometimes vulgar myths—that question had lingered with him: "Who are you?" It galled him that he hadn't yet come up with a satisfying answer.

So it was her image that Kauth fixed in his mind as he began to read the scroll, as she had appeared to him in that dream, wearing the face of the martyred paladin Dania ir'Vran and bathed in argent light. Perhaps Kalok Shash would smile on that mental image of silver fire and favor Vor because of it.

He reached into the scroll with his mind, gingerly touching the magic bound in each letter, amplified in each syllable, straining against the bonds of each word. One by one, he wrapped his mind around the knot of magic in each word and felt the knot loosen as he spoke. Magic streamed from the letters on the page, dissolving the ink it left behind, and poured from his mouth like sound. A cloud of divine power swirled around him like a brewing storm.

In that shadow of that storm, he felt infinitesmal, and he felt infinite. He felt himself dissolved in divinity, stretched across the universe and beyond, as though if he looked he could see everything and if he thought he could know anything. But he was far past sight and thinking. He was a tiny mind and a feeble hand reaching to touch a far greater power, speaking words that hallowed his tongue, daring to command the power of the gods.

It seemed to him, for a fleeting instant, that the gods deigned to be commanded, as he felt the power of the divine storm break and pour into Vor's body. He was empty, every mote of energy scoured from his body and mind. A shimmer of silver ran over the fallen orc, and some part of his mind heard Zandar next to him gasp, then hold his breath.

There was a moment of perfect silence. No one breathed, no waft of wind stirred the dusty ground, nothing moved. They hung suspended in time.

And then the sky rumbled with thunder somewhere in the distance, the gravel shifted and crunched under Sevren's foot, and the last flicker of silver faded from Vor's blood-soaked armor.

Nothing. There was nothing. His failure was complete.

* * * * *

Zandar couldn't bear the thought of Vor's body becoming a feast for whatever carrion feeders might crawl through the Demon Wastes, but there was no wood to build a funeral pyre. So he and Sevren collected rocks and piled them in a cairn over Vor, hoping that would do the job but not really believing it. Kauth sat alone as they worked, trying to recapture some of what he'd felt as he read the scroll and agonizing over his failure. Against the magnitude of that failure, turning his back on his mission and the Royal Eyes seemed paltry.

One other problem nagged at Kauth's mind—how to tell the others they were turning back. He had told them their mission was to scout the Demon Wastes for sign of an imminent invasion of the Eldeen Reaches. Something told him that Sevren and Zandar would want to complete that mission to honor Vor's sacrifice. He considered telling them the truth—that their true mission was to stir up an invasion and lose their lives in the process. He wasn't confident they'd be understanding. Somehow, he had to figure out how to prevent the rest of them from meeting the same fate as Vor.

Zandar and Sevren finished their work before he came near a solution to that problem. With some hesitation, Sevren took up the sword Vor had carried, the one they'd found in the serpent's lair, surrounded by the words of Prophecy. It was more fitting, Zandar had argued, to lay Vor's greataxe over his chest, the weapon he'd wielded in battle for years. Sevren initially handled the sword as though it were tainted by Vor's death, but after giving it a few trial swings he clenched it more tightly, evidently pleased with its heft. Then he looked between Kauth and Zandar.

"Onward?" the shifter said. "Vor said we should clear the Labyrinth today."

Kauth looked at Zandar, hoping he would be the first to suggest they turn back. The warlock was staring at the ground. No help from that quarter.

"Do you think you can get us the rest of the way through the Labyrinth?" Kauth asked Sevren.

"I have about as much chance to get us out on the far side as to take us back the way we came."

"Couldn't you follow our tracks back to the mountains?" Zandar asked. Good—the warlock was considering turning back.

"It's possible. This gravel doesn't show much sign of our passing, though. And the ground here has a tendency to change. Kauth, what do you think? This is your job, after all."

"My job got Vor killed. I'm about ready to damn it." And Kelas, he thought.

"I can see that," the shifter said, scratching his head. "On the other hand, if we turn back now we don't even get paid for our trouble."

"Five thousand galifars split three ways," Zandar said. "That's what? Sixteen sixty-something? I suppose that's the upside of Vor's death—an extra four hundred gold."

Kauth stared at the ground. Zandar was making a valiant effort at regaining his cynical mask, but no one believed it.

"If we survive," Zandar added.

"I think we need to find our way out of here," Kauth said at last.

"Zandar?" Sevren asked.

The warlock nodded, staring at Vor's cairn.

"I don't know how well I can follow our tracks," Sevren said, "but at least I know we start going that way." The shifter pointed a sharp claw in the direction they'd come.

For a moment, no one seemed willing to move. Zandar's eyes were wet, and Sevren watched him. Finally Kauth took the first step, and the others trailed behind. Zandar kept looking back at the cairn until the canyon turned and shut it off from his view.

* * * * *

Each time they reached a branch in the canyon, Sevren examined the ground, sometimes ranging a hundred yards in both directions in search of any sign of their prior passing. More and more each time, it seemed to Kauth that his final decision was little more than his best guess. Kauth kept turning around, hoping the canyon would look familiar from the other direction, but there were no clear landmarks, the canyon all looked more or less the same, and he hadn't really been paying close attention the first time around. He began to wonder if they might not end up on the far side of the Labyrinth after all, in a cruelly ironic trick of the Traveler.

They made camp early, to ensure that Sevren had enough light to look for their tracks. His hope was that sometime the next morning he'd find some sign of the camp they'd made the previous night, indicating they were still on the right track. But Kauth couldn't help noticing the uncertain tone in his voice.

The night passed in deathly silence, their third night in the Labyrinth. Kauth wondered how many travelers had survived three nights in the Labyrinth before. Perhaps it was many—travelers who managed to avoid the Ghaash'kala and any monsters that haunted the Labyrinth, only to die of starvation, hopelessly lost in the maze.

The next morning was slow going. Sevren stopped more than usual, looking for signs of their previous camp, and spent longer at each branch. As the day wore on, the shifter grew increasingly tense, snarling at any interruption of his concentration. He was beginning to believe he'd led them astray. Shortly after the sun passed its zenith, he threw himself on the ground.

"What was it Vor said?" Sevren said. "Something about abandoning hope?"

"Abandon all hope for your body or your soul," Zandar said, crouching near the shifter.

"We should have done that days ago."

Kauth sat to rest his legs, a little away from the others, and stared at the ground. Days ago, he thought, I should have realized that I couldn't lead these men to their deaths. Now it's too late.

Wrapped in his thoughts, it took a moment for his mind to register what his eyes had seen. In a tiny spot beside him, there was a disturbance in the sea of gravelly ground. Larger pebbles cleared away to the sandy soil below. And in the soil, the faint memory of a pattern—a pattern traced by Vor's finger!

"We're here!" he shouted, startling Sevren to his feet.

"We're where?" Zandar said, looking around the canyon walls.

"This is where we camped the night before last. Look—Vor was tracing his finger on the ground while we talked that night."

Sevren crouched beside him and examined the ground. He threw his head back and laughed. "Well," he said, "it's taken the better part of a day's travel, but I've finally managed to retrace a half-day of our journey. Only a day and a half to go!"

"Excellent," Zandar said, his old grin returning to his face. "We should be out of here by the middle of next month."

Despite Zandar's affected gloom, their mood was high as they continued their journey. Sevren chose their path with more confidence, and from time to time pointed out other signs he remembered from their earlier course—a place where Zandar's foot had slid in the gravel, a particularly large boulder Sevren had scrambled on top of to get a sense of the land. Kauth almost dared to believe they might all get out of the Demon Wastes alive—and he could carry the guilt of only this one last death, Vor's death, back into the Eldeen Reaches.

As Sevren pointed out what might have been one of Vor's heavy footprints, though, a terrible ululating cry arose from the cliffs around and above them, gripping Kauth's heart with icy fear. By the time he could pull his mace from his belt, warriors were running down the steep canyon walls like a swarm of insects, continuing their eerie wailing.

"The Carrion Tribes," Sevren said.

They were filthy and wild, matted hair jutting from beneath their battered helms and old blood staining their leather armor. They swung their weapons—clubs and spiked chains—in whirling arcs as they charged. Their rush was so chaotic that many tumbled down the steep canyon walls, only to be trampled under the feet of the barbarians behind them. They numbered in the dozens.

"Back to back," Sevren said.

Zandar took his position close to the shifter, each of them facing out to the onrushing horde. Kauth completed the triangle, glad to feel his companions so close, but acutely aware of Vor's absence.

CHAPTER
20

Haldren pulled Cart aside while the soldiers broke camp. "What's your assessment of our position?" he said.

Cart thought a moment. "We're making an assault into an enemy territory we haven't scouted, trying to secure an objective we haven't identified. We have no idea of our enemy's numbers, and very little sense of their capabilities. And we have eight soldiers, in addition to ourselves, Ash—Lady d'Cannith, and the wizard from Arcanix. We've already lost one-seventh of our original force."

Haldren listened and nodded. "And in our favor?"

Cart thought longer. "Very little. Your spells seemed effective against them, so your magic is a strong weapon in our arsenal. Lady d'Cannith is able to keep wounded soldiers alive. I didn't see what the wizard—"

"Caylen." Haldren said, a note of disdain in his voice.

"What Caylen accomplished during the attack, but I assume he's competent."

Haldren snorted.

"Perhaps not," Cart continued. "But I count him as a mark in our favor, however small."

"Anything else?"

Cart shook his head. Put in those terms, their situation seemed grim indeed.

"We'll begin, then, by rectifying our weaknesses," Haldren said. "We need to scout the land, determine our objective, and assess the strength of our foes."

Cart ticked off the problems he'd listed for Haldren. "And reinforcements?" he said.

"We avoid any further engagements with the enemy until the soldiers marching from Fairhaven arrive," Haldren said. "Pick two of our soldiers and scout ahead. Take Caylen with you," he added, almost an afterthought. "He should at least be able to help you find the canyon we're looking for."

Cart gave a sharp nod.

"Don't let the worgs catch you," Haldren said. "And keep those two soldiers alive. Dismissed."

Those two soldiers, Cart thought, striding away from the Lord General. He evidently doesn't care if Caylen survives.

He summoned the two sergeants and conveyed Haldren's orders. He asked them to select his scouts, then went to find Caylen. He found the young wizard perched on a rock, flipping the illuminated pages of a slender tome. Caylen looked up as he approached.

He wasn't sure how to address a wizard of Arcanix, so he got directly to the point. "The Lord General has requested that you assist me on a scouting mission." Based on Caylen's earlier outburst, Cart thought it best to present Haldren's orders as a request.

The wizard raised his eyebrows—surprise, Cart thought. "Scouting? I'm no scout."

"He believed your magic would be able to locate our destination."

"Surely his magic is sufficient—"

Cart interrupted him. "The Lord General is in command of this operation and cannot be spared for a scouting mission." Not surprise—Caylen's eyes were wide with fear. Cart began to understand Haldren's disdain of this wizard. "Therefore you are the only one available with the particular skills we require. Skills that, I was led to believe, were the primary reason for your inclusion in the operation."

Caylen glanced around as though looking for an avenue of escape. "How many . . . ah, how many of us will there be?"

"Four. You and I, and the two best soldiers we can spare."

"Will that be enough?"

"It will have to be," Cart said. "We have been instructed to avoid any engagement with the enemy, so I plan to return as a party of four."

Caylen slumped, resigned to his fate. "When do we leave?"

"Immediately."

* * * * *

The mission was not Cart's area of expertise any more than it was Caylen's, but the sergeants had chosen two fine scouts for the task. Verren and Tesh were more than able to compensate for Caylen's weakness. They made their way south into the foothills of the Blackcaps with Verren watching for tracks or other signs of the worgs, Tesh taking note of the lay of the land, and Caylen scanning for any great concentration of magical power in the area. Cart actually began to feel extraneous, but he kept his senses alert for any approaching danger, figuring that he was along on the mission primarily to keep the others alive, as Haldren had said. And he intended to keep Caylen alive as well, annoying as the wizard was.

Tesh led them along high ground that provided good vantage points over the valleys below, crawling along the crests of hills and creeping along narrow paths cut into canyon walls. At one point, Verren steered them off-course in order to make a wide circle around an area he said the worgs traveled heavily. Cart couldn't say whether he was right, but in any case they didn't encounter any of the demon-wolves. Finally, lying flat on a high bluff with a commanding view, Caylen proved his worth.

"That way," he said, pointing southeast, toward a narrow canyon.

Tesh looked to Cart, who nodded. "If Caylen says our destination is down there," Cart said, "that's the way we go."

"Captain?" Verren said. "I can't be sure, but I believe that will lead us into the thick of the worgs."

Of course it will, Cart thought. Sovereigns forbid this should actually be easy.

"Tesh," he said, "find us a place where we can see into that canyon without being seen. Verren, stop watching the ground and keep your eyes and ears open for any sign of approaching worgs. Caylen . . ." He shrugged. "Keep doing what you're doing, unless you have a better suggestion."

The wizard looked pale and shook his head.

Tesh found them a path down to the canyon. Motioning for the others to stay back, the scout crawled to the edge and peered down.

"This is definitely the place," Caylen whispered. "It's ablaze with magic."

"Holy Host," Tesh breathed, scampering back from the canyon's rim. He got shakily to his feet, white as chalk.

"What is it?" Cart demanded.

"They're everywhere. It's like a temple down there, all laid out around the canyon wall right below us."

Cart dropped to the ground and crept forward to see for himself. As his eyes cleared the ledge, he saw what had so disturbed Tesh.

The canyon was indeed alive with worgs. More commanding from this vantage point, though, was what the scout had described as a temple—more like a mosaic laid out as a maze radiating out from the canyon floor directly below him. The lines of the maze were bones, neatly piled, sometimes driven into the ground like stakes. Colored rock marked the pathways between them, clearly distinct from the ground outside the maze.

Shaking his head in bewilderment, he tried counting the worgs. Five, ten, perhaps twenty—

He lost count when the worgs began to howl.

* * * * *

There was no place to flee except back to the camp, even though Cart was certain the worgs were pursuing them. He sent Verren ahead on the most direct route to warn Haldren of a possible attack and give him some idea of the worgs' numbers, though he had no idea how many worgs were wandering or patrolling outside the canyon when he did his quick count. While they fled at top speed, Tesh covered their tracks as well as he could and led them along routes he thought the worgs would have trouble following. The worgs kept up their unearthly howl, and though it never sounded any more distant, it also didn't seem to be getting closer.

Sending Verren ahead was a risk, Cart knew. It meant the worgs would find branching tracks, one of their number splitting off from the other three. He hoped they would follow the larger party, but it was certainly possible that the worgs would split their group as well. He wasn't sure how smart the demon-wolves were. There was some chance they would follow Verren as a group, reasoning that he would lead them more directly to the new camp.

On the other hand, the worgs probably didn't need Verren's help to find the camp. In all likelihood, they were only giving chase because of the thrill of the hunt——and because a small group of scouts seemed like easy prey. Perhaps they were also trying to prevent the scouts' report from getting back to Haldren.

Cart tried to remain mindful of that mission, even in the midst of their headlong flight. He had a vague sense of the mouth of the canyon, but his attention had been focused on the nearer end, with its strange labyrinth of bones. He knew their objective and had some idea of the strength of their foes, but didn't yet have a clear sense of the defenses they faced. Haldren would be angrier about an incomplete report than about a renewed worg attack.

Tesh led him and Caylen along a high ridge that afforded some view into the canyon. The valley opened toward a wide mouth, which would make its defense difficult. The worgs would have to spread their defenses thin across the canyon mouth—although their speed meant reinforcements would arrive quickly. And the worgs might make their defense farther up the valley, where it was narrower.

Their path took them out of view of the valley for a while, and then Cart saw the mouth of the valley. He immediately revised his assessment of the worg's defenses—and their intelligence. Enormous piles of boulders blocked almost the entire canyon mouth, leaving only a narrow gap against the far wall. A gap easily narrow enough to hold with only a few worgs.

He was trying to formulate plans, anticipating Haldren's questions, when they crested a hill and found their path blocked by three of the enormous demon-wolves. As soon as the wolves saw them, they raised a howl—a howl that was quickly answered from close behind Cart's party. Cart saw Tesh pale and Caylen jump in alarm, fear written large on both their faces.

"Hold it together," Cart said. "We need quick thinking, not panic."

Fear was not so much a physical sensation for Cart as it was for humans, though he felt a slight clenching in his chest. He was incapable of blanching the way Tesh had done, and the phrase "spine-tingling" had always struck him as odd. But he knew fear—the raw, abject terror of the battlefield that makes a soldier swing his weapon in a wild frenzy, trying above all to keep the foe away, as well as the panic that makes him drop his sword and run for his life. Good soldiers learn to control their fear, to rein it in and channel its power into skilled ferocity. Soldiers who couldn't marshal their fear, who let it control them, ended up dead.

Tesh was a good soldier. Cart saw the way he drew his sword and held it, the determination he hammered out of his fear. Caylen, though, was not a soldier at all. As soon as the foremost worg stepped forward, Caylen yelped a word of arcane power and sent a bolt of flame hurtling toward the creature. It yowled in pain as fire licked across its hide, and then all three worgs sprang to attack.

Cart stepped in front of Caylen to meet the charge of the fire-seared worg. Holding his axe back, he thrust his shield at the leaping beast and deflected it to his left, away from the wizard. As the worg hit the ground, Cart's axe sliced down and bit into its armored hindquarters. Not a serious wound, but Cart hoped it would at least keep the worg's attention away from Caylen.

With a rumbling growl, another worg slammed into Cart's shield and shoulder, knocking him back and scrabbling to pull him to the ground. As he brought his axe around to swing at that one, still another one nipped at his right arm, trying to hold back the blow. With all his strength, he wrenched his shield around, smashing its top edge into the jaw of the worg on his left and hurling it off him. He used that momentum to pull his axe-hand away from the worg on his right and bring it around to cleave into the skull of the one he'd just thrown to the ground.

Keep them alive, Cart thought grimly.

He couldn't see Tesh, and Caylen was circling nervously around him, trying to keep Cart between himself and any worg. That game would end soon—two worgs were stalking toward him from both sides.

The worg he'd nicked on the flank took advantage of his distraction. Its jaws clenched around his right shoulder and its weight knocked him to the ground. A blaze of agony seared through his chest and arm as the worg bit and tore. His shield arm was pinned beneath him, and his axe was between his body and the worg's. He tried rolling the creature over, but it was too heavy.

Panic welled in his mind—fear without discipline, a burning and impotent need to run away. Rational thought was no longer possible, and he no longer gave a damn whether the others survived. Flailing his legs in search of leverage, he managed to roll the worg's weight off, but he still couldn't free his pinned arm with the shield attached. The worg rewarded his efforts by twisting its teeth in his shoulder, and he heard as well as felt crushing metal and splintering wood. The pain and fear burst from his mouth in an agonized howl.

Three yelps of pain answered Cart's, and the weight of the worg suddenly lifted off him. His panic got him to his feet before he had any idea what had happened, then his eyes fell on Caylen. The wizard stood in the burning center of a swirling galaxy of tiny stars, his mouth moving in a silent incantation. His tome floated on a column of fire before him, its pages fluttering as light danced across them. Threads of fiery radiance ran from him to three of the worgs and held them suspended in cages formed of searing flame.

Cart glanced around. Tesh was on his knees, shakily getting to his feet next to one of the imprisoned worgs. One worg lay dead where Cart had cleaved its skull, and three were hanging in the air. That left one—

It sprang at Caylen with a growl, yelped as it passed through the motes of light surrounding the wizard, then slammed into him. The three worgs dropped to the ground as Caylen fell. Cart leaped over the one that had pinned him, swinging his axe at the one on Caylen. In the instant before his blow connected, the worg sank its teeth into Caylen's throat.

Cart buried his axe in the worg's skull and sent the creature rolling on the ground away from the wizard, where it lay still. Caylen's tome fell to the ground, its pages rustling as they settled into place.

CHAPTER
21

Despite the fury of their uncontrolled rush down the canyon wall, the barbarians were disciplined fighters. Without Vor, Kauth and his allies were crippled—they couldn't coordinate their attacks or cover each other's defenses. They were hedged in, unable to maneuver into favorable positions, slowly forced apart until each was an island in a sea of enemies. Kauth fought fiercely, mustering all the magic he could to ward himself from the barbarians' attacks and to make his own weapon strike harder, but he knew it was a futile effort. Zandar was the nexus of a storm of eldritch energy, but Kauth saw the storm drift farther and farther away from him and slowly wane in fury. Sevren growled and roared as he cut around him, tearing flesh and splintering bone, but he soon disappeared under the raging sea.

Kauth saw the Traveler leering at him from the faces of the enemies surrounding him, mocking the foolish convictions that had turned him back from his mission. It was what many people would call the perfect gift of the Traveler—a sudden attack of conscience, an attempt to do the right thing, that immediately ended in disaster. By deciding to save his friends, he somehow led them to their deaths.

His body and his will were flagging. His mace was a heavy weight in his hands, blood ran from a dozen small cuts, and drawing breath wracked his chest with the pain of broken ribs. Using a wand to restore his strength would mean dropping his guard and inviting a killing blow from one of the barbarians pressing in on him. If he didn't keep his weapon in constant motion, he felt, he would die.

He had one last, desperate hope—a trick worthy of the Traveler herself. Smashing his mace into the nearest barbarian, he changed. He didn't have time for more than a quick sketch—paler skin, longer hair, scarred cheeks in place of his beard, a thinner nose, a bit shorter and slimmer. He tore off his cloak, threw off his leather cap, and dropped his mace, then scooped up the club of a fallen foe. Kauth died in that instant, and the Carrion Tribes gained a new member.

The barbarians who saw him transform shouted and lunged at him. He barreled into the midst of his foes, let the chaos swallow him, and then completed his transformation. He was one of them—shouting his alarm at the apparent disappearance of his enemy, staring at every nearby face to find the imposter.

"There he is!" The barbarian who had been Kauth pointed at a man about his height and build, and watched as the other barbarians bludgeoned him to death. As he watched, he changed his features again, making his face an exact duplicate of the dying man's. While his new allies stared at the corpse and struggled to make sense of what had happened, he stooped to pick up another dead man's heavy iron helm and put it on his head.

A name—he needed a name. What sort of names did the Carrion Tribes give their children?

"Aric, look." A man next to him hit his arm and pointed. Aric, then—that would be his name.

Aric's stomach sank as he saw a long pole rise erect in the midst of the barbarians. An iron ring at the top of the pole held a heavy chain, and Zandar hung by his wrists from the chain. A cheer went up from the barbarians, and Aric joined in, celebrating the death or capture of the warlock who had been his friend—in a different life, under a different name. He wanted to vomit.

A second pole went up beside the first, and Aric saw Sevren's broken body hanging from the chain at its end. Another cheer. Aric remembered riding the Orien coach to Varna and spotting the shifter for the first time.

No, he told himself, that was Kauth, not me.

Both men were still alive, as far as Aric could tell. The gift of the Traveler was complete—in addition to leading his friends to their deaths, the changeling would complete his mission as soon as he decided to abandon it. He cursed the goddess's ten thousand names.

Two strong barbarians held each pole upright by handles at the bottom, and they started moving at the front of the horde, carrying the prisoners like battle standards. Aric fell in among the mob as the barbarians began a hasty march toward whatever sinkhole they called home.

* * * * *

The barbarians jogged through the Labyrinth for the rest of the day and through the night without stopping. Aric's muscles burned, but he dared not fall behind the mob or attract attention of any kind. Aric recognized morning by the vague brightening of the blood red sky as he emerged from the narrow canyons of the Labyrinth into the expanse of the Demon Wastes.

The gravelly soil of the Labyrinth gave way to a broad expanse of blackened sand and jagged obsidian, broken here and there by geysers of fire reaching toward the belly of the red clouds. On this desolate plain, an army was encamped, a horde that dwarfed any single military force Aric had seen during the Last War. Campfires shone like stars in an obsidian sky, far too numerous to count.

Despair threatened to swallow Aric. Here was a barbarian horde already poised to scour the Labyrinth and spill over the Shadowcrags into the Eldeen Reaches. The work Kelas had sent him to do was done already—Vor had died for nothing, Zandar and Sevren were about to suffer torture and die for no reason, no pretense of greater good. Kelas sent him into the Demon Wastes, into the path of this horde, to die.

"Prisoners!" the men carrying the poles shouted as they approached the camp. "Prisoners for Kathrik Mel!"

That cry sent the camp into a frenzy of motion, the main effect of which was to increase the size of the mob sweeping Zandar and Sevren forward. Aric rode the tide, terrified of what lay ahead but seeing no avenue of escape.

"Prisoners for Kathrik Mel!" The mob took up the cry and turned it into a chant. Here and there, Aric heard a nearby barbarian shout "sacrifice" rather than "prisoners," and dread clenched his chest.

Aric felt himself jostled as the mob in front of him came to a stop and the people behind continued to push forward. Peering over shoulders and between heads, he caught sight of an enormous black pavilion adorned with banners of blood red and bone white. To one side of the tent was a high platform built of bone, and Aric saw three people climbing makeshift stairs to the top. Two of them looked like the barbarians around him, with unruly black hair and pale skin, though their armor was dirty scale armor rather than hide, presumably scavenged from the Ghaash'kala, and they both wore cloaks of black fur.

The one in the middle, though, was not of the Carrion Tribes—he was not human. He stood taller than the people to his front and back, and he wore the plate armor of a knight, stained red-brown with blood. Two long horns swept back from his forehead, and a bony ridge jutted from his jaw as if it were a beard. His skin was brick red, and a long tail twitched and coiled behind him as he walked. His right hand gripped the haft of a wicked-looking glaive.

As this man reached the top of the stairs, the mob's chant changed to a simple repetition of his name: "Kathrik Mel! Kathrik Mel!"

This, Aric knew at once, was the warlord Kelas had described. His hold over the barbarians was unmistakable, the sheer force of his personality palpable even from this distance. This was a man who could unite even the warring Carrion Tribes. He held up his clawed left hand, and the mob fell instantly silent. His voice was low and loud.

"You bring prisoners before me?" he said. "A blood sacrifice to me?"

The barbarians raised a shout of "Kathrik Mel!"

Kathrik Mel strode to the front edge of the platform and examined Sevren. "A shifter, a brave explorer from the Eldeen Reaches, no doubt." His voice dripped with scorn—and so powerful was his hold on the crowd that Aric found himself loathing Sevren, pitiful and broken in his chains. The warlord took a few steps and looked down at Zandar. "And a human from the soft cities beyond the forest."

He traced a finger below Zandar's jaw in what seemed at first to be a gentle caress. Zandar gave a weak cry, though, and blood welled up in the wake of the warlord's claw.

"See how soft they are!" Kathrik Mel shouted. "The cities of the east will fall before our might as easily as these two fell before our smallest band!"

The mob howled its approval, and Aric joined in.

* * * * *

The scratch on Zandar's neck was only the first of many small cuts the prisoners suffered. The barbarians toyed with them as if examining how much pain they could endure before finally dying. Aric heard Zandar confess that he was an Eldeen spy sent to scout the Demon Wastes, and he heard Kathrik Mel promise the utter annihilation of the Reaches. The barbarian horde would burn the Towering Wood to the ground, the warlord said, until not a single tree remained standing.

Mission accomplished, Aric thought bitterly.

And rather than watch Zandar and Sevren endure any more torture, he slipped through the bloodthirsty mob and lost himself in the Labyrinth.

CHAPTER
22

Gaven felt the nearness of the shrine before Lissa pointed it out to him, as though the words of the Prophecy contained inside were calling to him. The building was not particularly remarkable, except for the two dragons, painstakingly sculpted in wood, that flanked the stairway leading to the open archway—one painted red, the other gold. White plaster smoothed the stone walls, and gold leaf decorated the edges of the peaked roof. But to Gaven's eyes, it seemed as if the Prophecy had written the building into existence.

An elaborate mosaic adorned the ground just outside the shrine, depicting the three primordial dragons—shriveled Khyber coiled at the heart, enfolded by the sinuous body of Eberron. Siberys formed a snaky ring around the others. The Dragon Above, the Dragon Between, and the Dragon Below.

Lissa gestured for Gaven and Rienne to enter ahead of her. Gaven held his breath as he stepped across the threshold, hardly daring to hope that he might find what he sought inside. Colorful murals of dragons and dragonborn decorated the inside walls—dragonborn prostrate before dragon-kings, dragons unleashing their devastating breath upon armies and cities, dragonborn soldiers and courtiers and heroes. A stone tablet rested on a carved wooden pedestal at the far end of the room.

And that was all. Gaven let out his breath in a sigh of disappointment. He had expected something more like a library, or at least walls covered in writing rather than space wasted on murals. But this—a single stone tablet. How many of these shrines would he have to visit in order to find what he sought?

"Welcome to the shrine of the Prophecy in Rav Magar," Lissa

said. "May you find here the insight you seek."

Gaven turned to her. "Where do we sleep?"

"On the floor, of course. In front of the tablet. Dream well." She bowed, then she was gone.

Gaven stared out the archway at the mural on the ground outside. "I don't believe it," he said, glad to slip back into the comfortable Common tongue.

"Not what you expected?" Rienne was examining the murals.

"Might as well at least see what the tablet says."

"There's writing on the walls as well. Maybe just captions, but you should check." Rienne sighed. "Here, take off your pack. I'll get our bedrolls ready while you read."

Gaven slid the pack off his shoulders and kneeled in front of the tablet. "Three shadows . . . stifle? . . . extinguish? Stupid verbs. They put out the light of three stars, and their blood—is that the blood of the stars or the shadows? Probably either one. Their blood scours or cleans or refines the *drakatha*—the dragonborn, maybe, or the spawn of a dragon, maybe the brood of Khyber." He sighed. "I don't think this is what we're looking for."

He turned to Rienne and saw her smoothing her bedroll next to his—the shrine wasn't large enough to allow any space between them. His heart ached.

No wonder she feels like a supportive wife, he thought. *She doesn't speak the language, and she's not invested in our purpose here. She's only here because of me.*

She looked up, and her eyes were full of sympathy. "I'm sorry, love. You'll find it, I'm sure."

He glanced around at the words woven into the murals. They seemed like captions to the illustrations, though they were couched in the language of the Prophecy. He figured the murals might have illustrated a particular interpretation of the Prophecy, but there was nothing that struck him as relevant to the Time Between. He'd examine them in the morning.

As he lay awake long into the night, Rienne's head on his chest, his heart still ached. He had the nagging feeling Rienne had only accepted him back into her arms to comfort him, to fulfill her role by supporting him.

* * * * *

Rienne's hair became a mass of snakes, then a knot of tentacles reaching for him. She was the Soul Reaver then, an abomination, a tentacled head crowning a slender body, great claws on shriveled arms grabbing at him, blank white eyes staring into his and whispers of malice flooding his brain. Gaven rolled on top of it, pinning it to the ground. His hand clenched the spear whose point was the Eye of Siberys, embedded in the Soul Reaver's chest. His mouth full of slime and bile, the creature's tentacles raking across his face, he thrust the spear down into the Heart of Khyber.

Through his own hand.

The blood from his hand became a spear of lurid red light, jabbing up from the depths of the earth to pierce the sky. Scarlet filled his vision, and he floated in blood.

Three drops of blood mark the passing of the Time Between.

A ring of silver, a serpent coiled into a circle, shone brightly in the field of red. The red turned to sapphire blue, and the silver ring burst into blinding argent flame. A sword slid through the ring, and then it became a stream of blood, mingled silver and black, flowing out through the ring of fire. Searing flames burst to life around Gaven.

The Time Between begins in blood and ends in blood. Blood is its harbinger, and blood flows in its passing.

Pain like he had never imagined woke him from his sleep.

* * * * *

Rienne stood in darkness. A hard floor, smooth as glass, was cool against her bare feet. The only thing she could see was Maelstrom, suspended in the air before her, the blade pointing up and shining a faint beam of light upward into the darkness. She reached out and grabbed the hilt, savoring the touch of the leather wrapping its hilt. With ground beneath her feet and Maelstrom in her hand, she was solid, rooted.

Maelstrom jerked her arm upward and then lifted her off the ground. She floated in a void. Maelstrom was all—all she could see, all she could feel.

Dragons fly before the Blasphemer's legions, scouring the earth of his righteous foes.

Carnage rises in the wake of his passing, purging all life from those who oppose him.

Vultures wheel where dragons flew, picking the bones of the numberless dead.

Rienne recognized those last words—Gaven had recited them on the airship as they approached the Starcrag Plain.

But the Blasphemer's end lies in the void, in the maelstrom that pulls him down to darkness.

Rienne's feet found solid ground again, and the world burst into light—into the tumult of a battlefield. Dragons flew overhead, their flames and lightning blasting the armies on the ground. A banner fluttered in the wind, bone white, marked with a twisted rune. Maelstrom was alive in her hand—did she control it, or it her? Together they cut through soldier after soldier in a languid dance of annihilation.

She cut a swath through the soldiers until they fell away before her. Then a demon stood before her, his sword burning with blood red fire.

Darkness again, the brief awareness of Gaven's arms around her, and then she fell back to sleep.

* * * * *

Lissa waited in the antechamber until her feet ached from the hard stone floor and her eyes drooped from sheer exhaustion. After days of hasty travel, she wanted nothing more than to collapse into her bed and sleep for the better part of a day. But duty demanded this one last thing of her.

The door swung open and two soldiers clad in armor made of blackened bone escorted her into the chamber of the dragon-king. She entered silently, but as she approached, the great dragon's skeletal head turned and rose up on its bony neck. Lissa fell to her knees and dropped her face to the floor.

"Why do you come before me?" The dragon-king's words were a whisper, spoken without breath or voice.

One did not mince words with a dragon-king, though of

course one used the more formal diction of the dragons. "My lord and king, I have found what you have long sought."

"What is that?"

"The touch of Siberys's hand."

The dragon-king shifted from his recumbent posture to put his feet on the ground. "Then the Time Between has begun," he said, his eyes fixed on the stars that shone through the open dome of his chamber. He deigned to grant Lissa one more glance. "You have done well."

She scrambled to her feet and fled the chamber before the dragon-king's pleasure turned to wrath.

* * * * *

The visitor appeared human, but Kelas knew she was not. He greeted her in the ruined sanctuary of the cathedral, which was unsettling once he realized that the large room gave her space to assume her natural form, if she desired.

She was tall and slender, almost willowy—beautiful, even sultry. Her shining silver hair and eyes hinted at her true nature, and she wore a shimmering gown of the same silver color. Her movements were smooth and graceful, and they gave him the mental image of a dragon soaring on a mountain updraft. Could she be planting such visions in his mind? A subtle method of intimidation—reminding him of what he was dealing with?

"Greetings from Malathar," she said, "dragon-king of Rav Magar." Her voice was clear as a tuning fork, melodious and stately. She gave the slightest bow.

Kelas bowed a little more deeply. "Malathar honors us with his greetings and his messenger," he said, his Draconic perfect and smooth. He smiled warmly—a smile that had begun many successful seductions, though in this case he hoped only for a successful negotiation. She was the first envoy from the dragons, the first response to his widespread inquiries, and she had come all the way from Argonnessen. He had hoped against hope for a response from some lone dragon in Khorvaire. But a dragon-king of Argonnessen?

"Malathar has heard of your efforts and would like to help you bring them to completion."

A surge of excitement rose in Kelas's chest, and he struggled not to let it show on his face. "I am most honored," he said.

"Malathar will send you three dragons to fuel the furnace of your forge."

"And in exchange?"

"In his beneficence, all Malathar asks in exchange is the privilege of providing its first subject."

"Its first—?" Kelas's mind raced. It was impossible—he was building the Dragon Forge to have only one subject.

"The city of Rav Magar has a most unexpected visitor," the messenger said. "He bears the touch of Siberys's hand in the Mark of Storm."

The Siberys Mark of Storm? Kelas couldn't keep his face impassive any longer. Could Gaven possibly have traveled to Argonnessen? Or did two Siberys heirs of House Lyrandar walk the earth? It didn't matter.

"Please convey to Malathar my grateful acceptance of his generous offer."

* * * * *

Sleep eluded Gaven for the rest of the night. From where he lay on the floor, Rienne still slumbering against his chest, Gaven could read a few of the snippets of text on the walls, but he realized that the importance of the shrine had nothing to do with the words or pictures it contained. Sleeping in the shrine—sleeping in the holy presence of the Prophecy—induced prophetic dreams. That explained Lissa's matter-of-fact assumption that Gaven and Rienne would sleep in the shrine.

He looked down at Rienne's head, at the hair flowing behind her across the floor. Was she dreaming as well? What visions was she seeing?

The memory of his own dream made him shudder, and Rienne shifted slightly, pressing closer to him. His nerves tingled with the lingering echoes of the pain that had jolted him from sleep, but her soft warmth soothed him. With her at his side, he felt he could face whatever the Time Between held in store for him and whatever horrors would come after. His eyes welled with tears, and he touched his lips to her forehead.

He heard footsteps outside the arch, and then a sound—something between a series of clicks and a throaty growl. He recognized the sound as part of the dragonborn vocabulary of social interactions, though he had no inkling of its specific meaning. A dragonborn figure appeared in the doorway, silhouetted against the moonlit sky. Gaven tensed, stretching a hand toward his sword where it lay nearby.

Lissa's quiet voice put Gaven at ease. "Gaven," she said, "can you step outside, please?"

Gaven glanced down at Rienne, sound asleep. Smoothly and gently, he lifted her arm and set it on her own side. Then he lifted her head, laid it on the floor, and got quietly to his feet. Lissa stepped back outside the tiny shrine as he padded out the door.

"What is it?" he said, and then he saw the soldiers. Eight of them stood in an arc around him, wearing plate armor and carrying heavy swords. He wheeled around to the door—he needed his sword, and Rienne—but his path was already blocked by two more soldiers. Total silence, obviously magical in origin, fell around him just as he started to shout.

No matter, he thought. He felt lightning start to surge in his blood, and shadow draped the city as a stormcloud appeared across the moonlit sky. The entire city of Rav Magar would know the fury of the Storm Dragon.

Just as he started to turn, a heavy pommel slammed into his head, bizarre in its silence. He fell against the shrine's wall but forced his eyes to stay clear. He spun to face his foes and staggered forward a few steps, struggling to focus enough to channel the lightning out from his body. A dragon had joined the soldiers, azure-scaled, with an enormous horn at the end of its snout.

The lightning burst out from his arms and engulfed the dragon, dancing across its hide and sparking at its horn and in its mouth. It stretched its mouth wide in what might have been a mocking smile, and its own lightning danced over its tongue and teeth. Instead of sending a return strike at him, the dragon leaped into the air and clapped its wings, and a concussive blast of air buffeted Gaven—like thunder without the crash. He fell to his knees, motes of light dancing across his vision. Two more hard blows smashed into the back of his head, one after the other, and the blackness swallowed him.

CHAPTER
23

Cart couldn't tear his eyes from Caylen's tome where it lay on the ground. When a worg growled to his right, he reacted too slowly—it came in low and bit at his leg before he wrenched his gaze away from the slender book. He swung his axe down, but the creature sprang back out of his reach and howled.

Two voices joined in the howl, and a renewed surge of fear rose in Cart's mind.

I am steel and stone, he thought. My fear just fuels my fury.

Roaring his answer to the beasts' howl, he advanced on the worg and slashed his axe low across its chest. The howl died in its throat.

The two remaining worgs had Tesh caught between them, but he was holding his own. Just as Cart rushed forward, Tesh felled one of the two, and Cart intercepted the last one just before it pounced on Tesh's back. Caylen's spell had weakened them, clearly, and it was just a matter of finishing them off. Cart wiped the gore from his axe on the rough coat of the last worg.

Cart turned slowly to face Caylen. He saw the tome first, one page flipping over in a soft breeze. Then his gaze fell on the wizard's body, and he walked slowly to stand beside it.

"I'll take care of it, Captain," Tesh said.

Cart waved him off. Caylen had been in his care, and he would extend that care to the dead man's body. He kneeled on the blood-soaked ground, closed Caylen's eyes, and lifted him over his shoulder.

"Get his tome." Cart pointed at the book.

"You—" Tesh hesitated. "You're not going to leave him here?"

Cart stared at the soldier. He sometimes wished he could achieve one of those glares that Haldren used to make soldiers quail, but that required muscles in the forehead and around the eyes that Cart simply lacked. Even so, the simplicity of his unwavering gaze, set in his expressionless face and accompanied by a pointed silence, often had the same effect.

Tesh lifted the book—a little gingerly, Cart thought—and led Cart back to the camp.

* * * * *

Haldren berated Cart, as Tesh had done, for burdening himself with Caylen's body when there was still a risk of attack, then went on to reproach him for sending Verren off alone—although the scout had returned safely—and for returning with only a sketchy estimate of the number of worgs they faced and any defenses that might lie between the camp and the mouth of the canyon.

Cart found that his impassive stare was also effective when Haldren blustered. Cart stood at attention, unflinching before the Lord General's tirade, impassive to his criticism, and eventually Haldren ran out of steam. Part of Haldren's enjoyment, Cart knew, was in seeing the fear and shame in the faces and bodies of the soldiers he chastised, and he didn't like to give so much energy without getting anything in return.

Despite its imprecision, Cart's report at least suggested that the worgs' defenses were too strong for such a small party to breach. Haldren would wait for the soldiers who were marching from Fairhaven, even if it meant a three-week delay in their mission. Better a delay than their reinforcements arriving to find Haldren's force destroyed, the mission a failure.

Two soldiers had died in the first worg attack, and Caylen's death meant that three of their original fourteen were dead. Like Tesh, the other soldiers showed no grief over the wizard—none of them knew him at all. To a soldier of the Last War, the death of an acquaintance of a few days was not cause for mourning.

Cart stood over the young wizard's gore-splattered body, lost in thought. He barely noticed Ashara coming to stand by his side, but her presence was a comfort.

"I can't understand it," he said after a moment. "Why should it bother me so much?"

"Why shouldn't it?" Ashara said gently.

"It took me days to remember his name. Haldren thought he was incompetent and I thought he was a coward. Why should his death mean anything to me?"

"He was part of your team."

His team? Haldren's command kept echoing in Cart's mind—*Keep those two soldiers alive.* Haldren didn't care a bit about Caylen, but Cart had extended the Lord General's command to include the wizard, and then failed in that self-imposed responsibility.

"And that's the other thing," he said, grasping for words to express the doubt nagging at his mind. "Haldren didn't see him as part of the team—he didn't care if Caylen died. Does he care whether I keep myself intact or not?"

"Of course he does."

"I'm sure he does, as long as I remain competent. But how many times do I need to fail to make him as . . . as callous about my life as he was about Caylen's?"

Ashara didn't have a ready answer to that question, and her silence only strengthened the dread that was growing in his mind. She couldn't argue with the fact that Haldren was a heartless bastard.

"I've always believed that my purpose is to obey, to be a good soldier and carry out my orders to the best of my ability. I've only disobeyed Haldren once." The memory of Starcrag Plain was almost physically painful—while Haldren watched his plans crumble in impotent fury, Cart left him to go fight alongside Gaven instead, to make himself useful in whatever way he could.

"You're more than a good soldier, Cart."

He turned to look at her for the first time. She stood close by his shoulder, craning her neck to meet his gaze.

"That's what you made me to be—your House, Lady Cannith. I'm a weapon of war."

"A sword is a weapon of war, or one of the construct titans. You're a man—a living, thinking, feeling man. My House intended you to think for yourself, to make judgments in the chaos of the battlefield. Not just tactical judgments, Cart, but moral judgments."

Cart looked back at Caylen's mangled body. Since Starcrag Plain, he had struggled with a growing sense that Haldren didn't deserve his complete loyalty and obedience. He had begun to wonder whether Haldren's years in Dreadhold had blunted his mind or hardened his already stony heart. He had never really considered whether following Haldren was right in a moral sense, but Ashara's words seemed to strike to the heart of the discomfort he was feeling.

"The world should stop," Ashara whispered.

"What?"

"It happens so often that we barely notice it, but the world should mark the passing of any mortal soul."

An image flashed into his mind of a soul—Caylen's soul—as a white bird suddenly caught and crushed in the black, oiled cogs of Haldren's schemes and Kelas's conspiracies. Ashara was right—sometimes on the battlefield he had felt a moment's pause, the tiniest slice of silence in the din when someone nearby choked out his last breath. The rumbling wheels of war and rebellion should cease for an instant at least, to give some acknowledgment of the sacrifice made in their name.

Haldren barked at two soldiers to drag Caylen's corpse outside the camp and bury it, before the stench of it drew the worgs down upon them again. The noise of the camp intruded back into Cart's ears, and the instant of silence came to an end.

* * * * *

Fortunately, when Haldren put a competent sergeant in command of the overland expedition, he made a wise choice. The sergeant, whose name was Mirra, was resourceful and had connections in House Orien. Rather than march ten soldiers along well-traveled roads for three weeks, which would be certain to attract attention, she secured seats on the lightning rail for them all. The group split up to board and reunited in Passage, completing more than half their journey in a mere twelve hours. From there, it was only a week's march to Arcanix and another four days to join Haldren's camp near the canyon. An advance scout from the overland party met the sentries from the camp fully two weeks before Haldren expected reinforcements to arrive.

Haldren was not accustomed to praising the soldiers under his command, even when they displayed initiative and creative thinking. So he left that task to Cart, who thanked Mirra warmly and briefed her and the other sergeant on the situation in the canyon. In the week since Caylen's death, the worgs had attacked the camp only once, and it had been a small group of scouts rather than a serious assault. Evidently, Haldren had withdrawn far enough from the canyon that the worgs no longer felt threatened by their presence.

Cart wasn't convinced that twenty soldiers were any more likely to take the canyon than ten, but the doubling of their numbers did hearten the soldiers. Compared to his original assessment of the situation, things had improved somewhat. Cart's team had scouted the canyon, identified their objective and its location, and determined at least a vague sense of the enemy's numbers— roughly two dozen, perhaps a little less since Cart and Tesh had killed five. The worgs still outnumbered them.

Haldren had spent hours with Tesh, drawing a map of the canyon and filling in as many details of the terrain as possible. Cart and Verren had sketched in their estimates of enemy positions, though of course those could change constantly. Haldren thought he had a reasonably clear sense of what they faced, and had crafted a plan he thought would allow them to overcome the worgs' defenses.

Cart's role in that plan was to keep Haldren alive—the Lord General still trusted Cart's ability to do that, despite Caylen's death. Haldren's magic, and even Caylen's, had proven the most effective weapon against the worgs in their two previous skirmishes, so the main force of their attack would consist of Haldren's spells. Cart and a single squad of soldiers would protect the Lord General, and Ashara would heal him—and Cart and the soldiers—as much as she could. The other three squads would harry the worgs' flanks, strike quickly, and flee from strong resistance.

Cart reviewed the plan one last time as the soldiers broke

camp, slowly shaking his head. It seemed workable, if a little blunt-edged. But given the way the mission had gone up to that point, he had little confidence in plans.

* * * * *

A single howl, long and high, greeted their first approach. As it faded into an echo in the canyon, another one began, immediately joined by two more, then a ghastly pandemonium of yips and wails. Cart saw the soldiers glance at each other, multiplying their fear as they saw it in their comrades' faces. He'd chosen what he considered the best of the four squads—Tesh's squad—to provide Haldren's escort, but fear could poison the strongest soldier's heart.

"Steady," he said. "They will learn to fear us, soon enough."

He glanced at Haldren and saw a couple of soldiers do the same. Cart and the Lord General marched together a few paces behind Tesh, with the sergeant a few paces out to Cart's right, another soldier opposite on Haldren's left, and the others trailing behind. Haldren strode ahead, arcane power brewing in the air around him, streaming behind him in wisps of red smoke and motes of purplish light. He wore the mantle of leadership proudly, accepting the burden that came with it—the burden of being this little squad's sole hope for survival.

The sight of him bolstered the soldiers' courage, and Cart nodded in approval. Haldren could persuade, could lead, could inspire fierce loyalty and tremendous courage when the need arose. At times his charisma did seem magical, as though spells were woven into his words to soften his hearers' fears or steel their resolve, but Cart didn't know how to draw the line between the Lord General's natural leadership and his sorcery. It didn't matter—his soldiers would follow Haldren gladly to their deaths.

Another chorus of howls erupted in the distance just as the canyon mouth came into view. The sound didn't seem to be coming from the gap in the wall of boulders, but farther into the canyon. With a sudden jolt, Cart remembered how the worgs had caught him off guard before, with Tesh and Caylen—the constant sound of distant howls that didn't seem to draw any nearer.

"On your guard!" he called. "Expect an ambush!"

Three worgs leaped out from hiding places in the brush and rubble ahead of them, and a quick glance behind showed him three more advancing on the rear.

Haldren didn't hesitate and didn't move an inch—he pointed at the three worgs behind them, the ones closest to each other, and engulfed them in a burst of flame. One of them staggered forward a few steps and then fell to the ground, its fur smoldering with foul black smoke. The other two hesitated, then turned and fled.

Cart could feel the elation of the other soldiers—with Haldren leading them, they felt invincible. They were chomping at the bit, ready to charge the remaining worgs. He reined them back— "Stay close. Let them come to us. Haldren is our sword. You're his shield."

At Cart's reminder, the soldiers pulled back into a loose ring around Haldren and waited. Two blasts of flame erupted from Haldren's hands and consumed another worg. The remaining two circled warily, careful to keep some distance between them so a single spell couldn't easily encompass them both. Haldren snorted, spread his arms wide, and channeled a bolt of lightning in a line connecting him to the two worgs, passing neatly between the soldiers in their defensive ring.

Magic charged the air. Cart's whole body, made and enlivened by magic, hummed with the echoes of the power Haldren had unleashed. The others must have felt it as well—they surged forward with Haldren as he resumed his stride, swept up in his storm of devastation.

CHAPTER
24

Haldren's magic blasted a path through the gap against the canyon wall. For every new group of worgs that stepped up to defend the narrow way, Haldren had another spell ready to scour them with fire or sear them with lightning. As the Lord General had predicted, the narrow gap actually proved a hindrance to the worgs rather than a defensive advantage. Perhaps recognizing that fact, the worgs soon fell back and ceded the gap to Haldren.

Haldren seemed as swept up in the thrill of his power as the soldiers were, ready to storm into the canyon and obliterate any resistance the worgs tried to offer. Cart, though, suddenly realized the flaw in their plan, and he tried to hold Haldren back.

"Lord General," he said, "there might be a problem."

"Damn right there's a problem," Haldren barked. "I'm thirsty. Somebody give me a drink."

Tesh tossed a waterskin to Haldren, who drank deeply while Cart tried to explain.

"We expected the worgs to concentrate their defense in the gap, but they don't fight like that. If they see a significant threat, they fall back and regroup."

"They can only fall back so far," Haldren said, wiping his mouth with his sleeve. "We'll catch them all."

"No, Lord General, that's just it. They'll do exactly what we hoped to do to them—they'll harry us and fall back, again and again, slowly wearing down our strength until we decide to retreat. But then we'll have to fight our way through the gap again—they'll block it from behind us."

Cart was relieved to see the Lord General pause at least long enough to consider his warning. "What do you suggest?"

From his tone, Haldren clearly had no expectation that Cart could produce a better suggestion. He bit back a soldier's curse that sprang to mind, and considered the situation. "I suggest we fall back and circle the canyon as the other squads are doing. We'll wear them down from the outside in, like peeling an onion."

Haldren grinned. "I suggest a different simile," he said. "I say we pit them like a cherry—continue in until we find their heart, then cut it out."

A chorus of cheers drowned out Cart's attempt to protest further, and he shrugged. Perhaps Haldren was right—he'd had no difficulty yet in dispatching every worg they met. There didn't seem to be any reason to expect more trouble. That was exactly why he did expect it.

* * * * *

Haldren's confidence seemed fully justified, even if Cart also had good reason for his trepidation. They advanced slowly through the canyon, encountering occasional packs of worgs who nipped at their heels briefly before retreating, usually with at least one worg dead and no serious harm done to Haldren or his squad. Cart had been correct in his reading of the worgs' tactics, but Haldren had apparently been right in assessing the threat they posed.

After routing the third group of worgs, the group advanced steadily for an hour without seeing any more of the demon-wolves. Distant howls assured them that there were still worgs to fight, but no more attacked them, even as they drew close to the end of the canyon. Near the canyon's head, it was a narrow, jagged cut in the earth, and Cart couldn't see more than a dozen yards ahead of them at any time. Tesh scouted at the front of the group, wary of an ambush.

When Tesh fell to his knees, Cart's first thought was that he'd been hit by an enemy arrow—but of course the worgs didn't use arrows. The scout had crept up to the next turn and peered around a rocky buttress jutting from the canyon wall, and whatever he saw sapped his strength. Cart ran to his side.

"What is it?" he demanded. "Keep it together, soldier."

Tesh got to his feet, but he was pale and unsteady. He said nothing, only waved a weak hand at the canyon ahead.

Cart looked around the corner, and his limbs suddenly felt like lead. He saw Verren first—spread-eagled on the canyon floor, his guts ripped out and strewn across the ground, linking him in a line with the other members of his squad, crossing the width of the canyon. As mangled as their bodies were, their faces were all intact, wrenched into expressions of terrible pain. The worgs had wanted to make sure the dead soldiers' friends would recognize them.

Haldren strode forward to stand behind Cart. "What is the problem?" he asked.

"It's one of our squads, Lord General," Cart said. His mind felt blank, and he couldn't remember the name of the squad's sergeant. "All dead."

"Idiots," Haldren spat. "Let me see." He pushed past Cart.

"The worgs left them as a warning."

"That's more than a warning," Haldren said. "That's a barrier."

"Lord General?"

"They used the bodies in a ritual to create a wall we can't penetrate, at least not right away. I can get it down, but it will take some time."

"A wall?" Tesh said. Wide-eyed, he looked back along the canyon. "That means we're trapped here."

"They'll attack here, certainly," Cart said. "We'll have to fight them off before you take the wall down."

For the first time, Haldren seemed nervous about the possibility of a worg attack. "I'll start on the wall now. There's a chance I can get it done before they attack, and we won't be boxed in. If not, I can pick up where I left off after we've killed them all." He turned the corner and started toward the bodies, but turned back after a few steps. "Cart, keep the others back. They don't need to see this."

Cart put a hand on Tesh's shoulder and steered him back to the rest of the squad. He addressed the sergeant, Kovin. "We wait here—there's a . . . an obstacle ahead that only Haldren can clear. Watch our rear, but catch your breath while we wait."

Kovin ordered Tesh and another soldier back to the last turn in the canyon, and told the other two to rest. Tesh still looked pale, and he hung his head as he walked. His companion was turned toward him, talking with her hands, inquisitive. She wanted to know what he had seen, but Cart could tell Tesh wasn't talking. Good, Cart thought. Perhaps in the act of lowering the wall, Haldren could also remove the bodies, or at least put them into a less unsettling position.

Cart was still watching when the pair reached the bend in the canyon and a worg erupted around the corner, slamming into Tesh's companion and knocking her to the ground. Tesh gave a shout and drew his sword, but four more worgs came around the corner.

"Tesh!" Cart called. "Fall back!" He broke into a run, yelling over his shoulder for Haldren. Tesh couldn't do anything for his companion, but maybe Cart could, if he could get there fast enough.

Tesh tried a cautious withdrawal at first, backing away from the worgs with his sword and shield in front of him. When the worgs started edging around him, threatening to surround him, he turned and ran. A large worg pounced at him but fell short, raking its claws along his back and making him stumble but not fall.

By the time Cart reached Tesh, there were half a dozen worgs between him and the corner where Tesh's companion had fallen, and he couldn't see her anymore. He paused, debating whether to charge into the midst of the worgs to save her, but quickly realized he was too late. In the instant of calm before the breaking storm, he raised his shield and checked his grip on his axe, bracing for the worgs' assault.

He let them push him slowly back toward the others, moving to intercept any that tried to get behind or past him, buying them time to ready their defense and—he hoped—get Haldren away from the wall. But the farther back he moved, the more worgs came into view around the corner. There were at least two worgs for every one in his party, and he was sure he hadn't yet seen the end of the demon-wolves.

At the edge of his vision, he saw something move behind him and almost lashed out with his axe before he realized it was Ashara.

"What are you doing?" he said. "Get back!"

"No. Cover me," she said. She put a hand on his back and he felt magic course through him, cool and exhilarating.

A swing of his axe pushed back a worg that was trying to get to Ashara. She touched his shield and it flared with blue light. His axe split the skull of a worg trying to come in under his guard. As he drew the axe back, she touched it as well, and the blade burst into flame. He almost dropped it in his surprise, but he caught it in time to swing it down into the shoulder of another worg. Even as the blade cut, the fire seared the hair and flesh around the wound, making the beast yelp in pain.

"That's all I have," she said. "Stay alive long enough to make it useful."

"Thank you." Another swing of his axe made sure that the worg trying to follow Ashara wouldn't move again.

An enormous burst of fire blossomed in the canyon ahead of him, and Cart's position suddenly seemed less desperate. Tesh and another soldier stood beside him—he'd made it back to the others.

"Remember your top priority," Cart said. "Keep Haldren alive." Please, he thought—or we're all dead.

Some of the worgs in the rear of the advancing pack raised a howl, and the canyon seemed to shake with it as more worgs joined the chorus and it reverberated off the walls. The creatures in front surged forward, all teeth and claws.

Steel and stone, Cart thought. He met the worgs' ferocity with his own.

Another blossom of fire drowned out the howl for an instant, and yelps of pain came in its wake. Cart fell into an almost mechanical rhythm, slicing and hewing, lifting his shield to block attacks or throw worgs back. No worg would get past him, and before long he was covering the other soldiers as their energy began to flag.

This is what I was made for, he thought. Tireless, unceasing battle. But in what cause?

Despite his efforts, the worgs were pushing them back, closer and closer to the barrier formed by their companions' bodies. He saw Tesh beside him becoming more agitated, and he hoped none of the others would turn and see the grisly spectacle.

Haldren's magic was thinning the rear of the pack, but the worgs in front—either unaware of or unconcerned with the fate of their fellows—fought with undiminished ferocity. Another howl rose in the back of the worg band, and grew to fill the canyon again. Tesh stepped back in fear, and then the line broke—the soldier on Cart's right turned and ran in panic. The worgs made no effort to stop him.

"Stop!" Cart cried. "Hold your position!" He turned far enough to keep the soldier, Avi, in at least the edge of his vision without leaving himself open to the worgs.

Avi yelled when he saw the mutilated corpses, but he didn't check his headlong flight. He tried to jump over the bodies—and stopped in the air, suspended inside the magical barrier that only Haldren could see. His shout of horror changed into an agonized scream and he writhed in agony. The last Cart saw before he had to turn his full attention back to the worgs was a cloud of blood spreading out from Avi's twitching body, staining the invisible barrier red.

Kovin and the other soldier saw it too, and it nearly broke them. It was their first indication that they were trapped, with death on both sides, and Cart recognized the terror in their eyes.

"Forward!" Cart yelled. "Push them back!"

He stepped forward against the front line of worgs, trusting the others to follow him, and the worgs fell back the smallest amount. Haldren shifted tactics, blasting individual worgs in the front with smaller blasts of fire, helping to clear the line for the soldiers to advance. The ground was slick with blood, and they had to step over or around the hulking bodies of dead worgs, but they succeeded in pushing the line back, away from the deadly barrier. The forward press seemed to be having the desired effect—bolstering the last three soldiers' courage and hope.

A chorus of barks and yips began somewhere in the middle of the worg pack, and the worgs in front fell back still farther. Cart scanned the canyon, then gave a shout of triumph. The two remaining squads under Haldren's command perched atop the canyon walls on either side of the worg pack, showering arrows down into the throng. The other soldiers saw their salvation and joined Cart's shout.

The canyon walls were too steep in that spot for the worgs to climb, so the archers above could loose their arrows without fear. Many worgs took three or four arrows before falling, but fall they did, adding to the number of the dead as Cart led the soldiers on the canyon floor in a renewed assault.

Soon it was over—the worgs broke ranks and fled back down the canyon, scattering into the hills. Cart ordered all three squads to regroup rather than give chase. Ashara tended to the wounded— Cart was surprised to see the number of breaks and tears in his own body—while Haldren turned his attention to the barrier again.

Ashara used wands to tend her living patients, manipulating the magic stored within the wands to flow into their bodies and knot up their wounds, refresh their spirits, and erase their fatigue. For Cart, though, she ran her bare hands over his wounds, unleashing the magic contained in his own body to help it repair itself. It was, Cart felt suddenly, strangely intimate.

"That was incredible," she said, working her magic on his shoulder. "I've never seen anyone fight like that."

"It's what I was made for."

"It's more than that. Not every warforged is capable of what you just did. You've devoted yourself to it, mastered the axe and shield, trained your senses and reflexes. You've chosen to become the best warrior you can be."

"What are you getting at?"

"You're a person, just as capable of choosing your path in life as any of us. Other warforged have chosen to excel in magic or artifice. I met a warforged painter in Lathleer once—very skilled, and getting better. House Cannith might have made you to be a soldier, but that doesn't have to be your purpose in living. You can do what you want—you can be what you want to be."

"Maybe I want to be a soldier."

"A soldier?" she said, getting to her feet. "You're a hero."

She walked off to treat another of the wounded.

* * * * *

Haldren broke through the barrier and summoned Cart, who helped him pile the bodies together and start a pyre. Once the fire was blazing, Cart gathered the others together to pay their last respects to their allies, then hurried them onward.

After three more bends in the canyon, they found themselves at its head. The worgs' labyrinth of bones spread out before them, and from the canyon floor Cart could see its focus. It seemed at first like a pool of deep blue water set vertically into the sheer cliff at the canyon's head. Only after staring at it for a moment did he realize it wasn't water, but crystal—a glimpse of a larger formation buried in the rock, from what Haldren had said. He couldn't see any worgs—it seemed they had put everything they had into that last assault.

"The canyon is ours," Haldren declared.

INTERLUDE

Kelas leaned close to the glass globe on his desk, straining to hear the voice coming from it.

"In all, we lost eleven of our twenty soldiers, and the wizard from Arcanix." The small voice from the globe was Haldren's. Kelas frowned—those were heavy losses. "But the worgs are routed. We still hear them howling, especially now that the sun is down, but there aren't as many. We can hold the canyon until you arrive."

"Good," Kelas said. "I'll try to get there before the wolves get reinforcements."

"Thank you."

Haldren expressing gratitude. Was his pride really so broken? Best to buoy it somewhat, he reasoned.

"Thank you, Haldren. The Dragon Forge couldn't happen without you."

He didn't wait for Haldren's reply, but waved a hand over the orb and saw its light fade.

It seemed that everything was in place. Time for him to make his report.

Resting his fingertips on the globe again, he closed his eyes in concentration. Nara ir'Galanatyr—he thought her name, then concentrated on fixing her face in his mind. He saw her severe face, dark eyes, and short hair. He concentrated on her most likely location, her villa outside Wyr, on the Eldeen border. For good measure, he framed his thoughts with the details of her identity: the former head of the Royal Eyes of Aundair, abruptly removed from her position at the end of the Last War. Few people knew why, but Kelas was one of them. Simply by working for her, Kelas would have been committing treason, even if it hadn't been treason they planned.

A ruby light flared to life in the heart of the crystal, and he opened his eyes to see Nara's face form in the glow. She looked tired and angry—she had probably been waiting up for his report.

"It's about time, ir'Darran," she snapped.

"My apologies. I only just received word from the canyon."

"Tell me."

"All appears to be going as we planned, except for the speed. Haldren ir'Brassek has secured the canyon. Baron d'Cannith is ready to send her aid, and Arcanist Wheldren has won the commitment of the Arcane Congress to our cause. Reports from the west indicate that the Carrion Tribes are already on the move."

"What about the changeling?"

"I have heard nothing from him, but that is not unusual. He might well be dead, but he's very resourceful."

"And the mark?"

Kelas smiled, quite pleased with himself. "I received a messenger a few weeks ago who promised to deliver a Siberys heir with the Mark of Storm to me. I'm not positive it's the same man, but I don't think it matters."

"Who sent the messenger?"

That was the question he wanted her to ask. "A dragon from Argonnessen."

"Another dragon." Nara did not seem as pleased as he'd hoped.

"Of course. We can't build the Dragon Forge without dragons. And we'll have dragons—the messenger promised that as well."

"Then all is ready."

"Yes," Kelas said. "All is ready."

Part
III

*Two spirits share one prison beneath the wastes,
secrets kept and revelation granted.*

*They bind and are bound, but their unbound whispers
rise to the Dragon Between,
calling to those who would hear.*

*Their whispers turn to flame,
the scouring flame, the refiner's fire,
to purify the touch of Siberys's hand.*

CHAPTER
25

Aric drifted through the Labyrinth. The maze of twisting canyons swallowed him, consuming his thoughts and senses. Nightmarish apparitions flitted at the edge of his awareness, some combination of the demonic spirits said to haunt the Wastes and his memories of the warlord, Kathrik Mel—a demonic spirit incarnate. When the wind whistled through the canyons, he heard the tormented screams of Zandar and Sevren. Nothing materialized to threaten him, as though the Labyrinth were content to let him torture himself. It was a much slower and more painful death than anything the demons could create.

The Labyrinth drove any thought of the future from his mind—there was no future, only the Labyrinth. He no longer thought he could escape the maze, so he gave no thought to what he would do if he did. Day wore into night and back to day, and he wandered. He didn't eat, he barely slept, and by the fourth day his water was gone. After that, he stopped counting days. All his thoughts melted away except one: Abandon all hope for your body or your soul.

His stomach had stopped complaining, but his throat screamed for water. All he knew was his most primitive need. He fell, gravel pressing into his cheek. He didn't think he could stand up again.

Abandon all hope.

He heard the gravel crunch, and again. Twice more, a pair of boots appeared before his eyes, and he realized the sound had been footfalls.

"Who are you?" he murmured, anticipating the Traveler's inevitable question.

A booted foot rolled him over, and his vision became a field of reddish sky, framed on two sides by canyon walls. A shadow appeared and blocked the sky—a pair of eyes, a face looking into his. This time, the Traveler had adopted the face of a different fallen paladin, Vor. Light shot out in rays from behind his head, a nimbus of silver.

"He's alive," the Traveler said.

"Kill him." The other voice had no body, and it was almost too far away to hear.

"Not until he's heard the challenge." The Traveler's orc-face bent nearer to his. "You lie on cursed ground. You may proceed no farther into this place of evil, and you may not leave to spread its taint. I offer you a choice: Commit your life to the service of Kalok Shash and the holy calling of the Ghaash'kala, or die where you stand—where you lie."

A word died on his lips, an echo of the Traveler's words— "Shash."

Darkness swallowed the Traveler's face and the ruddy sky, and lastly the silver halo.

* * * * *

There was no pain. His first experience was absence—no pain. No light. No ground beneath him, no red sky above him. He floated in a void.

He couldn't move, and panic seized him. He tried to shout, but no sound would come from his mouth. He couldn't draw breath.

The first sense to return was touch—there was something beneath him after all, a hard bed supporting him in the void. And something heavy weighed on his chest, squeezing the breath out of him and keeping him immobile.

Suddenly air poured into his lungs in a shuddering gasp, and dim light nudged at his vision. His eyes shot open, and all his senses came back to him in a flood. He lay in a windowless room lit by a guttering oil lamp. Except for the lamp, it was bare as a prison cell. The thin door was slightly ajar.

One hand flew to his face to feel his features. Who was he supposed to be?

Scarred cheeks, a thin nose, wide jaw—Aric's face, he remembered. It seemed he had kept the proper face while he was unconscious. He wondered how long he had been there.

He remembered becoming Aric, taking the face of a barbarian foe. He remembered running with the horde, and shuddered as he remembered Kathrik Mel. Then grief clutched at his heart as he saw the agony of Zandar and Sevren—the torture he'd brought on them. He had stumbled into the Labyrinth, but the rest was a blur. He had no memory of where he was or how he got there, but unless he had somehow escaped the Labyrinth, he reasoned, he must be in one of the cities of the Ghaash'kala.

Which means I'm safe, he thought. For now.

He drifted back into a less troubled sleep.

* * * * *

The door swung open with a creak, jolting Aric awake. An orc leaned through the doorway, and seeing he was awake, came to stand at the foot of his bed. He looked a little like Vor, with an almost triangular face, wider at the jaw than at the brow. Two prominent teeth jutted up over his upper lip, suggesting a young boar's tusks.

"You are in Maruk Dar," the orc said, "refuge and capital of the Maruk Ghaash'kala. You are here, rather than being dead where we found you, because I thought you might have uttered the holy name of Kalok Shash before you completely lost consciousness. Tell me clearly now. Will you commit your life to the service of Kalok Shash and the holy calling of the Ghaash'kala?"

The alternative, Aric knew, was death. The Maruk Ghaash'kala would not hesitate to kill him, even after making the effort to nurse him back to health.

"I will," he said. What was another broken oath? He felt sick.

The orc smiled, revealing the full row of crooked teeth between the tusks. "Then you have heard the call of Kalok Shash, the beacon of hope in the Demon Wastes?"

Aric nodded.

"You are most welcome in Maruk Dar. I am Farren Dorashka. What is your name?"

"Aric."

"From what tribe do you come?"

Aric cast his mind back over his brief time among the barbarians. Had he heard a tribal name mentioned? He couldn't remember one—but then he recalled what Kelas had told him.

"Kathrik Mel bound my tribe into his horde. My tribe no longer exists."

Kathrik Mel—speaking the name brought his face clearly to Aric's mind, and he shuddered. The brick red skin and lashing tail, the clawed hand tracing a line of blood across Zandar's neck.

"The tiefling," the orc said, as though uttering a curse. "What information can you give us about him?"

"Many tribes now march under his banners. He plans to strike east. He swore to level the Towering Wood on his way to the cities beyond."

"As we feared. But he will have to get past us first. Are you ready to stand against him?"

"I am," Aric said—and he found, to his surprise, that he was.

* * * * *

The next morning, Aric put on a new leather cuirass, hefted the club he'd taken from a fallen barbarian, and stood with ten other warriors of the Ghaash'kala in the front courtyard of the fortress-city of Maruk Dar. Stone walls and bridges towered around and above him, carved into and built out from the walls of the Labyrinth. A great curtain wall shielded the city from the horrors beyond, with a dozen soldiers patrolling its battlements. Inside, homes were cut into the walls from the ground almost to the uppermost heights, stacked atop one another, stairs and ladders leading to the higher levels.

He'd learned earlier in the morning that the citizens ate in great mess halls, rather than buying or selling food in a market, and his new armor was further evidence that living in Maruk Dar was much like serving in the military. All of its residents were soldiers, except those too young to fight. None of its citizens was too old.

Farren Dorashka paced in front of the assembled warriors as

he addressed them. He spoke in Orc, and Aric wondered whether to reveal that he understood the language—would a barbarian of the Carrion Tribes know the language of his orc neighbors? Farren had addressed him in Common, assuming he didn't speak Orc, so he decided to feign ignorance, to keep his face impassive and his expression blank as the orc leader spoke.

It wasn't easy. Farren's passionate oration about the task before them reminded Aric of Haldren ir'Brassek—a memory from three lifetimes ago, it seemed. Farren was inspiring. Aric felt courage steel his nerves, pride well up in his chest, and reverence for the warriors of the past humble him. Kalok Shash—the collective spirit of those great warriors—seemed to form a nimbus of light around Farren as he spoke, a light that danced among the warriors like tongues of fire.

Like the Silver Flame, Aric thought. He increasingly understood why people tended to think of the Binding Flame and the Silver Flame as the same purifying fire. Was it wrong to equate them? Did that somehow dishonor the noble Ghaash'kala warriors whose spirits made up Kalok Shash, or the knights and paladins who had given their lives in service to the Church of the Silver Flame? He couldn't see how. He imagined the souls of all those warriors would be proud to say they had fought and died in pursuit of the same noble calling.

When did I start thinking like this? he wondered. Have Vor and Dania poisoned my mind? Or perhaps pretending to be a barbarian who's heard the call of Kalok Shash is rubbing off on me.

Farren finished his rousing speech and led the warriors through the mighty gates of the city that swung open before them. The city was situated at a bend in a wide canyon, so a plain spread out before the city walls and split into broad paths leading off to either side. They took the one on the right, and within the space of an hour Aric was again completely lost in the Labyrinth.

* * * * *

Days wore on, until Aric began to wonder whether Farren himself was lost. It seemed clear that the monsters and barbarians of the Labyrinth avoided the large band of warriors—Aric's small party hadn't traveled more than a day or two without meeting something that tried to kill them. It made him wonder whether they were actually doing anything to keep the Labyrinth safer, or just herding its inhabitants through the canyons.

Then he realized that was exactly what they were doing. Farren gave a signal, and the warriors fell silent. He led them slowly and quietly to a bend in the canyon, and told them to ready their weapons. He repeated the command in Common for Aric's benefit, then led the charge around the bend, into a dead-end canyon.

A small band of Carrion Tribe barbarians met their charge, trapped in the canyon. Aric had to admire Farren's skill—he had pressed the barbarians along exactly the paths he wanted them to go until he boxed them in. Now he closed in for the kill.

"They're Plaguebearers!" Farren shouted in Orc.

Then Aric was in their midst, and he understood the warning. Bleeding sores ringed by dead black flesh covered the barbarians, and gangrenous rot disfigured their faces. They reeked of death. Their disease didn't seem to weaken them, however—a club caught Aric in the ribs and knocked him back. He swung his own club wildly to stave off his attacker while he caught his breath, cursing the clumsy weapon.

"Die, traitor!" the barbarian growled, stepping past Aric's guard and swinging for his head.

As he ducked, Aric cursed again—the disguise he had adopted for the sake of survival had become a liability. He realized that every barbarian he could see was trying to fight past the orcs to reach him. They loathed a Carrion Tribe traitor more than their Ghaash'kala enemies.

Time to start killing. He swung his club to take the barbarian's legs out from under him, then brought it down on the man's head. In that moment's respite, he wove threads of magic into his borrowed club and tripped it, ensuring that it would swing faster and harder. He was fairly sure his allies were too busy to notice anything strange about his actions.

An orc to his right shouted, "Aric, watch out!" and tried to block an onrushing barbarian with a cut to his belly. It was a killing blow, but the barbarian's momentum carried him on to crash against Aric, knocking him to the ground. The dying man bared his rotting teeth in Aric's face, a leering grin of triumph even as his lifeblood spilled out over his prone foe.

Disgusted, Aric shoved the barbarian off and scrambled to his feet. Gore covered his armor, and his enchanted club was lost on the ground somewhere. The nearest weapon he saw was a two-handed hammer with a large, jagged stone for a head, so he lunged for it.

"Don't!" someone yelled.

Aric swung the hammer at a barbarian charging him and smashed the man's face. He appraised the hammer in his grip. Crude, he thought, but quite effective. He drew it back for another blow, then something knocked it from his hands.

He whirled on this new attacker and saw Farren instead.

"Plaguebearers!" the orc leader said. He pulled a battle-axe from a sling on his back and tossed it to Aric. "Use this."

Plaguebearers. The word finally registered in Aric's mind, and bile rose to his throat. The rot-infected man who had fallen on him—of course, he'd been trying to ensure that Aric contracted the same plague that had ravaged his own flesh.

He made a clumsy swing with Farren's axe at the nearest foe. He hated axes—it was too hard to make sure they hit edge-first. Too many glancing blows.

Orcs fought close around Aric, beating back foes that tried to reach him, parrying blows that might have hit him. He felt awkward and ineffective, and the thought of his flesh rotting away preoccupied him. He only realized the battle was over when the nearest orcs lowered their weapons and drooped with fatigue.

"We're not done yet," Farren shouted. "Burn the Plaguebearers."

Careful to avoid touching any of the bodies, the Ghaash'kala poured a viscous liquid over every corpse—human and orc alike—and set them alight. Aric watched black smoke rise into the air, a dark smear across the red sky.

CHAPTER
26

Cart spent the next few weeks supervising the soldiers' work in the canyon. They fought off a few half-hearted worg attacks, but the worgs' strength was broken. They cleared away the bones that formed the worgs' labyrinthine temple and built a palisade using lumber from the surrounding hills. And they built scaffolds up the wall at the canyon's head and began chipping away at the stone toward the buried crystal within. First they cut down from the top of the canyon wall until they reached the azure pool, then they began chipping the rock away from it.

Ashara supervised the excavation, which meant that she spent most of her time on the scaffolding, watching soldiers swing their picks to make sure that they didn't strike the crystal. Once in a while, she called a halt and put her hands against the stone. Then she either told them to continue or ordered a switch from picks to chisels. The rhythm of the swinging picks changed to a rattle of tapping hammers as the last thin layer of stone fell away to reveal the gleaming blue stone beneath. Then the soldiers lowered the scaffold and swung their picks again. Every few days, they raised the scaffolds again and cleared more stone away from above the jutting crystal.

Haldren paced like a caged tiger, yelling at soldiers who flagged in their work or made any errors. He had earned some good will from the soldiers in the battles against the worgs, but he squandered it away until the soldiers burned with resentment toward him. Either he was oblivious to it or he thrived on it—with every passing day his vitriol grew more caustic. Cart was sure that if he had not been there, the soldiers would have killed Haldren in his sleep, and he wasn't sure how long his influence could stay their hands.

Three weeks after the excavation began, Kelas arrived at the head of a caravan. A platoon of soldiers escorted a train of carts laden with food, lumber, and a jumble of metallic objects Cart couldn't begin to identify—tubes and cylinders of all sizes, gears and wheels, and a staggering variety of other shapes. A team of artificers and magewrights from House Cannith walked in the middle of the caravan, and miners and smiths rounded out the convoy. Haldren's soldiers cheered when the caravan first came into view, and laughed and clapped the newcomers on the back as they passed through the palisade.

Kelas and Haldren disappeared into the Lord General's tent, leaving Cart to supervise the expansion of the camp and the placement of supplies. Though it was hectic, everything went smoothly. The sheer number of new arrivals made the work go quickly—until a problem arose with the Cannith contingent. They wanted to place their tents and supplies near the scaffolding and commanded the soldiers and miners who were already established there to move. When Cart came to sort the problem out, they ignored him, continuing to yell at the other soldiers as though he weren't there.

It had been years since Cart had encountered that kind of treatment. As the only warforged in a squad of human soldiers during the Last War, he'd had to earn their respect—but he'd done that in their first battle. As he worked his way up the chain of command, he occasionally met resistance from his subordinates, but the army did not tolerate insubordination. On the Lord General's staff, he commanded absolute obedience. But many of House Cannith—because they had made the warforged during the war—refused to acknowledge the warforged as equals, let alone superiors.

Cart turned to a soldier beside him. "Get Ashara," he said. He hated to resort to that—bringing in someone else to bolster his authority—but he couldn't see any other option. He stood, arms crossed and impassive as he listened to the argument continue, until Ashara arrived.

Ashara approached quietly, unnoticed by either of the bickering factions. She stood behind his shoulder and spoke quietly. "What is it?"

The Cannith representatives were junior members of the House, technically subject to Ashara's command, and when they noticed her presence they slowly fell silent. She said nothing, but put a hand on Cart's back.

"House Cannith, your place in the camp is to the south," Cart said.

An artificer, a young man with pale hair and a constant sneer, stepped forward and looked up at Cart. The Mark of Making covered one of his arms, left bare by the sleeveless silk shirt he wore.

"We do not take orders from you," he said. His arrogant condescension was what he had first expected from Ashara.

Ashara remained just behind Cart, her position reinforcing his authority. "There are two people in this camp who outrank Cart," she said quietly. "Lord General Haldren ir'Brassek is one, and Kelas ir'Darran is the other."

The blond man stepped sideways to face Ashara. "You expect us to obey a cart? A tool?"

Ashara's hand flew like lightning to slap him across the face. A gasp went through the entire Cannith contingent.

"I told you his rank," she said coldly. "You will behave accordingly, or the Baron will hear of it." She turned and strode away, confident that her command would be obeyed.

His hand on his burning cheek, the blond man looked up at Cart again.

"House Cannith," Cart repeated, "your place in the camp is to the south."

The artificer spat on the ground at Cart's feet and rejoined his contingent. Cart watched, seething with anger and grateful for his immovable face, until they had gathered their belongings and moved to the south of the camp.

* * * * *

Cart didn't have a chance to seek Ashara until evening, with the new arrivals settled and the next day's plans set in place with Haldren and Kelas. He found her walking alone near the palisade.

"Lady Cannith," he said.

"Cart, how many times do I have to—"

"Ashara. I owe you an apology."

"Oh, no—I should be apologizing to you. Their behavior was outrageous. I'm ashamed for my House."

"It's nothing. And certainly not your fault. But I'm sorry for the way I've been treating you. You've shown me nothing but kindness since we met, and I . . . I questioned your motives."

"You thought I was trying to manipulate you."

Cart nodded.

"Isn't it funny?" she said, looking away. "We get so used to deception that we see it everywhere."

"I'm sorry," he repeated.

"I don't blame you. You trust me now?"

"You took my side against members of your own House."

Ashara smiled up at him, all warmth and affection. "You were in the right."

They walked together around the perimeter of the camp until the second watch of the night.

* * * * *

The excavation progressed quickly. The miners extended the head of the canyon from the top down, slowly revealing the bluish crystal, like a great glass monolith jutting up from the ground and leaning out into the canyon. Cart began to worry that if they cleared the stone around it all the way to the canyon floor, it would topple forward, but Ashara assured him that it extended at that angle deep into the earth, far deeper than they would dig.

As more and more of the crystal came into view, Cart started thinking he saw movement within it. At times it seemed like a faint light shifting inside, at other times like a dark smear. He tried to get a clear look, but it seemed to resist his gaze, vanishing into the azure depths as soon as he fixed his eyes on it. He hated it, somehow—looking at it made him inexplicably angry.

He wasn't alone in feeling perturbed by the crystal. Arguments broke out more often among the workers and soldiers, sometimes escalating into violence. As Cart broke up the fights, he had to keep a tight rein on his own anger to make sure he didn't injure the people he was trying to calm. Energy flagged, work on the excavation slowed dramatically, and the night was filled with the moans and whimpers of tortured dreams.

"Do you feel it, too, Cart?" Ashara asked. They stood together, looking up at the crystal from the greatest distance possible as the crimson sun of another day sank below the horizon.

"Anger, unease. At least I'm spared the nightmares."

"Be grateful."

"What is it?" he asked. "What's going on?"

"It's them." She pointed to the crystal. "The Secret Keeper and the Messenger."

"The imprisoned fiend?" Cart said.

"And the spirit that binds it. They're both angry. The Messenger fears that we'll release the fiend, and the Secret Keeper is furious that we haven't done so yet. I think it also suspects what we actually plan to do."

"Which is what?"

"You don't know?"

"Haldren only tells me what he needs me to know."

"They're going to power the Dragon Forge. They're the enormous knot of magical power our artificers will tap. And we think we can do it without breaking the bonds that hold them."

"You *think?* What if you're wrong?"

"If we're wrong, it will be disastrous. So we can't be wrong."

Cart felt tired. Not in his body—muscle fatigue was alien to his construct body. But his mind was weary, sick of the schemes and plans and ambition. He shook his head.

"I hope you're right," he said.

* * * * *

The situation grew bad enough that Haldren got involved. He put his own force of personality to work to counteract the influence of the imprisoned spirits and even used magic to soothe

the emotions of the soldiers and workers. The pace of the work increased again and fewer fights broke out, but the nights still seemed disturbed. Cart circled the camp while the soldiers slept in shifts, and the things he heard made him jump at shadows in the dark—fevered whispers and fearful whimpers, soft groans and sudden shouts.

Cart walked in his own nightmare, though his body needed no sleep. Shadows seemed to stalk at the edges of his vision, shapeless figures lurking behind corners or flitting across the sky. At times he wheeled to confront an approaching attacker, sure he'd seen the flash of steel in the darkness, but he found nothing. Whispered voices nagged at the limit of his hearing, wordless murmurs that seemed to threaten pain and destruction. All the soldiers, miners, and artificers he passed on his patrols looked suspicious or actively hostile until Cart fixed his eyes on their faces.

Disaster struck on the ninth day after Kelas's arrival. A miner's pick struck exactly the wrong place, as far as Cart could determine afterward, and a sheet of rock split away from the crystal beneath. Its collapsing weight caused a landslide that swept away the scaffolding and buried a dozen workers under a cairn of boulders. Cart felt the earth rumble, saw the rock begin to crumble, watched workers fall and then disappear beneath the rocks, but before he crossed three paces toward the scaffold it was over. A cloud of dust hung like a stormcloud over the ruin left behind.

He was thunderstruck. As he stared at the wreckage, though, a movement in the crystal caught his eye—the black smear within seemed to grow, or to surge to the surface. For a moment he thought he saw the shape of enormous hands pressed against the glass of the crystal column. He heard a sound like the beat of a muffled drum, quiet but clear, and a howl arose in answer—then another, then a chorus of faraway howls, as though the worgs were responding to a distant call. There could not have been many worgs left in the canyon, but they must have all joined that sinister choir.

Cart saw soldiers he knew as brave and battle-hardened fall to their knees and cover their heads, crying out in prayer or despair.

Others just sank to their knees in silence, overwhelmed by the combination of grievous loss and the possibility of a renewed assault. He knew he should take command, get the soldiers doing something—anything—to get their mind off the cries of the wolves and dealing with the disaster at hand. But he was as frozen as the others.

Kelas emerged, took stock of the situation, and began giving orders. He sent soldiers to the palisade, to prepare for another worg attack. Miners and more soldiers started picking through the rubble, hoping against hope to find any survivors, and others carried the rubble away to fortify the palisade.

Kelas was no more forgiving than Haldren when a soldier, overwhelmed with grief and horror, walked away from her work for a moment or fell to his knees at the discovery of a comrade's crushed body. There was work to be done—work that would take their minds off the horror.

CHAPTER
27

The dragons came one at a time into the presence of Malathar the Damned, dragon-king of Rav Magar. Copper Aggrand flew to a high window in the audience chamber and perched there like a dragonet, and black Surrun wormed his way in through a small back passage. A red dragon, Yavvaran, strode through the main entrance like nobility, shoving the dragonborn guards aside. Green Forrenel, last to arrive, came along a higher passage to appear at an arch ten feet above the floor.

When they were all present, Malathar turned his skeletal head to let his gaze fall over each in turn.

"I sent Vaneshtra ahead to prepare our way," he said. The silver dragon had been his messenger to Kelas ir'Darran, the human who dared build the Dragon Forge.

"The bronze is dead," Yavvaran announced. He was too bold. His tone was a challenge.

"Yes." Vaskar had been a fool.

"The Time of the Dragon Above draws to a close." The high voice was Aggrand.

"Our time has already begun," Malathar said. He stretched his wings, fingers of bone linked by tatters of desiccated skin. "The first blood is shed."

All the dragons showed their surprise, except Yavvaran—too proud by far. Aggrand even gasped.

"Three drops of blood mark the passing of the Time Between," Malathar whispered.

Forrenel was first to pick up the chant. "The three dragons are joined together in the blood."

Aggrand joined in as well. "And the blood contains the power of creation." Yavvaran grumbled the last four words.

Malathar silenced them all with a hiss. "One drop is shed where the Dragon Above pierces the Dragon Below, the Eye stabs at the Heart."

"What has happened?" Aggrand asked. "What blood was shed?"

"The Storm Dragon found the Eye of Siberys and used it to pierce the heart of the Soul Reaver, the Heart of Khyber."

"But the blood—what about the blood?" Aggrand was so enthusiastic, so excitable. A useful trait at times, but more often irksome.

"The Eye passed through the Storm Dragon's hand when it pierced the Heart," Malathar said.

Forrenel repeated the Prophecy. "One drop is shed where the Dragon Above pierces the Dragon Below, the Eye stabs at the Heart."

Even Yavvaran spoke the next words with the others—"Blood joins them, and so begins the Time Between."

"One drop unites Eberron with the Dragon Below," Malathar said. The others waited in breathless expectation. "Blood is drawn from a serpent binding the spawn of Khyber and the fiend that is bound. Bound they remain, but their power flows forth in the blood."

"The Dragon Forge," Forrenel said.

"One drop unites Eberron with the Dragon Above. The touch of Siberys's hand passes from flesh to stone, held within the drop of Eberron's blood."

"You have found the Siberys mark," Yavvaran said.

Malathar glared at him, and the red dragon actually stepped back from the baleful magic of the undead dragon's burning eyes. He would have the satisfaction of announcing his triumph. "I have found the Siberys mark," he said.

* * * * *

For a moment Gaven thought he was in Dreadhold and his taste of freedom had all been one fevered dream. He lay in a stone cell, crumpled on the floor where his captors had thrown him.

There was no bunk, no furnishing of any kind. A high window let in some feeble light, but shadows pooled in the corners of the room and closed in around him.

He ran a hand over the bumps on his head, still tender, and slowly the events of his capture came back to him. Lissa had betrayed him—but why? Why bother winning his trust at all? And Rienne—the dragonborn hadn't seemed to have any interest in her. That suggested to him that either his facility with Draconic or his dragonmark had drawn their attention, and he strongly suspected it wasn't his language skills.

Gaven got to his feet, aching in every joint, and stumbled to the door. It was windowless and almost perfectly joined to the wall. He sagged against it and turned to take in the whole cell. He could touch the walls on either side by stretching out his arms, and the far wall was only three paces away. A blast of lightning might knock the door open, he reasoned, so he stepped forward.

Before he reached the opposite wall, the shadows took shape. A slender man loomed in the corner where no one had been a moment before, then he emerged to face Gaven. The shadows seemed to cling to his long, dark hair and black clothing, contrasting with his pale skin. His long, pointed ears and high cheekbones marked him as an elf, but his eyes were lifeless pools of darkness. The Mark of Shadow began on his cheek, ran down his neck, and disappeared beneath his leather armor.

"Welcome to Rav Magar, Gaven," the elf said. "I have waited a long time for the privelege of meeting you."

Gaven didn't move. The elf was either a Thuranni or a Phiarlan, and either way he had good reason to hate the man who had helped orchestrate the schism between the two dragonmarked Houses. He fully expected a knife to appear in the elf's hand.

"I am Phaine d'Thuranni," the elf continued. He watched Gaven's face closely—did he expect Gaven to recognize his name? Or did he expect some reaction to meeting a Thuranni?

"What's a Thuranni doing in Argonnessen?" Gaven said, still on his guard.

"One might ask the same about a Lyrandar. Or perhaps not,

when the Lyrandar is an excoriate and a fugitive. You thought you could hide here, did you? Safe from all pursuit?"

"Pursuit? Are you telling me you followed me here from Khorvaire? Just to put me back in Dreadhold?"

Phaine chuckled, and Gaven's eyes dropped to the elf's hands again.

"You're going to kill me, then?" Gaven asked. "Get your revenge for what I did to your House?"

"I will kill you—eventually. But not until I've seen you suffer. And not until you've played your part in this drama."

Gaven felt blood rush to his face in anger. "My destiny is in my own hands, Thuranni. I won't be manipulated."

"Tell me that again when you've found your way out of this cell." As he spoke, Phaine faded into the shadows again. His mocking grin and cruel black eyes were the last to disappear.

Too late, Gaven lunged at him, but his hands hit the wall. Wheeling in frustration, he let a blast of lightning flow through his body to the door. It hit with a resounding crash, scouring the stone wall, spraying gravel in all directions, and rebounding to course harmlessly through his body. The door didn't move. He slid down the wall to sit on the floor, his dragonmark stinging and fury burning in his chest.

* * * * *

In fits of rage, he blasted the door and the walls with lightning until he collapsed in exhaustion. He slammed his fists against the door until they left trails of blood along the stone. He summoned a wind to lift him up to the window, but he found it barred with adamantine that proved as resistant to his lightning as the door was. He slept only moments at a time, propped in a corner or curled on the stone floor. He stood poised, waiting for the door to open so he could blast his way out.

The door didn't open. Out of either fear or cruelty, his captors gave him neither food nor drink, and he didn't see another guard after Phaine's brief appearance. Phaine had said he wasn't interested in killing him, but after what must have been four or five days, Gaven sat in the corner—arms limp at his side, legs splayed out in front of him, eyes half-closed. If the door had opened, he couldn't have responded except perhaps to beg for water.

Rienne seemed to step through the door then. Lines of concern creased her lovely face, and she fell to her knees beside him.

"Oh, Gaven," she said. "Please don't leave."

"I didn't mean to, Ree." His throat was parched, and his voice was little more than a harsh croak.

She cupped his cheek in her hand, but he couldn't feel anything. "You need to stay alive, love."

"Why?"

"You have to save the world, remember? That's why we came here."

"I could have been immortal, Ree. I could've stepped into the Crystal Spire and been a god. Do you know why I didn't?"

"Tell me."

"Because of you, Ree. I wanted to be with you."

Tears streamed down her face, and she clutched him to her. "So don't leave now. I love you."

He still couldn't feel her touch. "You're not really here, are you?" he murmured, his eyes drooping.

"No, love. You're all alone."

* * * * *

A dragonborn stood in the open door, and Gaven waited for his latest hallucination to deliver its message. Chains rattled in her hands, and she stepped close, cautiously, to clap a manacle on Gaven's wrist. When he didn't move, she rolled him over and pulled his arms behind him, binding his hands together. A longer chain went on his ankles, then Lissa tried to pull him to his feet. He couldn't stand.

She breathed a hiss or a sigh from the corners of her mouth. "Stop the river, and the city will fall," she said. "Perhaps we let the siege go on too long, but we thought you a worthy and dangerous foe." She lifted him over one shoulder. "We couldn't risk your escape."

Gaven's head turned enough as she walked to give him a vague sense of stone halls, dimly lit with oil lamps, but mostly he saw her back or closed his eyes, expecting at any moment to wake up in his cell.

Lissa set him down on his feet, but he slumped back to the floor—smooth, polished marble, rich black laced with veins of purest white. He saw Lissa drop down beside him, pressing her face to the floor.

"He is weak." The voice sounded like bones rubbing together, a whisper.

Lissa raised her head only slightly, still facing the floor. "He has been denied food and water for six days," she said. "We had to be sure he would not try to escape."

"There certainly seems to be no risk of that."

Gaven tried to raise his head to see the one speaking, but he couldn't.

"Is he strong enough to endure the Dragon Forge?" the whisper asked.

Lissa brought her face lower again. "I fear he is not."

"My lord." Another whispery voice, this one familiar—the Thuranni. It took Gaven a moment to remember his name and his face. Phaine. "If I may be so bold, I suggest that we transport him to the Forge in his weakened state and bring him back to a semblance of health once we arrive."

"You may not be so bold." The whisper grated harshly. "You suggest nothing I have not already planned. You will remember your place, *randravekk.*" Giant-slave—a harsh word recalling the ancient history of the elves among the giants of Xen'drik. Phaine didn't respond.

The voice grew closer. "Let me see his mark."

Lissa stood and lifted Gaven to his knees, and he looked for the first time on the dragon-king of Rav Magar. No flesh covered the bones of the enormous dragon, except for tatters of leathery skin between the bones of its wings. Its bones were blackened as though by fire, but deep violet light shone in the grooves of arcane lettering carved into nearly every surface. Purple fire danced in its eye sockets, set deep between two long horns curving forward around its tooth-filled snout.

The skeletal head came close and the burning eyes peered at

his neck, his bare chest, and his arm. Gaven's dragonmark tingled, a faint memory of his agonizing dream. He remembered Rienne's finger tracing the lines of his mark and the glimpse of his destiny he'd seen.

"Why does the Prophecy mock us so, writing itself on the flesh of these creatures? Is it not defiled when it is written on meat?"

The dragon-king stretched out a bony claw and scratched a bloody line down Gaven's chest. "No matter," the dragon said. "The Dragon Forge will purify it."

CHAPTER
28

F arren led the Ghaash'kala back to Maruk Dar, unerringly choosing a path through the twisted and branching canyons of the Labyrinth. When they neared the city, Aric was surprised to see another band approaching the city from the opposite direction and still another group already inside the walls.

Reading his face, Farren explained. "Four times a year, the Maruk Ghaash'kala return as one to Maruk Dar. We celebrate the victories of the past season, mourn the fallen, and renew our vows. You will make your formal vow at a ceremony two days hence."

My formal vow? Aric thought. That's right—the one where I commit my life to Kalok Shash and the calling of the Ghaash'kala. The one I'll break as soon as I think I can find my way out of here.

He wondered if he could escape the city before two days had passed.

The mood in the city was celebratory—friends and relatives from different warbands were coming together again for the first time in three months, embracing and laughing and trading stories. Children, dressed like warriors in uniforms of leather armor, ran through the streets to find their parents. Food appeared, such as it was—ground squirrels and rabbits caught near the Shadowcrags, the scant produce of dry gardens within the city walls, all heavily spiced and salted. Aric wandered the streets and squares for a while, enjoying the vicarious experience of community and fellowship. Then fatigue crept into his legs and a dull ache gnawed at his heart, and he tried to find the barracks he had briefly called home before setting out with Farren's band.

Just as he thought he'd spotted the right place, he found himself encircled by humans—black haired, scar-faced barbarians like . . . like himself, he remembered. They wore grim expressions but spoke words of welcome, inviting him to join them at their table, half-dragging him when he tried to refuse. They pressed a wooden cup into his hand, and the evident leader of the gang, a tall and wiry man with his face so covered with scars that it was barely recognizable as human, put an arm around Aric's shoulders.

"I'm Dakar," he said. "I keep an eye on this lot."

"Aric."

"What's your story, then?" His face was too close to Aric's, and his breath reeked of whatever strong liquor they were drinking. "How'd you hear the call?"

Aric stared into his drink, trying to identify the viscous liquid. How did one hear the call of Kalok Shash? He decided to tell a story that was close to the truth—such lies were usually easiest to maintain.

"Pangs of conscience," he said, shaking his head. That was all too true, and he still wasn't sure how it had happened. "My tribe was torturing some men they captured in the Labyrinth, and it made me sick. I wandered off and into the Labyrinth." He paused to gauge his audience's reaction. He needed a touch more. "I must have heard the call of Kalok Shash, even if I didn't recognize it at the time. Or why would I flee into the Labyrinth?"

Several of the others nodded, staring into their own drinks.

The woman on his left leaned in close as well, her black hair streaked with red and her face half-covered by a blotchy red birthmark. "What happened?" she said.

"I wandered for days, and finally I collapsed—hunger and thirst, exhaustion, maybe despair. And that's when Kalok Shash lifted me up." He saw a few eyebrows rise, and he wondered if he'd made the sacred flame sound too human, too physical. "Farren found me. He issued the challenge, and I just had strength to call on Kalok Shash. So he brought me here."

"That's it?" the woman asked. Her S was slightly slurred from her liquor.

Aric shrugged. He had no idea what further elements a conversion story should contain, at least among these people. "There might have been more," he offered. "I was half-dead for quite a while."

The woman laughed. "For me," she said, "Kalok Shash came as I was fighting against the Ghaash'kala. My companions were dead. I had killed fourteen orcs myself, and only three were left. They offered me mercy and I promised them a swift death like their fellows." She wore a savage grin, and as she looked around the table most of her companions returned it. This was the warrior pride of the Carrion Tribes, Aric realized. Probably no more than half true.

The grin dropped from the woman's face as she continued. "Then all the dead ones, they got up and surrounded me. Or at least their spirits did. They closed in on me, and started blowing around like a whirlwind of fire. I couldn't move, and my skin burned. I fell, and Kalok Shash burned the evil out of me."

"And the Ghaash'kala spared you," Aric said.

"No. I was forced to kill them. I did my penance when I took my vows."

"When was that?"

"This past Highsun, the last gathering."

Aric turned to Dakar, whose arm was still casually draped around his shoulder. "What about you?"

Dakar's scarred face twisted into what might have been a grin—Aric was reminded for a moment of Zandar. "My conversion happened when *he* took over my tribe," he said.

He—that could only mean Kathrik Mel.

"I was advisor to the chieftain," the man continued, "so encountering Kalok Shash seemed like a good idea."

That explained the sardonic smile. Dakar's "conversion" was a sham, and his oath was pretense. Aric wondered how many of the others here had similar stories. Most of them looked disappointed, and the woman on his left shook her head in disgust. But they tolerated this pretender as their leader.

"How long have you been here?" Aric asked.

"The longest of any of us. This is my third gathering."

Aric looked around the table. "You've all been here less than two seasons?" The half-dozen other barbarians nodded, looking perplexed by Aric's amazement.

"We don't last long here," Dakar said. "This will probably be my last gathering."

"But you've already survived one excursion," the woman said to Aric. "That's a good start."

"See any action?" the man asked.

"Some. We killed a band of Plaguebearers."

Dakar withdrew his arm from Aric's shoulder, to his relief, and everyone else at the table seemed to shrink away from him. Aric took advantage of the moment of stunned silence to choke down the foul-tasting liquor they'd given him.

"You were lucky," the woman said. "Sooner or later, they get us all. You can never really leave the Carrion Tribes."

* * * * *

After his mention of Plaguebearers, none of the barbarians were willing to touch him, so he managed to escape and make his way to the building he'd identified as his barracks. He slept heavily and woke feeling groggy. His body ached from too many days and nights in the Labyrinth, and he lay in his hard bed for a long time, hoping in vain to fall back asleep.

He gave up and found his way to the mess hall, but no sooner had he sat down with a plate of food than a great bell tolled somewhere in the heart of the city. He saw the orcs around him look up, shovel a last bite or two into their mouths, and head for the door, so he did the same. As the bell continued its somber tolling, crowds filed into the central city square, where a slender bell tower ornamented with carved flames rose high overhead. No one spoke—each citizen walked slowly, head bowed.

An orc woman stood at the center of the square, and Aric realized that the square was actually depressed like a shallow amphitheater, making it easier to see over the heads of orcs in front of him. The priestess was draped in ceremonial robes dyed emerald green. A length of silver chain hung around her neck almost to the ground. As the last toll of the bell faded into a lingering shimmer of sound, she raised her arms.

"Maruk Ghaash'kala," she said, and her booming voice carried easily through the plaza. "As the sun begins its slow descent into winter's night, we gather again to mourn the dead. We celebrate that their spirits have joined Kalok Shash, strengthening our case, even as we grieve the loss of their blades and their physical presence beside us."

Aric tried to imagine Sevren and Zandar incorporated into Kalok Shash, their spirits merged with those of all the Ghaash'kala who had died protecting the Labyrinth and the world beyond from the evils of the Demon Wastes. Joined, perhaps, with the noble knights and paladins of the Silver Flame across the world who gave their lives in service to their higher calling.

He couldn't. They hadn't died in any noble pursuit—he'd killed them, leading them into the nightmare of the Labyrinth in order to spark a new war. How many of the Ghaash'kala would soon die because of him?

His thoughts turned to Vor, and there at least he found some comfort. He had no difficulty whatsoever imagining the noble orc's spirit joined in the eternal Silver Flame—joined with Dania's spirit, perhaps.

A line had formed among the crowd, and people were filing forward to stand before the priestess and speak the names of those who had fallen. After each name, the priestess chanted a simple response: "Kalok Shash burns brighter." Aric imagined Vor's spirit as a brilliant mote in a stream of fire.

Silently, Aric mouthed his own list of names: Vor Helden. Sevren Thorn. Zandar Thuul. Dania ir'Vran. Kalok Shash burns brighter.

Farren stood by the priestess now, and he recited a dozen names, some of which Aric recognized—they were warriors who had fought beside him against the Plaguebearers and fallen. Some of them had died trying to protect him.

His voice choked with grief, Farren spoke one more name: "Durrnak Durashka, my brother."

The paladin who had stood against them in the Labyrinth, the old friend Vor had killed—Durrnak was Farren's brother.

"Kalok Shash burns brighter."

Aric felt suddenly light-headed, and his stomach churned.

This ceremony is not for me, he thought. I'm not part of this community—I have no business prying into their grief.

He worked his way out of the crowd and back to his bed. Finally, sleep claimed him again.

* * * * *

The war drums of the Carrion Tribes beat a slow cadence as the hordes marched eastward, spilling into the Labyrinth. The cadence shifted to double time, then resolved into a knocking at the door. He bolted awake with no idea of where he was, and he reflexively put a hand to his face.

He had no face—it was a blank canvas waiting for someone to paint features on it. Another knock rattled the door, and he tried to remember who he was supposed to be. He had never, since he was a child, awakened without a face. He was ashamed.

Aric, he remembered. Wide jaw, thin nose, long black hair. Scars on his cheeks. He'd never seen Aric's eyes. He could only hope he made them the right shade of blue.

"Come in," he murmured.

Farren pushed the door open and stepped in. "Are you ill?"

"I was dreaming."

"What did you dream?"

"War drums." Aric forced a grin—just a matter of moving the right muscles. "Must've been your knocking."

"I neglected you yesterday," Farren said. "We need to prepare you for the ceremony tonight."

"Prepare me? How?"

Farren tossed him a bundle of white linen. "Put that on," the orc said. "We'll spend the day in the tower. I'll teach you about Kalok Shash, and about the vow you'll be taking tonight. I'll leave in the early afternoon, and you'll spend the rest of the day in prayer, until the ceremony begins at sundown."

Aric nodded, and Farren stepped back into the doorway. He started to pull the door closed behind him, then turned back. "Aric, listen," he said. "There are some humans here among us purely out of expedience—they took the oath without any sincerity and they don't give a damn about Kalok Shash. They're only trying to prolong their lives a few months."

"So I've seen."

"You are my responsibility, and you will not be one of those. I will know what's in your heart, and if I don't see at least the glimmerings of true faith, you will not take the oath tonight."

"Then what?"

"I'll kill you myself."

* * * * *

"Make it solid," Aric whispered. Eyes closed, he reviewed every detail of his face and body, cementing them in his memory. He immersed himself in the persona of a Carrion Tribe barbarian who had heard the call of Kalok Shash, a man wracked with remorse over his past evils and truly aflame with his new-found faith. That part was not too difficult, but Farren's warning had made him worry that the paladin might see deeper into Aric's heart than either of them would like.

Farren returned much too soon. Aric looked hopefully in at the mess hall as they passed, but it was deserted. Farren explained that the third day of gathering was a fast day, making Aric wish he'd eaten more the night before. They walked in silence to the bell tower at the central plaza and climbed a long stair to a room near the top.

The rest of the tower was deserted. Aric had expected to see at least a handful of other new arrivals who would take the vow with him tonight. The thought of standing alone before a gathering of the whole Maruk Ghaash'kala made him nervous. His work generally demanded that he lie low, avoiding attention that might lead to discovery. He'd been good at his work, once. Now here he was, preparing to stand up and face the attention of the whole orc clan.

He had trouble concentrating as Farren ran through the teachings of Kalok Shash, but it didn't matter much. Farren thought he was an ignorant barbarian and presented his faith in the simplest possible terms. Even with only half an ear on the paladin's words, he had no trouble following the simplistic theology—

The spirits of the Ghaash'kala's dead warriors were gathered into the Binding Flame, a spiritual power that warded off evil and kept the fiendish beings of the Demon Wastes imprisoned in their shattered land. As servants of the Binding Flame, the Ghaash'kala shared the same mission—preventing the evils of the Wastes from spilling out into Khorvaire.

"Listen well now," Farren said, forcing Aric back to attention. "The day I found you in the Labyrinth—you died that day. You are a ghost now, privileged to spend your last, fleeting days on this world serving Kalok Shash, proving yourself worthy to join its holy flame. You are already dead. So when a man's club smashes your skull or a fiend's claws rip out your heart, that is simply the completion of your spirit's journey from life to Kalok Shash. You have already given your life to Kalok Shash, and you will never live again."

I was dead the moment I left Fairhaven, Aric thought—as soon as I left Kelas's office. Sevren, Zandar, and Vor died when they agreed to accompany me. The rest was just the completion of the journey.

"I will leave you to meditate on that thought," Farren said, standing. "I've seen your heart, Aric."

Aric looked up sharply, not sure what to expect. The orc paladin's face looked troubled.

"You take your vow tonight."

CHAPTER
29

T he catastrophic avalanche in the canyon had cost over a dozen lives, but—as Haldren pointed out—it saved what might have been weeks of work chipping away at the stone. When the rubble and bodies were cleared away, Ashara led a team of artificers and magewrights to examine the crystal and the rock that remained around it, and they declared that the excavation was complete—the front face of the azure monolith was fully exposed, and the work of building the Dragon Forge could begin.

Ashara tried to explain to Cart what the various parts of the forge were for, but it was mostly lost on him. The first step was the construction of some sort of reservoir, to hold the magic energy that poured out of the crystal. Two large cylinders studded with gemstones flanked the blue slab, and a delicate tracery of swirling gold inlay connected them to an ornate ring at the center point between them. The inlay took as long to complete as the enormous cylinders—the work was excruciatingly slow, as artificers scratched the shallowest possible grooves in the crystal's surface and filled them with minute amounts of gold. The forward-leaning angle of the monolith made the work more complicated, requiring the artificers to defy gravity with their magic to keep the gold in place.

As a further complication, the darkness within the crystal shadowed their every move—watching over their shoulders, as it were, in case they made any slip that might allow its escape. Ashara put the artificers on short shifts, so no one had to endure the fiend's scrutiny for too much time at once. Even so, its constant, visible presence heightened the anxiety that already gripped the camp, shortening tempers beyond even Haldren's ability to soothe.

The miners, meanwhile, began digging into the canyon floor, creating the trenches and chambers that would ring the forge itself. Though they were well away from the crystal and the darkness inside it, they were just as edgy and unsettled as the artificers. Cart hoped they would not turn their mining picks and shovels on each other.

During this phase of construction, the soldiers had nothing to do, and what Cart had thought would be a much-needed respite, helping them calm their nerves and rest their weary bodies, actually gave them opportunity to drink heavily and brawl. Cart had to break up at least one all-out fight each day, as well as a few smaller squabbles. When a soldier actually stabbed him, he decided it was time to bring the matter to Haldren's attention.

"And what do you propose we do about it?" Haldren asked.

"They need work," Cart said, shrugging. "Ashara tells me that it will be another two or three days before she can give them anything to do."

"Let them hunt the damned worgs." The worgs had been howling each night, further troubling everyone's sleep.

"I'm loath to risk their lives like that. Every fight with the worgs has ended with at least one soldier dead."

"That wasn't a suggestion, soldier," Haldren snapped. "It was an order. You may organize the parties as you see fit, but I want everyone in this camp who doesn't have other work to do hunting worgs. Today."

Cart stared at the Lord General. He had not noticed the lines of fatigue on Haldren's face, the darkness under his eyes. His hair was growing long again, and he looked almost as old as when he first left Dreadhold. And no wonder—of the three allies who had rescued him, only Cart was left. Darraun had been a spy, and he was dead. And neither Cart nor Haldren had seen Senya since the battle at Starcrag Plain. Haldren might as well have been in Dreadhold again, and he knew it. He had nothing left—nothing except Cart, at least, and now he seemed determined to drive Cart away as well.

"Is there a problem?" Haldren said. "Do you take issue with my orders?"

Cart was the soul of obedience. He was made to be a soldier, and he would be the best soldier he could be. "No, Lord General." He turned and strode out of Haldren's tent, Ashara's words nagging at his mind. *You're a hero.*

* * * * *

Cart gave Tesh a promotion, putting him in charge of half the remaining soldiers. Cart led the other half himself. By dividing the soldiers into only two parties, Cart hoped he'd increase their chances of surviving contact with the enemy—and perhaps decrease their chances of encountering the enemy at all. He'd made their orders clear. They should kill any worg they found. To Tesh, he stressed that they should make no particular effort to find any worgs. The real purpose of the excursion was to keep the soldiers busy for two days, to make sure they didn't kill each other. If worgs killed them, it defeated the purpose.

Cart's team would make widening arcs around the head of the canyon, while Tesh's group patrolled the length of the canyon itself. They'd go out from the camp for a day, then work their way back on the second day. Ashara promised him that she'd speed the artificers along so there would be work for the soldiers when they returned.

"I wish I could come with you," she told him as he prepared to go.

"You'll be much safer here," Cart said.

"What makes you think I want to be safe?"

"I . . . I don't—"

She smiled and clasped his arm. "Good luck, Cart," she said. "Sovereigns keep you."

Cart led his team a short way down the canyon, to a point where they could scale the wall and begin their first arc around the head of the canyon and its terrible crystal. They stayed close to the edge of the canyon for their first pass. Cart was pleased to see the mood of his soldiers lighten, especially once they realized that they weren't really looking for worgs. He was sure it helped that they'd put some distance between themselves and the fiend imprisoned at the camp.

But tensions grew again as the morning slipped by and they spotted the camp below. At about the time the azure monolith came into view, one soldier stepped on the heel of the man in front of him, who wheeled and shoved the offender, nearly sending him over the edge into the canyon. If Cart hadn't lunged to grab the toppling soldier, he would have fallen. At that point, he ordered the soldiers into a wider formation and they marched in silence. He caught himself warily eyeing the crystal as it came nearer, and he noticed the others doing the same. They were not fools. They could sense the evil trapped inside.

As they rounded the canyon, it was hard to take his eyes off the blue stone below, and the course of their march always seemed to drift closer to the edge. When another soldier nearly toppled over, this time just because he wasn't watching where he was going, Cart called a halt. He altered their course to go directly away from the crystal, widening their arc around it.

That new course led them up a narrow ridge and back down a gentler slope into a valley running parallel to the canyon. Mounds of dirt and rubble piled at the bottom of the valley told Cart immediately that something was very wrong, and he put the soldiers on guard. As they continued down, Mirra—the resourceful sergeant—pointed ahead and to their left.

"Captain," she said, "there's a mine shaft."

Cart called a halt, and the soldiers stopped their march, shuffling uneasily as they came to rest. "Has anyone heard of mining activity in these hills?"

"We had to bring miners from Breland," Mirra pointed out.

"Can't teach a farmer to mine," another soldier added. Aundair was known as an agricultural nation, not for its mineral wealth.

At a glance, Cart guessed that the shaft drove into the hill in exactly the direction they'd come— straight back to the crystal. Had the worgs found another way to access the object of their devotion? Could worgs dig? He'd seen dogs bury bones in the ground, but dig a shaft through solid rock? He ran his fingers absently over the plates covering his chest, remembering the wounds the worgs had dealt him. They had claws and teeth that could tear into adamantine—certainly they could dig a tunnel through rock.

"We didn't go looking for worgs," he said, "and we all hoped we wouldn't find them. But I think we have, so we need to prepare."

As he spoke, he was trying to formulate a plan. They needed more information, but his group was too large to watch the mine without alerting the worgs. Were there worgs inside? They couldn't attack them there—the defenders would have a decisive advantage, even discounting the worgs' innately superior strength. And Cart wasn't about to discount that factor. He wanted to keep as many soldiers alive as possible.

He decided to gamble on worgs being inside. They hadn't seen any worgs in the area, and he would have expected at least a single guard at the shaft if the rest of the pack was elsewhere. So he led his soldiers closer to the shaft entrance, fanning them out to form defensive lines around it. The shaft was dug into a low bluff in the side of the valley, one place where the gentle slope formed more of a wall. He hoped to close the wall with a ring of swords and spears to hold the worgs in place, but he didn't have time. A warning bark erupted from the shaft entrance, answered by what seemed like a symphony of howls. The howls echoed in the shaft, certainly, suggesting that the worgs had greater numbers, but that knowledge didn't keep him from fear's grasp.

"Steady," he said. The worgs wouldn't erupt from the shaft unless they saw that they would soon be trapped.

And just as his soldiers were about to close the trap, worgs sprang out of the entrance and bolted for the narrow gap that remained between Cart and the rocky bluff. They came like arrows loosed from a single bow, one at a time in a stream of a half-dozen.

There was no way Cart and the soldiers with him at the front of the line could stop all of the charging worgs, and only a handful of other soldiers were close enough to help. He fell back, leaving room for the worgs to pass. The worgs weren't any more interested in a fight than Cart was, so he let them go. As soon as they had passed the soldiers' line, they scattered to the winds.

"Mirra," he called, and the sergeant scurried to stand before him. "Take two squads back to the camp. Tell Haldren what we found, and come back here with miners—as many picks as the camp can spare."

Mirra saluted and went to gather her two squads. Cart pulled the other soldiers together and started preparations to spend the night at the worgs' den.

* * * * *

No one slept. Camped outside the entrance to the worgs' shaft, the soldiers were in constant fear of worgs, and the shaft itself loomed like a constant, vigilant presence. Soldiers who glanced that way turned away quickly, and Cart felt a slow pulse that resonated in the metal cores of his limbs, a sensation that hovered just at the edge of pain. He wondered how far the shaft went—had the worgs already succeeded in clearing a path to the crystal, opening a channel for its awful presence to extend into the neighboring valley?

As soon as the sun's light faded completely from the sky, the worgs launched their first attack. They struck at the weakest point—a relatively small cluster of soldiers a short distance from any reinforcements. It was a quick and brutal strike, leaving two soldiers dead, then the worgs retreated before any help could arrive. Cart pulled the troops closer together, and they nervously awaited the next attack.

The worgs always came just as the soldiers began to relax or grow tired, letting their attention wander and loosening their grips on their weapons. Each time, they left at least one soldier dead or grievously injured, and as far as Cart could tell, the worgs had suffered no significant wounds. As the night wore on, the attacks became less frequent as the tension among the soldiers grew, but each one took a greater toll as fatigue slowed their reactions and weakened their hands. Cart managed to bring down one worg when the beasts made their only significant mistake—attacking too close to where Cart stood guard.

With dawn's light, Cart looked down at a row of six bodies. It could have been worse, he told himself, but that was little comfort.

What was supposed to have been work to busy idle hands had become a costly engagement.

By the time the soldiers had constructed and lit a pyre for their fallen comrades, Mirra arrived with her two squads of soldiers, a platoon of miners, and Ashara, who insisted on inspecting the crystal and supervising the collapse of the tunnel.

Cart took one of Mirra's squads into the shaft first, to ensure that no worgs remained inside. At the shoulder, the worgs were taller even than Cart, so the height of the ceiling gave plenty of room. It was the width that made Cart nervous—if they did find any worgs, it would be a series of one-on-one fights in the narrow tunnel, and the soldiers would have trouble swinging their weapons at full strength. They made it only a short way inside before Cart called a halt and withdrew to replace his axe with a spear more suited to fighting in close quarters. So armed, he advanced into the tunnel alone, holding a sunrod before him to light his way. If only one soldier could face a worg at a time, he wanted that soldier to be him.

The shaft was straight, with no branches, and ran deep into the rock of the ridge. To his surprise, he found the tunnel shored up with wooden beams. How could the worgs have brought the beams into the tunnel? To imagine them digging into the rock like dogs burying a bone was one thing—but the idea of them carrying lumber into the shaft to support the ceiling seemed absurd. He resolved to have a miner examine the construction after he had scouted to the end.

As he expected, the light from his sunrod soon sparkled blue against what seemed like a doorway cut into the rock, outlining a crystal wall. A few paces farther in, he realized that the shaft widened and rose higher before the blue rectangle, as though the worgs had built a subterranean temple to replace their scattered labyrinth in the canyon.

Steeling himself for an ambush, he advanced slowly and as quietly as he could to the end of the shaft. He found himself in the entry to an impressive chamber carved from the stone. The walls were polished smooth except around the blue doorway, where a demonic figure was chiseled into the rock. Its feline head snarled in rage, and its clawed hands held the limp form of a winged serpent. The blue crystal gleamed between its legs, framed by pillars and a lintel that were also carved from the stone. The sculpture, more than the shores, convinced him that the worgs had not built this temple.

No worgs lurked in the chamber, but as he looked around, something moved within the crystal. First he saw a silver swirl—the serpent swimming through the mineral sea. Its movements had a sense of urgency that drew Cart a little closer. Other feelings surfaced in his mind, awe and wonder, respect and compassion for the sacrifice the spirit had made, giving its own freedom to bind the evil here in the earth. Cart wanted to honor that sacrifice.

Then a shadow moved behind the serpent. Two claws took form within the shadow and tore at the serpent, pushing through the barrier it had tried to make. He felt a flash of the serpent's fear, then an overwhelming sense of anger. The shadow pressed against the surface of the crystal, and Cart stared into the incarnate face of evil.

* * * * *

A tool of war, like a sword or a siege engine. Is that what you are?

Cart was trapped in shadow floating in a sea of blue. He heard a whispered voice, not in his ear, but in his mind.

What god cares about the warforged? I will be that god, and you will be my champion.

The owner of the voice had plumbed the deepest reaches of his mind and soul, the heart of his desire.

You will lift my banner, and the warforged of all the world will rally to it. And there will be war, glorious war, the glory of battle and conquest. Khorvaire will be yours.

I was made for war, Cart thought.

And what is a warforged to do in a world without war? They built you for war and then abandoned you. But you will show them what they have done. They have brought war on themselves. War now has a mind and a will of its own.

It's true, he thought. When the humans built war machines with minds, free-willed beings whose sole purpose was war, they condemned themselves to perpetual war. Until the last warforged lies dead and broken on a battlefield, there will always be war.

There will always be war. But these humans—Kelas, Haldren, Ashara and the rest—they try to use war as a tool, an instrument of their politics. You will bring war for war's sake, war without pretense. War with no goal can have no end, for it will never attain its goal.

The mention of Ashara's name stirred something in Cart that seemed to drive back the shadow just the slightest bit. To her, he was not a tool. In her eyes, he was something more than a machine built to be a soldier.

Of course you are more than a mere soldier—so much more. You are a hero, and you will be my champion.

To be a hero and to be your champion seem like two different things, he thought.

You will be whatever you desire. At my right hand, your destiny will be yours to choose.

Destiny. That word brought different memories to mind, memories of Gaven at the gates of Khyber, seizing his destiny and the Prophecy by the horns and wrenching them to his own will. Gaven had convinced Cart that his thoughts of godhood were illusions, that the path to greater good did not lie with the acquisition of greater power. Gaven had forsworn the power of divinity.

Gaven cannot be the Storm Dragon. He didn't fulfill the Prophecy of the Storm Dragon. The Storm Dragon is yet to come.

No, Cart thought.

A flash of silver drove the shadow back still farther, and Cart found himself standing before the crystal doorway, both hands pressed to its surface and his forehead leaning against it. He heaved himself backward, sprawled on the floor, and the darkness was gone.

* * * * *

Ashara was the first to reach him, rushing from the chamber's entrance to kneel beside him while two soldiers behind her gawked at the carvings around the crystal door.

"Stay back from it," Cart groaned. "Ashara, take a look, but be careful. We need to bring this temple down as soon as possible."

Ashara ran a hand over the blue crystal, and a shadow fell over her face. She seemed to shake it off quickly, and she pulled away. Glancing around the rest of the chamber, she nodded, apparently satisfied.

"Bring it down," she said.

CHAPTER
30

"Vaneshtra has sent word," the dragon-king's rasping voice said. "All is prepared for our arrival."

Gaven managed to raise his head and look around. This was a different chamber than the other one, darker and a little smaller, though still larger than most cathedrals. High windows let in little light, and Gaven saw storm clouds churning the sky. The dragon-king stood at the edge of a gigantic circle inscribed into the stone floor and inlaid with crushed gemstones of various colors, combining abstract patterns with Draconic characters. Four other dragons stood around the circle. One was a deep forest green, its head pronged with vicious-looking spikes and its mouth dripping with venom. The next was black, shining in the dim light as though it had just emerged from water, its horns curving forward like the dragon-king's and its face suggesting the skeletal appearance of the undead dragon. The third was red as autumn leaves, with great horns swept back from its proud head. The smallest of the four enormous dragons was a gleaming red-brown, with the faintest hint of a green patina as though its scales were cast from copper.

Phaine d'Thuranni knocked his face back to the ground and Gaven groaned. They had given him water, trusting that his weakness would prevent him from attacking guards who opened his cell door long enough to throw him a waterskin. He still had not eaten, and he felt stretched, like cotton being spun into yarn. A rumble of thunder from the clouds overhead reminded him, though, that he was still the Storm Dragon—there was still power in his blood and in his dragonmark, if only he could marshal the strength of will he needed to channel it.

"Step now into the circle," the dragon-king said.

Gaven felt all the dragons move closer, as though each one exuded an aura that pressed against him, squeezing him from all sides. Then the dragon-king began a chant, its words already burned into Gaven's memory.

"Three drops of blood mark the passing of the Time Between.
The three dragons are joined together in the blood,
and the blood contains the power of creation.
The Time Between begins with blood and ends in blood.
Blood is its harbinger, and blood flows in its passing."

Thunder is his harbinger and lightning his spear, Gaven thought—that was the Storm Dragon, described in the Prophecy. Wind is his steed and rain his cloak.

Another rumble of thunder made Gaven smile.

Without a pause, the dragons launched into a different chant, formed not of words but of syllables of power. Almost as soon as it began, Gaven felt the engraved circle spring to life beneath him, energy coursing along its channels and magic stirring the air.

Lightning struck the roof of the chamber, and he heard one dragon's voice falter, then pick up the chant.

Gaven felt a surge of elation that began to overpower his fatigue. I am the storm, he thought. I am the Storm Dragon!

Another lightning strike shook the building, and a shower of gravel fell from one of the windows. Rain drove against the roof and walls, and wind swirled inside the chamber. Gaven lifted his head again, and Phaine did not push it down. The elf had his sword in his hand as if to menace Gaven with it, but his eyes were on the roof and walls. Another strike made the copper dragon falter again, and the red growled a warning even as it continued the chant. Gaven saw cracks start to form across the roof, and the swirling air lifted him to his feet.

I am the Storm Dragon. You cannot contain me!

He began to rise into the air on a column of wind, power surging through his body, giving life to his muscles. He could feel the incantation building to its conclusion, and he lifted his arms to the sky to summon the full power of the storm. Lightning hit the roof again, and it began to crumble.

Had someone called his name?

The copper dragon pounced and brought Gaven to the ground beneath its claws. Flat on his back, he saw a huge stone slab break off from the roof and fall. The dragons uttered the last syllable of their ritual chant, and magic flared in a shimmering aurora along the lines of the circle.

Before the falling roof reached the ground, they were gone.

* * * * *

Gaven lay on broken ground, looking up at a clear blue sky that framed the angry face of the copper dragon. Its horns were similar to the red's, but their bases met between the dragon's eyes to form a V shape atop its skull. Its eyes were smooth pools of liquid turquoise, burning with fury.

"You thought to escape us, meat?" the dragon growled. "You think your power is a match for ours?"

Phaine, the other dragons, and the undead dragon-king stood around them in the same positions they had occupied in the chamber. Gaven's body ached from the dragon's attack, even though its claws hadn't torn his flesh. He was utterly spent.

"Enough, Aggrand," the dragon-king hissed. "He has failed."

Still snarling, the copper dragon stepped off Gaven and backed away to its place in the circle. There was a circle traced in the ground here, a faint echo of the elaborate carving in the chamber they'd left behind. It might have been scratched in the dirt with a stick, but its lines were carefully drawn to match the whorls and words of the original. Rocky canyon walls rose up on two sides, framing the sky.

He tried to sit up and look around, but the tip of Phaine's sword appeared at his throat. His head fell back to the ground, and he watched a cloud begin to form in the cloudless sky.

"Knock him out," the dragon-king said. "We will have no more storms to ruin this perfect day."

Sword still at Gaven's throat, Phaine kicked at his head. It was a precise blow despite its savagery. Gaven struggled for a moment to keep the darkness from closing in on his vision, but a second kick tipped him over the edge into oblivion.

* * * * *

Blue light. Gaven blinked, trying to clear his vision. Two human men propped him up between them, eyeing him warily as he lifted his head. They were burly soldiers in metal-studded leather, their hair matted with the dirt of weeks in the field. They stood facing an enormous mass of blue crystal that jutted up from the ground at the head of the canyon. At the top and sides, large facets blended into the surrounding rock of the cliff wall, but the front was a smooth plane, like a window into a vast blue sea.

Near the canyon floor, a tracing of gold wound its way from the edges of the crystal to a circle engraved in the center. Two great metal cylinders stood on either side, connected to the inlay with fine gold threads and covered with gemstones arranged in precise patterns. Glass tubes extended out from these cylinders, greenish liquid lying quiescent in their bottoms, linking them to what seemed to be construction in progress—the shell of a metal building surrounded by a deep trench.

Something nagged at the edge of Gaven's memory, disjointed scenes from a dream that made no sense. The crystal—he'd seen it, a coil of silver writhing inside, a smear of darkness trapped in its grasp. On the lightning rail in Zil'argo he'd dreamed it, jutting from the ground in this canyon. Two spirits bound in a single prison.

A man stepped in front of Gaven, blocking his view of the construction. Another human in studded armor, this one was older than the soldiers holding Gaven up, and carried an air of authority. He wore a midnight blue coat over his armor and fashionable boots that marked him as something more than a soldier or even a military officer. He smiled warmly at Gaven.

"I'm so glad you're awake to see this, Gaven," he said. "It would be a shame for you to sleep through such a turning point in history, since you play such an important part in it."

Gaven looked around and saw other people arrayed around the crystal, many of them familiar. Phaine d'Thuranni stood just off to his left, his sword still in his hand. Haldren ir'Brassek stood away to the right, arms crossed, glaring at Gaven with barely contained fury. Cart was in his accustomed place behind the general's shoulder. Gaven felt a pang of disappointment and grief—Cart could have been so much more than Haldren's lackey.

The dragon-king perched on the edge of the canyon above the crystal, but there was no sign of the other dragons. A scattering of soldiers with spears and swords, miners hefting picks and shovels, and what might have been magewrights—Gaven saw the Mark of Making on one or two of them—filled out a rough arc centered on the crystal. They watched him and the man standing before him with expectation.

"I'm Kelas ir'Darran," the man said. "I see you recognize some of your old friends."

Gaven scanned the crowd for Rienne, but of course she wasn't there. His gaze fell on Cart again, and he thought of Darraun.

Could the changeling be here? he wondered. Perhaps wearing a different face? No, of course. Darraun is dead.

"I have no friends here," Gaven said, his eyes still fixed on Cart. He saw the warforged shift, and he wondered if that were true.

"Indeed." The smile fell from Kelas's face. "However, at this point you are here merely as a witness—the Dragon Forge is not ready for you yet."

Gouts of dragonfire in a furnace below him—another scene from a dream. The same dream? He wasn't sure.

Kelas turned his back on Gaven and looked up at dragon-king. "The Prophecy, Malathar!" he shouted in Draconic. "Tell us!"

The dragon-king's voice was undiminished by the distance to the top of the canyon. "One drop unites Eberron with the Dragon Below," he said.

Kelas repeated the dragon's words in the Common tongue, his arms spread wide like a priest in prayer.

Gaven whispered the Draconic words along with the dragon-king. "Blood is drawn from a serpent binding the spawn of Khyber and the fiend that is bound." His eyes fixed on the crystal and the vague shapes within it. "Bound they remain, but their power flows forth in the blood."

From somewhere inside his coat, Kelas produced a large silver ring, a torc in the shape of a twisting serpent. He held it up, and silver light flashed within the crystal in answer.

"The Torc of Sacrifice," he said, addressing the entire assembly, "an embodiment of the power that allows the serpent of the crystal to bind the fiend. With this torc around her neck, a paladin of the Silver Flame took a possessing spirit into her body and bound it there, then gave her own life to destroy it. With the torc at the heart of the Dragon Forge, we will siphon power from the mighty beings in this prison—without setting them free."

"Bound they remain," Gaven said, "but their power flows forth in the blood."

Kelas turned, all warm smiles again. "Very good, Gaven."

Gaven looked at Cart, a willing participant in this . . . the only word Gaven could find to describe it was blasphemy. The emblem of a paladin's sacrifice, used to draw power into this Dragon Forge. For what purpose?

Kelas walked to the crystal prison, holding the torc in both hands, and carefully placed it over the ring of gold at the center. It flared with brilliant white light, and white fire ran along the intricate gold inlays, outward from the ring, turning the gold to silver. Kelas stepped back and watched the transformation, flexing his hands in anticipation. When the fire had burned to the gem-covered cylinders and gone out, he drew his sword and held it above his head.

"The Ramethene Sword," he said, "forged by fiends for their champion to wield in battle against the dragons of the world's dawn. Haldren, what say the *Serpentes Fragments?*"

Ramethene Sword, *Serpentes Fragments*—the names meant nothing to Gaven, but the sword drew his attention. It was heavy and angular, almost as though it had been carved of stone. It looked like it might have come from the ruins of Paluur Draal or Xen'drik, but it was not really like anything Gaven had seen before.

Haldren cleared his throat and recited a verse, unfamiliar to Gaven.

The Sunderer smote to the dragon's heart,
  and its blood formed a river upon the land.
The Fleshrender drew forth the serpent's life
  and its blood gave life to the gathered hordes.
For the blade drinks the blood, and the hand that wields it feasts
  on the life."

The Sunderer seemed more like a name from the Prophecy, and Gaven racked his brain in an effort to dredge up anything pertinent.

"The Sunderer, the Fleshrender," Kelas said. "This is the weapon that will smite to the heart of this prison and draw forth the blood to power the Dragon Forge."

Gaven wondered whether Kelas had any idea what he was doing. He had noticed that the dragon-king omitted any mention of the Time Between from his recitation of the Prophecy. Almost without doubt, Kelas was a tool in the dragon's claw, fulfilling the Prophecy of the Time Between while vainly pursuing his own ends.

Once again Kelas stepped up to the crystal. He put both hands on the hilt of the Ramethene Sword, drew a deep breath, and shoved it through the circle of the silver torc.

There was a sound like the plucking of an enormous string, almost too low to hear, but making the air thrum with its vibration. Gaven felt a wave of nausea pass through him, and his muscles felt even weaker. The soldiers supporting him staggered as well, and his knees buckled. Everyone standing around the crystal clearly felt it—they lowered their heads, staggered backward, or fell to their knees. The dragon-king and Cart alone seemed unaffected.

The canyon was hardly vibrant with life, but something was happening to it—the thin patches of grass dissolved into ash, bare rock blackened, the dry shrubs that grew here and there on the canyon walls shriveled and died. Desolation spread out in a wave from the crystal. Gaven looked in sheer terror at the shadow, expecting to see it burst forth from its azure prison.

Both the silver serpent and the dark fiend were agitated,

moving quickly, almost frantically. The Ramethene Sword glowed so brightly it hurt his eyes to look at it. The inlaid tracery pulsed with light as well, and gemstones came to life on the surface of the cylinders, glowing in a mosaic of different colors. The liquid in the glass tubes began to bubble and churn.

Then fire burst from the earth to fill the trench that surrounded the Dragon Forge.

CHAPTER
31

Rienne awoke, and Gaven was not there. She frowned at the place where he'd lain—usually she awoke long before he did and had time to exercise and meditate before she roused him for the day's journey. Something was wrong.

She sprang up with Maelstrom in her hand and rushed out of the small shrine. The dragonborn city was only starting to come alive with the first light of dawn. She saw dragonets flapping at open windows where dragonborn placed scraps of meat in tiny houses. She heard strange singing, low droning chords and high chanted melodies, that might have been a form of morning prayer. But she couldn't see Gaven.

"Gaven?" she called. Several pairs of eyes turned her way and quickly turned back. Louder—"Gaven!" He did not appear or call an answer.

The sky was cloudless, which gave her an odd reassurance that he was not in serious trouble. If he were fighting somewhere, certainly a storm would be brewing. At the same time, it was disappointing—if nothing else, she could have found him by heading to the heart of the storm.

"Gaven!" She heard the desperation in her own voice.

"Rienne!" The voice was not his, and she barely recognized her own name. A dragonborn was running toward her—the one who had led them to this city and shown them the shrine. Lissa.

As the dragonborn drew nearer, Rienne clenched the hilt of Maelstrom more tightly and called out. "Where is he?" Even as she said it, she realized the stupidity of it—Lissa didn't understand Common, and Rienne knew only a few words of Draconic, mostly words related to obscure aspects of the Prophecy that resisted translation.

Lissa's axe was slung at her belt and her shield at her back, so Rienne sheathed Maelstrom out of courtesy. The blade could be back in her hand in an instant if she needed it. When the dragonborn reached her, spewing a torrent of Draconic babble, she put a hand on Rienne's shoulder and tried to guide her back into the shrine. She seemed anxious, so Rienne followed.

When they were in the shrine and safely out of view, Lissa slumped against the wall beside the archway. Rienne could read the fear on her face, but couldn't determine the cause of it—was she being pursued? She should, perhaps, not be here with Rienne.

"Gaven?" Rienne asked desperately. Could Lissa give an answer she could understand?

Another gush of Draconic, but Rienne heard Gaven's name. She stared blankly at the dragonborn, and Lissa started again, slowly as if talking to an imbecile, but accompanying her words with pantomime, watching to make sure that Rienne understood each concept.

"Gaven," she said . . . hands bound together—a prisoner. Lissa pointed at Rienne . . . *go, go quickly*, Lissa wiggled her fingers like legs at top speed. *Run. Run away.* Lissa shook the axe at her belt and then pointed again at Rienne.

Flee or die.

"Not without Gaven," she said, more to herself than Lissa. She took the dragonborn's hands and put the wrists together, as Lissa had done to show Gaven's imprisonment. Pointing at Lissa, she said, "Gaven." Then she pointed at herself, and chopped her hand between Lissa's wrists. "I must free him."

Lissa's eyes went wide with fear, and she shook her head. Rienne guessed that meant the same thing to the dragonborn that it did to her.

"I can't leave him here," she said, her voice pleading. Lissa's eyes softened—she recognized the tone, at least. Rienne held up one fist—"Rienne"—and the other, "Gaven." She brought the two hands together, entwined the fingers. "Together." Hands still together, she moved them in imitation of the gesture Lissa had used to mean go away. "We have to leave together."

Lissa's face mirrored her own sadness. She took Rienne's wrists gently in her big, clawed hands and slowly pulled away the hand that was Gaven, lowering it back into Rienne's lap. "Rienne." Rienne alone.

Tears welled in Rienne's eyes, and she shook her head. "How can I leave without him?"

Lissa took the Gaven hand back in hers and led Rienne to the back of the shrine. High on the wall behind the stone tablet of the Prophecy, a mural depicted a dragon's skeleton, proud and erect, its eyes burning with purple flame and its entire form surrounded by a nimbus of deep violet. The dragon's bones were carefully marked with writing—perhaps another fragment of the Prophecy, Rienne couldn't tell.

Still holding Rienne's wrist, Lissa pointed at the undead dragon and said a single word, "Drakamakk." Then she lifted Rienne's hand up toward the dragon. Rienne understood. Gaven was a prisoner of this undead dragon, who was perhaps the ruler of this city. Lissa shook her head slowly, sorrow in her eyes. There was no hope of freeing him.

Rienne wrenched her hand away from Lissa and drew Maelstrom. She swung the blade high, toward the image of the undead dragon. Lissa caught her wrist again, stopping Maelstrom a hand's width from the mural image. Her eyes had hardened, just slightly. So Lissa was willing to help Rienne flee, but not to help her fight the dragon-king.

Thoughts racing, Rienne turned away from the dragonborn. What could she do? She couldn't hope to be inconspicuous in a city where she was the only half-elf—the only one these people had ever seen, as far as she knew. She couldn't secure help, couldn't bluff her way past the guards, couldn't exert the influence of her noble birth—she couldn't interact in any meaningful way with the dragonborn without speaking a word of their language. She wasn't sure the money she carried would buy her food or assistance. And if Lissa wouldn't help her against the undead dragon, how could she expect anyone else to?

She blinked back tears. "I can't leave him, I just can't," she said. "All those years he was in Dreadhold, I died without him." Lissa laid a hand on her shoulder, and Rienne was surprised at the tenderness of the gesture. The dragonborn seemed so large, so strong—so inhuman.

Rienne looked down at her feet, at the fine silver chain wrapped several times around her ankle. With barely a thought, it would take her home. Gaven had one, too, unless they took it from him. She could look for him, even in the palace of the dragon-king, and break the chain if she found herself in trouble. But using it would seem so final. If she fled at the first sign of danger, she would never have the chance to return.

"I have to look for him, at least," she said.

Lissa seemed to read the resolve in her face. She shook her head, breathing a hiss from the corners of her mouth, then stepped back toward the shrine's arched entrance. The dragonborn said a word of farewell—or perhaps it was a blessing or a warning—and then she was gone.

* * * * *

It was worse than Rienne had imagined. She was accustomed to the gawks and rude comments of the lowest classes in the streets of Khorvaire's cities, even used to fighting off attackers in the most dangerous neighborhoods, when business took her there. But she also expected polite treatment from her social equals and the middle class, and in Rav Magar she found none of that. Everyone stared at her, nearly everyone pointed, and many gave threatening hisses in her direction. Several dragonborn accosted her, puffing out their chests and shouting, sometimes roaring, until she guessed their meaning and made her best attempt at a display of submission.

She wandered through the city, searching for roads to take her to the higher parts of the city, toward the dragon-king's lofty palace. Few roads connected the city's different levels, but each time she did find her way to a higher tier, the size of the buildings, the ornateness of the decoration, the sheer displays of wealth grew more impressive. The layout of the city enforced the division

among the different castes of its people, she realized. Silver inlays
and then gold, marble, and alabaster taking the place of wood and
granite; silks and jewelry adorning the people she passed—they
all spoke of the greater status of the residents of the higher tiers.
More elaborate displays also marked the distinctions between
these dragonborn and the lower-tier citizens who did business in
the higher levels.

When the sun had not yet reached its zenith and she had
climbed only as high as the fourth tier, four armed dragonborn
challenged her. They wore metal armor like what Lissa had worn
in the forest, and sashes of rich black silk draped across their chests
seemed to indicate some official status. As a reflex, her hand started
for Maelstrom's hilt, but she pulled it back—four dead soldiers
would not help her any. She held her hands out in front of her.

What if I let them take me? she wondered. Will they bring me
to Gaven? Then I might not be able to help him, but at least we'll
be together. But what if they don't?

The guards inched forward around her with wide eyes. Rienne
dropped her hands and ran.

The streets of this tier were wide, and no narrower alleys ran
between buildings. Unencumbered by armor, she had a speed
advantage over the dragonborn, but she kept slowing to avoid
colliding with bystanders who stepped into her path and reached
their clawed hands to grab at her. For a moment she imagined she
felt the wind hurrying her along, as it had when she and Gaven ran
through Stormhome, and tears sprang to her eyes again.

She reached a branch where another wide road wound up
to the fifth tier, and she sped around the corner, praying to the
Sovereigns that she'd find someplace to hide. Instead, less than
a hundred paces up the street, she found her path blocked by
another group of guards, pointing heavy-bladed polearms at her.
She glanced over her shoulder and confirmed that the other soldiers were still behind her. Trapped.

Rienne struggled to quell her panic and quiet her mind,
reaching for the still point of energy within. It eluded her. She
stopped running, mindful of the positions of both groups of soldiers, closed her eyes, and drew a deep breath. Letting it slowly

out through pursed lips, she found her focus, and the still point rippled out through her body. With a sharp burst of breath, she resumed her run. One foot landed on a carved stone dragon by a doorway and she leaped.

She turned once in the air, then landed on her feet on a peaked roof, looking down at the astonished soldiers. Another slow breath, then she turned and ran. She dropped from her perch to another roof, crowning a building on the street where she'd first met the guards. Turning then, she ran up the sloping roofs and down the other side, leaping from building to building without breaking her stride. When she neared the far end of that street, she was confident that she had eluded the guards, and she dropped down into an enclosed garden behind what might have been a temple or another shrine of the Prophecy.

Her hand on Maelstrom's hilt, she stood silent in the garden, listening for any sign of approaching movement. An emerald green dragonet screeched at her and flew away, and then all was still.

As her pulse slowly calmed to normal, she sat with her back against the smooth stone wall and wept.

* * * * *

For three days, she huddled in the shadows of Rav Magar. She ate from the magic journeybread that had sustained her and Gaven since they made land and wondered what Gaven was eating. She wrapped herself in her silk, trying to cloak her appearance, perhaps pass as a withered and elderly dragonborn shielding her skin from the sun. By day, she slept fitfully in gardens or courtyards, starting awake at every sound. At night, she skulked in the darkness, avoiding any contact with the dragonborn and working her way slowly up to the highest tiers of the city.

Rav Magar was quiet and mysterious at night. In contrast to a busy city like Stormhome or Fairhaven, where any hour of night saw some people about on business, whether legitimate or not, the streets of Rav Magar were all but deserted by a few bells after sundown. The dragonborn marked the onset of night much as they did the dawn, with strange songs and what seemed to be simple household rituals conducted at window-side shrines. Dragonets crowded the air, jostling for the scraps of meat offered to them in these rituals. As the dragonets flew off, satiated, lamps winked out and the city drifted into silence.

In the silent night streets, Rienne drifted as well, thinking of Gaven and staring up at the ten full moons that began to wane as the two others waxed to prominence. Slowly, she navigated the maze of streets to the highest tiers of the city. Only once in three nights of wandering did she encounter another patrol of soldiers. She crouched beside a large dragon statue and watched them pass, drowsy-eyed and completely unaware of her presence.

On the third night, she reached the pinnacle of the city, where the dragon-king's palace raised its single tower to the sky. Every entrance was a great archway large enough, she realized, for a dragon to pass through. Four entrances opened onto the street, and three more yawned in the walls up the entire tower's height. She saw dragonborn guards, clad in armor made of blackened bone, posted at all seven arches. Staying to the shadows, she watched the palace for the rest of the day and through the night, noting when the guards switched shifts, observing the few dragonborn who entered and left the palace.

Sneaking in seemed impossible. When the guards changed, there was no lapse in the watch—the guards didn't leave until their relief was settled in place. The guards searched all who sought to enter the palace, confiscated their weapons, and questioned them extensively. There was no entrance that had fewer than four guards, and the ones she could get to without sprouting wings all had at least six.

She could fight her way through six or eight guards with little difficulty, but then what? The alarm would be raised, wave upon wave of guards would arrive to block her way. Gaven would get extra guards—they would know she was there to find him. Assuming he was actually in the palace and not in some prison elsewhere in the city.

Three more days passed in watching, waiting for something to change, some opportunity to arise, some sign to appear. On the morning of her sixth day of watching, something like a sign appeared. A dragon flew overhead, its scales gleaming copper in the sunlight. Its wings rippled rather than flapped as it swooped down and landed in one of the high arches of the palace. It perched there like an enormous bird for fully half an hour before jumping down into a chamber below.

Rienne wanted desperately to be that dragon, to spread great wings and fly to an open archway, to peer down and see, she imagined, Gaven on the floor of the chamber below. She would jump down beside him, let him climb on her back, feel his hands on her smooth scales, and then she'd fly back up and out, far away from Rav Magar—she'd fly until Argonnessen was a distant memory and the lands of Khorvaire spread out before them, until the towers and docks of Stormhome came into view.

A rumble of thunder jolted her from her reverie. The sky was clouding over, clouds forming from nowhere, directly over the dragon-king's palace. Gaven was inside and alive! And in danger.

She sprang into action, tossing aside the tattered rags that wrapped her. Maelstrom had already begun its deadly dance by the time she reached the guards at the nearest gate, and two of them fell before they knew what was happening. Thunder rumbled again, and she lifted her voice in elation. Two more guards lay dead. Lightning struck the palace, very near, shaking the ground and walls around her. She was past the guards, but more were charging down the passage toward her.

She heard rain on the roof, and she laughed as she cut through the guards. He's here! she thought. He is the Storm Dragon, and his storm will lift us out of here, together.

Another blast of lightning shook the palace, and wind howled through the passage, blowing at her back as though Gaven were calling her to him. The second wave of guards was dead or dying, and she ran unhindered with the wind. It led her unerringly through a maze of corridors until the passage opened into a chamber. Lightning struck again as she hurtled toward the archway. She saw the wind lifting dust and rubble into a whirlwind, and she knew that Gaven stood at the top of that column of air.

"Gaven!" she cried, but the wind swallowed her voice.

A flash of copper broke the whirlwind and brought Gaven to the ground. A shimmer of white light filled the chamber. She was almost there—in a moment she would be with Gaven again.

An enormous slab of stone fell from the roof of the chamber and crashed to the ground. The wind died, and she peered through a cloud of dust to the empty chamber beyond.

CHAPTER
32

A ric spent the remainder of the afternoon in the only form of meditation he knew—concentrating on every part of his body in turn, top of the head to soles of the feet, fixing the details in his mind. Seeking perfect focus, but constantly struggling to banish memories of Kelas, thoughts of his companions on this journey, and worries about the ceremony ahead.

"Who are you?" he asked himself.

"Aric," he answered, unsure what else to say. "From the Carrion Tribes, but I don't know the name of my tribe. I'm about to join the Ghaash'kala, because the alternative is death. I'm a coward, a soft-hearted fool, and a travesty of a spy."

Once more, head to toe. "Who are you?"

"I don't know. I'm not sure I care anymore. I'm dead."

His head felt light. He realized he'd been speaking aloud—pathetic. He closed his eyes, trying to clear his head, find his focus. Instead, he fell asleep, eventually slumping to the floor.

* * * * *

"Deep in meditation, I see." Farren's voice jolted Aric from sleep.

Aric scrambled to his feet, but Farren seemed more amused than angry.

"Are you ready?" the paladin said, clapping him on the shoulder.

He nodded, too tired to speak, and shuffled behind Farren down the tower steps to the plaza.

Just like the night before, orcs of the Ghaash'kala crowded the plaza, but this time there were humans scattered through the crowd in small clumps as well. The Carrion Tribe converts apparently participated in the recommitment ceremonies, but not the memorials. Aric wondered whether they had their own ways of honoring the dead.

A clear path opened up before him, leading to the center of the plaza where the same orc priestess stood waiting, though today her robes were yellow. There was one other person waiting to take his vows, an orc boy of perhaps twelve or fourteen—ready, among the Ghaash'kala, to pick up a sword and fight the evils of the Labyrinth.

As he stood before the priestess, he felt the eyes of the crowd on him, and he felt naked. His heart pounded, and his eyes darted around as if he could somehow find a way to escape. He had never been more trapped or more exposed. How could everyone present not recognize him for a sham, even as a spy?

"Maruk Ghaash'kala," the priestess said, her arms lifted and spread wide. "On this third night of gathering, we come as a tribe to witness the vows of these two men and welcome them among our ranks, warriors who will fight beside us. Hearing their vows, we will remember our own—our promise to serve Kalok Shash and participate in its work. Many of our tribe have fallen, but tonight we celebrate the replenishment of our numbers."

Replenishment? Aric thought. How many names were lifted up the night before? How many of the Maruk had died in the past three months? Farren alone had listed a dozen. And now two men came to fill their places. The Maruk Ghaash'kala were dying out.

"Ghaarat," the priestess said, standing before the boy and looking solemnly into his eyes, "today you die. As a ghost, you will fight the demons of the Wastes and their human servants, the foul beasts and mighty warlords. You will fight until at last you have proved yourself worthy of joining Kalok Shash. Are you ready?"

"I am," young Ghaarat said, no hint of fear or hesitation in his voice.

"Do you swear, before Kalok Shash and all the Maruk Ghaash'kala, to fight against evil in all its forms?"

"I do."

"Do you swear, before Kalok Shash and all the Maruk Ghaash'kala, to permit nothing, living or dead, to pass through the Labyrinth, either to leave the Wastes or to enter them?"

"I do."

"Do you swear, before Kalok Shash and all the Maruk Ghaash'kala, to fight without fear, to fight until your foes are dead or you join Kalok Shash?"

"I do."

The priestess turned, and a warrior stepped forward from the encircling crowd, a sword clutched in both hands.

"Ash Ghaal," the priestess said to this man, "do you swear to guide Ghaarat in the ways of the Maruk Ghaash'kala, so that he might be found worthy to join Kalok Shash?"

"I do," the man said, his voice choked with emotion.

The priestess turned back to the boy. "Ghaarat, you die this day." She nodded to the man.

Ash Ghaal stepped forward and swung his sword at Ghaarat's neck. The boy didn't flinch, and the sword stopped a finger's breadth from his flesh.

"Ghost of Ghaarat, join the Maruk Ghaash'kala."

The man embraced Ghaarat—his son, Aric realized with a start—and drew him back into the encircling crowd. Aric stood alone before the priestess. She came and looked into his eyes. Her eyes were rich brown, and he lost himself in them, aware of nothing else. Her brow furrowed for a moment, as though she were troubled by what she saw in his eyes, but she continued with barely a pause.

"Aric, today you die. As a ghost, you will fight the demons of the Wastes and their human servants, the foul beasts and mighty warlords. You will fight until at last you have proved yourself worthy of joining Kalok Shash. Are you ready?"

Am I ready? Aric wondered. Will I ever be worthy of joining Kalok Shash?

"I am," he said, but he did not believe it. His voice was a croak, and he cleared his throat.

"Do you swear, before Kalok Shash and all the Maruk Ghaash'kala, to fight against evil in all its forms?"

Aric opened his mouth, but he could not speak. He could see only the priestess's brown eyes, darkness closing in around them. "I—" he managed, but then the darkness swallowed him.

* * * * *

He was running, leaves lashing his face, thin branches grabbing at him as he passed. He was hunched, looking for something on the ground, and he had no face. He caught a glimpse of her—a doe rabbit bounding through the brush—and then she was gone.

Then he was a rabbit, fleeing a hungry fox. He ran as fast as he could, but the fox was faster, and no matter how many times he darted in a different direction, the fox always seemed to be drawing nearer. With one great pounce, it hit him, its claws pressing against his skin, its great fanged muzzle staring down into his face that was not a face.

"Why do you run?" the fox asked.

He was pinned beneath a boulder, part of an avalanche, and he stood at the top of a sheer slope and knew he had caused the rocks to tumble. He saw the swallow he'd been chasing swoop and swerve as it flew away, forever beyond his reach.

A gust of wind came up the slope and lifted him into the air, and he was in a whirlwind, lightning flashing all around him. An airship circled with the wind, and Gaven stood on the deck, reaching an arm out to him. Rienne walked to him, straight across the whirlwind, smiling. As she drew near, she extended her arms to embrace him.

Her two arms became four, and then six, and then she grinned cruelly as her legs became a long, snaky tail. There were swords in her hands, and they whirled and flashed like the storm, they cut and cut and cut and he screamed—

"Plaguebearers," said a voice whose source he could not see. "They were trying to infect him, and he lifted one of their weapons."

The demonic figure fell on top of him, and her face was no longer Rienne's face but Dania's. Her six arms were two again, and her legs straddled him. Her body moved against his, and she smiled down at him, her short red hair falling into her face. She reached up to push it back, and said, "Why do you resist me?"

Then she was the Plaguebearer lying on top of him, leering at him, infecting him, and he pushed the body off and stood in a deserted cathedral, like the one in Fairhaven but larger, and dozens of doors lined the walls of the enormous sanctuary. He walked across the mosaic floor, leaving footprints in the dust, and grabbed a door handle at random. The door swung open and a skeleton tumbled toward him. He stepped over it to enter the dark hallway beyond.

He walked in darkness, sure that his destination lay at the end of the hall. There was no light, nothing leading him onward except his certainty that the object of all his desire lay ahead. He couldn't even imagine what it might be, but the thought of finding it at last filled him with joy and excited anticipation. On and on through the darkness he walked, untiring. The hall began to slope upward, and he walked, and he climbed, and then he saw light, but it was overhead, and the hall was too steep to climb. The floor was smooth, then slick with blood, but he clawed for purchase, he refused to let it slide him back.

A coolness spread through him, quenching the fires that burned in his veins, and the darkness dissolved into soft red light. He floated, warm and comfortable. He couldn't see his body, he tried to lift a hand to his face but saw nothing—he was no longer sure that he was in his body.

"Aric," came another voice. "Or whatever your name is. Can you hear me?"

He could not answer, couldn't move, couldn't breathe.

"Who are you?"

The water pressed in around him, squeezing the breath and life from him, and he kicked furiously to reach the surface. His lungs screamed for air, but the water was so deep, so dark, he was no longer sure he swam in the right direction. Was there a hint of light above him, a faint glow in the blue? He kicked harder, but something tangled his legs, seaweed or—

He drew a great gasping breath, but the tentacles still held him, drew him in, then he was looking into a single great staring eye.

"Why do you struggle?"

A mace appeared in his hand and he swung it over and over, beating back the tentacles. Vor stood over him, hacking at tentacles as they appeared through the portal. "I'll hold them back," Vor said. "You seal it."

He kneeled beside the portal and laid a hand on it, trying to feel the knot of magic inside. It was too complex. His mind couldn't fathom its intricacies. It was a labyrinth—

And he was walking it, smooth crystal walls stretching as high above him as he could see. Straight corridors crossed and branched, and again he knew that everything he wanted was waiting for him at the exit from this maze. He wandered and wandered, then the maze was the Labyrinth, and he stumbled along, weak from hunger and thirst, half-blind from sun.

He fell, gravel pressing into his cheek. He didn't think he could stand again. Feet crunched the gravel and rolled him over. A field of blood red sky, framed by canyon walls.

"Who are you?" the Traveler asked him, her face shadowed by a brilliant sun behind her.

"Kalok Shash," he said through parched lips, and the Traveler withdrew from him.

"He changes constantly, a new face every few moments. Is he possessed?"

A hand on his forehead, and again coolness washed through him. "No."

"What, then? A demon? Should we not kill him now, before he regains his strength?"

"He is no demon, and no warrior kills a man while he is helpless. And he is a man, though he is obviously a man of many faces. He is ill, and we will care for him until he recovers."

"He deceived us."

"He didn't deceive me. I've seen his heart, and I know both the goodness and the evil there. Has anyone else seen what you saw?"

"No."

"Good. Then no one but you is to care for him, and you will admit no one but me to his presence. Do you understand?"

"I understand."

The Traveler withdrew from him, and he chased after.

* * * * *

Haccra approached the black pavilion, fear gripping her stomach. She hated approaching the chieftain, hated what she endured every time she entered his presence. But it was her duty.

She looked up at the banners as she passed, bone white with the chieftain's rune painted in blood. They made her heart beat faster—with excitement at the conquest they promised, and with fear.

Two guards stepped forward and seized her arms. She did not struggle.

"Do you bring news the chieftain wishes to hear?"

"I do."

"What tribe are you from?"

"I have no tribe. I serve only Kathrik Mel."

Not releasing her arms, they shuffled her forward into the pavilion, forcing her head down as they entered, then pushing her face to the ground. Only when she was prostrate did they release her.

"Haccra." His voice glided over her skin, smooth and exciting. "You may lift your head."

Slowly she did, and he grew into her vision—first his armor-clad feet and the twitching tip of his fleshy tail, the bloodstained plate armor he wore and his strangely delicate hands, fingers tipped with razor-sharp claws. She shivered at the memory of those claws tracing lines of blood in her skin. She could not look at his face.

"What news do you bring me?" Tingles ran down her spine.

"Our scouts found the stronghold of the Maruk."

"At last." He stepped closer. "This is excellent news, Haccra. What reward would you choose?"

"Pain." Pain hurt so much less than the pleasure he offered.

CHAPTER
33

S omeone sat beside Aric where he lay, and he was surprised to realize that it was not the Traveler, Dania, Rienne, Vor, or any of the bizarre figures that had haunted his dreams. It was Farren, laying a cool hand on his head and driving away the last of his fever.

"How do you feel?" Farren asked. There was concern in his voice, but his eyes didn't meet Aric's.

"Am I still dreaming?"

Farren smiled and drew his hand away. "No, I'm really here. You must have been having some strange dreams, based on what Lharat and I have heard. And seen."

Aric's heart leaped, but he steadied it with a thought. He had been completely out of control for—how long? It might have been hours or days. What had he revealed?

"Very strange," he said.

Farren stood and turned to look out the window. "Kathrik Mel's horde will be here soon. I fear that our city will fall."

"No!" The word burst from Aric's mouth, surprising him with its passion.

If Maruk Dar fell, one feeble beacon of hope in the Labyrinth would be extinguished, and it would be his fault.

"We're ready," Farren said. "We are already dead, and Kalok Shash will burn much brighter when Maruk Dar falls."

Aric envisioned the Binding Flame, growing brighter with each soul added to it, stretched across the Labyrinth as a barrier against the advancing horde. But he could not imagine it holding Kathrik Mel back. Not without a living army to back it up.

"You could flee the city, join with the other Ghaash'kala,

make a concerted defense where they leave the Labyrinth—"

"The Maruk Ghaash'kala will make their stand here, defending their homes. Though we cannot triumph, we can at least make their horde smaller." Farren turned away from the window to look at Aric again. "But you are not Maruk Ghaash'kala."

"I would have been. I was ready to take my vow."

"But you did not. Your illness saved you from joining the ranks of the dead."

"I will join them soon enough, defending this doomed city." The thought made Aric proud. The idea that he, too, could die in the service of something he actually believed in—perhaps the only thing he had ever believed in. . . .

He imagined standing beside Vor, Dania, and Farren's dead brother Durrnak, all smiling.

Horns sounded from the walls of Maruk Dar. "They're coming," Farren said. "I do not want you to die defending Maruk Dar."

"What?" How strange it felt, to have his chance at martyrdom snatched away. For a moment, he feared that Farren was about to draw his sword and make sure Aric didn't have a chance to die defending the city.

"Listen." Farren sat on a stool beside the bed. "I don't know who you really are, and I don't know what allows you to change your face, as I've seen you do."

"You lied to me," Kelas said, his voice wounded, almost piteous.

Laurann felt shame well in her chest, and she lowered her head.

"After all I've done for you, you betray me like this?" Kelas added. Tears were welling in his eyes, grief etched his face.

Something was wrong—this was not like Kelas.

"Aren't you ashamed?" he whined.

Laurann nodded, and Kelas flew into a rage. "Never be ashamed!" He slapped her. "You're supposed to lie to get what you want. Deception is your life!" One more slap, for good measure.

Laurann stood her ground, staring straight ahead, her shame dispelled by a rising tide of hatred.

"Never confess to a lie," Kelas added. "And never, ever feel shame! Shame is weakness, and your enemies will exploit it."

That had been the first time she felt shame, and the last—

Until now. All the time he'd convinced himself that he believed in the ideals of Kalok Shash, he had been lying to Farren and all those who sought to live out those ideals. After all they'd done for him, he had betrayed them.

"Farren, I—"

The paladin cut him off. "I no longer care. I know there's nothing demonic about you. I know that your desire to fight and die alongside the Maruk Ghaash'kala is sincere, that the call of Kalok Shash is real to you. I want you to heed that call in a different way."

"What?" After all Aric's deception, Farren called him sincere?

Farren glanced at the door. "The Carrion Tribes will attack within the hour. We will hold them back as long as we can, but within a week Maruk Dar will fall. Then there will be nothing between Kathrik Mel and the eastern mountains. They'll cross the mountains, and they won't stop until a big enough army makes them stop."

Aric thought of the Towering Wood in flames, the fields of Aundair razed. How far would the warlord go? South into Breland? He might be stopped by Scions Sound and the Mournland. But he might not—what was the Mournland to Kathrik Mel, used to life in the Demon Wastes?

"What is it you want me to do?" he asked.

"I want you to make sure that a big enough army meets him soon, before his evil can spread far."

"But how—"

"You will flee Maruk Dar and leave the Labyrinth and go back across the mountains to warn the peoples of the east."

"Leave the Labyrinth? But your vow—"

"Even sacred vows must sometimes be broken. I'll let one man I know is mostly untainted escape into the Labyrinth if it means the greater taint of the Carrion Tribes can be contained."

"Silence!" Durrnak cried. "You knowingly allowed a demon to escape the Labyrinth and enter the world beyond! There is nothing to discuss."

"A pregnant woman, Durrnak!"

*"Carrying the taint of evil in her womb as well as in her blood!
You knew our holy command, and you disregarded it. Your sentence
has been passed, and you will die here today."*

Mostly untainted, Farren had said. Yet it had been Kauth's
mace that staggered Farren's own brother, a paladin who held so
strictly to his vows. Kauth had led Vor, Sevren, and Zandar to
their deaths—he had provoked Kathrik Mel into this eastward
march!

What greater taint could I possibly bear? he wondered.

"I don't think you really know my heart," Aric said.

Farren looked directly into his eyes. "Yes," he said. "I do."

*   *   *   *   *

As he fastened the straps of his armor, Kathrik Mel could
barely contain his excitement. He pulled each strap just a little
too tight, savoring the exquisite nips of pain as leather and metal
pressed into his skin. For far too long, his hordes had done his
fighting for him, exterminating pockets of Ghaash'kala scouts
long before they presented any serious threat. But they had
reached the stronghold of the Maruk clan, and it promised to be a
battle worthy of his involvement.

His armor on, he snatched the sword from Haccra's hands. It
was the sword he'd claimed from the dead shifter, who was not
worthy of such a blade. "Bloodclaw," he whispered. The sword had
consented to reveal its name to him, but the secrets of its power
were still a mystery. Perhaps when the Maruk had fallen, the
blood-drenched sword would tell him more.

He strode from his pavilion, blinking in the unusually bright
sunlight, and surveyed the walls of Maruk Dar. The orcs were
sounding horns, calling their fellows to the city's defense. His
scouts had told him that all the Maruk were within—it was one of
their gathering times. Haccra had warned him to wait until they
had dispersed again, and he had cut out her tongue. With all the
Maruk gathered in one place, he could destroy them all in a single
blow.

It was time.

* * * * *

After making sure Aric was equipped with new armor, a new mace, and a pack full of food and water, Farren led him to the back of Maruk Dar, where the city nestled into the wall of the Labyrinth. Half a tower seemed to grow from the stone, reaching up the cliff face. Together they climbed a narrow stair, spiraling partly in the tower and partly through the cliff, until they reached a large room at the top. It, too, was a full circle, half embedded in the cliff, strengthening the impression that the tower had somehow sunk into the cliff or been partly engulfed by it. The room was bare.

"It's over here," Farren said, walking to the wall in the room's cliff-facing side.

"What is?"

In answer, Farren passed his hand over the wall and tripped a catch Aric couldn't see, and a section of wall detached from the rest and slid toward them. When it stopped moving, Farren pushed it to one side, revealing a tunnel descending into blackness.

"It's a long tunnel. From time to time some burrowing creature stumbles upon it and uses it for a nest—we don't patrol it very often. So be on your guard. When you come out, you'll still be in the Labyrinth, but from that point, if you go left at every branch you will soon find yourself at the feet of the mountains."

Aric nodded, peering down the tunnel.

"Aric. I have only shown this path to one person before, and I am still not sure I did the right thing. Please do not disappoint me."

One person before—Aric knew in a flash of insight. "Vor," he said. "Voraash. You helped him escape."

Farren's eyes shot wide and his mouth fell open. "How did you know?"

"I traveled here with Vor. He's dead now—and Kalok Shash burns brighter. You did the right thing."

Except that Vor killed your brother, Aric thought.

"I knew he had not truly fallen," Farren said. "I knew his heart, just as I know yours. Go now."

Aric struggled to find words, but Farren hurried him into the tunnel and closed the door behind him without another word.

* * * * *

It was time for a new face. He would emerge from the tunnel, and from the Labyrinth, a new person.

As he walked through the tunnel, he began by casting his memory over past identities. Haunderk, Faura, and Laurann—those were faces he had worn during his earliest training at Kelas's brutal hands. They would not do. Laurann, though, whose grief at killing Kyra had been so strong, and who confessed to shame, made him think of other sympathetic women. There was Caura Fannam, the soldier who escaped Haldren's camp with Jenns, then left him alone in the forest to die. No. Maura Hann, who had been a mother as well as a lover to so many foreign spies, coaxing secrets from them when she held them close. No. He thought of Rienne, the kindest and most caring woman he had known. But he had never been that kind of woman. He had bruised too many hearts.

Baunder Fronn. He could not believe that he had lived three months as a simple Aundairian farmer. No, Baunder was not the kind of man who would walk out of the Labyrinth alive. Auftane—no, he had betrayed Dania, taking the torc from her body. Dania ir'Vran—he had thought of her when he chose another name, Vauren Hennalan. Vauren infiltrated the Knights of Thrane and found their morality rubbing off on him—perhaps he'd started this whole mess, nurtured the first seeds of conscience in the changeling's heart. Vauren had been unable to kill the unconscious dwarf, Natan Durbannek. But Vauren was still a spy, posing as a Knight while gathering intelligence about Thrane's troop movements before Starcrag Plain. Still Kelas's tool.

He had always been a tool in Kelas's hand. It was time for a new face entirely—the face of a free man.

Tall—tall and proud. Like Kauth and Aric, but less bulky, less hard. Short, straight hair, dark but with a sprinkling of gray at the temples, distinguished. Brown eyes, warm—he would need a mirror to do those properly, but he sketched them in. Skin tanned from travel but not too weathered. He would retrieve a cache of money when he returned to civilization and use it to buy new armor and clothes, so his garb would match the nobility of his face and body. He liked this person already.

Now this noble figure needed a name. Haunderk Lannath, Auftane Khunnam, Darraun Mennar. Aura, Caura, Faura, Maura. He was not very creative when it came to names—they were all variations on his real name, with the AU in the first name and the double N in the last. Laurann only needed one name. Couldn't he just be Aunn? No more secrets, no more lies?

"My name is Aunn," he said aloud. "I am Aunn. No, just Aunn."

Like Gaven—no family name. But Gaven was excoriate—he'd lost the right to use his name.

"I am Aunn," he said again. "And don't be fooled by my handsome face—I'm actually a changeling."

He didn't think he could be that honest.

CHAPTER
34

It was better than the prison of the dragon-king in Rav Magar, but Gaven was no less a prisoner in Kelas's camp. The shackles never came off his wrists, and his legs were chained to a stake in the ground as well as each other. He might have been able to pull up the stake, but Haldren had spoken some ritual over it to root it in the ground. He got some food and ample water, but he remained out in the open, day and night, and the midday heat was nearly unbearable. He tried once to shade the sun with clouds, but any time clouds began to form in the sky, his guards beat him savagely. His head felt like more bump than bone.

He barely slept, and when he did nightmares plagued him. Looking for meaning, he sifted through the scraps of dreams, but found only horror and despair. He dreamed of Rienne—he saw her killed in terrible ways, wrenched from his grasp by demonic figures, and transformed into a hideous aberration or a demonic creature. He always woke with tears in his eyes, facing the Dragon Forge and feeling the evil presence at its heart. It filled him with loathing, and he was certain that it was responsible for the nightmares.

With every passing day, the Dragon Forge grew. He caught some glimpses of the apparatus the artificers were constructing at its heart—a strange thing with moving arms and long levers—but the walls going up around it soon shielded it from his view. Upon a framework of arching beams, the workers built a structure that vaguely resembled a crouching dragon. They shaped a sort of dome to resemble a dragon's folded wings, open at the back around the blue crystal and the cylindrical receptacles, with enough space for the dragon-king to enter there. At the end of a long hall stretching forward into the canyon, they built a dragon's head, its mouth open in a small archway leading into the heart of the forge.

From time to time, a new caravan of parts and supplies arrived in the camp, sparking a flurry of activity and some confusion. Each time, Gaven watched for an opportunity to escape, some kind of opening, but his guards remained as vigilant and brutal as ever. Wagons passed right by him, sometimes sending him scrambling to avoid their turning wheels, but only his guards seemed to notice him at all.

The days and nights blurred together. Weeks might have passed, but he could not track the time. As the Dragon Forge neared completion, Gaven started piecing together the fragments of his dreams. He was quite certain now that he had seen this forge—completed, burning with dragonfire—more than once in all his visions. He remembered looking down into the canyon, being led down an iron hall, the heat and bursts of fire—and when he followed the memories too far, excruciating pain. The memory of the pain was so vivid that it made his flesh tingle, particularly on his neck and chest, around his dragonmark.

He dreamed of that hall again, entering through the arch of the dragon's mouth. He descended amid clouds of smoke billowing up from the heart of the Dragon Forge. Chains bound his hands and feet, clanking against the iron floor as he walked, then stumbled. A hand on his shoulder steadied him. Then it was shaking him gently, and he woke to a dark night.

"Gaven?" It was Cart.

Gaven tried to sit up, starting his chains rattling, but Cart gripped his shoulder again to stop him.

"Quiet," Cart whispered.

"What do you want?" Gaven asked, too loudly.

Cart looked around nervously at the sound. "Gaven, please. If Haldren sees me talking to you—"

"He can't make it any worse for me. The rest is your problem."

Cart looked down. "We parted on good terms, Gaven."

"I think that changed when I found you in league with the people who captured me, the ones who've been starving me and beating my head in."

"I had nothing to do with your capture."

"But here you are. What's happening, Cart?"

"Haldren only just told me, this evening. I swear, if I had known before, I wouldn't have let them—"

"If you'd known what?"

"What the Dragon Forge is for."

Gaven's breath caught in his chest as a vague memory of dreams full of fire and pain stirred in his mind. "And what's that?" he asked.

"They intend to harness the power of your dragonmark. To strip it from you—"

"They're siphoning the power of the things imprisoned here in order to harness the power of my mark? Then what? Use it to get power from something else?" Cart's words finally caught up with Gaven. "Strip it from me?"

"I told you, if I'd known—"

"Cut it from my skin, like they used to do with excoriates?" Gaven shuddered with the memory of pain, the excruciating pain of his dream. "And then use it . . ."

"As a weapon of war."

"When?"

"I'm not certain. I don't think Kelas is either. They'll use the weapon as leverage with the queen—"

"I mean when are they taking my mark?"

Cart hesitated. "Tomorrow."

"So we have to get out of here tonight." Gaven's chains rattled again.

"I'm sorry, Gaven."

"What?"

"I told you before, my place is with Haldren."

The pang of disappointment Gaven had felt when he first saw Cart returned, accompanied by a sick feeling in his stomach. "You could be so much more than Haldren's aide."

"Why do people keep telling me that?"

"Because it's true. Once you stood on the threshold of godhood—"

"And like you, I turned away."

"Yes, and now you need to take your destiny into your own hands. As I did."

"I have." Cart's voice was quiet and low. "I've chosen to do my duty."

Gaven's disappointment soured into disgust. "Duty? Duty is a soldier's excuse for his crimes, a coward's excuse—"

"You call me a coward?" Cart's voice was more incredulous than offended.

"—for not doing what he's too afraid to do. It's the master's hold on the slave, the father's claim on his son." His father's face flashed into his mind, the forced smile he wore after Gaven's failed Test of Siberys. Gaven had always failed to live up to his duty.

"Duty is what holds society together," Cart said.

"That's what the generals, queens, and fathers want you to think. Duty's what keeps you from protesting when they enslave you."

"The words of a true fugitive from Dreadhold."

Gaven bit back a retort about Haldren and shook his head. He was making no progress, and he wasn't sure why he was trying. "Why did you come here, Cart? Why warn me? Is that part of your duty?"

"You were never a soldier," Cart said. "Let me tell you something. Sometimes in the war we fought the Brelish, sometimes we marched beside them to fight the Thranes. Once I met a warforged soldier from Breland, Dodge was his name. We fought the Thranes together at Harrow's Pass in the Blackcaps—not too far from here, actually. We talked in the camp while the others slept."

The Blackcaps were not too far—that was Gaven's first hint of where they were.

Cart's voice grew hard. "A month later, the tides of war shifted and Breland was our enemy again. At the battle of Silver Lake, I met him on the field. Now, we were enemies. That didn't mean we hated each other. We saluted each other with the greatest respect. He had been my friend. But duty demanded that we fight, because the victory of one of us could mean victory for his nation. So I killed him."

"And did Aundair win the battle?"

Cart stood and looked down at Gaven where he lay, still in chains.

"You completely miss my point," the warforged said. "But yes, we did."

"What is your point, then?"

"I salute you, Gaven Storm Dragon—with nothing but respect. I hold no hatred for you. I am proud to have known you."

"And Dodge returned your salute, did he? Faced death like a dutiful soldier?"

Cart stared down, impassive as always.

"Well forget that." Gaven spat at Cart's feet. "The war's over, Cart. You're as much a criminal as I am, and a more cold-blooded killer. I used to respect you, but I don't any more."

Cart's unblinking eyes fixed him for a long moment, then he turned away without another word.

A crash of thunder brought two guards running to knock Gaven out again.

* * * * *

He stood on a floor like glass, traced with coiling lines of light. He walked along the twisting path they formed, and they rose up behind him as he walked, a tangled spiderweb hanging in the air. Recognition slowly dawned on him. The lines were his dragonmark, the Siberys Mark of Storm. Suddenly the path was not a line of light anymore, but a round tunnel carved through rock. He trailed his fingertips along the rough walls as he walked, and the winding tunnel spoke to him of the Prophecy and his place in it.

The dream-words made no sense to his sleeping mind, but they made him sad. He was lying in a swinging cot, and Rienne's fingertip was tracing the path on his skin, and he kissed her forehead. Her eyes, full of tears, looked into his, then she was wrenched away from him into the darkness.

He slowly surfaced toward consciousness, dimly aware that he had not said good-bye to Rienne and he might not have a chance to. Then a kick to his stomach jolted him fully awake.

It was the Thuranni, Phaine, standing over him, wearing a

malicious grin. "Wake up, Gaven," he said in his whispery voice. "It's time to play your part."

His head still muddled from his dreams, Gaven allowed himself to be lifted to his feet. They led him on a winding path to reach the rim of the canyon. Phaine followed behind until they reached a spot directly above the Dragon Forge. The dragon-king was there, head high as it looked down on the completed forge. Kelas, looking somber and suspicious, watched Gaven approach. Haldren watched him too, but Cart did not look his way. There was a woman at Cart's side, whispering to him and pointing down at the forge, but Cart seemed oblivious. A few others Gaven didn't recognize filled out the knot of people.

"It begins," the dragon-king said, and a burst of fire rose up around the forge below. In the distance, a horrible rumbling howl arose, starting with a single voice and growing into a ghastly chorus before fading away again. The guards led Gaven to the cliff edge and he saw the forge complete and ready for him.

He was back in his dream—the vision he'd had months ago, as he and Senya rode the lightning rail out of Zil'argo. In stark contrast to his first view of the canyon, the earth around it was desolate, and the canyon had taken on the appearance of a gash torn into the earth. At the heart of this gaping wound was a cloud of smoke and steam billowing up from the canyon floor, from the trenches dug into it, from the base of the Dragon Forge.

The dragon-king's neck swung around and its burning eyes took in the people gathered at his feet, lingering longest on Kelas. "You suspect the significance of this moment," he said, "but you know only a glimpse of it. To you, the completion of the Dragon Forge is the climax of your plans and schemes, or this stage of them. It paves the way for the next, greater stage."

Gaven wondered how many of the assembly understood the dragon-king's words. Kelas, certainly. How would he react to the revelation that his mighty schemes were a tiny part of Malathar's much larger plans?

The dragon-king raised his head higher, so he was looking down at Kelas. "It plays much the same role in the history of the world," he said, "though you see it not. We stand at an axis point, the very center of history around which all the rest revolves. An age of the world has ended, a new one is about to begin, and we are in the Time Between."

The center of history—Gaven had described it to Rienne as a point that history revolves around. He'd been right, then. To Malathar's mind, the Time Between was the pivotal moment in history, with the Time of the Dragon Above merely its prelude, and the Time of the Dragon Below its aftershock.

The Time Between begins with blood and ends in blood.
Blood is its harbinger, and blood flows in its passing.

"At the birth of time," the dragon-king continued, "the three dragons were united, but they broke apart. In the Time Between they are united again. At the end of the ages, they will be united a third time. What you have accomplished here speeds the world on its course to completion."

Kelas shifted impatiently, and Malathar dropped his head to stare right into his face. Kelas stumbled backward. "Do my words bore you, meat?"

"Of course not," Kelas said. "Only look at the sky."

The dragon-king swung his neck to look upward, to see the clouds gathering there in answer to Gaven's distress. "No matter," he said. "The storm will not answer him much longer."

The dragon-king raised his skeletal wings and took to the air, their tattered flesh lifting him without a breath of wind. He swooped at Gaven and snatched him up in one great claw, tearing him from the grasp of the guards who held his chains. Gaven watched below as he fell with the dragon-king into the canyon. The ground and the metal wings of the Dragon Forge rushed up at him as it had in his dream among billowing clouds of hot smoke.

Malathar swept into the wide gap between the crystal prison and the walls of the Dragon Forge and set Gaven down inside. Waves of heat assaulted him, rising from the furnaces below. The iron dragon's wings formed a dome that arched high above Gaven's head, leaving the dragon-king just enough room to rear up to his full height. The bizarre apparatus Gaven had glimpsed during the forge's construction towered over him like a massive pillar, silver tracing forming twisting symbols across its surface. Tubes and rods, gemstones and glass clustered around its lower portions like barnacles encrusting a stately galleon. Its bottom disappeared into the smoke and fire below.

Metal grates formed the floor around the apparatus, covering a trench dug like a moat protecting it. On scaffolding below, a few people moved around, wielding strange tools to adjust a pipeline here or a cylinder there. Jets of flame burst in erratic rhythm from spouts shaped like dragon heads beneath them, the crimson light of the fire turning them into sinister shadows, like devils tending the flames of Fernia. A dragon snaked into his view, crouching low to the scaffold, wings folded so they didn't brush the grating above. It looked up and met his gaze, then hissed angrily, loosing plumes of smoke from its nostrils. A wave of vertigo washed over him as he stared down into the raging furnace.

A heavy hand on his shoulder steadied him, and he grabbed at it. The metal of Cart's hand was warm against his skin. He tore his gaze from the fire and turned to look at the warforged, but the sight of the crystal prison behind Cart stopped him. The dark figure inside was clearer than Gaven had ever seen it, pressing its hands against the inside surface, an impression of a snarling feline face above them. A silver serpent writhed around it, clearly trying to pull it back, to hold it fast. Palpable waves of fury emanated from the blue stone, and silver fire sparked from the slender filigree connecting the torc to the receptacles on either side.

"Gaven," Cart said beside him.

"Two spirits share one prison beneath the wastes, secrets kept and revelation granted." Gaven spoke as if in a dream. "They bind and are bound, but their unbound whispers rise to the Dragon Between, calling to those who would hear."

"Gaven, you were right."

Flame burst up from the furnace below, great spouts of it erupting around him, searing his skin. He heard the clank of metal as Cart's adamantine axe cut through the chains that bound his legs.

"Now, Gaven!"

Cart had his axe in hand, and with his shield he pushed Gaven forward. Gaven stumbled toward the fire, then realized that Cart was hurrying him toward the narrow entrance at the far side of the Dragon Forge. Cart was trying to help him escape.

Gaven's dragonmark tingled cool in his hot skin, and he felt power prick his scalp and his arms. Soldiers running to intercept him were blasted aside with thunderous explosions of air. But then Kelas and Phaine blocked his path, and Haldren behind them, and they stood their ground as the wind whipped at them ahead of Gaven's charge.

Gaven saw Haldren raise his hands, and waves of freezing air crashed over him. His legs went numb and he stumbled. Every muscle, already weak from hunger, felt too stiff to move. Another spurt of flame warmed him, but it also brought back memories of his dreams. His fate was inevitable, it seemed—was it not bound to take place as he had seen? The agony—

A jolt of pain ran up his leg as Kelas kicked at his knee, which buckled under him. Chains still weighing down his wrists, Gaven felt like a captured beast, harried by goads and unable to fight back. He roared in pain and fury, and the air shook with thunder. A blast of lightning shot from him—from his arms, his chest, his whole body—and shot through Kelas first, then Haldren. Then Cart was pushing him forward again, toward the tiny doorway that seemed to whisper freedom.

"What in the Realm of Madness do you think you're doing?" Haldren, looking scorched from the lightning blast but keeping his feet, barred their way now, giving voice to Gaven's thoughts. But he was addressing Cart. "Do your duty, soldier!"

"I am," Cart growled. He ran at the Lord General, his metal-plated feet clanking against the steel floor, lifting his axe above his head. The fibers and cords in his joints creaked and stretched with his effort as he buried the axe head deep in Haldren's shoulder, shattering bone and cleaving flesh.

Gaven watched entranced as blood flecked the cracked lips he had seen through their prison doors so many times. Cart, too, seemed momentarily fascinated, or perhaps appalled by what he had done. Then they were running again, and Gaven leaped over Haldren's body as the life spilled out of it, ran ahead as soldiers scattered out of his path.

A shadow passed over him, and then the dragon-king blocked his path. Black fire burned in the dragon's mouth, and his bony wings spread as wide and high as the walls of the forge would allow.

Gaven would not back down. He heard Cart behind him, ready to fight—a hero in his own right, finally seizing his destiny. Together, they could escape, against all odds. Gaven raised his hands to the sky, and lightning crackled down from the metal ceiling to flow into him. He glowed like a shining white beacon in the red light of the Dragon Forge. Then he lowered his arms to point at the dragon-king.

The roar of thunder was deafening and the lightning burned its path into his eyes. Malathar reared up with the force of the blast, writhing as lightning danced along the edges of every bone, sparked in the runes carved into his ribs, and doused the black fire in his mouth. His forelimbs fell back to the ground, and for a moment Gaven thought they would collapse under him, but the dragon-king fell into a crouch instead, ready to pounce.

"I am Malathar the Damned," he said. "Even you cannot stand before me, Storm Dragon."

Storm Dragon! The dragon-king recognized him as the figure of Prophecy, and still thought to face him in battle? Wind whipped around Gaven as he drew breath for another lightning blast.

Malathar breathed first, crackling black flame engulfing Gaven, searing his skin and sapping his strength still more. It was the excruciating pain of his dream, wracking his body and bringing him to his knees. Suddenly Gaven saw the dragon-king for what he was—one of the most ancient creatures in the world, preserved beyond even the tremendous natural lifespan of a dragon for what might have been hundreds or even thousands of years. Inconceivable power was bound to his blackened bones.

The pain ebbed, and Gaven somehow found strength to regain his feet. He glanced back at Cart—

Just in time to see Phaine d'Thuranni slide his blade out of Cart's back. Cart dropped to his knees, his eyes on Gaven, but the spark had already gone out of him. He fell forward, onto his face, and was still.

In Gaven's moment of shock, a bony claw coiled around him again, pinning his arms to his sides and lifting him off the floor. The dragon's touch was icy cold, and Gaven's strength and will drained out of him as Malathar carried him back to the far side of the forge.

PART
IV

Thunder is his harbinger and lightning his spear.
Wind is his steed and rain his cloak.
The words of creation are in his ears and on his tongue.
The secrets of the first of sixteen are his.

At the dawn of the Dragon Above he rises,
and lays claim to what belongs to him.
The blood of the evening sky is his,
joining day to night,
what is above to what is below.

In twilight he becomes a pilgrim,
seeking what he has lost,
what lies beyond his grasp.
His storm flies wild, unbound and pure in devastation,
going before the traitor's army
to break upon the city by the lake of kings.

In the darkest night of the Dragon Below,
storm and dragon are reunited,
and they break together upon the legions of the Blasphemer.
The maelstrom swirls around him.
He is the storm and the eye of the storm.
His is the new dawn.
In him the storm cannot die.

CHAPTER
35

Aunn. He decided to use his real name, even if he wasn't prepared to show his true face or admit his nature. It felt strange—like his name alone was a secret and revealing it would make him vulnerable. But he was willing to expose that one weakness, at least, as a sign of the new life he intended to begin.

He emerged from the tunnel and felt a strange air in the Labyrinth. There was . . . an expectancy about it, a sense that the Labyrinth itself was waiting for the hordes of Kathrik Mel to pass through it. It did not feel malevolent but eager, welcoming. It took Aunn hungrily in and wanted more. He couldn't help hurrying along, stumbling as though the ground were pushing him onward.

Left at every branch.

Farren's instructions were easy enough. Still, as Aunn wound his way through the canyons, he felt like he was going around in circles, though it might have been an ever-widening spiral. Always left. Farren had not said how far he would have to travel—the vague word "soon" might have meant a few hours, but as he spiraled always to the left he suspected it might have meant a day, maybe two. There could be no sense of progress, no idea that the mountains might be nearby or that he was getting at all closer.

He rounded a bend, chose another left branch, and came up short. Rubble blocked his way, the result of a landslide—a recent one, it seemed, for smaller rocks still tumbled down the pile. Panic seized him. If he couldn't follow Farren's directions, he wasn't sure he could find his way out of the Labyrinth. Perhaps he could scramble over the rubble and continue on the other side? He hurried forward, but the ground seemed to buckle beneath him, sending him sprawling on his face.

When he looked up, he saw a pair of booted feet before him. There had been no warning sound of crunching gravel—the figure must have just appeared. Half-expecting another visitation of the Traveler, he scrambled back and looked up at the man's face.

The man was tall, and he held himself proud and strong like a nobleman. His dark hair was cut short and sprinkled with gray at the temples. His warm brown eyes looked at Aunn, and Aunn realized that he was looking at his own new face. He had never seen it in a mirror, but the eyes—

The eyes were wrong, or at least they were not as Aunn had envisioned them when he sketched them in. Had he done them wrong? There was a hardness to them, an edge of cruelty. No, that would have to change.

"Who are you?" the vision asked—the Traveler's eternal question of him.

This time he had an answer, one he would stand by. "I am Aunn."

The man's warmth vanished into anger as he took in Aunn's face. "You've stolen my face! You're a fiend of the Wastes!"

This was no vision of the Traveler. Was it possible Aunn had given himself a copy of this man's face without ever having seen him? Or had he seen this man before? His thoughts felt muddy. He couldn't remember. Even the strange man's clothes and armor were identical to his—it didn't make sense.

The strange man roared in fury and ran at Aunn, his hands raised like claws before him. A vision flashed into Aunn's mind—a monster like a horned bear, fire in its eyes, a gaze that was fixed on him as it rushed toward him. He felt again the freezing cold of Frostburn Cut, the icy grip of fear he'd felt when he saw this monster before.

"We are in the Demon Wastes now," Vor said. "Do not trust your senses."

The man had become the bear-thing, massive claws raised to tear Aunn to shreds. An instant before those claws reached his throat, he brought his mace up and smashed it into the monster's face, knocking it aside. It sprawled against the canyon wall, changing back into a human form as it fell and rolled. Aunn followed it, raising his weapon.

The man chuckled and turned his face to Aunn. It was Vor's face now. "Well done, Kauth," he said. "You penetrated my disguises."

Aunn stopped short and nearly dropped his mace. It couldn't be Vor, but how did it know Kauth's name? How did it recognize him as Kauth? Was this the Traveler after all?

"You tried to lead me to my death," Vor said, his chuckle turning into a snarl. "If you had but known the extent of my power . . ."

"No," Aunn said. "I saw you dead. You're not Vor."

"You're right," Vor said, and his face melted away. Dania stood before him.

It was a nightmare, just like the fevered dreams of his illness, but Aunn was sure he was not sleeping. "What are you? Kalok Shash—the Silver Flame? Incarnate in the paladins—"

Dania roared, and the beast's massive paw slashed across Aunn's face, knocking him to the ground. "Paladins? Me and Vor? Not at all, Auftane, not at all."

"There was holiness in you both. So much good."

"Evil can wear the guise of good when the need arises."

"Evil—you—you're the fiend of the Wastes . . . You're dredging my memories!"

"Perhaps I am a fiend," Kelas said, "but does it follow that I am not also Dania, and Vor, and Kelas? Think about it, Haunderk. I've been with you all this time. I have guided you all your life. I've made you what you are."

Aunn cowered on the ground, terrified that what Kelas said might be true. Kelas *could* be an incarnation of evil. He was capable of such cruelty. But could he have been Dania? Vor? No, it couldn't be—

"Where did I fail, Haunderk?" Kelas loomed over him, powerful and intimidating. Aunn cringed, awaiting the inevitable slap or kick. "What flaw in your education allowed this . . . this *conscience* to take root in you?"

Conscience.

Kelas said the word like it was the name of the most loathsome, despicable creature he could imagine. And Aunn remembered exactly how it had come about. He stood up, face to face with Kelas.

"You did fail," he said. "You taught me detachment, taught me not to love. But you didn't teach me not to care. You made me hate you, and you never punished me for hating you. Hatred is just as strong as love, Kelas, and my hatred for you is my greatest strength. Because I hate you, I care—and because I care, I learned to love."

Kelas laughed—a low chuckle that grew into a great, booming laughter that echoed in the canyon. "Then you have learned to fail," he said, his face suddenly grim.

Then the bear-beast leaped at Aunn again, knocking him to the ground. With its massive paws pinning him down, its fiery eyes met his gaze. As it spoke, droplets of spittle fell on his face and seared his skin. "I am everything you've ever cared about. Except for Kelas, it's all been a sham. My evil is the only thing that's ever been real in your life, changeling."

Despair sank into Aunn's chest like the weight of the fiend's paws, and he waited for its teeth to close around his neck. Instead, it brought its mouth close to Aunn's and drew a deep breath.

Aunn's lungs screamed their protest as the demon sucked every last scrap of air out of them and still continued its inhalation. His vision swam, and darkness closed in at the edges. The paws lifted off his chest and Aunn felt his body rise off the ground with the force of the monster's breath. He closed his eyes.

He was a husk, left with nothing inside him but his despair. Kelas had been manipulating and controlling him his entire life, and Kelas was an incarnation of evil. Everything else had been a lie—Dania, Vor, and Farren. The ideals of the paladin that had seemed so virtuous, they were nothing but a quick path to a noble death. And now his own death, hardly so noble, was upon him. Kalok Shash would not burn brighter, he felt sure. If it existed at all, it would soon be extinguished.

In the midst of the blackness, Dania lay atop him as she had in his fevered dream. She moved against him, smiled at him, and asked, "Why do you resist me?"

"I can't anymore," he said. "Take me."

A blast of white fire shattered the darkness, and air poured into Aunn's lungs. Hope seeped back into his heart as well, and as his eyes regained their normal vision he saw the bear-thing scrabbling at the ground, trying to get its feet under it again. When it did, it vanished from sight, and a moment later Aunn felt its absence.

But there was still a presence with him, a presence that had taken root in his soul and flowered at last into that burst of fire. It was Dania's smile and Vor's courage, Rienne's care and Gaven's fierce power. It was a flame burning against all the world's darkness, a purifying fire.

Who are you?

He knew, with every last spark of his soul he knew. He smiled and answered, "I am Aunn."

Then he climbed up and over the rubble that had blocked his path.

* * * * *

The Demon Wastes lay behind him and the Shadowcrags rose up ahead. Aunn turned for a last look back. The Labyrinth had not changed since his first view of it—an endless maze of winding canyons, scorched as if by the acidic touch of corruption, all spread out beneath a blood red sky. But it felt different. He had approached it with dread, afraid of losing his soul. But he looked back on it with a strange mixture of grief and ... something else, something that was hard to name. He lost Vor there. He led Sevren and Zandar to their deaths. He helped kill Durrnak and the orcs under his command, and finally left all of Maruk Dar to the hands of the Carrion Tribes. That grief and remorse might have overwhelmed him, except that he had gained something as well. Vor had warned him to abandon hope, but instead he had gained a shred of hope.

A thin plume of smoke to the right caught his eye, and he wondered whether it was a sign of Maruk Dar's fate. As he watched, more plumes arose, and more, until they were joined into a great billowing cloud of black smoke rising up and spreading out to cast a deeper pall over the whole Labyrinth.

Maruk Dar is burning, Aunn thought. I should have been there to die in its defense.

He fell to his knees and watched the smoke and occasional flashes of fire rising above the canyon walls. He thought of Farren, probably one of the first to die as he tried to shield the city from the onrushing hordes. He thought of Dakar and the woman with him, and the other Carrion Tribe "converts" among the Ghaash'kala. They, too, were probably early victims, sought out for special punishment by those they had deserted. Or perhaps they turned on the Ghaash'kala, hoping to redeem themselves and rejoin the winning side in the conflict. And what of young Ghaarat, who had just sworn his vow to defend the Labyrinth? How long would a boy last in battle against the Carrion Tribes, even a boy of the Ghaash'kala?

Farren had allowed him to escape the sack of Maruk Dar. Farren had ensured that he would be alive at that moment, able to look back on the billowing smoke that told of the city's destruction. Farren had broken his vow and allowed Aunn to escape the Labyrinth, and for one purpose: to warn the people of the east, of the Eldeen Reaches and perhaps Aundair and Breland. The Carrion Tribes were on the march, their sights set on the cities of the east, and it fell on him to try to stop them.

Aunn felt the weight of that burden as he lurched to his feet. He gave one last look toward Maruk Dar and said, "Kalok Shash burns brighter." Then he turned his back on the city and set off to find his way back into the Shadowcrags.

Chapter
36

Gaven was barely aware of guards putting new chains on his wrists and removing the ones that had bound his hands together. Winches rattled on either side, and the chains pulled his arms up and out, then harder until his shoulders burned with pain. The pain jolted him from his stupor.

Kelas stood before him. "Storm Dragon," he said, snarling with contempt. He reached up and ran a fingertip across the dragonmark at Gaven's neck. "Will the storm still obey you after this? I wonder."

He turned away, reaching into his coat, and produced a dragonshard larger than his fist, at least the size of the Eye of Siberys. Its substance was light red, and a swirl of blood coiled in its heart—an Eberron shard. Kelas set the stone into a fine gold setting, and adjusted an array of fine metal arms around it, cradling it aloft and apart from the rest of the forge's workings.

"The Dragon Forge is a refinery, of sorts," Kelas said, satisfaction in his voice. "It's made to separate gold from dross."

"To purify the touch of Siberys's hand," Malathar whispered behind him, "by removing it from the tainted flesh on which it is written."

Gaven gazed at the dragonshard with growing horror. Eberron shards were often used to contain magic—wizards recorded spells in them or attuned them to specific spells to make wands or even the relatively mundane everbright lanterns. Could it contain his dragonmark?

Kelas placed his hands on a golden orb below the dragonshard and gasped as silver flame leaped out from the orb to engulf his hands. He trembled with what might have been torment or ecstasy, his eyes rolled back in his head, and the dragonshard flared with crimson light.

The light washed over Gaven, searing into his dragonmark, and then the pain struck him.

* * * * *

The worst of it was over. The chains binding his wrists held Gaven as he hung, limp and drained. His skin still burned where his dragonmark had been, blood oozing from the raw skin it had left behind. The manacles bit into his wrists, and he lacked the strength to find his feet and take the weight off his arms. He could barely lift his head to look around.

Kelas cackled with delight as he lifted the enormous dragonshard from its golden setting and gazed into its depths.

"It's here!" he crowed. "The dragonmark is perfectly preserved within the shard!"

Gaven could just make it out. What had been a mostly formless swirl of darker red within the pinkish stone had taken on a definite shape, but he did not recognize it as his mark. Then Kelas turned it slightly in his hands, and Gaven gaped. There they were—the familiar lines of his dragonmark, the Siberys Mark of Storm. There was a depth to the mark in the stone, so it changed when viewed from different angles. Kelas moved it again, and Gaven caught a fleeting glimpse of another shape before Kelas turned away, blocking his view. There was meaning in the depth of the mark, Gaven was certain. Through a haze of pain and weakness, a knot of resolve formed in his gut—he had to get that dragonshard, to untangle the Prophecy he'd carried on his skin.

Still chuckling with pleasure at his success, Kelas placed the dragonshard in another setting embedded in the apparatus, this one made of glass pipes and studded with gemstones.

"Wait," the dragon-king whispered, and Kelas froze. "I must examine it first."

"You'll have your chance," Kelas snapped.

Malathar lifted his head to loom over Kelas. "I will. And it will be now. Or at my command, the dragons that fuel your forge cease their work."

Kelas stood looking up at Malathar, fists clenched at his sides, his face growing deeper red. The dragon-king returned his stare blankly. Finally Kelas broke. He lifted the dragonshard from its setting and handed it to Malathar, who held it gingerly between his two front claws.

Gaven found his feet and strained for a better view of the shard as the undead dragon held it, to no avail. A movement at the corner of his eye drew his attention to Phaine, who also gazed at the dragonshard with longing. Several pieces of the puzzle fell into place in Gaven's mind.

Malathar and the other dragons helped Kelas build the Dragon Forge because of their interest in the Prophecy, and particularly in the Time Between. They had fulfilled their vision of that Prophecy, with three spillings of blood joining the primordial dragons in pairs. Gaven's blood joined the Eye of Siberys and the Heart of Khyber. The Ramethene Sword spilled symbolic blood—the magical energy that powered the forge—to join the spawn of Khyber with the spirit that bound it, which must somehow represent Eberron. And Gaven's blood again joined his Siberys mark with an Eberron dragonshard. By their reading, the Time Between must be drawing to a close, and the Time of the Dragon Below beginning.

More than fulfilling the Prophecy, though, Malathar sought to learn more about it, particularly as it was scribed on the skin of Khorvaire's dragonmarked heirs. He had said that the Prophecy was defiled by being written on the skin of meat, and that the Dragon Forge would purify it. He wanted to study the marks separated from the skin of the mortals who carried them, and the Dragon Forge allowed him to do that.

Phaine's interest in the dragonshard was more surprising, but Gaven suspected it arose from the same intent. The elves of Aerenal had almost as much interest in the Prophecy as the dragons, and House Thuranni might be making a study of it for their own ends. Or perhaps Phaine—or all of House Thuranni—wanted to understand dragonmarks better, or even to control the power of the other Houses' marks. Could they harness the magic contained in a dragonmark that was held within an Eberron dragonshard? If so, they might be able to compete with all the other Houses—build and operate their own lightning rail, open their own message stations, control the weather and pilot airships and galleons.

Enough, Gaven thought. It's time for the Storm Dragon to get out of the Dragon Forge. I am the storm. . . .

But he was not the storm. It had grown easy for him, since walking the Sky-Caves of Thieren Kor, to submerge his mind in the atmosphere, to join himself with the storms that always accompanied his anger or distress. But there was no storm to join—he couldn't find the weather at all.

It was not just his dragonmark they had stripped away. He was no longer the Storm Dragon.

* * * * *

Ashara's hands moved over Cart's inert body, finding the damage, the places where the knots of magic that gave him life were broken. Eyes closed, she saw him as a tapestry nearly ripped to shreds, almost every strand of warp and weft broken in one place or another. It would be some time before she could make him fully alive again, but he was not dead.

It was a strange thing about the warforged, and something that the living armies of the Last War had often forgotten to their detriment. A human soldier dealt a mortal blow would die before long, his life ebbing out with his blood. A warforged, though, could linger in that state of unconsciousness—still alive, but so badly wounded that he couldn't function—for days, weeks, or months. She had heard stories within her House of warforged who lay in remote battlefields for years, then were repaired and rose up ready to battle.

She wondered what Cart was experiencing as his body lay inert. The warforged didn't sleep, so they weren't accustomed to dreams. Would he dream in his unconsciousness? Or was his mind simply blank, unaware of the passage of time? She would ask him when he awoke at last.

It was hard to work in the little tent, with Gaven's screams of agony in the background, but by nightfall she was confident that Cart would be up and around. Then, under the cover of darkness, they could flee. Together.

* * * * *

Gaven's resolve had drained away, and he hung from his manacles again. Without the power of the Storm Dragon, he had nothing to rely on but a sword and a handful of spells—and he had no sword. Before the Sky-Caves, before Dreadhold and his Siberys mark, sword and spell had been enough. But now, against Kelas, Phaine, Malathar, and a small company of soldiers, his situation was hopeless.

Malathar gave the dragonshard back to Kelas without a word. Gaven had neither strength nor will enough to strain for another look at the stone, though he saw Phaine shift again in hope of a better view. Kelas turned back to the eldritch machine and returned the dragonshard to the new setting of glass and gems.

"Now," he said, "we learn the true power of the Dragon Forge."

He grasped two crystal rods that jutted out beneath the shard, and a brilliant light flared to life between them. Gaven couldn't look at the light, but he didn't need to—the tracings of the dragonmark, his dragonmark, now filled the enormous room. Lines of scarlet fire etched the ceiling's arch and turned slowly as the machine rotated the dragonshard in its setting. A cluster of artificers flocked around the machine and manipulated its controls.

The sky rumbled with thunder, a brewing storm that had nothing to do with Gaven.

It was all around him, the mark he had carried for five years, the Prophecy that had been written on his skin but out of reach of his understanding. His gaze darted around the room, trying to take it all in.

The Storm Dragon flies before the traitor's army to deliver vengeance.

The storm breaks upon the forces of the Blasphemer.

When Rienne traced his dragonmark on his skin, it had been only a vague foreboding, a sense that his end might come at the hands of the Blasphemer. Now it took concrete shape in his mind, spelled out in the breadth and depth of his mark.

But did it apply to him? Without the Mark of Storm, without

the Storm Dragon's power, he couldn't fulfill that part of the Prophecy. But if he was no longer the Storm Dragon, then who was?

A deafening clap of thunder made the soldiers cover their ears and even Phaine looked up nervously. Rain fell in huge, splattering drops, and shouts of fear and pain arose from outside, from soldiers and laborers seared by the acidic downpour.

I am the storm. . . .

Gaven remembered losing himself in a storm over the Aerenal forest, fighting off a pack of beasts with his bare hands and summoning lightning to spear them. He made one more effort to reach his mind up into the storm, but his mind was as tightly bound as his hands.

My hands . . . ? Gaven thought.

He looked at the manacle holding his right wrist and the chain that pulled his arm out straight, almost wrenching it from its socket. The chain disappeared into an extension of the forge machinery, presumably attached to the winch he'd heard.

Perhaps the manacles were constraining more than his body. Maybe with his arms free he could command the storm again. Or at least die trying to fight his way out of the Dragon Forge.

Once he'd been known for his strength. Especially for a Khoravar, he was mighty—his body had none of the slender grace of his elf ancestors. Whenever he was in Stormhome, delivering his latest cargo of Khyber shards for use in his House's elemental galleons, he used to arm-wrestle at taverns, to Rienne's utter embarrassment—and he never lost. He defeated Cart at the goblin wrestling game in Grellreach. Even without a sword, he had that strength to fall back on.

The winches creaked slightly as he began to pull. He glanced around at Phaine and the guards, but none of them paid him any mind. He'd become irrelevant.

He shifted his weight to his left side and was pleased to find some relief to the burning pain in that shoulder. He'd already created some slack in the chains. With one more glance around at his guards, he pulled the chain on his right. The winch groaned and pain stabbed through his shoulder, but the chain didn't give.

Another clap of thunder shook the roof and walls, and sparks shimmered down along the metal walls to the ground. Kelas looked up for the first time, then looked at Gaven. He strode over to stare Gaven in the face.

"Did you do that?" he demanded.

"I thought you were making the storms now," Gaven said. His throat was raw from screaming, and his voice came out a rough scratch.

Kelas's face flushed with anger. "I am," he said. "I made it. Did you make the lightning strike the forge?"

"Lightning is a willful mount. Sometimes it goes where it wants to go." Gaven's heart thrilled at the idea that he might still have influence over the storm, might still be able to control it. "It especially likes metal buildings."

Kelas slapped him, surprisingly hard for a man half Gaven's weight. "Before treating me like an idiot, remember who has done this to you."

Anger flooded Gaven's body, surging into his muscles and pounding in his heart. He would never forget who peeled the dragonmark from his skin. The winch on his right creaked again, louder, making Kelas wheel to look.

Just as Kelas called out—"Knock him out! Get him out of here!"—something cracked inside the forge and the chain rattled loose. Gaven yanked the chain free, grabbed a loop of it, and swung it hard into Kelas's face, sending him reeling backward.

A needle of pain lanced Gaven's shoulder and his arm went limp. Gathering more chain in his left hand, he wheeled to see his attacker. Phaine stood there, the very tip of his dagger stained with blood. Gaven glared—of all his captors, Phaine had managed to make Gaven loathe him most of all. He aimed right at the elf's smirking face, but the chain, still attached to the winch, caught him up short. Phaine vanished into the gloom, then another quick stab of pain numbed his left arm.

"Do you like that?" the elf whispered over Gaven's shoulder. "We use that to incapacitate people we aren't quite ready to kill. Yet."

Gaven's foot shot out behind him, cracking into Phaine's shin. He tried to tangle Phaine in the chain binding his legs, but the elf stepped nimbly away. At least Gaven had the satisfaction of seeing Phaine favor his injured leg.

In a panic, Gaven tried to shake his arms, to bring feeling back into them or make them move, but they just swung from his shoulders, useless. Phaine vanished into shadow again, and Gaven spun just in time to see the Thuranni appear right in front of him. He jerked his head forward and down, smashing his forehead into the bridge of Phaine's nose. As the elf stumbled back, clutching at his bloodied nose, Gaven kicked at his knee. Gaven had almost reached the end of the chain that held his left arm, but he just had room to bring his foot down on the prone elf's neck—

His right arm jerked up across his chest, pulling him back and off balance before his foot came down. Kelas had hold of the chain, and Gaven's limp arms now crossed in front of him, holding him firmly in place.

"Damn it, Thuranni!" Kelas yelled. "Stop playing games and get him out of here!"

Gaven threw his weight away from Kelas, yanking the chain from his hands. Some feeling was returning to his right hand, and he fumbled trying to grab hold of another loop of chain to use as a weapon.

A sharp jab of pain in his neck made his whole body go limp, and the world went black as he slumped to the floor.

* * * * *

Ashara laid her hands on Cart's shoulder, giving him one last infusion of magical power, and he was as strong as when he'd come out of his creation forge. He watched her as she worked, bewildered by the attention she gave to him, by the concern in her eyes and the care in her hands.

"There." She sighed. "Feeling better?"

"Why are you doing this? I turned against Kelas, killed Haldren—" The memory of what he'd done overwhelmed him. He killed the Lord General, the man he'd sworn to serve, the man he'd helped break out of Dreadhold.

"You really don't know?"

Cart shook his head.

"You're my friend," she said. Then her brow furrowed, unsure of his reaction. "Aren't you?"

Friend. Cart cast his memory back over the thirty years of his life. He'd been one of the first warforged, born as a slave to House Cannith and then sold to Aundair's army. He was a successful soldier, not just surviving year after year of battle, but rising through the ranks to Haldren's right hand. Soldiers had called him comrade, or they'd called him Captain. Haldren had described him once as his most trusted ally, and he'd included Cart when addressing his "friends"—but Cart knew full well that Haldren used that word to manipulate his audiences. Always in the plural.

No one had ever called him friend before, not really.

"I . . . I hope to be," he said, and she smiled.

"Good. Then let's get out of here." She stood and held out a hand to help Cart up.

"Wait. What happened to Gaven?"

The smile fell from Ashara's face. "I'm told the Dragon Forge worked perfectly, and that Kelas is very pleased with me."

"Is he dead?"

"Dead? No, not yet." She looked at the ground. "But the Thuranni has him in custody. It might take a while, but death will come."

"I need to free him," Cart said, getting to his feet.

Ashara sighed. "I thought you'd say that. But look where it got you last time. It's far easier for you and me to sneak out of this camp than for us to break Gaven out of Phaine's hands."

"You were right about me, Ashara. It's not enough for me to be a soldier. Now Haldren is dead and no one gives me orders. It's time for me to be a hero."

She put a hand on his arm and looked up, her face a mixture of pleasure and grief. "You already are," she said.

"Time to act like one, then. Where is Gaven?"

* * * * *

"You have led me on quite a chase, Gaven."

Phaine was clearly enjoying himself. With every prick of his blade, he leaned close to Gaven's ear and whispered some new taunt or imprecation. He had bound Gaven to a wooden chair and continually pricked at his nerves to deaden his limbs, ensuring he never mustered the strength to break his bonds. Blood trickled from a dozen tiny wounds.

"From Dreadhold to Q'barra. When we found your room in Whitecliff, the bed was still warm."

"You've been following me since Dreadhold?" A personal or House interest in dragonmarks couldn't explain that kind of interest. Had Phaine come looking for the Storm Dragon as soon as he escaped?

"Indeed. Then to Aerenal, which was most enlightening. It had been some time since I visited my ancestors."

"It took you this long to catch up to me? Three other Houses got to me first, you know."

"And failed to capture you. You killed the Deneith Sentinel Marshal, of course. House Tharashk, too, has abandoned the search. House Kundarak is probably still scouring Khorvaire, stinging from the blow of losing two prisoners from Dreadhold. But then, none of them knew what you were."

"And what am I?"

"You *were* the Storm Dragon. Now, you're nothing. Nothing but a man who's responsible for the extermination of the Paelions and the fracture of my House."

"You can blame your own baron for that."

That must have angered Phaine—he jabbed his dagger more deeply into Gaven's upper arm.

"The baron acted on information you planted."

Gaven's memories of that period of his life were shrouded in a haze. It had been nearly thirty years, but more than that, he had barely known his own mind at the time. But he knew there was some truth to what Phaine said. He had helped plant false evidence to suggest that the Paelions were plotting against the other Houses. But it had been Baron Elar d'Thuranni who ordered the slaughter of the entire Paelion clan.

"So you've followed me all this time to get revenge?"

"That is merely the sweet finish to the chase." Another jab of pain showed Gaven how much Phaine enjoyed the taste of revenge.

CHAPTER
37

Rays of sunlight from the shattered ceiling lit clouds of dust as the rubble settled in the great chamber. Smaller rocks shifted and fell within the pile and tumbled from the cracked roof above. Gaven had been there. Rienne was certain of it. But he was gone, and whoever or whatever he had been fighting was gone as well.

She walked in a dream into the chamber, circling the largest pieces of the fallen roof. Something moved in the rubble, and she hurried to the spot, lifting slabs and pushing rocks aside until she found bare floor beneath. There was nothing, no sign that he had been present.

A sparkle of color at the edge of the room caught her eye. Crushed gemstones in pieces ranging from powder to granules filled a pattern of lines engraved into the floor. Shattered granite covered most of the pattern, but she guessed it was a circle lining the perimeter of the room. Magic. Some ritual had taken Gaven away.

The thunder of approaching footsteps filled the hall. She turned to face the doorway, Maelstrom limp in her hand. She wasn't sure she could muster the energy to fight anymore. Why bother? Gaven was gone.

I could escape, she thought. If I can't find Gaven, perhaps he can find me.

Sheathing Maelstrom, she bent down and unfastened the slender chain around her ankle and held it up in the sunlight. She could almost feel the magic contained in its fine silver links, promising freedom.

"Rienne!" Lissa appeared in the doorway, more footsteps resounding behind her.

"I have to go, Lissa," Rienne said.

Three more guards crowded behind Lissa, but she held up a hand to stop them. Her voice was tender and calm when she addressed Rienne.

Tears sprang to Rienne's eyes. "Promise me that if you find him, you'll tell him where I've gone." There was no way the dragonborn could have understood her words, but there was understanding in her eyes, and sympathy, and grief.

Rienne snapped the chain. She blinked as one of the tiny links broke, and when she opened her eyes she was in a green courtyard surrounded by orange trees. The citrus smell was intoxicating, but it was carried on a sea wind that told her she was home.

* * * * *

The courtyard was part of a stately house with a blue-tiled roof and white plaster walls. A fountain burbled against one wall, opposite a hall leading to the front door. Rienne looked around nervously. Jordhan had not told her where he got the magic chains, though she trusted his discretion. Presumably, this place belonged to whatever artificer had crafted them.

The roof framed a square of dark sky, dawn just beginning to light one side—or evening fading in the west. It had been morning when she entered the dragon-king's palace in Argonnessen, far to the east. Morning to the east meant that dawn was still approaching in Stormhome, and the house's owner was probably still asleep. She crept to the hall, then stopped short.

If Gaven had already broken his chain, he would have come here as well, and the artificer might have seen him appear. If he hadn't yet, the house's owner could tell him that she'd been there and give him some message, some idea of how to find her.

But that would mean she'd have to know where she was going. At the moment, she had no idea. She crossed the courtyard again and settled herself on a stone bench beside the fountain to plan and wait.

Stormhome was not a safe place for her. She could go to her own family, but the Sentinel Marshals had come to her house when Gaven first escaped. Thordren's house had been watched the last time she and Gaven appeared there. Would they still be watching it? Gaven and Rienne had been gone for months. How badly did House Kundarak and the Sentinel Marshals want to find him?

Stormhome had no poorer neighborhoods where Rienne could remain anonymous and unseen. House Lyrandar controlled who lived and worked there. Anyone who couldn't afford the rather steep price of a place to live in Stormhome went back to the mainland, one way or another. Rienne had no place to hide. She couldn't linger there, waiting for Gaven to appear.

She had struck out on her own once before—she'd flown to Vathirond, found Gaven, and rescued him from his pursuers. She could do it again.

On the other hand, leaving Stormhome presented its own set of challenges. House Lyrandar operated the only ships passing to and from the mainland, and it would be hard to find a captain who didn't know her, at least by reputation. Jordhan would have helped, of course, but he might still be half the world away, as far as she knew. What, then?

She had called in plenty of favors before leaving in search of Gaven the first time, but that was no longer an option. She had also turned much of her wealth into a more portable form, a small bag of tiny, perfect gemstones she kept next to her skin. Selling a single stone would provide her with living expenses for weeks. The money, at least, would serve her well.

If she only had some idea of where to look for Gaven.

Her thoughts were going in circles, running through every possibility she could imagine of finding help, departing the city, and leaving word for Gaven. She replayed the last few days in her mind, from her arrival in Rav Magar to Gaven's sudden disappearance and Lissa's farewell. Her dream in the shrine of the Prophecy played itself over and over in her mind—Maelstrom in her hand, portentous words describing the Blasphemer, and the tumult of a battlefield.

A battlefield where she, in her dream, had played a decisive role. Perhaps Gaven had been right and Maelstrom was indeed a sword of legend, the weapon of a champion. In her dream, she had faced the demon at the heart of an army. Could it be that her destiny was to kill that demon, thus preventing or at least putting an end to the devastation described in the Prophecy? The idea turned her stomach. She didn't want the crowning accomplishment of her life to be ending another life. *Any* other life.

Her eyes drooped and her head nodded, and she slept where she sat beside the fountain.

* * * * *

Maelstrom clashed against a sword that burned red, a ceramic urn shattered on the cobblestones, and a girl's shriek jolted Rienne from her sleep.

The sky was a little brighter, and sounds indoors suggested that the household was beginning to stir. A girl of perhaps thirteen cowered behind a pillar, peering out at Rienne with round eyes, pieces of the urn littering the floor around her bare feet. She must have been a serving girl, sent to fetch water for the kitchen or bath, shocked to find a stranger sleeping by the fountain.

"I'm sorry," Rienne said, and the girl stood a little straighter. "I didn't mean to startle you."

"What are you doing here?" the girl said, but her voice was more curious than frightened.

"I need to speak to the master of the house. But first let me help you clean up that mess."

"No no, I'll do it, Lady. After I take you inside."

Rienne grimaced. Her accent betrayed her noble birth, despite the dirt and dust of travel matted in her hair and plastered to her skin, after months at sea and weeks spent slogging across a distant continent.

"Please," she said, "it's my fault. I'll help you."

She crouched down and started gathering the larger fragments, stacking them carefully and setting them aside. Hesitantly, the girl joined her, working from the other side.

"What's your name?" Rienne asked.

"Ava."

"I'm Rienne." She smiled at the girl, and Ava finally seemed at ease. "Is the master of this house an artificer, Ava? Working with magic?"

"Not the master, Lady. But my mistress is very skilled."

The mistress, of course. Why had Rienne assumed it was the man? A thought jolted her to her feet. A female artificer in Stormhome—"Is this Chanda's house? Chanda ir'Selden?" Chanda and Rienne had been childhood friends and stayed close up until the time that Rienne fell in love with Gaven. Chanda disapproved of Gaven's adventuring lifestyle, prospecting for dragonshards. Rienne had made a few efforts to get back in touch with her after Gaven's imprisonment, but she had always been rebuffed.

Ava looked puzzled, but she nodded. "Shall I take you to her, Lady?"

Would Chanda help her now? Not if word had spread that Rienne had helped Gaven after he escaped from Dreadhold. For the sake of their old friendship, Chanda might refrain from summoning the Sentinel Marshals immediately, but she would not help.

"Actually, Ava, it's probably best if I just get on my way."

"Should I tell her you were here?"

"Will she punish you for the broken urn?"

Ava shrugged. "She'll take it out of my wages."

Rienne produced a silver coin and pressed it into Ava's hand. "Best not to tell her I was here. Thank you."

Ava stood gaping at the coin as Rienne slipped out the front door and into the quiet morning street.

* * * * *

As a girl, Rienne had practiced her sword play on a bluff just outside Stormhome, overlooking the crashing waves of the sea. Under the city's perpetually crystal blue sky, she learned to still her mind and harness the energy flowing through her body. In her adolescence, she came to the same spot to find quiet and search for some sense of peace. She hadn't been back there in years.

So she slipped out of the city before the streets grew crowded and noisy and retreated there, seeking the same stillness and solitude she had found there in her youth. As the sun cleared the horizon, she drew Maelstrom and moved through the forms of her fencing style, quieting her racing thoughts and focusing in on the still point at her core.

She froze, Maelstrom's blade before her face, her sword hand pressed against her other palm. "We balance on the razor edge between past and future," she had said to Gaven, "but that edge is what matters." She saw Maelstrom's sharp edge and it became clear.

On one side of the blade, eternity. The unchanging landscape of Argonnessen's wilds, untouched by the passage of time except the cyclical turning of the seasons. On the other side, history, the constant churn of events, wars, nations, people, and relationships— motion with progress, destination. She felt she stood on the razor edge between, not past and future, but history and eternity. The edge was her destiny, the intrusion of history into the eternity of the world. It was not a foreordained destination, but the result of her action. Her destiny, she realized, was the ultimate consequence of her actions.

What did she want that consequence to be?

She swung Maelstrom in a circle around her. It caught the sun, surrounding her in a ring of blazing light. Sliding the blade back into its sheath, she walked back to the city, a plan forming in her mind.

* * * * *

Leaving the city was a challenge, but one she could overcome. She couldn't buy passage on a ship to the mainland, so she'd have to stow away. She knew the routines of the harbor well enough to sneak aboard a galleon bound for Thaliost, and she knew the galleons well enough to find hiding places aboard. It was risky, but it was nothing she couldn't handle, nothing she needed Gaven's or anyone's help to accomplish.

She made her way to the harbor, her bedraggled appearance drawing some stares. Among the sailors and merchants at the wharves, she blended in to the crowds. A few inquiries revealed that a galleon would be sailing for Thaliost in a week's time. She would have liked to leave sooner, but in the meantime she could enjoy a taste of life in the city again. She sold one of the small gemstones she used as a portable form of wealth, since she could no longer access her Kundarak accounts, and spent freely. She savored the taste of anything that wasn't journeybread. She slept in a bed, on a filthy mattress under scratchy blankets, grateful to be out of her bedroll and off the floor. She bathed and bought new clothes, with the unfortunate consequence that she drew more attention as she walked in the streets. But the sword at her belt frightened off the lonely sailors and drunken revelers who might otherwise have accosted her.

Finally, the night before the *Windborn* was to sail, she slipped down to the galleon's berth, dodged the guards, slunk past the sailors on deck, and disappeared into the hold. There among the barrels and crates, she made herself as comfortable as she could and settled in for the journey, clutching Maelstrom to her chest.

* * * * *

Getting off the ship would be more difficult, she knew. They'd dock in Thaliost sometime on the third day of their journey, probably early in the morning. Passengers would disembark, then the sailors would unload the cargo and there would be no place left to hide. Rienne's best hope was to sneak back up to the deck amid the bustle of their arrival and mingle among the passengers. It would be easier to mingle, she thought ruefully, if she looked like she could afford the hundred and fifty galifar fare. The clothes she'd bought in Stormhome were those of a street vendor or laborer, not a noblewoman.

Still, she knew from experience that adventurers who made their fortune by pillaging ancient ruins and selling dragonshards sometimes bought extravagant fares on Lyrandar vessels, so that was the role she adopted. When the morning of the third day broke, she stole out of the cargo hold and up on deck, and scanned the other passengers. One human woman wore a necklace that looked like a relic of the Dhakaani empire, so Rienne approached her and struck up a conversation about the jewelry.

The woman was an instructor at Morgrave University in Sharn, Rienne learned, and had retrieved the necklace herself from a goblin ruin near Tranthus, in Zil'argo. Goblin history was not one of Rienne's strengths, but she kept asking questions, drawing long responses from the instructor. When the ship docked at the cliffs below Thaliost, they strolled together off the ship, lost amid the other passengers, to all appearances a pair of friends traveling together.

The docks of Thaliost were down at sea level, over the waters of Scions Sound. Overhead, the crumbled remains of White Arch Bridge jutted out from the cliff where the city perched, stretching out across the sound toward Rekkenmark in Karrnath. The bridge had been a sign of the united Galifar before the war, joining two of the Five Nations, but it quickly became one of the casualties of the Last War. One by one the passengers grew silent as they crossed the docks, looking up at the shattered bridge and remembering what it meant.

Before they could board the magical lifts that would carry them from the docks to the city itself, the passengers had to file through a checkpoint where Thrane soldiers checked their identification and traveling papers. Rienne had no traveling papers, but she was not concerned—the identification papers that showed her to be a member of the nobility, combined with a "processing fee," would certainly be enough to get her where she wanted to go.

"Papers, please." The soldier stuck out his hand without looking at her, listening to the soldier on his right tell a story about his mother-in-law. Rienne put her identification papers in his hand, and he glanced down at them momentarily. "And your traveling papers?"

"I'm afraid I don't have traveling papers."

That got the full attention of the soldier and the man with the mother-in-law. "You don't have traveling papers? What do you think you're doing?"

"I was called away from my family estate in rather a hurry," Rienne said, adopting the tone of a noblewoman faced with impertinence from the lower classes. It had the desired effect—the soldier examined her identification, raised his eyebrows at her family name, and compared the portrait on the papers to Rienne's own face. As he did that, Rienne placed three galifars on the table in front of him. "This will cover the cost of processing the papers," she added.

"I'm very sorry, Lady Alastra," the soldier said, and as his eyes fell on the gold coins his face showed deep sorrow indeed, "but there's no way I can let you into Thrane without traveling papers. Not these days."

"Ever since Aundair attacked up north," the other soldier added, "we have to be a lot more careful." He, too, eyed the gold coins with regret and longing. "On the lookout for spies and such."

Rienne drew herself up in outrage. "Are you suggesting that I am a spy?" This was a disaster. She was already drawing some stares. Her erstwhile companion, already past the soldiers, lingered to see what the problem was, and other soldiers were looking up from their own tables to find the source of the disturbance. She had left Khorvaire almost immediately after the battle at Starcrag Plain—she'd had no idea of the political repercussions of Haldren's aborted attack.

"Of course not, Lady," the soldier with the mother-in-law said, holding his hands up to shield himself from her wrath. "It's just that the rules are so much stricter now—"

"The rules do not apply to me, soldier." That was an attitude Rienne encountered all too often among the nobility—one she despised. If she could have followed the rules, if there had been any way she could get traveling papers, she would have.

The first soldier seemed to take offense at that. "The rules apply to everyone, *Lady.*" He sneered. "We're all equal before the Flame."

The other soldier shuffled out from behind the table as Rienne's mind raced through her options. Arguing with the soldiers was getting her nowhere, and she suspected that her appeal to her birth had hurt her cause more than helped it. With the magical lifts between her and the city, breaking past the soldiers and fleeing into the streets and alleys wasn't an option. She couldn't return to the ship without showing her papers there, where the Lyrandars who crewed it would know who she was.

Two other soldiers stood at her shoulders, and the one with the mother-in-law stood in front of her, looking down severely. "I'm sorry, Lady, but we're going to have to take you into custody until we can sort through this matter."

That was the fourth option, and it was the only one that seemed viable. She gave herself up to the soldiers, who escorted her into the city, into a guard tower, and into a bare stone cell with iron bars.

CHAPTER
38

Despairing of finding Frostburn Cut or any other pass through the Shadowcrags, Aunn staggered through the foothills, trying always to make his way to higher ground. The mountains rebuffed him, spilling him back out onto the plateau above the Labyrinth, and leading him much farther south than he would have liked. From time to time he saw shadows in the clefts of the hills—stalking creatures watching him, waiting for him to tire and falter. Sevren's words echoed in his thoughts, warning of predators making their way out of the mountains—bears, panthers, and girallons. And flying predators as well, griffons and wyverns.

Flying predators . . . Aunn looked up at the sky, glowing red with sunset. At first he saw nothing, but then a dark shape rose just above the line of the mountains before swooping back down. The shape was miles away to the south, but a flying predator needed prey. And the most likely place to find prey in the mountains was in a pass. He scanned the mountains as the sky darkened, hoping to see something closer, but all he saw was another flap of mighty wings in the same general area. That had to be his destination, his gateway back to the Eldeen Reaches and the civilized world beyond.

He walked in that direction until his legs threatened to give out beneath him, then he staggered into a crevice and dozed, clutching his mace and jolting awake at every sound. A tingle on his neck made him leap out of the crevice, swatting at what proved to be a scorpion the size of his fist. After smashing it with his weapon, he tried to sleep with his back against the cliff wall, but sleep evaded him.

When morning's fire lit the sky, Aunn heaved himself to his feet and continued on to where he'd seen the hint of wings. Shadows kept stalking him, but as he climbed higher into the hills, farther from the Labyrinth, they resolved into less sinister threats—a red panther that watched as he passed beneath its clifftop perch, a silver bear that shambled away, more interested in the sparse growth of bushes on the higher ground ahead than in him.

This time he climbed and kept climbing, continuing higher and higher until the Demon Wastes lay spread out behind him like the slowly fading memory of a nightmare. The rising ground led him at last into a narrow cut through the mountains, chilly rather than cold, only a faint dusting of snow on the rock above him. The bushes grew thicker and greener, and he could see trees ahead and above him. The air tasted sweet after the acrid fumes of the Demon Wastes, and he drank it in like water.

Before the sun even reached the horizon—still too far to his right, not at his back—he decided to stop, desperate for rest and certain he'd sleep better on higher ground. He spread out the bedroll Farren had given him, wrapped himself in the warm wool, and stared up at a sky that was beginning to clear of clouds. Three of the smaller moons were rising nearly full in the east, and two bright crescents shone high overhead. As the sky darkened, the gleaming Ring of Siberys took shape, a golden band linking the moons. When the sky reached its perfect blue, within a hair's breadth of black, Aunn smiled and closed his eyes.

A high, distant shriek jolted him awake. He sat up, looking around for the source of the sound. A hint of shadow on the ground made him look up—just in time to roll away from the talons of a griffon as they raked across his back. He fumbled with his bedroll and onto his feet, scooping his mace into his hand on the way up. Another beast swooped at him, its vicious beak open wide and its front talons stretched forward as its leonine rear legs kicked at the empty air.

Aunn threw himself aside as it reached him, swinging his mace into its ribs. He could only see two griffons—a dangerous threat, but manageable, as long as there weren't more he hadn't seen yet. It would help, he thought, if they were the sort of predator that fled from prey that could defend itself.

The griffon he'd hit, knocked off balance by the blow, made a clumsy landing and emitted a sound that combined a high screech and a rumbling growl as it turned back to face him. So they were not that kind of predator.

A strange calm settled over him, even as he hit the other griffon in the wing, knocking it out of its dive. He still didn't fully understand what had happened when he wrestled the fiend in the Labyrinth, but whatever it was, it was staying with him—the supporting presence of Kalok Shash, perhaps, the spirits of the dead Ghaash'kala warriors fighting beside him.

The grounded griffons circled warily, on opposite sides of him, watching for an opening. He turned with them, keeping them at either edge of his vision, ready for them to pounce. But then the one on his left slowed its pace slightly, dropping out of his field of vision.

Damn, he thought, these things are smart.

He ran forward and whirled to face them as they sprang in unison toward him. He used the momentum of his turn to swing his mace in a wide arc across his body, knocking one griffon into the other and keeping both their claws away from his body. A feathered shoulder slammed into his exposed chest, knocking him to the ground. The griffon landed on him, squeezing the breath out of him.

Its rear claws scratched at his legs as it scrambled to its feet, and its mate lunged in to bite at his weapon arm. Its beak tore flesh, and his mace tumbled out of his hand. Shouting in pain, he kicked the griffon off him and rolled to grab his weapon with his other hand. Talons bit into his back.

A manageable threat? he thought. What was I thinking? And why aren't the dead warriors of the Ghaash'kala covering my back?

He heard Zandar's voice in his thoughts, the warlock's cynical wit, and it shamed him. As much as he had liked the warlock, it was Vor's faith he wanted to emulate, Vor's confidence and strength.

Aric, today you die. As a ghost, you will fight . . . You will fight until at last you have proved yourself worthy of joining Kalok Shash. Are you ready?

His initiation into the Ghaash'kala had not been complete—until he faced the fiend in the Labyrinth, he realized. In that battle, he had died. He was already a ghost, fighting to prove himself worthy.

"Make me worthy," he breathed.

Biting back the pain, he found his feet again. A beak already washed with his blood lunged at him again, but his weapon came down on the griffon's skull and crushed it. The other beast shrieked in fury and jumped forward. One swing knocked its head to one side, and a second smashed it the other way, breaking the creature's neck.

Silence, except his own breathing and the pulse of blood in his ears. A gentle chill seized him and he closed his eyes to savor it—a presence that defied all names, holding him up and soothing him. His breath stopped and his pulse no longer pounded, all sound was shut out in that moment. When the moment began to fade, he clutched at it, tried to hold the presence near, but then it was gone, and he heard the movement of breath and blood, the stirring of a gentle wind coming down from the mountains.

The corpses would attract scavengers. He slung his pack, threw his bedroll over his shoulder, and made his way farther up the pass to find a new resting place.

* * * * *

Aunn lost track of the days he spent climbing the pass, but before long he stood overlooking the Towering Wood once again. The sky was clear but pale. Here and there, orange and gold were scattered among the leaves of the forest, hinting at the winter to come. Soon, the trees would shed their leaves, standing bare and dark between the snow-covered ground and white sky.

An image flashed into his mind of bare trees burning, snow melting into steaming blood, a sky shrouded with smoke. He tried to believe that his imagination was poisoned by the taint of the Demon Wastes, but even so, the vision spurred him on, through the pass and down toward the forest. Aundair and the Eldeen Reaches had to be warned, or Greenheart and Varna and soon Fairhaven itself might face the same fate as Maruk Dar.

The forest covered the foothills and reached up the sides of the mountains, and soon Aunn walked among smooth-skinned trees that stretched to the sky, every leaf and branch straining toward the sun. The ground was a twilight world of shade and silence, only thin beams of sunlight filtering down through the canopy screen. The musty scent of fallen leaves hung thick in the air. Colorless fungus jutted from gray and brown tree trunks, and dead leaves covered the ground. But when he looked up, the trees lifted him up with them—he felt he was soaring among their highest branches, enveloped in green, glorying in the sun above. Even the air smelled cleaner, clearer. Many times he stumbled over a root or stone because he was watching the sky instead of the ground where he walked.

More days passed as if in a dream. If predators stalked these woods, they never showed themselves. Even birds and squirrels were sparse. He saw a single leopard hare, its mottled pelt helping it hide on the leafy forest floor. Insects crawled on the ground, but none buzzed around his ears or tickled his skin. He used the sun to keep to a roughly southeastward course, toward where he imagined Greenheart would be. From dawn to sunset he walked with few stops to rest. He slept peacefully, untroubled by hungry beasts—or haunting dreams.

Slowly the forest became greener—moss clung to the sides of trees, willowy saplings with bright new leaves sprouted between ancient trunks, shocks of grass emerged from the fallen leaves. Then one night as twilight descended, the forest lit up with fireflies, flashing to each other from the sides of trees and hovering in the air. The forest seemed to come alive at their signal—a nightingale began its anthem, squirrels chased each other along high branches, a rabbit dashed past.

Aunn felt himself drawn forward, toward the flashing fireflies, along the path of the hare. A soft glow arose before him, pulsing gently yellow-green, as though gigantic fireflies were lighting their lamps on the other side of the tree trunks ahead. As he walked on, globes of light appeared among the trees, swaying in a dance to the music of singing birds and chirping insects. Then he heard soft flutes join the melody, the gentle strum of harp strings, and distant voices singing high and clear. Only then did he realize he was no longer alone.

Tall figures emerged from among the trees all around, slender and lithe, beautiful but somehow terrifying, like the splendor of a firestorm or a whirlwind. They walked like royalty, slow and stately, but he saw swords, spears, and wands in their hands, caution etched on their faces. Their eyes were pearly orbs of swirling colors, unmarked by pupil or iris, seeming to glow in the twilight.

"Valatharanni, usharan, ka halatha na-dravanni kelos dar ben." It was a woman's voice, right at his shoulder, soft as silk but clear in its threat. The language sounded similar to the tongue of the Aereni, but his knowledge of Elven was fragmentary, and this was beyond him. He spread his empty hands away from his body and shook his head.

"Your name," the voice at his shoulder demanded, now in heavily accented Common. "And why you are here. Tell us."

"Aunn—my name is Aunn." He felt clumsy beside these graceful folk, and his voice was rough from disuse, grating against their melody. "I'm trying to reach Greenheart."

"Why?" Her voice was a dagger held at his throat.

"To warn them—I should warn you. Barbarians are massed in the Demon Wastes, ready to spill over the mountains and raze the forest."

He saw no surprise on the faces of the people around him, though their expressions were grim.

"Travelers are not our enemies, Aunn," the woman behind him said. "We are just . . . *dravan* . . . cautious. Join our feast, as our guest."

* * * * *

Aunn ate—sweet fruit, salted nuts, greens, roots, and roasted mushrooms, all of it delicious. Some part of him suspected it only tasted so good because he'd eaten nothing but journeybread and the rough food of the Ghaash'kala for so long, because he could never have imagined that a meal free of meat and grains could be so flavorful. He drank their ethereal wine, like drinking pure air that made his head swim. The eladrin, as they called themselves, welcomed him into their midst.

The woman who had stood behind him and invited him to the feast stayed distant throughout the meal. She was stunning—every time his gaze fell on her, her beauty struck him like a gust of wind, drawing the breath out of his lungs. She alone of all the eladrin had black hair, like the wings of a raven, and her eyes were smooth mirrors of pearl and green. As the night stretched on, she took in the radiance of the fey lamps and shed it from her skin, glowing in a nimbus of light.

The other eladrin who reclined on soft couches around Aunn were fair-skinned—pale was not the right word, he thought, for skin that seemed so healthy and alive. Their hair was various shades of silver, gold, and white, though a few were a more human-like blond or very light brown. Their eyes shone blue, violet, and green, milk white, or liquid gold.

In choosing his new persona's appearance, Aunn had strived for an aura of nobility—but among the eladrin, he felt like a baboon. They held cups made of leaves in their slender hands, and it was all he could do to keep from crushing his own cup. They reclined languorously on their couches, and he could not get comfortable. He felt all angles and rough edges compared to their smooth and graceful curves.

He would have been content to lie back and watch these folk and listen to their melodious voices, slipping freely between speech and song, but they plied him with questions, some of them speaking in fluent Common, others stumbling over the unfamiliar words. He told them he came from Aundair, that he worked for the queen—tantamount to admitting he was a Royal Eye—and he thought later that he might have admitted he was a changeling. They showed no surprise, and their attitude toward him didn't change. He told them all he could about Kathrik Mel and his horde, and he wept as he spoke of Maruk Dar's fall. He described Vor's death, and then Durrnak's, and he confessed his guilt and described what he thought might be his redemption. He told them of his dreams, his battle with the fiend in the Labyrinth, his surrender to . . . to Dania, in his vision, to Kalok Shash or the Silver Flame or the Traveler, he wasn't sure.

He had never spoken so freely or felt so deeply. The eladrin could move from laughter to tears in a moment's time. Their anger was almost palpable, like a charge in the air, and their joy made the lights shine brighter. In their midst, Aunn's passions and emotions took hold of him, carrying him in their currents, surging strong to break free of the tight reins of his control. All his discipline, his lifetime of training under Kelas's firm hand, came to nothing.

When he tried to turn the questions back on them, they gave evasive answers and shot back new questions of their own. They had him outnumbered, so every time he finished an answer another eladrin asked a new question, keeping him on the defensive, never allowing him an opening.

Dawn's approach brought the feast to an end. The globes of light drifted off and vanished among the trees, and the eladrin followed, one by one. Sadness gripped Aunn's heart as he watched them go, and the journey ahead of him seemed long and hard. If they would let him, he thought he might stay among them forever.

As the last of his dinner companions said farewell and drifted away, Aunn looked up to find the raven-haired woman standing over him. "Walk with me," she said, and she offered a perfect hand to help him stand.

Her touch was cool, exhilarating as autumn dawn. Her beauty took his breath away, but her touch restored it, washing away the fatigue of the long night and the long journey behind him. When she withdrew her hand, he thought he might never be able to draw enough breath.

"Wh-what is . . ." he stammered. "May I ask your name?"

Her laugh was the stirring of dry leaves on the ground. "Marelle," she said, and she walked on in silence.

"Your people—are you related to the elves of Aerenal?"

"Distant cousins, you might say."

A panic seized him as he remembered his mission. "Kathrik Mel—you should flee, you can't hope to stand against him!"

She stopped then, turned to him with the slightest smile, and put a hand on his cheek. "Listen," she said, and he could hear nothing but her voice. "The barbarians can not harm us. But there is more here than the barbarians. More than our people and your nation. The *Harath-Vadrema*—the Secret-Keeper calls, and his people answer. His power flows into the world. If not stopped, soon he will be free. Go. Warn your nation. Raise their armies to fight the barbarians. But be careful that they don't use weapons more terrible than their foe."

Aunn blinked, utterly uncomprehending. His cheek burned when she pulled her cool hand away, but her cryptic words were inscribed in his memory.

"Farewell," she said. "You stand at the edge of the Eldritch Grove. Lake Galifar is to the west, the Blackcaps to the south."

Aunn gaped. "I'm in Aundair?" That was impossible—the Eldritch Grove was over a month's journey from the Shadowcrags.

Marelle shook her head. "There is more here than your nation, Aunn." She took two steps backward, and with the third step she was gone.

Chapter
39

"Come in, Kelas."

Kelas pushed open the door and strode into the warm room. After weeks encamped in the miserable canyon, he was glad to be back in Fairhaven. He had teleported away from the Dragon Forge the day before, then spent the night in a soft bed, washed in hot water in the morning, and put on new clothes. He felt like himself again, prepared to play his part in the unfolding plot.

Thuel Racannoch sat in a comfortable chair, half turned away from the door, before a crackling fire. Kelas knew the appearance of comfort was an illusion—though he didn't look at the door as Kelas entered, Thuel was perfectly aware of his movements and warded against any attack. The Spy Master of Aundair's Royal Eyes did not take security lightly.

Kelas settled himself into a chair beside Thuel, enjoying the warmth of the fire, and waited for Thuel to speak first. He cast a few sidelong glances at his superior, trying to assess the Spy Master's mood.

Thuel was the picture of Aundairian nobility—though his birth among the merchant class, his freedom from noble entanglement, had been one of the reasons he'd been selected to fill the position left vacant by Nara ir'Galanatyr's removal. He held himself erect in the chair, feet flat on the floor and fingers laced casually at his waist. His chin was high and his eyes closed, savoring the warmth of the fire. Kelas imagined him as a lizard resting in the sun, warming his cold blood.

Thuel was known as a great lover of music, so the slow turning and bobbing of his head might indicate that he was listening to a symphony playing only in his mind. To Kelas, that suggested a pleasant mood, which would make his task difficult. It was much easier to turn an agitated Thuel into a fearful and anxious man.

At last the Spy Master opened his eyes and turned a hard gaze on Kelas. "You have news?"

Kelas was taken aback by his tone, not at all indicative of a pleasant mood. Was it possible that Thuel had some inkling of Kelas's recent activities?

"I do."

"News that will concern the queen?"

"Yes."

Thuel sighed. "Let's hear it, then."

Kelas chose his words carefully. "First, Haldren ir'Brassek is dead." Thuel's eyebrows rose slightly. "Our agents discovered him encamped in the foothills of the Blackcaps. He resisted arrest, and they were forced to kill him."

Thuel did not look away from the fire. "Just like Yeven."

"Exactly." And now that both of the men supposedly responsible for the debacle at Starcrag Plain were dead, Aurala would appear to be absolved of responsibility.

"And his body?" Thuel asked. The queen would want to display it publicly, of course. As she had with Yeven's.

"Our agents are transporting it here now."

"Excellent. And second?" Thuel was quick, efficient. He liked to get the information he needed and move along. Despite his relaxed appearance, he was in constant motion.

"Our concerns about the western border have proven justified."

Now Thuel turned to look Kelas square in the face. "The barbarians?"

Kelas nodded. "Several of the Carrion Tribes have joined under one chieftain's banner, and they have already started eastward."

Thuel brought his hands up, putting one finger to his lips in thought. "Several tribes," he said. "How many tribesmen are there in this army?"

"They number in the tens of thousands."

That provoked the reaction Kelas was looking for—Thuel clutched the arms of his chair and leaned toward him, eyes wide.

"They'll annihilate the Reaches!"

"Yes," Kelas said. He would let Thuel reach his own conclusion. There was only one possible conclusion.

"And they won't stop there. They'll be at our border in no time."

"Without doubt."

Thuel sat back in his chair. His eyes darted around the room, chasing his thoughts. Kelas could guess at those thoughts. The logical course was to send aid to the Reachers, reinforcing their border so the barbarians never got close to Aundair. But so soon after the debacle at Starcrag Plain, the Reachers weren't likely to welcome Aundairian troops into their lands—they would suspect Aundair of trying to reannex the Reaches. It was no secret that Aundair still considered the Eldeen Reaches its western province.

But the Reachers' attention would be focused on the west. They had been mollified by Queen Aurala's assurances that the attempted invasion of Thrane had occurred without her knowledge or approval, and the public execution of the general responsible, Jad Yeven. The Aundairian border would be poorly defended by little more than a token force. With the full support of the queen, Aundair could strike with enough force to sweep through the Reaches and meet the barbarian horde in full strength.

"The chieftain who leads them," Thuel asked, "what do we know of him?"

"His name is Kathrik Mel. He inspires tremendous loyalty in the barbarians, an almost religious fervor."

"He's a demon?"

"I don't think so. The Ghaash'kala call him a *sak'vanarrak*—it translates as something like 'fiend-touched.' A Karrn scholar coined the word *tiefling*. I think he's some mixture of fiend and mortal, more like a savior than a god."

Thuel frowned. "Their savior, our damnation."

Damnation—that was a strong word. But then, Thuel had been very vocal in his support of the Treaty of Thronehold, very eager to stop the hostility between Aundair and its neighbors.

Outspoken in his condemnation of Haldren, who attacked the Reaches after the signing of the treaty. It made sense for him to describe a return to war in such stark terms.

"Is there anything else?" Thuel asked.

There was so much more. But the time would come for that. "No," Kelas said.

"I'll advise the queen. Thank you."

Kelas rose and left the room. The hall felt cold after warming his blood by the fire.

* * * * *

Cart had never been particularly good at sneaking. The adamantine plating of his body tended to clank, if only slightly, when he moved in certain ways, and it made crouching behind cover hard for him. More than that, it ran counter to his training and his attitude toward battle. Enemies were to be faced and slain.

But practical concerns sometimes forced him into unfamiliar ways. He was the lone warforged in a camp full of soldiers. He was known as a traitor and thought to be dead. If anyone saw him, there would be fighting, and he didn't want to fight the soldiers who blindly followed Kelas's orders. There was at least the possibility they might overwhelm him with sheer numbers, and in any event there would be a large number of needless deaths.

So he draped himself in a voluminous cloak, trying to hide his nature, and moved as quietly as he could through the camp to Phaine's tent. The elf had chosen a spot near the Dragon Forge to pitch his tent, far closer to the crystal prison than Cart would have wanted to be. It was also, apparently, closer than anyone else in camp was willing to sleep. No other tents stood within fifty yards of Phaine's. Also to Cart's advantage, once he reached the wall of the forge and started creeping along it, the hissing steam and occasional bursts of flame covered any noise he might have been making.

Ashara had an easier task, given her prominent position in the camp. First, she ensured that Cart was armed, and found a sword for him to give Gaven and a shirt of chainmail she would bring for him to wear later. Then she left the camp, promising to provide an escape route for Cart and Gaven—a way to scale the cliff near

Phaine's tent. From the top of the cliff, it would be a simple matter of evading or disabling a handful of guards and disappearing into the foothills.

A growl of pain from the tent ahead of him told Cart that Gaven was still alive, at least. He felt a surge of anger, on Gaven's behalf as well as his own. The blow had been quick and precise, and Cart had been only vaguely aware that Phaine's hand held the blade that had nearly killed him. He would repay that strike.

Gaven yelled again, and Cart sprang into action. He seized the pole supporting the nearer end of the tent and heaved it upward, ripping two pegs from the ground. The canvas billowed up, and in a flash he saw Phaine standing over Gaven, a blood-tipped dagger in his hand. Cart swung the pole into the elf's gut, doubling him over and tangling him in canvas and rope.

With the sword in his other hand, he hacked at the ropes holding Gaven to the chair, careful not to cut into flesh. The tent flew free, and Phaine wasn't there.

"Look out," Gaven said. His voice was weak and his throat raw from shouting.

Cart whirled and brought the sword with him, cutting a wide arc through the air. Phaine leaped back, almost out of reach, but the point of the sword still sliced into his upper arm and across the leather armor that covered his chest.

The weight of the sword pulled Cart off-balance, and Phaine sprang into the gap in his defenses. The elf's blade found the softer substance between the metal plates of Cart's arm, making him nearly lose his grip on the sword. Cart pushed Phaine off him and dropped the unwieldy weapon, yanking his own axe from his belt. Fury nearly blinded him, shutting out Gaven and the rest of the camp. He saw only Phaine.

The elf circled warily, wearing a smirk that only intensified Cart's rage. "I don't know how I failed to kill you before, war-forged," he said. "But I never repeat my mistakes."

"In all my years, I've never encountered a more loathsome, honorless, traitorous scum." Cart swung carefully, sizing the elf's reactions without leaving himself open. Phaine was amazingly quick on his feet, his movements a shadowy blur.

"Thank you," Phaine said. He darted to one side, and his blade was at Gaven's throat. "I wish I could say I held you in such high esteem."

Cart cursed himself. He'd been careless, oblivious to the field of battle while he focused on his enemy. He let the head of his axe droop to the ground. He'd hoped to be a hero, but proven himself a fool.

Gaven's hand shot up and grabbed Phaine's wrist, pulling the blade away from his throat. With a grunt, Gaven heaved Phaine forward, dragging the elf over his lap and slamming a fist into his gut while he passed over. Phaine landed in a crumpled heap on the ground.

"Give me the sword," Gaven said. Cart saw that he'd worked his hands free, but his feet were still bound to the legs of the chair.

As Cart stooped to retrieve the sword, he saw Phaine vanish, and an instant later he felt Phaine's blade slide between his armored plates. Strange lights danced in the darkness at the edge of his vision, and his thoughts clouded. With a final surge of effort, he lifted the sword and swung it and his axe together. It was a solid blow—he felt both blades hit flesh. Phaine's body dissipated into wisps of shadow, and then he was gone.

Cart held both blades at the ready, waiting for the elf's inevitable reappearance. Pain raged in his chest, but he managed to fight back the darkness in his eyes, clear the shadows from his mind. A moment passed—nothing. He stepped over to Gaven and handed him the sword, still watching—still nothing. Gaven cut the rest of his bonds and stood beside him, holding his sword in both hands, but the elf did not reappear.

A shadow took form amid the pulsing light of the Dragon Forge's fires, and Cart and Gaven both whirled to face it. It was not Phaine. The enormous form of Malathar the Damned rose up from the forge, smoke and steam billowing around him, his blazing eyes fixed on Cart and Gaven as he leaped into the air.

Gaven crouched, preparing to cleave into the dragon's bones when it drew near enough. Then he lurched forward, gasping with a jolt of pain. He tried to resume the stance, but he was favoring one leg.

"Come on!" Cart shouted, pulling at Gaven's arm.

Gaven gave a fierce shake of his head. "Not before I've dealt with him."

"You're mad." Cart managed to pull Gaven back a few steps before the half-elf wrenched his arm free. "You're in no condition to fight him."

The dragon-king wheeled in the sky and dived toward them.

"I have to!" Gaven cried.

"Not now. It's suicide!"

Gaven turned and fixed his gaze on Cart's eyes. "If I leave here without that dragonshard, I might as well be dead."

Darkness coiled and congealed in the dragon's mouth, then burst forth in a spray like black fire. Cart rolled away from the brunt of it, but the blast drove Gaven to his knees. A purple-black light coursed along the edges of Gaven's clothes, festered inside the many wounds on his skin, and sparked in his hair. He lifted one leg, but he didn't have the strength to rise.

Shouts arose in the camp beyond the Dragon Forge, and Cart saw soldiers emerging from tents, donning helmets and seizing their weapons. Malathar circled around in the air for another attack. Cart stooped over, wrapped an arm around Gaven's legs, and lifted the half-elf to his shoulder. Gaven went limp, and Cart ran.

He started for the cliff near Phaine's tent, where Ashara had said she would provide a way up. He scanned the cliff face as he ran, looking for a rope or any other indication of Ashara's presence. He saw only the sheer blue crystal jutting up and out from the jagged edge of the cliff. Had she been hindered or captured?

A rope dropped from inside the crevice between the crystal and the rock, above the strange metal strands that linked the crystal to the forge. He saw a glimpse of Ashara's face, wide-eyed and pale, before she pulled back into the shelter of the gap.

"The excoriate cannot leave here alive," the dragon-king said, its whispery voice somehow louder and more intense though still eerily voiceless.

Cart didn't know or care whether Malathar was addressing him or the gathering soldiers. As he seized the rope, another surge of eldritch fire washed over him. It was at once searing hot and deathly cold, numbing his senses and his mind to everything but the burning pain. He shielded Gaven with his own body as best he could, but he felt the strength siphoned from him—his arm dropped from the rope and he staggered under Gaven's weight.

"No!" Ashara called from above him. He wanted to raise his head, to reassure her, but he couldn't.

Cart's head drooped and touched the azure crystal, itself alive with black flame. He heard the voice of his despair in his mind, the same voice that had addressed him in the worg's temple.

It is no use. You cannot hope to fight him, and you cannot escape him.

Cart lacked the strength of will to argue.

You and Ashara can't stand against Malathar the Damned, dragon-king of Rav Magar! And Gaven is nothing more than dead weight.

"Cart! Up here!" It was Ashara's voice, desperate with fear. He lifted his head and saw her face in the crevice again, her hand reaching down to him. "Take my hand!"

"Take her hand, Cart—the hand of a friend."

It was the softest sound, so utterly unlike the dry voiceless whisper of the dragon-king or the rasp of his despair—it was the rustle of silk, almost too fine for his rough senses. A writhing coil, bright in the blue, moved within the crystal, and he took Ashara's hand.

"We need to get out of here before he does that again!" she shouted.

"No!" Cart cried.

Malathar slammed down behind him, shaking the earth. Bone claws raked across his back, scrabbling at him as Ashara helped him climb, clumsily trying to pluck him from her grasp.

Wordlessly, the paired voices of the crystal—the silken rustle and the harsh rasp—fought for his attention, but Ashara's hand held him, tight and strong, and he climbed up beside her. The crevice was narrow, and for a moment he feared he wouldn't fit, but Ashara took Gaven from his shoulder so he could work his way through into a wider channel.

Malathar spewed one more eruption of unholy fire. The flames licked at the edges of the gap, and a few made it just inside, but the crystal inhaled the greater part of the fire. Cart saw it shimmer along the outside, and seep like rain inside.

"He shouldn't have done that," Ashara said, her eyes wide with fear. "He should know that. His fury blinds him."

Cart heaved Gaven over his shoulder and Ashara took his hand again, pulling him deeper into the fissure, away from the raging dragon-king. He stumbled blindly after her, her touch the only respite from the pain. She led him up a spiraling ledge around the crystal column, glancing from time to time at the crystal as if she were afraid it might lash out at her.

They reached another crevice where the rock jutted closer to the crystal, and Ashara peered through. "It's clear," she said. "Can you get through?"

It would be a tight fit. "I'll try. You go first and I'll hand Gaven through."

Gaven's broad shoulders had trouble, and Ashara winced as the rock scraped the skin of his chest. But then he was through. Ashara staggered under Gaven's weight but let him down as gently as she could on the ground beyond.

"You'll never make it," she said, her brow creased.

"Stand back."

Ashara obeyed, and Cart pounded his fist against the edge of the rock. The adamantine plating on the back of his hand was harder than the stone, and soon chips were falling free and the gap grew wider. On his third try, he made it through and found himself in the smooth stone chamber, the temple where they'd found the worgs before.

"I thought we collapsed this chamber," he said.

"Kelas refused. Make of that what you will."

A week ago, that news would have surprised him. Now that he'd seen what Kelas was capable of, it made perfect sense.

"Now rest a moment and let me see to Gaven, then I'll help you."

Cart dropped to his knees then eased himself down on the ground. Ashara crouched beside Gaven, murmuring softly and touching a wand to the half-elf's wounds. Cart watched skin knit itself together at her command, blackened flesh fade to angry red and then its normal tanned color, the lines of pain slowly disappear from Gaven's face. Before she was finished Gaven opened his eyes, started at the unfamiliar face and then smiled as the healing washed through him. When she was done, he looked better than Cart had seen him since his first arrival at the canyon.

Ashara turned her attention on Cart then, putting away her wand and laying her soft hands on him. He could feel her coaxing his substance back to wholeness, weaving him together. Her touch was a soft caress, gentle and cool. She called him friend. He reached out to run a finger along the line of her jaw, as soft a stroke as his clumsy hand could manage.

She looked up, startled.

"I'm sorry, Lady—"

"No, no." She seized his hand before he could pull it away, and cupped it to her cheek. "You surprised me, that's all. I don't mind."

Cart's hands looked like armored gauntlets, but they could sense touch like the rest of his body. His fingers were not very sensitive to details of texture, but he could distinguish hot from cold, tell a sharp blade from a dull one, discriminate between rough and smooth or soft and hard. He could tell that her face was warm, smooth, and soft, as were the hands that held his in place. He had never felt anything like it before—it was warmer than silk, and softer than the hands of a dying soldier clutching his to hold back the pain.

Her eyes were moist and bright when she finally released his hand and turned her attention back to his wounds.

CHAPTER
40

L ake Galifar is to the west, the Blackcaps to the south," Aunn
     repeated to himself. He turned the directions Marelle had
     pointed—first west, then south. The forest seemed thinner
to the south, so he walked that way.

His mind felt addled. Marelle had brought him from the
western edge of the Towering Wood to the south of Aundair—
they must have traversed nearly a thousand miles in a matter of
moments! He tried to review the night's events, but his memories
of them were shrouded in fog. At some point, he reasoned, the
eladrin must have shifted him between worlds, drawing him
in to the Faerie Court of Thelanis and dropping him back in
a different place. How long had he really been gone? Nursery
stories warned of travelers disappearing into the Faerie Court
and emerging a hundred years later, convinced that only a week
had passed.

A thorn-studded thicket marked the edge of the forest. Aunn
pushed through and found the morning sun, then turned west to
get his bearings. There was a shimmer on the horizon that might
have been Lake Galifar, farther away than he'd hoped. The tip of
the Blackcap range also jutted up just to the south of west, and he
followed the line of mountains around to the south.

There was a storm over the Blackcaps—a very strange storm.
For miles around, the sky swirled with black clouds, but beyond
that vortex it was bright and clear. At the center, lightning flashed
in a roiling mass of red and violet cloud, brilliant bolts striking
down to the ground every few seconds. That could not be a natural storm.

It has to be Gaven, he thought.

Having found a destination, he set off as quickly as his legs would carry him.

* * * * *

In his office the next day, Kelas leaned over his glowing crystal. Nara was smiling this time, a smile that reminded him of when she'd first taken him under her wing as a new recruit. He was pleased to bring her good news—very good news.

"Queen Aurala has agreed to send troops into the Reaches. A full force."

Nara laughed, a cackle of raw delight. "So all Thuel's talk of peace is undone, and I am vindicated at last."

The mention of Thuel made Kelas's face fall. "Thuel is having me watched," he said. "It's getting harder to move around."

"Stay where you are, then. Do you still have agents you trust?"

"I've never trusted an agent," he said, echoing her teaching from so many years ago. Even as he said it, though, he thought of Haunderk. Reliable as the orbit of the twelve moons—but trustworthy? "Never. But I don't think any of them are reporting back to Thuel."

"Use people outside the Eyes for anything important. But make sure the agents have things to do as well, or a traitor might report back that you've grown suspicious."

She wasn't telling him anything he hadn't already put in place, but it was comforting to hear his old mentor confirm his judgment.

"And all is running smoothly at the forge?" she asked. "The dragons?"

"The dragons are still cooperating. Their king is studying the shard while it's not in use, but so far he seems content to stay and observe the situation as it develops."

"Why? If you're giving him access to the shard, what's to stop him from taking it and going back to Argonnessen, taking his dragons with him? Then we have no forge, and Aundair has no weapon."

"If he decides to take the shard, there's little we could do to stop him in any case. I think he's staying because he wants to see what happens. He's very interested in what the Prophecy has to say about all this, and he's going to stick around to see it all come true."

Nara frowned. She didn't like being told there was nothing to be done—she wanted plans and backup plans constantly prepared. Kelas had some ideas about what to do if the dragon-king did leave with the shard, but he was confident it wouldn't come to that.

"What about the excoriate?"

"The Thuranni is keeping him in a great deal of pain."

"Better to kill him. He must not escape, Kelas. You know that."

"Yes." Gaven was physical proof of the power of the Dragon Forge. The Cannith heirs at the forge were already under close watch, as the people most likely to have qualms about their work. Jorlanna went along with the plan despite serious reservations. If Gaven escaped to show the dragonmarked Houses what Kelas was doing, the Dragon Forge would be leveled in a matter of days as every resource the Houses could muster was brought to bear against it.

"When will Jorlanna and Wheldren go to the queen?"

"In the morning. If all goes well, they'll bring the queen to the forge the day after tomorrow for a personal demonstration."

"I think you should accompany them for the demonstration."

"Me?" Kelas said. "Why?"

"I want to hear the queen's response from your mouth, first of all. And it will bring you to the queen's notice."

"That's exactly what I was hoping to avoid."

Nara grinned. "One of Thuel's subordinates taking such initiative without his knowledge or approval—it makes Thuel look bad."

"Does it matter?" Kelas asked. "Queen Aurala's opinion won't be important for much longer."

"It matters to me. I want Thuel humiliated as quickly and as greatly as possible."

"Very well," Kelas said. "I will bring the queen to the Dragon Forge."

* * * * *

"We can't stay here, Gaven," Cart said patiently. "Kelas knows about this temple. He ordered it preserved. Which means that Malathar probably knows about it as well. They'll find us here."

"They'll find us if we go running across the hills," Gaven said. "I'm ready to fight that damned dragon-king and get my dragonmark back."

Ashara's ministrations had removed Gaven's wounds and the numbness that lingered behind Phaine's pricks and jabs. Now they were enjoying a good meal Ashara had prepared with food she brought from the camp, and it was starting to restore Gaven's strength as well, after weeks of near-starvation. Another artificer with excellent cooking skills. . . . Gaven shot Ashara a sharp glance.

She didn't seem to notice. "You're not even close to ready," she insisted. "One full meal isn't enough to fortify you after all this time."

"You're a changeling," Gaven said, watching her face carefully for her reaction.

Her surprise seemed genuine. "What?"

"You faked your death at Starcrag Plain, took on a new face and rejoined Haldren. You're Darraun." Gaven was on his feet, pointing a trembling finger down at Ashara, who looked up at him incredulously. Of course she was surprised—surprised to be found out.

Cart put a hand on Gaven's shoulder. "Gaven—"

"You don't fool me," Gaven continued, ignoring the warforged. "Cooking was your mistake." His certainty gripped his mind like a fever, and he felt unsteady on his feet.

"In case you hadn't noticed," Ashara said, getting to her feet, "I carry the Mark of Making." She pulled back the arm of her shirt to make sure he could see the lyre-shaped tracery clearly, swooping across her upper arm. "That's a difficult thing to imitate."

"But you've done it before. You piloted the airship, you faked the Mark of Storm and even fooled the elemental."

"You're mad," she said, and turned away. "As crazy as they said you were."

Cart placed himself between them. "Gaven, I think you should sit down and finish your meal. We need to get out of here."

Gaven whirled to put his back to Cart and Ashara. "Fine," he said. He sat down and returned to his half-finished meal.

* * * * *

The storm faded quickly, leaving the sky a richer blue with its passing. Aunn carefully marked its location in the mountains, though, and he hurried on well into the evening, hoping that the end of the storm did not mean that Gaven was dead. He slept fitfully and rose before dawn, hurrying on toward the cut in the mountains etched against the slowly brightening sky.

He wasn't sure what reaction he could expect from Gaven. As far as the Storm Dragon knew, Darraun had died at Starcrag Plain—assuming that Gaven had found the body he'd made to look like his. If he hadn't . . . well, that might be worse. Gaven would believe that Darraun abandoned him, fleeing with Haldren, or perhaps chasing Haldren. He finally had to admit that he didn't know what Gaven would think. But he knew that he'd misled Gaven, lied to him, and that he had to rely on the half-elf's forgiveness.

Rienne, on the other hand—he was sure Rienne would forgive him. Rienne had seen him at his most vulnerable, weak from piloting the airship and tormented by his dreams, unable even to remember the name he'd chosen. And her first question had been, "Are you all right?" She had been all concern and care, not a hint of anger or condemnation. Rienne would welcome him back, glad just to see him alive.

It wasn't until the third day, as the ground started rolling toward the foothills of the Blackcaps, that he began to wonder why he was seeking Gaven at all. Gaven and Rienne had struck him as two people he could trust—potential allies, perhaps his only possible allies, in warning Aundair and the Reaches about Kathrik Mel. But they knew he wasn't trustworthy. Why should they help him?

He had no one. Except for the single evening he'd spent with the eladrin, he had been alone since leaving Maruk Dar. Everyone he had trusted or relied on up to that point was dead: Farren, Vor,

Sevren, and Zandar. Kelas had betrayed him, and he had betrayed everyone else, including Gaven and Rienne. He would have to complete his mission alone.

Besides, he reasoned, the storm had appeared in the mountains and since disappeared. Three days had passed, meaning Gaven and Rienne could already be three days away from the mountains in a different direction. What hope did he have of finding them in that enormous swath of wilderness and farmland? They might have traveled north to the forest along a path parallel to his own, or deeper into the Blackcrags. Or they might be bound for Arcanix, west on the shores of Lake Galifar, or Cragwar, in Breland to the southeast. The spires of Vanguard Keep rose above the middle of the plain. They could have gone there, or perhaps they were prisoners in the fortress outpost.

By the dawn of the fourth day, he had convinced himself that his journey wouldn't be in vain. The storm had been a sign of more than Gaven's distress, he decided, but some indication of destiny. He felt that his destiny was bound to Gaven and Rienne in some way he didn't yet understand, and that fate would draw them back together after their long separation. Proof would come soon enough—he was close to where he had seen the storm, close enough that he could no longer see the cut in the mountains that had been his landmark.

The sky, brilliant blue for days since the storm faded, started clouding over again in late morning. A shadow fell over the sunlight, and Aunn looked up to watch the unnatural storm take shape, just off to the east. Dark clouds appeared in the air like steam churning up from a boiling pot, writhing in the air like a living thing. They swirled outward to coat the sky, whirling around the vortex where they had appeared. A boom of thunder nearly knocked him off his feet, and rain began to fall into a canyon just east of Aunn's hilltop vantage point. He hurried down toward it.

* * * * *

As Gaven ate the last of his meal, Cart came to sit beside him. The warforged sat in silence for a moment, his face turned toward the blue crystal and the snarling demonic figure that framed it. He waited until Ashara was at the far side of the ancient temple, busy with the pack she'd brought from the camp.

"Darraun was a changeling?" Cart asked quietly, still looking at the crystal.

Gaven cursed himself. He'd forgotten that Cart didn't know, and he'd violated the changeling's trust.

It doesn't matter, he told himself, if Darraun really is dead.

"He was." He wasn't sure how much else he should say, or wanted to.

"So perhaps he's not really dead," Cart said.

Gaven felt his pulse quicken. Even in more lucid moments, he had half-wondered the same thing while building Darraun's cairn—why didn't he wear his true face in death?

"He can disguise himself," Cart continued. "Why not disguise another corpse to look like him?"

"But why would he do that?"

Cart shrugged. "Why did he do anything? Why was he spying on the Lord General . . . on Haldren? Why did he help Haldren escape from Dreadhold in the first place?"

"He . . ." Gaven drew a blank. "I don't know."

Cart glanced over his shoulder at Ashara. "I don't think she's a changeling," he said. "But I would have said the same thing about Darraun. How can we ever know for sure?"

"No, you're right," Gaven said. "I think I wasn't quite in my right mind. Raving."

He knew he hadn't been raving. But it occurred to him that Ashara might somehow be listening, and he wanted her to think he'd abandoned his suspicions. She'd be more likely to slip up.

Cart got to his feet and helped Gaven stand.

"I need to go back to the forge," Gaven said again.

"I didn't rescue you just so you could go back and be captured again—or killed," Cart said. "My goal was to get you to safety, and I'm going to do that."

"It's still all about duty, isn't it, Cart? You're always working on a clearly defined task, one after another. You can't think about taking on another task until you've completed that one you set for yourself. But I'm telling you I don't want to go to safety. The forge is where my enemies are, and they have something that belongs to me." He ran a finger over the tender skin his dragonmark had left behind.

"I'm not a machine."

"Of course not. But you're also not flexible. The world doesn't conform to our plans. People never do what we want them to. You have to live with that."

"Or you have to convince them that they're being stupid and stubborn, and show them why your way is right. I'm not an idiot and I'm not naïve, Gaven. I'm perfectly capable of changing plans midstream when I need to. But only when a better plan comes along. And going back into Malathar's claws is not a better plan."

Gaven clenched his fists at his temples. "I'll do it alone if I have to." His voice resounded in the chamber, uncomfortably loud. "I need her back."

"Her?" Ashara spoke for the first time.

That was it. Gaven's hands dropped to his sides and his shoulders slumped. He was being stupid and stubborn, he realized. It wasn't his dragonmark he wanted back. It was Rienne.

"Rienne," he said. "I need her back. I need her more than my dragonmark, more than revenge on Phaine and Kelas and the damned dragon-king. I—"

Cart put up a hand to stop him, turning his head toward the entrance. Then Gaven heard it as well—a rumbling like distant thunder, echoing in the tunnel that led out of the temple.

Cart stepped cautiously to the tunnel mouth, and Gaven circled around to the other side, staying out of the opening. Just as they started to peer into the tunnel, a hiss like the threat of an enormous serpent roared in the tunnel, then a spray of thick, black liquid gushed out at them. Gaven jumped back out of its way, but Cart shouted in pain. The warforged fell down, frantically wiping at the liquid that clung to his body. It bubbled and smoked, warping the metal plate of his face and searing the wood in his neck.

Ashara rushed to help Cart, so Gaven risked a look up the tunnel. It was long but straight, sloping up to where he could just make out the light of day beyond. A hulking black shadow blocked his view of the light, though—the source of the acidic spray. Another dragon.

Faint echoes of voices outside told him that some of Kelas's soldiers were there as well. Rage burned in Gaven's chest. These people and that dragon had taken everything from him—Rienne, his dragonmark, his freedom. He tried to channel that rage and release it, to send a blast of lightning back up the tunnel at his enemies. Nothing.

"Gaven, get back!" Cart said.

Gaven heard the dragon's deep intake of breath and leaped back away from the tunnel mouth just in time. More black acid sprayed out past him, spattering on the stone floor. Some reached as far as the blue crystal, and Ashara gasped as it burbled and disappeared into the azure pool.

"Get away," Cart said. Ashara had repaired some of the acid's damage, but his neck still looked seared and warped.

Gaven leaped past the tunnel mouth and crouched beside Cart. "We're trapped," he said.

"We're under siege," Cart answered, "but it could be worse. We can't get out, clearly. But they won't come in because we'd fight them right here, three of us against each one of them who came to the tunnel mouth. It's a waiting game."

"One we can't win," Gaven said. "They'll starve us out, if nothing else. Or send the dragon into the tunnel first."

"They won't wait here forever," Ashara said. "I have a feeling something will take their attention off us before long."

"What do you mean?" Cart asked.

"The Dragon Forge."

CHAPTER
41

S o this is how Gaven felt in Dreadhold, Rienne thought.
Trapped in a cage.

She looked through the barred window of her cell, out
onto the bustling streets of Thaliost, and wondered if Gaven had
a window in Dreadhold. Probably not. She felt the morning sun
warm her skin, and realized that she had no idea what Gaven had
experienced. Twenty-six years in a prison far worse than her bare
cell—it was still beyond her comprehension.

The worst part was that she didn't know where Maelstrom
was. They'd taken the sword as soon as they took her into custody,
and when they led her to her cell the guard carrying it had gone
a different way. She'd been tempted to break free of the guards
and seize the sword, fight her way free, but she couldn't imagine a
conclusion to that course of action that didn't make her situation
worse than it already was.

The morning wore into afternoon, casting the tower's shadow
across the town below her window. A guard brought her a pass-
able meal sometime between midday and evening, and shortly
after that a man came to see her. He dressed like a nobleman, all
frills and frippery, but he walked like a soldier, intense and direct.
He'd probably received a noble title as a reward for his service in
the Last War, and tried his best to act his part in an alien world of
diplomacy.

He looked down at the identification papers in his hand, then
back up at her face. "Lady Alastra?"

"Yes." Best just to answer his questions, simple and direct.

"I'm Padar ir'Hollen. The borders of Thaliost are ultimately
my responsibility, and the soldier at the docks report to me. Were

you mistreated in any way while in our custody?"

"No, and I thank you for asking." Rienne liked this man's approach—he was direct, he didn't bother with titles except to make sure she knew he was a noble. She'd never heard of the ir'Hollens, of course, and Padar might very well have been the only member of that recently formed noble house.

"Lady Alastra, I'm sure you can appreciate how seriously I take my responsibility for our security, particularly now. Since Aundair's attack, we have been even more concerned with possible breaches of our borders."

"I do understand. But the attack in the north was the action of a rogue general, not the Aundairian government."

"So Aundair claims. But if that's true, he had a remarkable amount of support from the army."

"Along with his flight of dragons, yes."

Padar's eyes went wide. "You seem to know a great deal about that battle."

Rienne drew herself up proudly. "I helped defeat that rogue general."

"You what?" Padar's mouth hung open after his question.

"I was there. I fought one of the dragons Haldren brought with him. I fought in the midst of the horde of monsters that rose from the earth. And as the battle wore down, I found Haldren and his—and the woman with him and I fought them. I'm no pretty noblewoman sitting in my estate, weaving and gossiping, Sir Hollen."

"I can see that," Padar said, scratching his head. "But now I'm far less sure how to deal with you."

"You're making it too complicated. It's really quite simple. Bring a scribe from House Sivis back here with you. Question me about my destination and purpose, have the scribe draw up traveling papers for me, and send me on my way."

"Why don't you tell me your destination and purpose now?"

Rienne had spent the morning formulating her answers to those inevitable questions. A fugitive following a vague sense of impending danger to the west would not quickly endear herself to any border authority. "I'm bound for Daskaran." As the other major town in the north of Thrane, Daskaran would give her a reason to leave Thaliost without raising the question of why she didn't sail on to Flamekeep—Thrane's capital gave better access to most of the nation. "My family wishes to forge an agreement with the ir'Cathra family there—they own mines in the Starpeaks and we can help them distribute the ore." As mundane as possible, not something that would arouse attention.

"From battling monsters to negotiating trade agreements? You are versatile."

"One reason my family values me."

Padar looked at another paper in his hand. "Your family is located primarily in Stormhome, correct?"

"That's right. Our ties to House Lyrandar give us an edge in our shipping deals."

"And you sailed from Stormhome? Before arriving here?"

"Yes.'

"I assume you purchased a regular fare on the Lyrandar galleon—the, ah, *Windborn?*"

Rienne forced her face to keep smiling as she cursed herself. She was a stowaway as well as a fugitive, and she had failed to account for that in her morning planning. "Of course," she said, as though it were nothing.

"It's strange that the *Windborn* carried no record of that purchase. Did they not check your papers when you bought the fare?"

"They did check my identification papers, but I'm afraid the young man was somewhat distracted. He never did ask about traveling papers, and he must have forgotten to record me in the passenger manifest."

"I see," Padar said.

He studied the papers in his hand once more, then stared at Rienne too long. She had the sense he was imagining what might have distracted the young Lyrandar agent, and his eyes made her uncomfortable.

"Well, Lady Alastra," he said at last, "I will need to discuss this situation. Perhaps I will bring a Sivis scribe with me when I return."

And perhaps not, Rienne thought as he disappeared down the corridor.

* * * * *

When the sun went down, Rienne's cell plunged into near-total darkness. Only shreds of light from the streets below reached her window, everbright lanterns and the lamps carried by the night watch—not nearly enough to let her see the walls, the bars, or even the cot she sat on. Sleep evaded her, so she sat and tried to focus her mind, find some rest in meditation at least.

"Where is he?" A gruff voice jolted her from her stillness, and she sprang to her feet.

A halo of light filled the far end of the corridor and lit the angry face of Ossa d'Kundarak. The dwarf stormed toward her, another pair of dwarves trailing at the edge of the light. Ossa wore her usual scarlet shirt beneath a heavy breastplate of cured leather, but it was wrinkled. Wisps of hair escaped the tight braid coiled at the back of her head, her face was drawn, thinner than Rienne remembered. She exuded a frantic energy that bordered on madness. The search for Gaven had not been good to her, Rienne thought.

"Where is he?" Ossa repeated when she reached the bars of Rienne's cell.

Rienne fought back a surge of anger. The last time she'd seen Ossa, the dwarf held a dagger pressed to her neck. But anger wouldn't help. She had to calm the dwarf, placate her as much as possible. Somehow, she had to get out of this prison, and an angry Ossa would make that impossible.

"I don't know," she said.

"I don't believe you!" Ossa seized a bar and thrust her face right up to it. "You've been with him since Vathirond."

"We parted company more than two weeks ago. He was captured, and his captors took him away. He could be anywhere."

"Who captured him? The Thuranni? Everyone else is dead."

"Everyone else?" There had been another one, a Tharashk bounty hunter with Ossa in Stormhome.

"Does that surprise you? You heard he killed a Sentinel

Marshal. And I would have thought you knew he killed Bordan. Bordan was a good man."

"Bordan? We saw Bordan in Stormhome. Gaven fled, and I got the airship."

"Bordan outpaced me in following Gaven. I found him dead on the beach, then saw your airship pass overhead, on your way to pick him up."

Bordan dead on the beach? Why wouldn't Gaven have told her?

Ossa sneered. "That troubles you? What did you expect, traveling with a fugitive? I told you in Vathirond he was dangerous."

"You don't know him." Rienne thought she did, after all this time. But he hadn't told her about Bordan.

"Of course," Ossa continued, "in Vathirond I had no idea how dangerous he was. He was involved with Starcrag Plain, wasn't he? Shall I add those dead thousands to the list of his crimes?"

"What? No—he prevented the death of thousands more. He closed the chasm where the spawn of Khyber were spilling out. Without him, the monsters would have overwhelmed—"

"He tried to clean up his mistake, then? Closed off the passage he opened?"

"He didn't open it!"

"What might have been merely a clash of two armies became a bloodbath. And witnesses say the chasm opened about the time a certain airship appeared at the scene."

"A clash of two armies with dragons on both sides! It was the Prophecy—"

"Don't insult my intelligence. He'll answer to that charge as well, when we recapture him. Now where is he? Who captured him, if that part of your story is true?"

This interview was not going the way Rienne had hoped it would. Ossa was no less belligerent—more so, if anything. She had to go back to being helpful. "It wasn't a Thuranni that captured him. It was a dragon."

"A dragon." It was a challenge, not a question.

"In Argonnessen."

"So that's where you've been hiding all this time." Ossa clearly didn't believe a word, and the dwarves standing behind her shared a laugh.

"That's right. We sailed to Argonnessen then walked into the interior. We found a city there, and that's where Gaven was captured."

"So Argonnessen has cities now? My dear Lady Alastra, it seems your lover's madness has warped your own sense of reality."

The truth wasn't working, Rienne saw. It was time for a well-crafted lie.

Rienne choked back a cry of despair and fell to her knees, burying her face in her hands. "Oh, why am I still trying to protect him?" she wailed.

"It will go better for you if you don't," Ossa observed. Rienne could hear the hope in her voice. The dwarf thought she'd broken Rienne at last.

"He left me," Rienne sobbed. "He went back to that elf trollop." That was a risky lie, she realized. Senya had escaped the Starcrag Plain with Haldren—if she'd been captured and Ossa knew about it, her story would collapse.

"Where?" Either Ossa believed her, or she was trying to trap Rienne in her lie.

"Stormhome." She and Gaven might have been seen together there, before boarding Jordhan's ship.

"Where did they go from there?"

"I don't know. They took a ship—I think they persuaded or forced some Lyrandar captain to take them off somewhere." If she could make Ossa believe that Gaven had left Khorvaire, moved beyond House Kundarak's reach . . .

"And where have you been all this time?"

"I stayed in Stormhome."

"Have you seen your family? Gaven's brother?"

Ossa would have had both her family's estate and Thordren's house watched. "No. I lay low, mostly kept to the wharves."

Rienne risked a glance at the dwarf. Ossa had passed the lantern to one of the dwarves behind her, shrouding her face in darkness, and she rubbed her temples with two thick fingers.

"Look at yourself," Ossa said at last. "I don't know whether to hate you or pity you. You wasted your youth following Gaven around. He went mad and ended up in the care of my House, and what? You tried to settle into a normal life, but you never stopped pining for him, did you?" Her voice dripped with scorn. "He escaped and you ran to him, ready to start following him again. And then he runs off with the elf trollop instead of you."

Rienne felt a weight in her chest. She had to remind herself that Ossa's words weren't true—Gaven hadn't gone off with Senya again.

"I can't punish you any worse than you've already punished yourself," the dwarf added. "Go ahead and live your pathetic life."

Rienne swallowed hard as Ossa turned and led her silent dwarves back the way they had come. Ossa's words weren't true—at least not the last part. But the rest still stung.

* * * * *

Morning brought another meal, and another one in the mid-afternoon. The guards shrugged off her questions, and then another night fell. Two more days crawled past. Exhaustion finally allowed her to sleep on the hard cot. When her stomach told her it was time for the afternoon meal on the fourth day, she watched as footsteps approached the corner of the hall. Padar emerged around the corner, turned and told someone else to wait, out of sight, and then approached her cell.

"Good afternoon, Lady Alastra," he said. "I am sorry that your stay here has stretched on so long."

"You brought a scribe?" Rienne's eyes darted back down the hall, eager to see the means of her deliverance.

"The situation has proven much more complicated than I had any reason to expect. Not exactly a routine case of missing traveling papers. Your family's ties to House Lyrandar initially made our government reluctant to touch your case." He referred to a sheaf of papers in his hand—an increasingly irritating habit. "But then we learned you've been connected to an excoriate who also happens to be a fugitive from Dreadhold. So House Lyrandar wants nothing to do with you."

Rienne's hands went cold on the iron bars.

Padar swallowed and continued. "House Kundarak, as you know, involved itself. But they decided to lay no claim on you, and the other Houses have followed their lead. That accounts for the delay. In fact, I'm somewhat amazed that we received responses from all the Houses so quickly."

"So what now?" Rienne asked. Her voice sounded more desperate than she intended.

"Now, in the end, your case turns out to be a routine matter of missing traveling papers after all." Padar smiled weakly. "I did indeed bring a scribe from House Sivis to complete your traveling papers. He is waiting downstairs."

Relief washed over her and she sank down on her cot. "Thank you," she breathed.

"In addition, it appears that you still have at least one friend in House Lyrandar." Padar turned and called down the hall, "You may approach now."

Rienne stood again, went to the bars, and looked down the hall. A young guard appeared around the corner first, a halberd in one hand and a heavy ring of keys in the other. Another man followed, a broad smile lighting his weathered face.

"Jordhan!" Rienne laughed with raw delight. Only Gaven's face could have been a more welcome sight. "You're back!"

As he approached, Rienne thrust her hands between the bars, and he took them in his own warm grasp.

"Only just," he said. "The return journey was somewhat harder without the Storm Dragon's help."

The guard's keys rattled as she unlocked the cell door. Rienne relinquished Jordhan's grasp long enough to let the door swing open, then threw her arms around his waist and held him tight. She hadn't realized how cold she'd been in the cell until she felt Jordhan's warm embrace.

"If you'll follow me downstairs," Padar said, "I'll get your belongings and we'll settle the matter of your papers—and the fine, of course."

"Of course." The fine would probably be outrageous, but she didn't care.

CHAPTER
42

art and Ashara insisted that Gaven get more rest while they waited out the siege, waited for the distraction Ashara predicted or some other change to the game. Gaven didn't think he could sleep, knowing that a dragon lurked in the tunnel, and soldiers beyond, but he was wearier than he had realized.

Nightmares troubled his sleep, dark whispers of despair and malice. He saw Ashara change form, taking on Darraun's laughing face and mocking him for being so duped. Malathar's flaming breath enveloped him and bony claws tore at his flesh. Kelas held the bloodstone containing Gaven's dragonmark, and the mark slithered out of the shard to wrap itself over his skin as he cackled in triumph. Rienne wept in a dungeon somewhere in Rav Magar, calling out for him. Cart stood against him, shielding Ashara/Darraun from his attack. A hideous, undead Haldren bombarded him with fire. He woke, over and over, in his cell in Dreadhold.

When at last he truly awoke, he thought at first he was still in Dreadhold. Ashara's slow breathing behind him was out of place, though. He sat up and saw the blue crystal, framed by a snarling demonic figure, then turned to see Cart, standing right where he'd been when Gaven fell asleep, just to the side of the tunnel mouth.

"Any change?" Gaven said.

"I hear thunder," Cart replied.

* * * * *

It stung Kelas to kneel before the queen, but he had to keep up the act a little longer. Baron Jorlanna and Arcanist Wheldren had persuaded her to come and view the Dragon Forge. He had to act as though he appreciated her condescension.

"Welcome, Your Highness," he said to the ground. "May I present to you the Dragon Forge—the instrument of your victory in your western campaign."

The queen deigned to address him directly. "Show me."

Hiding his grin, Kelas rose. Queen Aurala stood at the center of the arcane circle, right where Malathar and Gaven had appeared weeks ago. She had a reputation for great beauty and in her younger days had a reputation for toying with her suitors and playing them against each other. Kelas had never understood that. She was too thin, too fair-skinned. Her blonde hair was fine. She looked fragile, easily broken. Her silk gown, fur-trimmed cloak, and delicate jewelry contributed to the impression that she was weak.

Soon she will be broken, Kelas thought with satisfaction.

With that thought in mind, Kelas led the little procession down into the canyon. Three of Aurala's bodyguards followed him, then the queen, Jorlanna and Wheldren, then four more guards. The air tasted thin, and Kelas's mind felt stretched. So much rode on this day, but he was prepared. He had accounted for every possibility. Malathar was out of sight in a nearby canyon—his presence would have been too alarming to the queen. Phaine had vanished when Gaven escaped, either in shame or hunting the excoriate, it didn't matter. One of Malathar's dragons, the black one, had gone in search of Gaven, and the others four ancient ones had long since left the area. Only three small dragons remained, safely hidden beneath the forge, fueling it with their breath. Nothing could go wrong.

He led the queen into the narrow entrance to the Dragon Forge. He felt the guards behind him tense as steam and flame roared along the walls, but he strode on to where the glorious dragonshard lay couched in its elaborate mechanism.

"The Dragon Forge has harnessed the power of a dragonmark," Jorlanna said to the queen. "Now it can use that power and amplify it—"

"Please, Baron," Kelas interrupted. "Let Her Majesty see for herself."

With a pull of a lever, the dragonshard came alive with the light of a sun, drawing the lines of Gaven's dragonmark on the walls and ceiling of the forge. Jorlanna's people sprang into action at the device's controls, but Kelas could see only the dragonshard. He placed both hands on its smooth, warm surface and felt a thrill shiver through his body. He caressed it with his fingertips—he imagined it gave way to his touch, ever so slightly, like the skin of a lover.

Thunder rumbled overhead, then a sharp crack. He tore his eyes from the dragonshard and nodded to Arcanist Wheldren as rain began to pelt the metal roof.

"Your Highness," Jorlanna said, "the Dragon Forge has created a terrible storm above us. Now we'll send the storm to the northwest."

Wheldren had drawn a circle in the air, and it shimmered to life like a mirror. "Your Highness," he said, "I invite you to gaze through this window to where your troops are gathering near Varna."

With a quizzical look, Queen Aurala stepped to the circle in the air and peered into it. Kelas smiled broadly. He could taste his success. He heard thunder rumble in the northwest, and the pounding of rain on the roof stopped.

"Greetings, Your Highness." The voice came through the window, and Aurala drew herself up in surprise. "I am Arcanist Fillian of the Arcane Congress. I will now direct your gaze south, across Lake Galifar."

The queen looked closer. Kelas knew what she was seeing—a hint of a dark cloud, growing quickly as it charged away from the Dragon Forge and across the lake. Soon it would be pouring devastation on the Eldeen troops defending Varna. Kelas counted slowly, barely daring to breathe.

Fifteen seconds, thirty. Aurala shifted impatiently, and Kelas bit his lip. Forty-five. A rumble of thunder came through the window, and the queen brought her face as close as she could to the magical window. A mighty crash startled her, but she shot a faint smile at a guard on her right. He had her.

"Your Highness," Fillian shouted over the roar of the storm, "I wish I could give you a closer look, but I am at the edge of the storm and perhaps too close as it is."

The storm had picked up strength as it crossed the lake, and its devastation was incredible. Kelas saw Wheldren tense—he was worried for Fillian. The storm did seem to be battering the Aundairian forces more than they had planned, but if the effects on the Reachers were terrible enough it wouldn't matter. Aurala watched in fascination, and Kelas could feel Jorlanna and Wheldren holding their breath, waiting. The noise of the Dragon Forge seemed to fade until the thunder and wind of the storm were the only sound.

Kelas broke the hush at last. "The siege of Varna is over, Your Highness. Before it began."

Aurala turned slowly away from the window, and Wheldren collapsed it with a wave. Jorlanna bit her lip, waiting for the queen's response before delivering her lines.

"Impressive," Aurala said. Her gaze swept between Jorlanna and Wheldren. "Am I to understand that House Cannith and the Arcane Congress have provided the use of this weapon at no charge to my treasury?"

That was what Jorlanna had been waiting for. Kelas smiled as Baron d'Cannith stepped up to the queen and fell to one knee.

"Your Highness, I pledge the work and support of House Cannith to the service of the crown of Aundair. We are yours to command."

Aurala was taken aback. "Baron d'Cannith, are you disregarding the Korth Edicts?"

Kelas's pulse pounded in his ears. Everything hung in the balance in that moment. For over a thousand years, the Korth Edicts had staked out the neutrality of the dragonmarked Houses—prohibiting marriage between heirs of the Houses and members of Khorvaire's nobility, preventing the Houses from owning land or building armies, and in exchange giving them a measure of independence from royal dictates. Disregarding them was exactly what Jorlanna was doing—sacrificing that freedom and swearing fealty to the queen. No, Kelas reminded himself—to the crown, which Aurala would not wear much longer.

"We are," Jorlanna said.

Aurala turned to the officer at her side. Without a word, the soldier drew his sword and handed it, hilt first, to the queen.

Gently she rested the flat of the blade on Jorlanna's shoulder.

"Rise then, Jorlanna ir'Cannith. I accept your fealty and offer you the protection of the crown."

Wheldren's pledge of fealty was less momentous, but Aurala treated it with no less dignity. The dragons had spoken of a turning point in history, and Kelas knew he stood at that moment. Centuries of tradition had just been abandoned. The political and economic landscape of Khorvaire would never be the same.

* * * * *

A sharp crack of thunder echoed in the tunnel, jolting Gaven fully awake. It was close, perhaps directly overhead. Or right over the Dragon Forge. Rivulets of water snaked down the tunnel, and the next thunderclap sent pebbles trickling from the temple's ceiling.

"It's the damned forge," Gaven said. "Using my dragonmark. Making another storm."

"The Secret Keeper . . ." Ashara murmured.

Shouts from the soldiers outside almost drowned out her voice. Gaven peered into the tunnel. He couldn't see the dragon, and the daylight at the far end was dim and gray, barely distinct from the darkness of the passage.

A more powerful storm than you ever created.

The voice whispered in Gaven's mind, as close as his pulse. It was the same malignance that had haunted his dreams while he was a captive at the forge, the same evil that coursed through the forge itself.

"The bastard stole my storm!" Gaven growled, and thunder crashed in answer.

Why don't you get it back?

Ashara tugged at Gaven's arm. "We have to get out of here," she said. Her eyes were wide with terror, and as Gaven turned to look for Cart, he saw why.

The azure crystal at the back of the temple had gone dark, drowned in inky shadow. At the center was a lighter portion, with a perfect black circle in its center. As Gaven looked, it moved, fixed its gaze on him. It was an eye.

The whisper in his mind erupted in growling, maniacal laughter as Gaven followed Cart and Ashara into the passage, terror racing in their veins.

* * * * *

The acidic rain and pelting hail of the storm had driven off the besieging dragon and the soldiers with it. Cart emerged from the passage as the last of the rain spattered on the dry ground and rays of sunlight broke through the clouds. Another peal of thunder drew his gaze to the west, and he saw the black clouds of the storm surging away from the canyon of the Dragon Forge.

"Where is he sending it?" Gaven asked.

"To the Eldeen Reaches," Ashara said. "Probably Varna."

Gaven came and stood over Ashara. "Varna? That's a city of thousands!"

"Yes." Ashara looked at the ground.

"You knew about this?" Cart said.

She nodded as she turned away.

"You helped them build it," Gaven added. "You helped them steal my mark and use my storm as a weapon."

Ashara sobbed and fell to her knees.

Crouching beside her, Cart rested a hand on her shoulder, then looked up at Gaven. "Then she brought me back from the brink of death—and did the same for you. Let her be, Gaven."

Gaven stared at Cart for a long moment, anger creasing his brow and the corners of his mouth. Then he turned to watch the retreating storm.

Ashara buried her face in Cart's shoulder. Words and tears spilled from her in a torrent. "It's all madness, Cart. Kelas is mad. They don't know the power they're dealing with here—the Secret Keeper is getting stronger. He could break free. Malathar's flames on the crystal, the other dragon's acid, the storm—they're all weakening his bonds. Oh, Cart, Varna is the least of the evils I'm to blame for."

Cart circled his arms gingerly around her and held her as she wept. When he looked up again, Gaven was gone.

* * * * *

Aunn stood at the top of the canyon and surveyed the wake of the storm. Little craters pocked the ground where heavy rain and hail had fallen. Lightning had struck a dry shrub here and there, and one still burned while others smoldered and smoked. His vantage point let him trace a path of devastation a mile or so toward the lake.

He looked down at the monstrosity of iron and flame squatting below him, like a swollen tick feeding on the magic of the blue crystal jutting up at the head of the canyon. He didn't have to touch that stone to sense the lines of magic flowing freely out of it and into the eldritch machine, and his stomach revolted at the powerful sense of malice emanating from the whole canyon.

"His power flows into the world," Aunn murmured. "If not stopped, soon he will be free." Marelle's words were engraved in his memory, and he thought he finally had some insight into their meaning. "Is this a weapon? More terrible than the barbarian foe?"

A line of people filed out of the iron building, and Aunn backed away from the edge. He found some cover and watched them walking to the edge of the canyon, then crouched down and peered over the edge. The people turned and began climbing a path along the canyon's edge, and Aunn gasped as he recognized Kelas at the front of the line. His head pounded with anger. The group had climbed well up the path before Aunn realized who else was in the procession. He recognized Arcanist Wheldren from Haldren's gathering in Bluevine, but the woman beside him was unfamiliar. The woman surrounded by a knot of soldiers, though—that could only be Queen Aurala.

What in the Traveler's ten thousand names is she doing here? Aunn thought.

They were approaching his hiding place, so he withdrew to a point where he could safely see the plateau overlooking the canyon. A few moments later, Kelas emerged from the path and led the cluster of people to a circle scratched into the ground. Arcanist Wheldren busied himself retracing the lines of the circle, which must have been nearly obliterated by the storm, as the queen and the other woman talked together. Kelas stood back from the pair, but Aunn could see the look of smug satisfaction he wore. Clearly, whatever had happened here was a part of Kelas's greater plan, but it was a part he had kept secret from Aunn.

Wheldren was preparing the circle for a ritual of teleportation, Aunn realized, which meant that Kelas would soon be out of his reach, and he didn't know where. He entertained thoughts of attacking Kelas where he stood, the queen and her soldiers be damned. Suicide. Charging into the circle as Wheldren completed the ritual, teleporting along with them? The same. What if he put Haunderk's face back on and approached Kelas as a friend? Kelas had sent him to the Demon Wastes to die—there was no reason to think he would not order Haunderk's death more directly.

His anger and hatred paralyzed him, and he cursed himself for it. Wheldren began his ritual, and it was too late. He might be able to knock Kelas out of the circle at the last moment—but then Kelas stepped out on his own, bowing a farewell to the queen. Another moment, and Kelas stood alone on the plateau, looking tremendously self-satisfied.

Aunn stood from his crouch and stepped around the boulder that had shielded him. It took Kelas a moment to notice him, but his sword flew into his hand while Aunn was still some distance away.

"Who are you?" he demanded.

"You don't know me?" Aunn said. "I'm an old friend, Kelas."

"I've never seen you—" Kelas's eyes went wide. *"Haunderk?"*

Aunn changed his face, and he was Haunderk. "Very good. A lifetime of suspicion has served you well."

"Haunderk! Your mission was a success!" Kelas smiled, but he didn't drop his guard as Aunn drew closer.

"It was. Kathrik Mel is on the march, probably spilling over the Shadowcrags at this moment."

"I commend you. Everything is falling into place."

"The barbarians have sacked Maruk Dar. Soon they'll set the Towering Wood on fire. If everything goes according to plan, they'll meet the armies of Aundair somewhere in the midst of the Eldeen Reaches. And then what, Kelas?"

"Then we'll crush them, and the Eldeen Reaches will sing the praise of their liberators."

"What if we fail?"

"We won't," Kelas said. He nodded toward the canyon. "The Dragon Forge ensures our victory. And that's enough questions. Come with me, and we'll discuss your next mission."

"Why don't you just stab me in the back this time? Wouldn't that be easier?"

"Tempting." Kelas took a menacing step forward, sword in his hand. "But you've got more use in you yet."

Aunn slid his mace from his belt and hefted it. "True." He charged, swinging his mace to bat Kelas's sword aside and slamming his body into Kelas.

Kelas staggered backward, caught off guard by the sudden attack. "Haunderk!" he snarled. "You'll pay for that!"

"I already have. I've paid over and over for the privilege of killing you. I'm done paying now." He caught Kelas's cut on the haft of his mace. He changed again, donning the face of General Jad Yeven.

"I own you," Kelas said. "You will obey me."

"Oh, I forgot. You hate looking at dead people." Aunn changed again, taking Kelas's own face. "Here's another dead face for you."

Kelas roared. He had long ago forbidden Aunn from wearing his face, a lesson he'd beaten hard into a young changeling. Aunn sidestepped a fierce thrust, but Kelas's blade still bit into his arm. Aunn brought his mace around into Kelas's side in return, doubling him over as he staggered back.

"That's enough," Kelas said. "This is no longer a matter of punishment. Drop your weapon now, or I will have to kill you."

"Kill me?" Aunn took Kauth's face. "You've tried to kill me already. You sent me to the Demon Wastes to die, but I didn't die. Maybe I can't die."

"We'll see." Kelas charged again. His sword went wide, and he took another blow in his gut.

Aunn felt that he was watching the battle from outside his body, totally calm as Kelas grew more and more furious. It was a game, and Aunn knew he was going to win.

He took Laurann's young and pretty face. "You made me a killer. Kill or be killed. No one lives forever."

"So you remember some of your lessons," Kelas said. "But you've forgotten what happens when you disobey."

Aunn stepped forward, swinging his mace back and forth, forcing Kelas back. "I have not forgotten."

Kelas stumbled on the rocky ground, and one more blow sent him sprawling on his back. His sword clattered out of reach. It was over.

Aunn took Faura's face. "Who do you want to kill you, Kelas? Does this form still arouse you? Do you want this beauty to kill you?"

Kelas tried to scramble away and get to his feet, but Aunn slammed a foot down on his throat, pinning him to the ground. He wore Haunderk's face again. "Or this one? You still think of me as Haunderk, don't you? You gripped my child hand and drove my blade into Ledon's throat. It was Haunderk you taught how to kill."

"Please . . ." Kelas whimpered.

"You're begging for your life? You don't know remorse or shame, Kelas. That's what you taught me."

He wiped his face clean. Colorless eyes set in blank, gray skin. "My name is Aunn," he said.

With one swing of his mace, it was over.

CHAPTER
43

Gaven emerged from his hiding place and called to Kelas's killer.

"Changeling," he said.

The figure whirled around, holding his mace on guard. When his pale eyes fell on Gaven, though, he lowered his weapon.

"You killed my enemy," Gaven said, "so I'm willing to call you friend."

The changeling's face changed. A mouth appeared and formed a smile. "I'm glad, Gaven." The face resolved into Darraun's. "I hoped I'd find you here."

"Darraun." Gaven didn't know what to think. A changeling was made for deception. Gaven had just seen this one adopt no less than six different faces, and he or she had clearly worked for Kelas before turning on him. How could he trust such a being? Maybe the Darraun standing before him was the same Darraun he'd known, but maybe it was just a fellow spy of Darraun's, one who knew Darraun's face and his connection to Gaven.

The smile fell from Darraun's face, and he took a few steps closer. "I'm sorry, Gaven. I wish I hadn't deceived you the way I did."

"So do I," Gaven said. "I trusted you."

Darraun's brow furrowed. "Even though you knew what I was?"

"I was a fool."

"No, but I was. You were right to trust me. I helped you—I freed you from the Kundaraks, I flew the airship, I led you to Haldren—"

"And then you let him go."

"Yes. That was where I betrayed your trust, and I—" Darraun's face looked strange, his eyes momentarily out of focus, distracted. "I'm sorry," he said to the air.

"That was not a very convincing apology."

Darraun turned his back, looking down at Kelas's body. "He beat it out of me. 'You are not sorry! You do not care!' I'm not sure I've given a sincere apology since then." He turned back and his eyes met Gaven's. "Until now."

"Haldren was here. He was part of what they did to me."

Darraun's eyes fell on the raw, bare skin on Gaven's neck and chest, where his dragonmark had been. Even Ashara's ministrations had not relieved the pain or healed the skin. He started as if noticing it for the first time.

"Your mark . . ." Darraun breathed. "Haldren did that?"

"He was here, but Cart killed him before Kelas activated the forge."

"I had no idea. Kelas never told me this part of the plan."

"What did he tell you?"

Darraun ran his fingers through his hair. "He stirred up the barbarians of the Demon Wastes to attack the Eldeen Reaches. That will give Aundair an excuse to move troops into the Reaches, to defend its own border. For all I know, they might be there already."

"So it's Haldren all over again, war for the sake of Aundairian conquest."

"Yes and no," Darraun said. "Haldren had dreams of reuniting all of Galifar under his rule, and I'm not sure Kelas ever had any aspiration to the throne. It's moot now." He nodded toward Kelas's body.

"The plan is larger than Kelas," Gaven said. "Dragons, a Thuranni—"

"The queen was here," Darraun interjected. "Baron d'Cannith swore fealty, the Arcane Congress—"

"And they're using my mark as a weapon. Did you see it? They made a storm and sent it to the Reaches."

" 'But be careful that they don't use weapons more terrible

than their foe,' " Darraun murmured. He drifted to the edge of the canyon and looked down.

"What?"

"A warning. You're right. This is much larger than Kelas."

* * * * *

Gaven led Darraun away from the canyon, toward the place where he'd left Cart. Darraun lost himself in his thoughts as they walked, turning Marelle's warning over and over in his mind. What Kelas had called the Dragon Forge might well guarantee Aundair's victory, not only over the Eldeen Reaches but also against the barbarians. Without it, Aundair's forces might not be able to hold the Carrion Tribes back—Kathrik Mel might lead his horde through the Reaches and across the Wynarn River into Aundair.

But at what cost would victory come? Darraun could still feel the magic coursing out of the crystal prison and through the Dragon Forge, and the evil of the imprisoned fiend with it. It seemed clear that the Dragon Forge was the weapon Marelle had warned him against. Was she right? She had seemed almost like a divine messenger, but did her words carry prophetic weight? Or was she simply expressing the way she would resolve Darraun's dilemma? Perhaps the evil of the Dragon Forge was actually a lesser evil than the marauding of Kathrik Mel's horde, or at least a less urgent threat. The eladrin, it seemed, could afford a long-term view of events. When Marelle warned that the Keeper of Secrets would "soon be free," what was her understanding of "soon"?

And what did dragons have to do with it all? Thinking about the dragons' Prophecy still made his head spin, and being around Gaven seemed to make its mysterious words and dire warnings a very present reality. For months he'd been out of Gaven's orbit, pleasantly isolated from any thought of the Prophecy, but as soon as he met Gaven again there were dragons involved and he had to wonder why.

There was another, no less disturbing consequence of being back with Gaven. He was wearing Darraun's face again, and he found his thoughts running along familiar channels—scheming, suspicious, convoluted. As Darraun, he was a spy again. He had tried to leave that person behind in the Labyrinth, but he'd slipped back into that mode in order to placate Gaven, to present a familiar face. He didn't like that familiar face.

That, at least, was a problem with an easy solution. As he walked behind Gaven, he changed again, taking the tall, warm, proud and noble form he'd created for Aunn. When Gaven indicated that Cart should be just over the next rise, Aunn put a hand on Gaven's shoulder.

"Gaven?" he said.

Gaven turned around and started with surprise at the man before him. "What's this?"

"My name is Aunn. That's my real name." He swallowed, waiting for a reaction that didn't come. "That's who I want to be."

Gaven looked at him for a long time. "Aunn it is," he said. "I'm pleased to meet you." He turned with a smile and crested the rise.

"Gaven!" Cart's voice sent a thrill of anxiety through Aunn's body. "Where have you been?"

"Look who I found." Gaven turned and took Aunn's elbow. "Aunn, I believe you know Cart, and this is Ashara d'Cannith. This is Aunn. Cart, you know him as Darraun."

"Darraun," Cart said. His voice carried a hint of amusement. "So who did we bury?"

"I found a corpse that bore some resemblance to Darraun's face, and did my best to disguise it. I'm sorry."

Cart laughed. "I told you, Gaven, didn't I?"

"You did." Gaven didn't share Cart's amusement.

"No matter, Darraun. Or Aunn. I'm glad to see you alive."

"And I'm glad you're not me," Ashara added, stepping forward to clasp his hand in greeting.

Aunn didn't understand the joke, but it made Gaven laugh at last.

* * * * *

To Gaven, the appearance of the storm above the Dragon Forge had seemed like a sign calling him back to destroy the eldritch machine that had stolen his mark. Knowing that the storm had been a weapon sent to devastate the Eldeen Reaches revolted him, and he felt responsible for the use of his dragonmark. Aunn's return and Kelas's death reinforced that message, and Aunn's concerns about the Keeper of Secrets, the chance the imprisoned fiend might escape, solidified it. He still burned to find Rienne, but the Dragon Forge seemed like a more imminent concern—even discounting the possibility of reclaiming his mark.

"Malathar is my greatest concern," Cart said, staring into their campfire.

"Malathar?" Aunn asked.

"The dragon-king from Argonnessen," Gaven explained. "He's ancient, mighty—"

"Undead," Cart added.

Aunn raised an eyebrow. "Well, to our advantage, we know what we're up against. There are preparations we can make, protective wards and enhancements to our weapons."

"His breath is devastating," Gaven said.

"I think I'm up to the challenge," Aunn replied, and somehow he bolstered Gaven's confidence.

"I hope you don't overestimate your skill," Ashara said. She had a hand at her chin, half-covering a bemused smile. "You are talking about significant infusions of power."

"I apologize, Lady Cannith," Aunn said. "I certainly didn't mean to discount your own skill at artifice. Between the two of us—"

"Do you know the ninth weaving of Merrix the First?"

Aunn's eyes showed no recognition, and Gaven's confidence faltered. "I'm afraid I'm not familiar with House Cannith's terminology—"

"Where were you trained?"

"I had a private tutor. I figured a lot out on my own."

"You figured it out on your own," Ashara repeated. "How can you hope to understand the weavings of artifice figuring it out on your own?"

"It's simply a matter of untangling the knots, Lady. I find it quite intuitive."

"I require a demonstration."

Gaven frowned at her. Ashara was always kind and mild with Cart, but her manner with Gaven, and now with Aunn, could be curt. Imperious—given her position in the House, she was used to issuing commands and having them obeyed. She had to remember that she was not in charge of this group, he thought.

"I don't think that's necessary," Gaven said. "I've seen Aunn do—"

Aunn interrupted. "It's all right, Gaven. I'll give a demonstration." He made a small bow toward Ashara. "Would you care to name the task?"

"Cart, would you let Aunn borrow your axe, please?"

Cart hefted his axe and passed it to Aunn, who looked at Ashara expectantly.

"Do your best," she said. "Prepare it for the battle ahead."

Aunn closed his eyes and placed his hand flat on the blade. A smile danced at the corner of his mouth. Gaven watched him carefully but couldn't make sense of what he was doing. He ran a finger down the edge, ran his hand down the haft, traced twisting runes on the head with two fingertips. After a long moment, he opened his eyes, let out his breath, and handed the axe to Ashara.

As soon as her hand touched the weapon, Ashara's eyes shot open wide. She examined the axe for only a few heartbeats, then handed it back to Cart.

"This will serve you well," she said. Turning her eyes back to Aunn, she returned his bow. "Your skill is at least the equal of mine. I'm sorry I doubted you."

Now it was Aunn's turn to look surprised. "That is high praise."

"Yes, it is. Now let's get to work on the rest of our preparations."

Gaven's sword was next, and when Aunn handed it back he could feel it sing in his hand, longing for the battle ahead. While Aunn worked on the sword, Ashara handled Aunn's mace, and then she put her hands on Gaven's back, weaving magic into his armor.

An ache fell on Gaven's heart, thinking of Rienne's hand on his back, the touch that always calmed and soothed him. Where was she? Then he thought of her bitter words on the *Sea Tiger:* "I'll

cover your back. I hope you can spare a thought to cover mine."
Did she still hold that bitterness in her heart? Did she think he'd
simply abandoned her in Rav Magar, forgetting to cover her back
once again? Facing Malathar would have been so much easier, he
realized, with Rienne fighting beside him.

On Jordhan's ship, they had talked about the Prophecy, about
the Time Between that was just beginning. Now it appeared the
Time Between had reached its end. The fleeting time it took for
the hourglass of history to reverse itself was over, or would soon
be. The Time of the Dragon Below was beginning, and he had
no more insight into what the future held than he had on the *Sea
Tiger*. The Blasphemer's legions . . . Who was the Blasphemer?
Malathar?

Gaven stared at the ground between his feet as Ashara finished
her work.

I'm lost without you, Ree, he thought.

Then the preparations were complete, and Gaven led the way
back to the Dragon Forge.

* * * * *

The dragon and the soldiers who had fenced them into the
worgs' temple hadn't returned, so they approached the forge the
same way Gaven, Cart, and Ashara had fled it. They squeezed
between the rock and the blue crystal, and worked their way slowly
through the tunnel.

You walk boldly to your doom.

It was the merest whisper at the back of Gaven's mind, but he
felt it gnaw at his resolve like a rat. Darkness stalked through the
crystal, shadowing his movements.

*You think to stand before a power that was already great when
Karrn the Conqueror took his first infant steps.*

The Keeper of Secrets, that darkness was called, and the Messenger strained to keep it bound. Gaven tried to feel the presence
of the Messenger, some shred of good or hope left in the crystal,
but he felt only the hatred of the other.

*Malathar the Damned will consume your body and annihilate
your soul.*

Gaven looked back at Ashara and Aunn and saw a grimness on each of their faces. Cart's steps were heavy and his head hung low. All of them heard the Keeper of Secrets. All of them were wrestling with doubt and despair.

"It lies," Gaven said. His voice sounded muffled in his own ears, as though he were calling to his companions through a thick fog. They looked up at him as though lost in that same fog, their eyes distant and distracted.

"It lies," he repeated. "Truth would burn its tongue. It's the Keeper of Secrets."

Aunn murmured something, perhaps a vague echo of the warning he'd repeated several times in their camp.

"It's trying to sow despair," Cart said.

"It's very good at it," Ashara said.

"Fight it! It speaks nothing but lies."

Gaven pressed forward, trusting the others to follow. If they could just escape the tunnel, he felt sure, the despair would ease.

You were the Storm Dragon. You bore the touch of Siberys. Now what are you? Nothing. Just another would-be hero marching to certain death.

I was the Storm Dragon, Gaven thought. Is it possible that I'm not anymore? Was my destiny stripped from me as well?

Your destiny is to die in Malathar's claws.

I am player and playwright. I will decide my own destiny.

Malathar will decide, and you will die.

CHAPTER
44

Gaven's voice sounded faint against the fog in Aunn's mind, as he called back some warning over his shoulder. Another voice was trying to drown Gaven's out—the harsh whisper of the evil held within the crystal. It grated against his ears but didn't break through into his consciousness.

All he heard was a velvet hush of words, soft and quiet and yet still more powerful than either Gaven's shout or the Secret Keeper's rasp.

He will soon be free. You must stop him.

"How can I stop him?" Aunn murmured.

Be not afraid. I will be with you.

Gaven plunged ahead through the tunnel, and Aunn followed as fast as he could. It felt like walking through water—the air was thick with the warring energies of the two spirits. He closed his eyes, and he saw himself in a raging torrent, power churning out toward the Dragon Forge, splashing and foaming against rocks that strained feebly to hold it back. The end of the tunnel came into view, visible to Aunn's senses as a lattice spidering out from a central point, where a blade, radiant with powerful magic, was thrust into the stone. Coiled around the blade was a shining silver corona. Aunn opened his eyes with a start. Distorted through the crystal, he could just make out the silver torc he'd taken from Dania's body.

Gaven squeezed and stumbled out of the tunnel and down the short jump to the canyon floor, and Aunn followed. He had expected his mind and his ears to clear once he left the tunnel, but the steam and flames of the Dragon Forge just added a sinister drone to the cacophony. He turned back to the crystal as Ashara, already through the gap, helped Cart squeeze out, and he closed his eyes again to see the intricate weave of magic that fueled the Dragon Forge.

Ashara and then Cart dropped to the ground beside him, and he turned to Ashara.

"It's incredible," he breathed. "I've never seen anything—"

Cart cut him off. "On your guard!"

Aunn whirled. A sudden wind kicked dust and gravel up into the air as a huge shadow fell across the canyon. He looked up, and laid eyes for the first time on Malathar the Damned.

* * * * *

"Into the Forge!" Gaven shouted. He ran without glancing back at the others, but then Rienne's voice rang in his mind again. "I hope you can spare a thought to cover mine." He turned his head to look over his shoulder as he ran.

Cart and Ashara were right behind him, but Aunn seemed paralyzed, his gaze fixed on the dragon-king. "Aunn!" he called, but the changeling didn't move.

"Go," he told Cart as the warforged drew near, then he turned and ran back to Aunn. There was a memory, distant and vague—

He stood in his shattered cell in Dreadhold, staring bewildered at Cart while Darraun spoke encouraging words and Haldren shouted overhead.

But Aunn didn't look bewildered. His mace was in his hand, and he stood at the ready. He looked intent, focused, and determined.

Black flame roared over them both as Gaven reached Aunn's side. Gaven roared and tumbled to the ground, reacting to the pain before he realized how well his newly enchanted armor had protected him, its warding magic extending even beyond the reach of its metal. The pain was not so bad, and his strength held up against the necromantic energy of the dragon-king's fire.

Aunn shimmered with silver as the black flame rolled off him like water and drained into the ground. He raised his mace to Malathar, a challenge or a salute, as the dragon-king wheeled in the air overhead.

"Aunn, come on!" Gaven seized the changeling's wrist and started to pull him toward the forge, but Aunn wrenched his wrist away.

"Why flee?" he said. "Didn't we come here for this?"

"I came here to get my dragonmark back and destroy that forge. *Then* I'll face Malathar."

"Go, then. I'll cover your back."

Gaven paused for just an instant, Rienne's words haunting him again, then he turned back to the forge and ran after Cart and Ashara. He saw Cart swinging his axe just inside the entrance to the iron building and hurried to join the battle.

With a rattle of dry bones and a rustle of leathery skin, Malathar landed before him. Dust billowed in a cloud around the undead dragon, stinging Gaven's eyes and biting his exposed skin. Even with all four feet on the ground and his body crouching low to the ground, Malathar seemed huge—the dragon-king's breastbone was at his eye level, his back out of reach, and his bony wings stretched far overhead.

"You have proven nuisance enough, meat," Malathar whispered.

Gaven checked his headlong rush and clutched his sword, circling more carefully around the enormous dragon's side. He spoke an arcane word and his body erupted in protective cold fire. "Let me show you what a nuisance I can be," he growled as he lunged forward.

His sword clattered against a bone, then Malathar's violet eyes appeared in front of him, blazing into his own. A deathly chill started behind his eyes and spread down his spine, numbing his limbs and freezing him in place. With a whispering hiss, the dragon-king's head snaked up on his long neck, then shot forward, jaws wide. Gaven was powerless to dodge—he could only watch the swordlike teeth coming at him.

Aunn's body slammed into his, knocking him aside, and the changeling's mace smashed up into Malathar's jaw. The weapon burst in a flash of white light and knocked the dragon's head backward. Aunn landed on top of Gaven, shouting in pain from the icy cold of Gaven's protective fire. He rolled quickly aside, dodging a blind rake of Malathar's claw. The chill was slow to ebb from Gaven's limbs, but he managed to scramble to his feet and stagger a few steps away.

"Go!" Aunn shouted.

Gaven stumbled into a run, then he was beside Cart. He swung his sword wildly, beating back the soldiers who tried to defend the Dragon Forge. The soldiers fell back in the face of their combined fury and he saw the dragonshard in its setting. Another sprint and he would be there.

For just an instant his heart sang—he thought he felt the wind at his back lifting him and speeding his run. But then a rush of fire followed the gust of air, engulfing him again in Malathar's flaming breath. The cold fire melted off him, his armor drew the flames away, but there was still heat to spare, searing his flesh. Even as fire licked at him, the cold essence of death sank into his bones, sapping his strength. He bent double, stumbling in his run.

It had been a deadly blast, and Gaven feared for his friends. Cart stood firm against the dragon-king, his axe flashing white against the violet shimmer that limned Malathar's rune-scribed bones. Ashara stood behind him, a hand on his back, reinforcing his defenses and healing his wounds. Aunn—where was Aunn?

There! Crumpled in a heap on the iron floor, as though the dragon-king had hurled him against the Dragon Forge and left him where he fell. Forgetting the dragonshard, Gaven started toward the changeling's side.

Aunn lifted his head and saw Gaven approaching. "No," he called. "I'm all right. Just get the damned dragonshard!"

Aunn didn't look all right. His arm was pinned beneath his body at what must have been a painful angle, and his other arm clutched his belly. But he was right—he could do more to help himself than Gaven could. Gaven turned again and ran to the dragonshard.

Malathar snaked in after him, ignoring Cart's furious blows at his side. "That no longer belongs to you," he said. "It won't help you."

Gaven knew better. Despite his words, the dragon-king was proving himself desperate to keep Gaven from his goal. Three more steps and Gaven's hand clutched the smooth stone.

It was still his, there could be no question. The dragonshard sprang to life at his touch. A crash of thunder shook the walls and the ground. Gaven felt a tingling surge starting in the shard, then building in his feet, then pulsing throughout his body. The skin of his neck and shoulder burned. With a snarl of rage and effort, he lifted his free hand to point at Malathar. Arcs of lightning danced between his arm and the metal floor, then a tremendous discharge linked him to the dragon-king. He roared with the thunder and saw Malathar's mouth open wide in voiceless pain. He threw his head back with the lightning and saw Malathar's head twisting back on his long neck. Suspended in that instant, they were united in the lightning flowing between them.

Joy flowed through Gaven's body with the lightning. *I am the—*

Gaven's hand slipped from the shard and the lightning died with a final snap that threw Gaven backward. He collapsed on the iron floor, and a dead silence fell around him. He looked around in a daze. Aunn was on his feet, smashing his mace over and over against the bones of Malathar's shoulders and ribs, sometimes his jaw. Cart was on the dragon-king's other side, his axe a blur of motion. Malathar was clearly on the defensive, but he was still a terror of gnashing teeth and raking claws. Even his tail swept around him, slashing at his foes. It was all happening in utter silence.

Gaven rose to his feet and took a step toward the dragon-shard. He had the strangest sense that he was dead, a spirit, and if he looked behind him he would see his body on the ground. He walked in a ghost world shrouded in silence, and he couldn't feel his feet on the ground. Shaking his head, he took another step. He wouldn't look back—if he was dead, he didn't want to know it.

He cupped both hands below the dragonshard, drew a deep breath, and raised them to lift the stone from its setting. He couldn't feel it, and for a moment he feared that his hands passed through the stone. No, it rose with his hands, and an instant later he felt it surge again in his grasp. The sounds of the forge and the battle burst into his ears again. His nerves sprang back to life, and there was no longer any question that he was in his body—he had never felt more alive.

Thunder crashed outside the forge, overhead, and a rush of wind swept through the building, eddying around Gaven's feet. His heart was racing. Another gust blew in, building at his back as he stepped toward the dragon-king. Soon a gale blew through the forge, seizing Ashara's cloak and Aunn's hair. Malathar opened his mouth and purple-black fire danced inside, but the wind tore it out and the dragon-king staggered back a step. Gaven's friends scattered for cover.

"Thunder is his harbinger and lightning his spear," Malathar said, his dry whisper undiminished in the gale. "Wind is his steed and rain his cloak."

"The words of creation are in his ears and on his tongue!" Gaven shouted over the howling storm. He didn't know where the words came from. "The secrets of the first of sixteen are his." More of the Prophecy—had he always known this?

"The Storm Dragon flies before the traitor's army to deliver vengeance. The storm breaks upon the forces of the Blasphemer."

Now Gaven remembered. He looked into the dragonshard in his hands and saw it, his destiny written in the lines of his dragonmark. "The maelstrom swirls around him," he whispered, and his words were lost in the wind. "He is the storm and the eye of the storm."

Malathar spouted another blast of black fire, but a whirlwind sprang to life around him and carried the flames away. Gaven's feet left the ground and he clutched the dragonshard to his chest. Lightning danced around him, joining him to the whirlwind. He spoke a word, a single syllable in the language of creation, and Malathar erupted in purple fire. Lightning sprang from the whirlwind to course along the dragon's bones. Thunder buffeted him, snapping his wings and beating him to the ground.

The dragonshard burned with red light as it had in the Dragon Forge, casting the lines of Gaven's dragonmark around the walls and floor once more. It shone right through Gaven's chest—he was wind and storm, not flesh—and traced lines of white fire across Malathar's body. The wind carried streams of ash and grave dust from his bones. A scream arose in the howl of the wind, issuing not from Malathar's body but from a black shadow that now streamed away from him in tattered ribbons. Malathar's damned soul, bound too long to his ancient body, was lost in the wind.

CHAPTER
45

Just before Dania died, Aunn remembered, she had kneeled at the pinnacle of a ziggurat in Xen'drik and let herself be swallowed in silver fire. When she stood and brushed her hair back from her face, Aunn—Auftane, at the time—had seen a silver torc around her neck—the same torc that was now part of the Dragon Forge, funneling the Secret Keeper's power into the apparatus. Then he had seen Dania's eyes, transformed into pools of quicksilver. When her gaze had lingered on him, he felt sure that she saw him as he really was. She moved with purpose, leading her companions to the heart of the temple where she met her end.

Purpose, Aunn thought. That's what this is.

He didn't think the Messenger within the prison had taken residence in his body the way the Silver Flame had filled Dania. He felt too . . . too present, perfectly aware of everything that happened around him. Even lying on the floor of the Dragon Forge, no detail had escaped him—he knew exactly where his bones were broken, where each of Gaven's footsteps fell as he foolishly ran toward him, where Cart circled carefully around the dragon-king. No, he was still in control of his mind, where Dania had relinquished control.

But there was purpose now in everything he did, a cascade of objectives and intentions that all built toward the greater goal of destroying the Dragon Forge and ensuring that the Keeper of Secrets remained imprisoned. Protecting Gaven so he could reach the dragonshard, Gaven summoning this storm, Malathar's annihilation—these were steps toward his greater purpose.

The wind whipped around him, snatching at his breath and stinging his eyes. Cart and Ashara had taken cover in the shadow of a boulder, Cart's armored body shielding Ashara from the driving gravel and biting sand. Gaven stood on a column of whirling air, halfway to the arched roof of the Dragon Forge, arms raised skyward, lost in the storm's fury.

A knife of lightning struck the iron structure, arced to Gaven's outstretched arms, and flowed through his feet to the ground. Gaven threw his head back and held the lightning in place. His every muscle strained, as if the lightning were chains that bound him to the walls, and Aunn saw him begin to pull the walls down.

It was time. Before Gaven leveled the forge, Aunn had to deal with the lattice of magic and gold that fed it. He stood up and slid his healing wands back into the sheath at his belt. Then he turned and walked, unhampered by the wind, to the hilt of the sword plunged into the crystal.

He recognized the hilt—Kelas had shown him the blade. The Ramethene Sword, which Janik had discovered in Xen'drik and Maija had stolen from him when the fiendish spirit possessed her. She had given it to an agent of the Order of the Emerald Claw, who had then sold the blade to Kelas. The blade, of course, went through the ring of Dania's torc as it entered the stone. The Torc of Sacrifice, Kelas had called it, when Aunn—Haunderk—had given it to him. An embodiment of the serpent's binding power. The torc formed the gleaming center of an intricate lacing of silver threads, which then joined to two cylindrical reservoirs. Inside those reservoirs, Aunn thought, must be pure, distilled magic.

No, he reminded himself—or the Messenger's velvet whisper reminded him. There was nothing pure about the magic fueling the forge. Every mote of its power was polluted by the fiend's incalculable evil. That Dania's sacrifice was connected to this abomination made him sick. Slowly, he stretched his fingertips to touch the silver ring of her torc.

He jumped as twin crashes of thunder boomed behind him, followed by the sound of wrenching metal. Then a monstrous roar made him wheel around in sudden terror.

Gaven had managed to wrench the roof over the forge open, and steam billowed up where rain fell into the open furnaces. The roar had come from a red dragon, small compared to Malathar, that had emerged from the furnace and was trying in vain to redirect its fiery breath at Gaven. Its wings grabbed at the air, flapping wildly, but the wind buffeted the dragon and would not let it fly. A second dragon leaped up from the furnace and well into the air, unfurling its wings as it reached the apex of its mighty leap, catching the wind and soaring away, jerking in the turbulent storm but unharmed. Then a third followed the second, just as the first dragon crashed down onto the jagged wreckage of the metal roof and lay still. A blast of lightning pinned the third dragon for an instant, but it flew on, quickly disappearing behind the lip of the canyon to the west.

Aunn drew a steadying breath and felt calm flow through him again, soft and warm. The wind raged at his back, but his mind was still and silent. Once again he stretched his fingers to touch the ring of the torc. He closed his eyes and let the web of silver threads trace themselves on his mind.

He was in the Labyrinth again, utterly lost and bereft of hope. A fiend stood close at his back, her arms wrapped seductively around his chest. "Why do you fight me?" she whispered, her breath hot in his ear. "Don't you want me beside you?" She ran her hands over his body, seeking some response, but receiving none.

Her gentle breath became a roar of fury in his ear. "You dare threaten me?" The fiend's face was now the horned bear of the Demon Wastes, fearsome in its rage. The hands on his chest were massive claws, and they tore into his chest. He threw his head back and screamed.

A voice called to him within the Labyrinth, "Over here, Aunn." The pain faded and he turned his head to see Ashara, her hands pressed to the blue crystal. Cart stood behind them, trying to shield them both from the storm. Aunn looked around, but saw no fiend. He looked down, and to his surprise saw no blood on his chest.

A shadow moved within the crystal as he stepped beside Ashara, keeping his fingers on the silver tracings. The fingers of one hand met hers, and suddenly he saw the latticework in its entirety, spread like a map before him. Ashara had been working to unravel the threads at one end, and he knew at once he should do the same at the other, near the opposite reservoir. The torc and the blade—those would come last.

Aunn stepped out from Cart's protection and the wind blasted in his face, hot and dry like the air of the Labyrinth, then frigid like the wind in Frostburn Cut. The bear-thing loomed before him out of the driving snow, then reared on its hind legs to tear at him.

"No," he said, and the fiend fell back before him. Still holding the entire network of silver threads in his mind, he found the place opposite where Ashara stood and he mirrored her work, thread by thread, with painstaking precision. The calm—the promised presence of the Messenger, he believed—settled into his mind and kept the fiend at bay.

Aunn and Ashara worked more quickly together. Their minds and hands were joined in the lattice, so each could follow every movement of the other. They worked like expert weavers, hands darting over the loom, barely conscious of the work. The earth rumbled and the sky roared behind them as Gaven's storm continued in its fury, but they worked on, moving from the outer edge in until they stood side by side before the Torc of Sacrifice and the Ramethene Sword.

A crack of thunder so loud it might have split the world—

Ashara sliding the sword out of the crystal—

The torc of sacrifice falling into his outstretched hands—

In a single instant the Dragon Forge was unmade and the Keeper of Secrets imprisoned once more.

* * * * *

Silence.

Aunn looked around wildly, trying to take it all in, everything his eyes could tell him. He floated in an ocean of silent, still air. No breeze brushed his face, no sound reached his ears. Dust and sand settled slowly onto the ground in the wake of the storm, while clouds parted and drifted off and faded into a perfect blue sky. Cart shifted beside him, turned to look at him, and his metal jaw opened, but Aunn could hear no voice. Ashara was curled on the ground, leaning against the column of blue-gray stone that had once been clear crystal, and Cart bent to tend to her.

Aunn wandered to the wreckage of the Dragon Forge, the gravel silent beneath his feet. The metal roof lay bent and sundered, a horse-sized dragon impaled on one jagged edge. The eldritch machine itself was a pile of rubble, half-collapsed into the trenches and furnaces beneath it. Clouds of steam still billowed up from the furnaces, and broken pipes here and there shot silent jets uselessly into the air.

He could see no sign of Malathar's bones—the wind must have scattered their dust across southern Aundair. He also couldn't see Gaven, and that started his heart pounding with fear. He scanned the rim of the canyon above him, then hurried into the wreckage of the forge, dreading what he might find.

He shifted rubble that made no sound, tossed aside pieces of metal that bounced silently against stone. He saw Cart move in alongside him, joining the search, and then a pale and frail-looking Ashara. He saw tears streaming down her cheeks, but could not hear her weep.

A gleam of red stone caught his eye—there! He gave a silent cry and pointed, then hurried to where he'd seen it. Gaven was on his knees, his back turned to Aunn, his shoulders and his head drooping, curled in around his gut.

Gaven? Aunn tried to speak, but if he had a voice he could not hear it. Gaven didn't respond.

Aunn glanced over his shoulder at Cart and Ashara. They'd seen him come this way, even if they couldn't hear his cry. He stepped closer to Gaven, trying to see his face, and his eyes fell on the dragonshard clutched to Gaven's chest. Gaven was rocking ever so slightly, forward and back, his head bowed, his glassy eyes fixed on the bloodstone.

Aunn put a hand on Gaven's shoulder. "Gaven, look at me." Still no sound, and Gaven didn't respond to his touch. He shook Gaven's shoulder, gently and then fiercely, he rocked Gaven's body from side to side, but Gaven didn't look up from the dragonshard.

Cart and Ashara stopped just behind him, and Cart put a hand on Aunn's shoulder.

For a moment, the stone in Gaven's hands was gold, not red. Ashara was a lovely elf, and Haldren was hurrying through the Aerenal jungle behind them. The whole mad adventure had just begun, and for just an instant he dreamed that he might have the chance to do it all over again, to do it right, to be true to Gaven this time.

But this time, Gaven was not coming out of his stupor. In Aerenal, he had looked up from the Eye of Siberys with a startling new clarity in his mind. Now, Gaven seemed lost in the depths of the stone, trapped in the coiling lines of his dragonmark.

Aunn fell to his knees, and the first sound to penetrate his ears was his own howl of grief.

* * * * *

Rienne stood at the railing of Jordhan's small airship and gazed at the placid waters of Lake Galifar below.

From Thaliost to Varna, everywhere they had seen signs of brewing war. They had crossed the broad peninsula of Thaliost, claimed by Thrane, and seen Thrane soldiers marching toward the Starcrag Plain, anticipating another Aundairian attack. On the second day of their journey, they saw a great storm far to the south, and Rienne thought of Gaven. She almost made Jordhan turn south, but the march of war drew her on to the west. They crossed all of Aundair, and saw most of Aundair's forces marching westward. On the sixth day, drawing close to the Wynarn River, they saw another storm arise in the south, but this one sped across Lake Galifar, growing as it came, until it was a hurricane tearing into the Eldeen city of Varna. Jordhan kept well clear of the storm until it waned.

They crossed the Wynarn the next day, and saw streams of Eldeen refugees fleeing the wreckage of Varna. They turned southward then, and saw the ruins for themselves. The city walls had crumbled, the buildings were leveled, the forest for a mile around was strewn with fallen trees, and half the city was under the surface of the lake. The soldiers of Aundair were picking through the ruins, assaulting refugees, skirmishing with scouts and rangers in the forests—but mostly they were massing on the road that led west from the city, along the lake shore, to Greenheart. One by one, more and more companies joined the body and melted in, row upon row upon row of soldiers in perfect lines.

Jordhan kept them high above the army, well out of bowshot. The brilliant noonday sun, blazing in a perfect autumn sky, gleamed on the helmets of the soldiers, glinted off their spearheads, sparkled on their armor. Their boots were a distant rumble of thunder on the road.

Epilogue

Vultures soared in the air, riding the updrafts along the edge of the Shadowcrags.

Magnificent birds, thought Kathrik Mel.

His gaze swept along the snow-capped mountains, which for so long had stood as a barrier between him and his destiny. He shook his fist at them, cursing them, and then laughed. He turned, and his eyes took in the grandeur, the majesty of his horde.

They swept down from the foothills and into the forest, killing every living thing they saw in a frenzy of bloodlust. The forest was ablaze, fire leaping in the dry autumn leaves. They had achieved their first victory—a trivial matter—and already the chants were gaining strength and drawing closer. "Sacrifice for Kathrik Mel!"

The prisoners were tall and slender, hideous with perfection, their faces serene. He would cut the placid stares from their faces. He spat, whirled, and sat on his throne, lashed together from the bones of his enemies. He slid the sword, Bloodclaw, from its sheath and admired its gleaming blade.

A rustle of scales arose behind him, and the dragon's neck snaked out around the back of the throne.

"Tell me again," Kathrik Mel demanded, and the dragon did.

He traced his finger absently up and down the edge of Bloodclaw's blade as the dragon whispered in his ear. Midnight blue sparks flared to life where he touched the sword, proof that the sword was fully his at last. The blood of the Maruks had sealed it, as he had hoped.

"Dragons fly before the Blasphemer's legions," the dragon hissed, "scouring the earth of his righteous foes."

Scouring the earth—he liked that. Not just washing or

cleansing. Scouring meant attacking a stain, a pestilent blot, burning it away or cutting it out. He would scour the earth.

"Carnage rises in the wake of his passing, purging all life from those who oppose him."

"Yes . . ." he murmured, biting his lip and tasting blood.

"Vultures wheel where dragons flew, picking the bones of the numberless dead."

There would be dead beyond counting. Kathrik Mel stood again, unable to contain his excitement.

The Blasphemer had come, and all the armies of Khorvaire could not stand against him.

KEITH BAKER'S
THORN OF BRELAND

As a child, Nyrielle Tam dreamed
of being a soldier. Instead, she
became a spy, a saboteur, and when
necessary, an assassin.

She became Thorn, Dark Lantern of Breland.

THE QUEEN OF STONE
Available Now

THE SON OF KHYBER
November 2009

THE FADING DREAM
October 2010

DON BASSINGTHWAITE'S

LEGACY OF DHAKAAN

From the ashes of a fallen empire,
a new kingdom rises.

The Doom of Kings

The Word of Traitors
September 2009

The Tyranny of Ghosts
June 2010

FORGOTTEN REALMS

Ed Greenwood
Presents
Waterdeep

Explore the City of Splendors through the eyes of authors
hand-picked by FORGOTTEN REALMS world creator Ed Greenwood.

They engulf civilizations.
They thrive on the fallen.
They will cover all trace of your passing.

THE WILDS

THE FANGED CROWN
Jenna Helland

THE RESTLESS SHORE
James P. Davis
May 2009

THE EDGE OF CHAOS
Jak Koke
August 2009

WRATH OF THE BLUE LADY
Mel Odom
December 2009

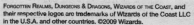

MAGIC
The Gathering®

**Everything you thought you knew
about MAGIC™ novels is changing...**

From the mind of

ARI MARMELL

comes a tour de force of imagination.

AGENTS
OF
ARTIFICE

The ascendance of a new age in the planeswalker
mythology: be a part of the book that takes fans
deeper than ever into the lives of the Multiverse's most
powerful beings:

Jace Beleren
a powerful mind-mage whose choices now will forever
determine his path as
a planeswalker;

Liliana Vess
a dangerous necromancer whose beauty belies a dark
secret and even darker associations; and

Tezzeret
leader of an inter-planar consortium whose quest for
knowledge may be undone by his lust for power.